THE WIDTH
OF THE SEA

Michelle Chalfoun

BLACK SWAN

THE WIDTH OF THE SEA
A BLACK SWAN BOOK : 0 552 99899 0

Originally published in Great Britain by Doubleday,
a division of Transworld Publishers

PRINTING HISTORY
Doubleday edition published 2001
Black Swan edition published 2002

1 3 5 7 9 10 8 6 4 2

Set in 11/12pt Melior by
Falcon Oast Graphic Art Ltd.

Black Swan Books are published by Transworld Publishers,
61–63 Uxbridge Road, London W5 5SA,
a division of The Random House Group Ltd,
in Australia by Random House Australia (Pty) Ltd,
20 Alfred Street, Milsons Point, Sydney, NSW 2061, Australia,
in New Zealand by Random House New Zealand Ltd,
18 Poland Road, Glenfield, Auckland 10, New Zealand
and in South Africa by Random House (Pty) Ltd,
Endulini, 5a Jubilee Road, Parktown 2193, South Africa.

Printed and bound in Great Britain by
Clays Ltd, St Ives plc.

For A.F.

I am grateful to the Massachusetts Cultural Council for its generous support.

Though the decline of the North Atlantic fisheries inspired this book, all events and characters are the product of the author's imagination. Any resemblance to actual persons, living or dead, is entirely coincidental.

The lyrics at the opening of each section are from traditional shanties passed from ship to ship, sailor to sailor, through the ages. They have no known authors and many variations. I learned the versions quoted here from many different sources. Special thanks to all the captains and crews with whom I've had the pleasure to sail, work, and sing.

—I love all waste
And solitary places; where we taste
The pleasure of believing what we see
Is boundless as we wish our souls to be:
And such was this wide ocean—
—Percy Shelley, 'Julian and Maddalo'

Virtually every major American commercial fishing region outside of Alaska is in severe trouble; nearly eighty percent of the nation's known commercial species are now overfished . . . Mankind has won. To the victors go the empty seas . . .

—*New York Times*, December 11, 1994

I

Now me boys we're coming up to dock,
and the pretty girls on the pier do flock.
There's my Jenny in her new pink frock—
Oh, Jenny, put your red dress on.

1

Early on a Saturday morning most people of Rosaline sleep in. A few lobstermen – RayRay O'Buck, Tomas Dugan, and Jim Salvatore – get up and out in the dark a.m. to check their pots, but they are far offshore now and the town is quiet. Out in the bay, small waves mirror the sky: deep blue troughs and dazzling caps like liquid light. The red and green buoys look dull against the brilliant water. It is going to be a hot one. Even the gulls seem to be feeling it. They are slow to discover a package of hot dog buns spilling from the dumpster behind the Finast. One finally swoops in, a few more follow, then suddenly a crowd gathers, fighting over the scraps.

'Hah! Hee-yah!'

Two men come through, one shouting and feinting kicks. The gulls scatter. The men are locals, fishermen. Their clothing gives them away. They wear home-knit sweaters frayed around the cuffs and waists, flannel-lined canvas trousers reinforced with extra swaths of fabric at the thigh, the colours so faded and dirtied and sun-and-salt-bleached the original shades are a guess. Their hair, too, is bleached and dried. On their feet, rubber deck boots – folded down – flop noisily about their ankles. Even if these men were to clean up and wear different clothes, their hands would mark them. Turgid, mottled palms; inarticulate fingers, thick as toes, curved as if permanently rigored around a fillet knife.

The big one, John Fitz, is thick-necked and broad-shouldered. He walks slowly, as if he is not yet awake. The other, Chris Albin, is small and wiry, and his path is not straight. He veers here to kick a bottle cap, there a pebble. As soon as the gulls resettle, he rushes them again, crying, 'Yah! Hee-yah!'

Satisfied, he swings back to his friend. 'It's warm,' Chris says.

'Yeah,' John says.

Chris trots alongside the bigger man, looking up at him. 'I'm thinking about fried egg sandwiches. I could use a fried egg sandwich right about now.'

'No dollars,' John says.

'We could stop at the ATM.'

'None there, either.'

The two cross the parking lot, duck behind Handleman's, and come out on the east end of Water Street. A banner over their heads reads: *Welcome to Rosaline – One Foot in the Past, One in the Future!* In small print, *Sponsored by CARP*; and in smaller print, *Citizens Associated for Restorative Projects*. There is no wind. The banner sags. They pass the old processing plant, still smelling of fish and metal. A few threads of graffiti decorate the barred steel doors. The temporary closure sign has rusted around the bullet holes. Most of the chicken-wired windows are broken.

After the fish plant, Water Street splits in three. One paved road heads to Charlesport as Route 412. One road, gravel and broken clamshell, runs to the tip of the southern spit, servicing the southern lighthouse. The third road, the one John and Chris take, is just a nub of asphalt leading to the bay. Not too long ago, it curved gently down to the Titus Fish Pier, but now the road breaks off abruptly as if it has been hacked by a giant hand. Last year's nor'easter blasted away the last hundred yards and left the Titus Fish Pier in shambles. The town hasn't had the budget for repairs. Now the fleet docks farther down the harbor, in front of the

Maritime Museum. The two men stop at the end of the severed service road and squint over the edge of the cliff to the shipyard below.

'Look at that,' John says.

Chris whistles.

For months the marine railway has been empty, but now an antique schooner sits between the catwalks. Half her rigging is down and her dories are gone, her sails are yellowed bundles on deck, but John says, 'She sure is something.'

There aren't many like her anymore. Her hull rises dramatically from her keel, as if defying gravity with perfect geometry. The shores and lines look too small to hold her. Though broad, she tapers to a graceful prow. She would sail well. Compared to the pleasure boats John sees scudding around the Charlesport Yacht Club, she is a giant. Length overall 125, length on deck a hundred or so, beam a quarter of that. Her masts — trees that tall don't exist in Rosaline forests anymore, but they did when she was built. John knows this boat well, though he has never seen her under way.

The whole town knows this boat. An exact replica sails in the Maritime Museum, in a glass aquarium in the middle of the Ship Models Room, on a plaster-and-paste sea. There, her tiny rig is in full repair. Her matchstick crew work about the deck cleaning fish, some lay aloft furling sail, a few more are out in the waters still, rowing their laden dories back. As a child, John loved the models. He would press his nose against their glass boxes, fogging them with his breath. He memorized the bronze plaques detailing the statistics and histories of each boat. This one, the *Shardon Rose*, was a dory schooner built in a Rosaline yard in 1902 for groundfishing off the Bank. She became a cargo vessel between Cape Verdes and New Bedford, made a scientific expedition to the Arctic, had a stint in the movies, and then spent a few years as a toy for a billionaire who made his money in adhesives. For the last

11

decade, she's been rotting off a Halifax pier. But now she has come home – this morning, at 3:14 according to the chalkboard on Carreiro's henhouse.

'So Sal won,' John says, pointing to the chalkboard.

Dora Schultz had a pool going up at the Whiskey Wind for when the *Shardon* would come in. She'd rigged a chart over the register, and every night she moved the pushpin a bit farther south, tracking the schooner's progress.

'Yeah.' Chris swipes his nose with his cuff.

'He'll be buying, then.'

'Yeah. Let's go.'

But John doesn't move off the cliff for the bar. Instead, he scrambles down the dirt slope.

'Come on, man!' Chris calls after him. But John keeps going and Chris follows.

At the bottom they hop the granite scree to Carreiro's yard. The barn doors to the shop are open, and Helio Carreiro putters about inside, readying the long-closed space for its new commission. He looks up and waves to them. He jerks his chin at the schooner and makes a thumbs-up sign, grinning. It is something of a victory that, after many empty months, he's got a boat back on the ways. He almost lost the job to a Charlesport yard.

John says, 'She's looking good, Helio!'

Helio wipes his hands on his coveralls and comes out. 'My friend, how are you?' He pumps John's hand and slaps his shoulder. 'How's the old man?'

'Good, he's good.'

Helio nods hello to Chris. 'And you. Tell Phil I expect him.' He spreads his hand toward the schooner. 'I expect him this morning first thing. I'm surprised he don't come.'

'Well, you know my dad. Busy man,' Chris says. He scratches his chest, looks bored.

'When do you start?' John asks.

'Monday. We give the crew a rest, you know. They have a long transit.'

'Can we take a look?' John asks.

Helio frowns, smooths his few strands of hair. He is short and round and neckless. He turns his whole body to survey his yard – a couch losing its stuffing beside the henhouse, the shack itself looking abandoned, with tar paper peeling from its roof and a window out. Still, the gears and chains have been recently worked: the sharp bite of fresh grease hangs in the air. From the shed floats the grassy perfume of new wood.

'I don't know,' Helio says. 'I got a work site here, you know? People walk around, something falls, I get a suit.'

'Oh well.' John starts to walk away.

'Okay, okay.' Helio holds his hands up as if surrendering. 'You only. I can't have everybody.' He shoos them down toward the schooner. 'Go on, take a look.'

John jumps the small granite boulders that line the gentle slope down to the marine railway. He steps onto one of the iron rails and teeters a moment, waving his arms back and forth. Then he walks it like a tightrope to the wooden platform where the great schooner sits. Chris follows him down.

The railway platform juts into the sea. Waves lick the boards, splash against the aftermost shores and over the toes of John's boots. Foam hisses back to the bay. The strong sun lifts the odor of evaporating ocean. The schooner looms over them; looking up, John is blinded. He steps around to the other side, into the boat's shadow. Now he can see clearly how rust stains the cleats and hawse holes. The dolphin striker looks nearly eaten through in parts. He strolls aft, inspecting the hull. Her timber has turned a slimy black, pocked and covered with barnacles. The prop looks chewed.

'She looks like shit,' Chris says.

'She's got some rot.' John gouges a finger-length splinter from a punky board. He rubs the bit between

13

his fingers, and it frays to angel hair. 'She just needs work.'

'I hear Joe's hiring.'

'So?'

Chris rocks from foot to foot. 'So it's just what I hear.'

'Well,' John says, 'you heard Helio. He's keeping the transit crew on. And I bet he's cut a deal for all his cousins.'

'Well, Walley says Joe says Helio still needs a few more men.'

John shrugs. Since Joe Ames runs the museum and the *Shardon Rose* is museum property now, even though the yard belongs to Helio Carreiro, it stands to reason Joe Ames will have a hand in hiring some of the restoration crew. Or so the logic has gone around the Whiskey Wind. Folks divide on whether to kiss Ames's ass or not.

'You got a job,' John says. 'So does Walley.' They fish with John and his father.

'I know, I'm just saying.' Chris stops rocking. He rubs his nose.

John holds the frayed wood fibers to the wind and lets go. The fluff sails toward the town. Not only does Joe Ames run the museum, he's also the president of CARP. He's also got a whole exhibit on cod in the Children's Discovery Center, but he doesn't seem to know that carp swim in fresh water.

2

Yve Albin stares a long time in the bathroom mirror. Her nose is red. She spent most of the day at the museum playground with her nephew Martin, and now she has a sunburn.

'I'm sunburned,' she says to Kate.

'At least you got some color. I look like a ghost.'

14

'I look like Rudolph.'

Kate sits on the toilet, smoking. Martin soaks in the tub behind her. The boy and Kate both have the same white skin. He doesn't look much like his father, Yve's brother, Chris. Their mother used to say Martin was delivered with the mail. He doesn't have much Albin in him at all. He's mostly McCormac, like Kate. Fair redheads. In his forehead, blue veins show through. Kate had them when she was young; as she grew older her skin grew thicker.

'What are you wearing?' Yve asks now.

Kate looks down. 'This. Why?'

Yve looks at her through the mirror. 'It's fine.'

Kate's wearing what she wore to work, but then again, she always dresses like she's ready to party. Blacks and purples, tight and cheap. She can get away with such clothes, even at thirty-two. Her figure, all soft white curves, hasn't sagged or fattened, though the most exercise she gets is tapping kegs. She bartends days at the Whiskey Wind. Normally Kate has week-ends off, and so Yve has weekends off from baby-sitting, but today Dora was busy with the arrival of the schooner and Sal Liro's getting half the town drunk. She called Kate in to work extra. As usual, Kate dropped Martin off with Yve. She didn't even bother to call first. After a half hour, Yve's mother wanted the boy out of the house, because she still had so much cooking to do, so Yve took him to the playground. She managed to keep Martin clean all day. When she brought him, still perfectly clean, to the Whiskey Wind to meet Kate, Kate had to go and buy him a cherry ice from Garenelli's. Now the boy is red around the mouth and all down his front. Somehow even his legs are stained. A cherry ice before supper! Kate spoils and ignores the boy alternately. She smoked all through her pregnancy, though Yve read to her about cigarettes and fetal development. Now the smoke from her cigarette curls bluely up to the bathroom

15

ceiling. Yve has the door open, but she still smells it.

'I guess I'll just have to go to the dance with a red nose.'

Kate ruffles through her bag. 'Try my foundation.'

'It's too pale.'

Kate shrugs. She lifts herself up off the toilet a bit, opens the lid, and drops her spent cigarette in. It hisses. She sits back down and lights another. 'All I know is, Chris better show up,' she said. 'I told him – him and John were there all day today, completely fucked up, and I said to the both of them, I said, Don't you dare come in here again if you don't show up tonight . . .'

Yve listens with half an ear. Her fingers play over her face: forehead, cheeks, jaw. Fine wrinkles spray around her eyes like hairline checks in dry wood. She squints and deepens them, then releases her hold. They don't quite disappear. She is twenty-nine. And her lips – they look flatter than she remembers. 'Look at my lips,' she interrupts. 'Do they look weird?'

Kate stops mid-sentence. 'Weird how?'

'Flat? Like they're going in sort of?'

'No.'

'They're definitely thinner though, right?'

'Try this.' Kate hands her a lipstick. Yve twists it open, and the smell reminds her of high school.

'Jesus. What a color. I can't get away with that.'

'You need *some* color.'

'I've got my red nose.'

'Lovely.'

Yve opens the cabinet mirror. The spotted shelves are cluttered with practical toiletries: an earwax-removal kit, a tin of Bag-balm, her father's shaving mug and brush and razor blades. Behind the Gold Bond Powder, Yve finds a lip pencil. It's old and dry. She mixes a chip with petroleum jelly on the back of her hand and carefully applies the smear with her pinky. Grins. Her teeth look yellow by contrast; too much coffee. She wipes the color off and decides it doesn't matter, she looks fine enough, even as she pinches her middle, stepping back and rising on tiptoe to catch a glimpse of her full self.

'I'm getting fat.'

'Where?'

'Here.' She pinches her waist for Kate to see. 'Soon I'll be big as my aunt.' She palpates her body as she did her face: hips, breasts, arms, and thighs. Her muscles are still round and hard under the pads of flesh. She tenses them to be sure, then lets go and is appalled by the looseness of it all. She'll end up heavy as Edna. That's the Larkin thickness, though her mother hasn't inherited it, of course. Somehow her mother has managed to stay tiny.

'She's putting all the single women on the serving line,' Kate says. She looks up at Yve expectantly.

'Who?'

'Your Aunt Edna. You're not listening.'

'I am.'

'Then what did I say?'

'She's putting all the single women on the serving line.' Yve turns to profile. She can still tighten her calves by pointing her toes; she can still move hand-fuls of thigh or stomach to better places, lift her breasts manually – her fingertips grip her collarbones, pulling the slopes taut until they are champagne-glass-round again. Those are John's words: *champagne glass*. That sort of thing sounds good at fifteen, seventeen, twenty. It gets tired. She sucks her belly in, lifts her buttocks. She can pretend it isn't so bad; just lose a few pounds and it'll be better, do a few sit-ups.

'Think about it,' Kate says. 'Everyone on the serving line is single.'

'Oh please. It's not a conspiracy. Dora, Jenny, and Mabel all have service experience – and you're married and she put *you* on the serving line.'

'She probably figures I might as well be single.'

'Kate, that makes no sense. She put me on serving too.'

'Well, you're single.' Kate crosses her eyes.

Yve makes an ugly face back. 'I'm practically not.'

'Oh please.'

'Please what?'

Kate blows blue smoke from her nostrils and waves it away from her eyes. She uses her left hand and Yve is sure she's doing that for a reason, flashing the tiny diamond and wedding band set.

'Please what?'

'Nothing.'

Warm smells rise from the kitchen below. Yve's mother is down there, baking a green bean casserole for the party. She will show up, casserole in hand, dance with Yve's father, enjoy herself. Twenty-nine. Her mother had Yve at twenty-two and Chris at nineteen. Kate had Martin at twenty-nine. It's Labor Day weekend, the last days of summer. In May, Yve turns thirty. She tries not to calculate how many years are left for children. If she has a son now, how old will she be by the time he's eighteen? By the time he has children? If she has a child next year? The year after? How old will she be before she sees her own grandchildren?

She tries to ignore biology: if there are approximately a thousand eggs in each ovary – she doesn't know the actual number, but thinks this is a generous guess – and every month another is dropped and flushed away like so much waste, how many are left her now? How many are damaged? How many dried up? Sometimes she takes Martin to the Children's Discovery Center in the museum. There's a display there. A wood-carved cod releases scattershot, representing her eggs. You turn the roulette wheel and watch probability. This many are eaten, this many are unfertilized. This many are damaged by heavy metals. A sign warns women of childbearing years not

18

to eat this, that, and the other fish. Scientific language rendered down for children explains how the metals are so heavy they sink into ovaries and lie there, breaking eggs. Yve grew up eating fish until there were so few no one gave them away free anymore. Before that, Warren Fitz gave her father fish in exchange for hardware and paints. He took Yve's brother, Chris, on as crew and Chris carried fish home. John Fitz brought fish when he came over for supper. Yve brought bonus gifts of fillets home from the fish plant. Her mother cooked chowders and stews and fishcakes. Fried, steamed, simmered fish, poached, broiled, boiled, grilled—

Yve piles the hair on top of her head. Lets it drop. 'It seems thin; is it thinning?'

'Your hair wants cutting,' Kate says in her best Red Queen voice. Martin giggles and splashes behind her. 'You like that, Martin? Your hair wants cutting!'

Yve bows her head to braid her hair. 'Are they definitely coming, do you know?' She means John and Chris.

'I told Chris come hell or high water. If he doesn't show, I'm going home with a sailor.'

'You are not.'

'Watch me.'

'I'm sure he'll be there.'

'Yeah, but so? Your brother has the amazing capacity to exist two places at once. He can be both here *and* in the Land of Nod.'

'Oh no.' Yve looks over at Kate. 'He's not again, is he?'

Kate snorts. 'Again? What makes you think he ever stopped?'

'He promised Mom.'

'Well,' Kate says. 'Oh well.' She starts shimmying and singing. 'Ohwellohwellohwell – Huh!'

Martin laughs and paddles the water.

'You like when Mommy dances?' Kate asks. 'You gonna dance with Mommy?'

19

Martin giggles and nods. He puts his hands up to his cheeks and Yve notices his tiny fingertips are wrinkled. His lips look bluish. She grabs a big towel off the rod. 'You should get him out. He's freezing. Look, he's shaking.'

'He's not shaking, he's laughing.'

'He is too shaking, his teeth are chattering.' Yve lifts her nephew from the tub and wraps him in the towel. She rubs his arms and takes his hands and kisses his fingertips. 'Pruney-boy. Let me see those little prune fingers.' She settles him on her hip. He clings to her with his thighs. He smells like soap and he is damp even through his towel and her bathrobe. His clothes, down in the laundry room, need at least another ten minutes drying.

'I'm taking him into my room.'

'Uh-huh.' Kate takes her place at the mirror.

Yve pads to her room. She puts Martin down on the floor and stands in front of the closet a good long time.

She calls to Kate, 'What should I wear?'

'How the hell should I know.'

Her dresses and skirts hang there, unchanged since morning. She's always dressed sensibly, and now she is disappointed by what she finds. She touches down the row of familiar cottons and wools. Easy to wash and wear. They slip under her dry hands. She finally selects a gray jumper and a white blouse, because the last time she wore it John said she looked like fog and she thinks, perhaps, he meant it as a compliment.

Two blocks from the Seamen's Fellowship Hall, people crowd the streets. Signs post the streetlamps – *Welcome Shardon Rose!* – and arrows point the way to the potluck supper and dance. Kate and Yve nod hello; Martin waves. They know everybody. The greasy stink of fried fish fills the air. Joe Ames, costumed as a pirate, works the streaming crowd. He's wearing an eyepatch and a felt parrot and big red pin with his name.

'Give one to your boy!' He holds a pencil set out to Kate, but her hands are hobbled by her grip on Martin. Yve takes it for her.

'Oh Lord,' Yve says, showing Kate. The plastic case has a black-line drawing of the schooner *Shardon Rose* in full repair with all her sails flying. Each pencil says *Rosaline Maritime Museum – Making Its Mark!*

Kate snorts.

'Here you go, Martin.' Yve gives him the pencils.

Up ahead, brisk music spills from the hall's open windows, and Kate feels a bit of excitement. She's thought of this party all day at work – the men talked only of the new schooner, the older ones pretending they could remember a time when it was all schooners and no draggers, and she poured their drinks and made their change and argued with Chris and imagined dancing and drinking and flirting just enough to get Chris jealous.

'Trot trot! Trot trot to Boston!' Kate bobbles Martin and gallops the last few steps to the back of the line. He bounces on her hip and she chants the whole rhyme for him, swooping him over backwards at the *All fall in!* Martin wants it again and again, so she trot-trots him in place.

'We're not getting anywhere,' she says to Yve. 'We haven't moved in ages.'

'Well, what's going on?' Yve stands on tiptoe and cranes her neck. A crowd blocks the door.

The confusion is being caused by Rita Barrett. She sits at a small card table blocking three-quarters of the landing, forcing people to squeeze around one at a time. She has a money box and a roll of tickets beside her. Her fingers and wrists sparkle, counting change and tearing tickets, stamping hands. Her hairdo, a mass of frosted curls, bobs with the effort of making money. She alternately smiles over her right shoulder at the paid and ticketed passing on in, and argues over her left with Susan Furlong, who argues back, loud enough for everyone to hear, that since she brought a lasagna, she shouldn't have to pay.

'That's not fair,' Yve says.

'She's a bitch,' Kate says. 'Rita, I mean, not Susan.'

'We better not have to pay. We're serving.'

'Tell that to the Profit Queen.'

'And Susan's working in the kitchen,' Yve adds.

'See? Married women in the kitchen, single on the serving line.'

Yve rolls her eyes, and Martin squirms on Kate's hip, reaching for his aunt. Kate shifts him higher. 'Christ, Martin, you're killing me.'

'I can take him,' Yve says.

'He's fine.'

Yve frowns at the boy. 'His shirt's still red. We should've stopped by your house to change him.'

'I covered it,' Kate says.

'It still shows. You could take the T-shirt off, leave him in just the sweatshirt.'

Kate looks down at her boy. She put a Mickey Mouse sweatshirt over his old T, but the cherry-ice stains show where the shirt peeks beyond the neck and waistband. 'He doesn't like the sweatshirt by itself. The Mickey scratches him.'

'You're a mess and your mommy dresses you funny,' Yve tells him.

'He doesn't care. Do you, Martin? No, say: I know I'm handsome, Mommy.' Kate kisses his cheek and leaves plum lips behind. She wipes with her thumb and he shakes his head, kicking his heels into Kate's stomach and back.

'Ow!' She puts him down hard. 'That fucking hurt.' She tugs her hair from under the baby-bag strap, then reaches under her cardigan and wriggles her dress back in place. He looks at her, his face screwing up for a cry. 'Don't you dare,' she warns him.

'Are you ready to dance, Martin?' Yve takes his hand and waves it in time to the music. This distracts him enough and he gives up on crying. He looks puzzled, though, turning his gaze between his mother and his aunt. The line inches forward, and Yve pulls the boy along.

Kate gets a cigarette. 'Ah, there's our man now, to the rescue.' She points her ash. Mayor Barrett sweeps through the crowd, sweating in his top hat and tails, ushering people past his wife with smiles and handshakes.

They start moving quickly.

'Soon we'll be dancing, hey Martin?' Kate laughs to Yve. 'They always kick you right in the cesarean.' She drags hard, then drops her butt; they are nearly at Rita's card table. 'You would think they'd've thought of childcare. The whole fucking town's here.' She props her bag on her knee and rummages for money. Throws Rita a few wrinkled bills.

'Come on, I got yours already,' she tells Yve.

Cinder blocks prop open the heavy doors, and people crowd the cloakroom: women in circle skirts, men in clean work chinos and good button-down shirts, new and still bearing the creases. The coat rack is full; outside shoes litter the floor beneath. The crush continues into the hall. Lights and balloons and banners string the ceiling; semaphore flags, though they have more to do with yachts than dory schooners or fishing, fringe the service table and the stage. Little girls in frilled and smocked dresses run the room's circumference, trailing crepe-paper streamers. Their patent-leather shoes canter and slide on the pine floor. In the center, two lines of dancers twirl and step. Already they've memorized the pattern and they whirl through the figures without the caller's cues. All the tables along the walls are occupied. Around one corner table squeeze the men of their crowd, the English-speaking groundfishers, but neither Chris nor John Fitz is with them.

'I don't see them,' Yve says, but Kate's already looking.

'Bastard. I'll kill Chris.'

'I'm sure he tried.'

'I'm sure not hard.'

'Maybe they're still at the Wind. I'm sure they'll come as soon as they leave there.'

Kate scans the room. In the corner farthest from the fishers' table, under a welcome banner, sit the transit crew off the *Shardon Rose*. They don't look very promising. A fat one with a walrus mustache, a skinny one with a wispy white braid. A few others have their backs turned so she can't really tell, but she clicks her tongue and says, anyhow, 'A regular halt and lame show.'

'Who?'

'The crew off that boat.' Kate tilts her head at the table.

'Maybe not,' Yve says.

'Why do you care? You're practically married.' Kate swipes Martin from the floor and plants him on her hip. She doesn't wait for Yve's answer, but cuts through the crowd of dancers to the serving table where Dora Schultz, Jenny Stewart and Mabel Dowd stand behind bowls and platters. Cleaned up, in their neat dresses and aprons, they look prim and tense, like a stiff little chorus waiting nervously to sing their few notes, hoping someone in the audience might notice.

'Hello, ladies,' Kate says.

The women all nod hello.

'Long time no see,' Dora Schultz says.

'How'd you get out?' Kate asks her. When she left the Wind, they were still stacked three deep at the bar and Dora was pouring pints like a madwoman.

'Sal ran out of dough, and the beer's free here. I closed about an hour ago.'

Kate gives Yve a withering look. Yve looks back at her with an annoyingly innocent, open face. 'I'm sure they're on their way,' she says.

Dora Schultz passes them aprons. 'What are you

24

going to do with him?' she asks Kate of Martin.

'Hand him off as soon as Alma gets through the line.'

'Rita's holding things up,' Yve says.

'Bitch,' says Dora.

'He's fine. Aren't you?' Kate tucks Martin under the table. 'It's like a tent, play camping.'

'You have turnips and fish,' Dora tells her.

Jenny Stewart says, 'You see the sailors?'

'Old farts,' Kate says.

'Good,' Dora says. She's the oldest of them all. Fifty with two husbands behind her.

'Not all,' Mabel Dowd says. 'I saw the captain before, but he's turned around now.' Her eyes are fixed on the table of sailors and she's blushing.

'Mabel and I saw him before.' Jenny's drawing a smiling face next to her name on her name tag. She frowns at her picture, adds a little squiggle under her name, then hands the marker and tags to Kate.

'He's handsome,' Mabel Dowd whispers.

'Christ,' Kate says. 'Would you listen to yourselves?'

'Well, I'm glad we're serving,' Jenny says. 'They have to talk to us even if it's just "More peas."'

'Jenny,' Kate says, 'you need to get out a lot more if you think that's what turns men on.'

'More peas,' Dora snorts.

Kate's gaze wanders over the table of the new sailors – there is no room for chairs, so many people have pulled around. Mostly CARP types: all the suits and yachties and washashores, all the people who stand to make money if the schooner brings the promised tourists. A short, stocky sailor stands with them. He says something and the crowd laughs. The sound is carried away by the music and stamping feet, but Kate sees their heads snap back and their mouths open and the man looking slyly from one side to the other. He must've made a joke. She wonders if he's the captain everyone's so crazy for.

'I wouldn't mind a dance,' Kate says to Yve.

25

'You want to? I could be the man.'

'Nah, I got Martin.' Kate lifts the hem of the table-cloth and peeks under at her son. 'You okay there? Handsome boy?' She's broken Martin out of a stare, and he takes a moment to focus. 'You okay? Say: "Okay, Mommy."'

He doesn't say anything, so she lets the cloth go. But she's woken him up and now he wants to play. A few rustles in the toy bag, then Martin's zooming his trucks over the landscape of feet. Engine noises, like small wet farts, bubble faintly up.

'Ow,' Yve says. 'He got me.'

'Watch it.' Kate kicks a little with her toe. She makes contact with some part of her son. Then tires run again, more gently, over Kate's ankles and knees.

The music ends, and couples clap and bow to each other. A few people come down the line; Kate spoons turnips on their outstretched plates. She spatulas slabs of fried fish. People say hello, please, and thank you, and Kate answers without seeing them. She's looking over their shoulders. In the far corner, the new sailors are rising from their table at Joe Ames's invitation. His hand extends to the buffet, and now the sailors are crossing the room. There are young ones, Mabel Dowd was right. They take the plates Joe Ames hands them and stand in line. They aren't all old. A few of them look about her age.

As they come closer, Jenny begins giggling. 'That's him,' she whispers. 'Oh Lord, oh Lord.' She grabs the spatula of fried cod from Kate and holds it to the man. 'Fish?'

The captain is short, shorter than any of the women except Yve. His face is clean-shaven. He has deep lines in the corners of his eyes that suggest he smiles often, as he is smiling now. He has all his teeth, unstained, set straight in a strong jaw – strong jaw, strong cheek-bones, strong everything as far as Kate can tell without obviously looking.

'Fresh?' the man asks.

Jenny bites her lip. 'Frozen.'

Kate says, 'The only fresh thing here is me.'

'Yeah, but I bet you're bad for my health.' The captain laughs and Kate laughs. She puts fish on his plate and peas from Jenny's casserole. He moves down the line.

'That's the captain!' Jenny whispers.

'So?' Kate holds a slab of cod to a fat sailor. 'Fish?'

'Isn't he handsome?' Mabel murmurs.

'Do you want me to do something about it?' Kate whispers back. 'Do you want me to go up to him and tell him Mabel Dowd thinks you're handsome?' She offers a spatula of fish to Joe Ames. 'Fish?'

'No.' Mabel blushes again.

'Well, anyway' – Kate puts her lips right to Jenny's ear – 'he likes *you*.'

'Oh please,' Jenny hisses.

Yve says, 'I can't believe you two,' but she watches with the rest of them.

'He's put his plate down on the table. He's coming back over.'

'His food's going to get cold.'

'I don't think he cares about food.'

'He's short.'

'You know what they say about shorties. Things get made up in other departments.'

'Oh Lord.'

'Shut up. He's coming.'

'Ewww! He's *cum*-ing?'

'Please shut up.'

The captain stops in front of Jenny Stewart. 'Care to dance?'

For a moment, Jenny stands frozen with her spoon of peas and pearl onions. She blushes. 'I can't. I have to work.' She gestures to the dishes and peas fly from the spoon, scattering across the tablecloth and onto the floor. 'Excuse me.' She drops behind

27

the table. The women burst into laughter.

'That's Jenny Stewart down there,' Kate says. 'She's very shy.'

'But you're not,' the captain says.

'No. Kate's never been known for modesty,' Dora Schultz says.

The captain smiles expectantly at Kate.

Kate wiggles her ring finger. 'Sorry.'

'Don't look at me,' Dora says. 'I'm too old.'

'How about Mabel?' Kate says. 'We were just saying how handsome you two'd look together, weren't we?'

'Well?' The captain holds his hand to Mabel Dowd. Her face turns scarlet and red blotches stain her neck and chest, but she hurries from around the table, untying her apron as she goes. The captain leads her to the floor.

'You blew your chance,' Kate tells Jenny. 'He wanted you.'

'Shut up.' Jenny throws the peas at Kate. They scatter about the table and roll to the floor, and Kate laughs again.

'He asked everyone,' Dora says.

'He didn't ask Yve,' Jenny Stewart points out.

'That's because she dresses like a nun,' Kate says.

Yve bends to get the peas before Martin finds them. 'Well, his food's going to be cold.'

On the floor, couples and contra-lines are forming. The captain leads Mabel Dowd to the head of the line. The caller walks the dancers through the steps while the band idles behind him, tuning and drinking beers. When the music starts up, the dancers stomp into a balance and swing.

Edna Larkin leans from the kitchen and taps Yve. 'You and Kate should go dance. Show those boys what they're missing, not asking you.'

Yve clicks her tongue.

'Go on,' Edna says. 'Everyone's dancing, they're not eating. Dance while you can.'

'No, I'm fine,' Yve says. 'When John gets here I'll take a break. Kate, you and Dora go ahead. I can watch the table.'

'Nah, it's all right,' Kate says. 'I just turned a dance down, didn't I?'

They all look to the dance floor. 'The captain steers her well,' Dora says.

He does steer Mabel well, and Mabel isn't known for her grace. She's awkward, hovering between her late thirties and early menopause, still at home with her parents – she's been working part-time at the Maritime Museum since the fish plant closed. Her hair is graying at the temples. Friday nights find Mabel drinking too many white wine spritzers at the Wind, and sometimes she gets loud. She tends toward crying jags. She's gone home with men who seem sympathetic, but always the following week she's back alone. Kate would feel sorry for her if she felt sorry for anyone – but she doesn't, after so many years tending bar. No one takes Mabel Dowd home twice. Last spring a rumor went around by way of Walley Larkin that Mabel wears a black garter and no underwear. Now, out on the floor, Mabel's cheeks are perfect red balls, and her graying hair bounces a counter-rhythm to her swinging skirt.

Kate plops her spoon in the mashed turnips, forming and destroying peaks. 'He's an all right dancer. Despite the short legs.'

'She's not doing so well, though,' Jenny Stewart says.

'You know what they say: if you can't dance upright, you can't dance horizontal.'

'And you've done enough research to know.'

'You guys,' Yve says.

'Well, she's wasting his time, anyway.' Kate points with her spoon. 'If she can't handle it, she should get out the way and give a chance to others better equipped.'

Dora laughs loudly.

'She's doing fine,' Yve says. 'She hasn't tripped anyone.'

'That credit should go to the captain—' Something metallic catches Kate under the knee. 'Ow, fuck!' She reaches down to rub the skin and her son bangs her again.

She crouches down and grabs Martin by the arm. He smiles at her, as if surprised at her sudden appearance under the tablecloth. Then he frowns. She is squeezing his arm. She squeezes his arm until the skin turns white around her fingers. He lets go of the truck. It clatters on the tile, and he looks from it to her.

'I don't have another pair of stockings, understand? You understand?' She gives him a little shake.

Martin's face starts turning red and screwing up.

'Don't you cry, Martin,' Kate warns. 'Don't you dare.'

His eyes shut and his mouth opens and he wails.

'Kate,' Yve says.

Kate is trembling. 'I don't have another goddamn pair of stockings, you understand that? Mommy can't afford a run – do you understand?'

'Kate, come on.' Yve presses Kate's shoulder, and she releases the boy.

Yve starts to kneel, but Kate says, 'Leave him. He's fine.' She looks from Yve to Dora to Jenny. They keep their eyes lowered. 'He's calming down,' she tells them. She puts her hand to her forehead.

Sobs come loudly from under the table, and Martin's got his hands around Kate's calves. His wet face presses into her knees. Yve stares at her. Kate reaches down and strokes the boy's sweaty hair. He jerks from her hand, and she hears a clunk, and the wails change pitch.

'Oh Jeez, now I've got him going again.' Kate laughs a bit. 'He must've hit his head on the table leg.' She lifts the hem of the tablecloth, sees Martin snuffling into the toy bag.

'He's okay. Say: "I'm okay, Mommy. Okay, Mommy."
See, there's a big boy.' She squats behind the table and,
careful not to scratch with her nails, wipes his tears on
her skirt. Martin's eyes follow her hands.

Dora clicks her tongue. 'You better get him quiet or
people coming down the line'll wonder.'

Kate looks up at Dora. 'I'm not planning on staying
on this line much longer.' It's news to herself, but as
soon as she says it, she knows it's true. Mabel Dowd
doesn't have a chance with the captain; she's just
wasting everyone else's time. And if Chris isn't here to
dance with her, Kate'll find someone else. She begins
packing Martin's trucks. She deserves to dance as
much as Mabel Dowd or any of them. She wrestles the
last truck from Martin's fist, and he whines.

'Mommy wants to dance,' she tells him. She pulls
him from under the table and plunks him on her hip,
struggles his bag onto her other shoulder. He rubs his
eyes and makes weak putting noises with his lips, as if
he isn't quite committed to a full-out cry so soon after
the last, and she hopes he'll please God stay quiet a bit
longer.

'Where's Granma?' Kate searches the line of dancers,
the tables. Phil and Alma Albin are sitting with Susan
Furlong. 'Take my station, will you, Yve? I'll spell you
later.' She doesn't wait for an answer. She skirts
around the dancers, feeling lighter already, dumps
Martin on Alma's lap, and two-steps back to the line.
The fringe on her boots sways with her swaying body.
Her hair is clean and freshly colored; curls fall across
her face, she flips them back over her shoulder. She
feels like an actress in a music video. She feels pretty.

She stands to the side, watching the rows of men
and women face off and weave through a complex
pattern of steps – promenades, stomps and bridges,
dizzying spins. They finish a series and start again,
foot couples advancing, head couples retreating. It
doesn't take Kate more than a few measures to see how

it goes. She sashays between Mabel Dowd and the captain, her movements so smooth the line doesn't have to break for her. In a twirl she's there instead of Mabel, gypsying with the captain. He looks surprised, but he smiles. Kate smiles back.

'Fresh and local,' the captain says.

'You got that right.'

They walk around and around each other, flirting with gypsy eyes just like the move says. Then the captain takes her hand and they duck under the uplifted arms of Patrick and Toddy Styles; Toddy's eyes widen and her loose jowls wattle with shock to find Kate, not Mabel, as the captain's partner. Kate beams at the staring old woman. So what, so what, let them stare!

The fiddles take front stage, firing off competing riffs, the washboard rattles a loud rhythm, and the dancers shake the floor with the balance and swing. The captain pulls her in. His right hand is strong in the small of her back, his strong left hand clasps her right. In his strong hands she feels soft. It's a feeling she likes and rarely gets. Their inside feet touch toe to toe for the pivot point, their outside feet push and pump them around, their arms strain against each other's backs, and their palms and their eyes are locked. He is so short she must look down to look into his eyes, but she doesn't mind. They swing in this tight waltz and the room spins around them so the people staring are just blurs. Mabel at the side, gaping like a dying fish, is just a blur. Kate can barely see the open mouths and hands held to cheeks.

Yve watches Kate dance until the song ends. It's the last of the set, and as soon as the band breaks, the line quickly fills with band members and dancers, but Kate doesn't come back. For a few moments Yve loses track of everything but doling out green bean casserole and roast potatoes and Kate's stations also, mashed turnips

32

and fish. The stragglers hurry through the line and settle into seats. Soon the tables are overrun and people must sit on folding chairs against the walls, balancing their plates on their knees. When Yve looks back up, Kate is nowhere to be seen.

'Ladies and gentlemen, please—' Mayor Barrett stands before the microphone in his top hat and tails. He carries a large foil-wrapped key in one hand and a scroll in the other, and he lays them ceremoniously on the podium. He has always been theatrical. When he ran, he actually delivered chickens in pots to every door, which was thought to be quite a feat until Dora Schultz found out his cousin had a chicken farm operating at a loss for tax reasons.

'Ladies and gentlemen.' It takes a while for the room to settle down. 'I figure I better do my talking while your mouths are busy with this fine food – provided for us by the SnugHarbor Ladies' Auxiliary – special thanks to Edna Larkin.' He sweeps his hand to the kitchen and everyone claps. Yve's aunt peeks through the service window, her glasses and plastic name tag fogged from dishwater steam. 'She wants me to read this announcement: "Send your letters to the council by the end of this week. The referendum is going up for vote, and we want to keep fishing!"'

A loud cheer rises from the kitchen and fishermen side of the room. The CARP tables clap politely.

He holds his hand to his ear and puts on a radio announcer voice. 'That little message was brought to you by the SnugHarbor Ladies' Auxiliary.'

His wife laughs loudly.

'Seriously—' He holds his hands up as if to quiet the crowd again. 'There are some who say the dory schooner is dead. But here in Rosaline, we respect tradition. One foot in the past, one in the future!' He joins his fingers at the tips and holds them there as a sign of this straddling philosophy. 'We take pride in our rich fishing past, a pride that will never die—'

33

A voice from the fishermen's table hollers, 'For some of us it ain't the past!'

Yve turns her head sharply, but only catches Walley Larkin hooting through his hands. The other men join Walley hooting and shaking their fists. From the kitchen, Edna Larkin puts her fingers in her mouth and whistles. The married kitchen ladies of the SnugHarbor Auxiliary cheer and clap. Yve joins in, as does the rest of the service table, as do every fisher and lobsterman and all their wives and daughters and girl-friends and children out on the floor. They keep it up even longer and louder than before. The mayor stands at the podium with his raised palms and stiff smile, as if they are cheering him. Finally the noise dies on its own. The mayor continues.

'A beautiful ship, like a beautiful woman, is a joy forever—'

'Mayor's talking about you.' John Fitz stands in front of Yve.

She takes his plate. 'You want everything?'

'Sure.'

'I'm afraid it's all cold now.' She fills the plate with fish and sides and hands it back.

'I'm sure it's fine.' He puts the plate down on the service table and half-turns toward the stage. The sailors off the *Shardon Rose* are up there now, along with Joe Ames in his pirate outfit, gathered in a half-moon around the mayor.

'You having a good time?'

'Not as good as some.' She scrapes the last few peas into the green bean casserole dish. Then scrapes all that into the turnip bowl.

'The dancing's done, I guess.'

'I had to work anyhow.' She gathers serving spoons.

'I'm sorry. I didn't think they'd end the music so soon. We just got talking—'

'It's fine.' She picks up her stack of serving dishes and goes to the kitchen.

34

Onstage, the mayor hands the captain the key and the scroll. He claps him on the back and holds out his hand for shaking, but the captain's hands are full. There's a little laughter and shuffling; Joe Ames takes the key and the scroll for the captain and hands are shaken.

John goes to the kitchen and leans against the doorframe. The room is filled with women, who all turn and look at him. Susan Furlong's scraping plates; Yve's mother and aunt are drying, flushed from beer or dance or dishwater – it's hard to tell, but they were laughing it up until he followed Yve in.

'Mrs. Larkin, Mrs. Albin,' John says. 'Ladies.'

'John,' Alma Albin says. She glances down at Martin, sleeping on the counter. Dried dishes are piled in stacks around him. She picks the boy up and says, 'I think I better get this one home.'

'Yeah,' Susan murmurs. 'Danny's tired too.' She follows Yve's mother out. 'See you, John.'

'Yeah, see you later.'

Yve has found something to do at the sink, scrubbing in hard circles that shake her whole back. Edna Larkin looks at John, then at Yve. She says to Yve, 'You don't need to clean, hon. You can go with John now. I'll take care of it.'

'I'm fine. I'll just do these few.' Yve turns on the faucet and hot water blatters the deep metal sinks.

'Okay, then.' Edna unties her apron and squeezes past John.

Steam rises around Yve. Her sleeves are pushed back and her elbows are red and chapped. She rinses a pan, puts it in the drainer to dry. John waits. She washes another, puts it up to dry.

'Do you think you'll be long?' John finally says.

She keeps her back to him. 'Does it matter?'

'Not really.' He steps into the room, stands behind her. The sink is empty of dishes. 'Just that we're going out in a few hours.'

She throws her sponge on the sideboard.

35

'Are you angry?' he asks.

'No. Just tired.' She sounds angry. 'You know, we expected you and Chris—'

'I'm sorry.'

'Yeah, so.' She suddenly turns and wraps her arms around his neck and leans her cheek against his chest. It's an awkward hug: she's trying to keep her wet hands off his back, and her elbows stiffen with the effort.

John holds her loosely. He kisses her scalp. Her hair smells like fry oil.

'Jerk.' She hits him in the chest with the side of her fist. Then she shoves away from him and turns back to the sink. She pushes the sponge around, scooping up sudsy scraps and tossing them in the garbage. 'Why do you have to go now when I'm mad at you?'

'Well, I'm not going right now.'

'So?'

'So maybe you won't be mad at me by the time I leave.'

'How're you going to work that?'

He comes up behind her. He moves her braid to one side; he kisses her neck and behind her ear. She shifts a little, making room for him. His hand drifts from her hip to the dip of her waist.

'Oh, I don't know.'

She slaps at his hands. 'Not here.'

'Where then?'

'Nowhere, because I have work to do.'

'How about while you work?' He moves the stacks of plates aside. 'You just climb up here—'

She lets him lift her up on the counter, then she pretends that isn't where she wants to be at all. She squirms and hops down. 'I'm still mad at you,' she says.

'Okay then.' John shrugs. He starts for the kitchen door. 'I might as well go home and get a couple hours' sleep. You want me to take the trash on my way out?'

'Yes please; that'd be a help.'

'Okay then.' He takes the trash bag from the can.
'See you in a week.'

'Yeah, see you in a week.'

'Bye then.'

'Bye.'

John carries the heavy bag to the back stairwell. It's
still relatively early, only a little after eleven by the
tower clock. They're leaving at four, when the tide
turns. It is still warm. The moon is down, but the stars
are out. Lamplight spills down the cement stairs. John
lifts the dumpster lid, heaves the bag in, and lets the
lid clank shut. A faint stink of rot puffs out. He should
shower before they go. He's been out all day, drinking
and sitting in a smoky bar. He won't get another
chance for a week.

'You're a real pain.' Yve's voice precedes her, then
she comes around the corner, struggling into an unnecessary cardigan.

'Are you done with the cleanup? Are you sure they
can spare you?'

'Well, I thought you could at least walk me home
before you leave me.'

'Oh, is that what we're doing? Walking you home?
That's fine.' He takes her hand and together they walk
up the stairs and onto the street. 'That's all I really
have time for anyhow. I have to shower and pack still,
and find Chris and roll him aboard.'

She drops his hand. 'Then maybe you shouldn't
even walk me. Maybe you don't have time.'

'Maybe you're right. See you.' He waves and pretends to be walking away. She lets him go a few steps,
then she hurries behind him, her heels knocking on
the cobblestones. He leaps from one circle of lamplight
to the next, she runs behind. When he finally lets her
catch him, she is breathless.

37

3

In Yve's dream, she is very young, too young for school. She is playing with her friend Kate McCormac. Her brother Chris, her cousin Walley Larkin, and their friend John Fitz are handlining off the Titus Fish Pier. Walley's father, Yve's Uncle Abel, works on John's father's boat. Fitzes, Larkins, and Albins have been twined together as long as Yve can remember. Now the children are waiting for their fathers, whom they haven't seen in a week, to come in. Yve and Chris – whose father owns the chandlery and therefore comes home every night – are waiting to see the off-loading. The big draggers catch so many fish the bodies slip over one another like water from a cupped hand. Soon the boat Warren Fitz owns will pull up, and fish will be hoisted from the hold in wire baskets, dripping chipped ice. Men with pads and pens will scream numbers and money will change hands and the fish will disappear into one of the great black buildings where all the children's mothers work, to be cleaned and sliced and wrapped in plastic.

The boys shout; they've hooked something. It tugs the line tight over Chris's fingers. He winds the nylon on its dowel, playing a bit, paying out, reeling in, as if the fish is an underwater kite and he's catching pockets of wind. Finally, a body breaks the surface and is pulled by all the boys, wriggling up past the piling, fighting still, its scales flashing with a rainbow sheen like oil spilled in a puddle. The boys are happy. They say *All right* and *Wicked*, and slap each other's palms.

The fish flops on the tarry boards. The line extends from its mouth like a thread of spittle. They circle it, even Yve and Kate are allowed in this circle – the boys are so stunned by their catch they don't think to exclude the girls. Their bowed heads cast shade on the simple silver body. They argue about what kind it is, but no one sounds quite sure. To Yve, it looks like the type of fish she draws with crayons, a pumpkinseed with a triangle tail. Its mouth and gills gape as if it has last words, and Chris and Walley Larkin make funny voices for it, saying silly things like *Remember me* or *I'm a goner, Joe*. Things they've heard in movies. They nudge each other, toe the fish. *Tell my wife I love her.* Then they stop because they've run out of things to say, and the ones they repeat become less and less funny. It has gone on too long. The eye stares blankly up at them, the gills slow, stop, the silver scales go gray, the eye goes milky.

Chris gives a little kick. The fish lolls and flops back. 'You want it?' he asks John. John shakes his head.

'It's too small to eat anyhow,' Walley says.

'Yeah, it's stupid small,' Chris says. He looks as if he's angry at its being small, his face drawn tightly toward his pinched mouth. 'It's stupid,' he says again. He raises his foot and his heel comes down hard. The fish makes a sound like a chicken bone snapping. It slips from under his boot and catches on a splinter. The scales open under the fin and the flesh is pinker underneath. A saltwater smell rises from the body.

'Dumb fish,' Chris says.

'Yeah,' Walley says, and he stamps on the fish.

The boys take turns, stamping and cursing; Chris calls it an asshole and Walley, daringly, says Cocksucker. John just says Bastard. When it comes around to Yve, her face burns. She doesn't have a bad enough word to say. She says Jerk, and Kate laughs at her, and the shame of it makes her angry and the anger makes her stamp the fish harder and she lifts her foot and crushes it again and lifts her foot—

'Wake up, Yve.' John kisses her eyes. 'Wake up.'

For a moment she is disoriented. Then she remembers this is John and she is in his bunk on the *Pearl* and he is going out fishing.

'No.' She buries her head in the sleeping bag. It smells of sweat and mildew.

John scratches her back. His other arm, under her neck, is pins and needles. He opens and closes his fist to get the blood back. 'Come on, Yve. It's time.'

'It's not.' She comes up for air. The cabin is blue and silver. 'It's still night,' she says. She paddles her feet on his. 'It's night, still.'

'It's morning in less than an hour.' He rolls from under her and their sweaty chests make a sucking sound. 'Listen.'

She listens. On the water side, the starboard side, the sea burbles along the hull. On the port side she hears the bump and creak of the draggers working against each other. They are moored three deep, gunnel to gunnel, with the *Pearl* outermost.

'I don't hear anything,' she says.

'Everyone's here,' he says. 'They're waiting for us to get out of the way. You can't hear them?'

She does hear voices and footsteps on the pier. She shakes her head no.

'You're deaf, then.'

'They're just walking back from the party. It's early.'

He taps the clock glued to the underside of the overhead bunk. 'It's almost four.'

'No.'

'Yes.'

She bumps her forehead against his chest. 'Why?'

'Because.' He swings his legs free of the bag with sudden energy. He is always a little excited just before leaving. 'Time and tide wait for no man!'

Yve stays in the bag. She doesn't want to get up and out into the cold air. She wants to stay in the bunk with him a whole night, wake up late, have eggs and bacon for breakfast and putter around. Read the paper all morning and then make love again.

He finds his boxers and wipes himself down. Then he leans and reaches – the foc's'le is small enough that from his bunk, with his long arms, he can touch nearly everything he needs if he stretches a bit – and he finds

40

the switch for the red night light. His skin glows red and shadows blacken.

'Turn it off,' Yve says. 'I hate that light.'

He turns it off. The cabin goes gray again and his skin goes pale.

'I had a dream.' She rolls to her elbow.

'If I didn't go every time you had a bad dream—'

'I didn't say it was bad.'

'Okay, if I didn't go every time you had a dream—'

'I didn't say don't go.'

'You're right, you didn't.' He looks at her a good, long time. Her hair has loosed from her braid and he pulls more strands free. They are dry and stiff, from saltwater or sweat, and they drift about her head so that it looks as if she is under water.

'I do have to go.' He kisses her.

'You stink,' she says. She pushes at him and sits up, the nylon bag whistling away. All business now, she wrings the elastic free from her hair and begins rebraiding, her fingers agile, her head craned forward, the cords of her neck tight like stays on either side of her throat. Her raised arms lift her breasts. John bends down to kiss her nipple and she slaps the top of his head. 'You wanted to get up!'

'No, I think you were right. I don't hear anyone now.' He tries to pull her back to the mattress.

'You have to go, John.'

'You're right, you're right. I have to go.' He finds his shirt, smells it, pulls it on. 'Why do *you* have to go, though?'

'Because if I don't, Walley and Dan'll be down here in a minute getting the show of their lives.' She slips off the bunk and dances naked around the cabin for a few seconds, shimmying and turning to wriggle her behind. Then she squeals and ducks, laughing. 'Christ, there are people on the dock already!'

'You give them their money's worth?'

'You'll have to radio them later and ask.'

41

'I most certainly will.'

'Jerk.' She scrambles around on the floor for her clothing and dresses in a half-crouch. He sits on the edge of the bunk, watching her body flick in and out of the shadows.

'Is there coffee?' she asks, when she's dressed.

'If you make it.'

'You really are a jerk.' She smiles and kisses him on the forehead.

A plastic curtain separates the sleeping quarters from the galley and mess. She pushes this aside and in two steps crosses the tiny room. In three steps she's up the companionway and poking her head into the night air and looking across the decks of the *Lady Bea* and the *Three Marias* to the dock. Edna Larkin, who is there to drop off Walley, waves and calls out, 'Yoo-hoo, Yve! Come on and I'll give you a ride!'

'In a minute!' Yve calls and ducks back below.

John is dressed and in the galley, pouring water into the coffee-maker.

'I should just go,' Yve tells him. 'My aunt's up there and everyone.' She starts back up the steps.

'Hold on.' John climbs up after her.

On deck, the slight rocking of the boat feels more pronounced. A gull ghosts about overhead. The moist air smells of salt. The red and green buoy lights bob along the channel, the twin lighthouses flash their four- and seven-second intervals, and headlights sweep toward the pier – women dropping their husbands and sons off. John and Yve hop across the decks of the boats to join the others.

'Hey Dan!' John calls out. Dan's the fifth man on their crew. John Fitz, Warren Fitz, Chris Albin, Walley Larkin, and Dan Furlong.

Dan lifts his hand to say he'll be right over. His wife, Susan, leans against the open door of their truck. Her arms are folded, and her face is turned toward the boats. Susan worked the fillet line with Yve at one time. When the fish plant closed, she landed a much-coveted position as cashier at Finast, through her mother-in-law, Joan. She can supplement her income with dented cans and day-olds. While Joan Furlong rattles around in the big house, alone, Susan, Dan, and the baby crowd into a tiny half-cape on Cooper Street. Dan is explaining something to Susan now, his chin jutting with emphasis, his hands hanging at his sides. She looks at the boats. Finally, he stops talking at her, and she reaches into the front seat of the truck, and she hands him a paper sack. When he goes to kiss her, she turns so his lips graze her hair. She always sends Dan off with a Thermos and lunch bag, even though he'll be out six days, and there's a full galley and mess aboard. Dan calls it his good luck lunch, and it's the first meal he eats every trip.

There's a certain sameness every time. Now Susan gets back in the truck and sits there looking out the windshield, while Dan carries his seabag over to John and Yve. Now Walley Larkin pecks his mother's cheek and joins them. The men say hello all around, then start talking about weather and fish. Yve traces the calluses on John's fingers, and John allows this, letting her hold his hand like a tool he isn't using at the moment. Now Warren Fitz and Chris roll in. They've been drinking and they swoop down upon the group, whooping.

'Lovely lovely night!' Fitz says, clapping his hands down on John's shoulders.

Chris pokes his fingers in Yve's ribs. 'Hey, sis. Heyheyhey.' He stumbles back and laughs and pokes her again.

'Waiting long? Find something pleasant to do?' Fitz winks at Yve. 'How're you, darling?' He doesn't wait for an answer. He turns to his crew and claps his hands together. 'How are you, Dan? Walley?'

'Chris,' Yve says, and he stops weaving and bobbing. 'You were supposed to be at the dance. Kate really wanted to see you.'

'Yeah, well, we caught up at home.'

'Did you now?'

'Yeah.' He has three scratches on his cheek, and she sees him see her see them. He stops smiling.

'Is she okay?' Yve says. 'Should I call her?'

'Do whatever you like.' He picks up his bag and jumps down onto the first boat.

'Well, we're all here,' Fitz says. 'Holding everyone up. Say your goodbyes, and let's get on with it.' Because the boats are tied three deep, the inner boats must wait for the outer boats to go, and so the *Pearl* must be the first to leave. Dan, Walley, and Fitz take up their bags and follow Chris.

'I have to go for real now, Yve,' John says.

'I know,' she says. But now that he's going really, she can't stop touching him. She takes both his hands and slides her fingers up to his wrists, his forearms, pushing her own arms up into his sleeves and grasping him by the elbows until he pulls away, embarrassed.

'Come on, now.'

'Okay.' She holds on to the hem of his sweater. 'Bye.'

'See you soon.'

'Okay.'

'Bye then.'

'Bye already.' She lets his sweater go. He taps the toe of his boot against her sneaker and quickly kisses her, then jumps from the pier to the boat below.

Yve walks over to her aunt. The old woman puts her arm around Yve and rubs her back. The other women, too, say their goodbyes and then gather together in a loose group. Susan Furlong gets out of the truck and stands with them – little Danny, in flannel footie-pajamas, straddles her hip. Bea Hopewell pecks her husband, Pete, on the cheek and then goes to stand beside Edna Larkin. The women watch the men moving about the decks of the boats.

'Sandy's not going?' Edna asks Bea.

Bea shakes her head. 'He got a job down at the yard. With that schooner.'

'Pete can't be too happy about that,' Edna says.

Bea clicks her tongue.

A bell rings, and the *Pearl*'s motor rumbles to life. Pete Hopewell, on the *Lady Bea*, throws the dock-lines to John and Walley. Fitz waves out the wheelhouse window and pushes the throttle forward, and the dragger pulls away. The boats go one by one, and the women wait together until the last rounds the northern spit. By now the sky is lightening, and Danny Jr. is stirring on his mother's hip. Susan rocks him still; she has been rocking him since she took him from the car seat. She says to no one in particular, 'At least they've got nice weather for it.'

'Good weather all week,' Bea says. 'I was hearing on the radio.'

'Yes, nice all week,' Edna says. She looks out over the black water. 'Well, you ready, Yve?'

Yve nods. She is suddenly very tired.

'We're off then, ladies.' Edna slips her arm through Yve's, and Yve is glad for the comfort. Her aunt smells like fish and butter, and dishwashing detergent. Edna calls over her shoulder, 'Don't forget, ladies. Wednesday, my house. Keep the pressure on!' She is heading another campaign against the most recently proposed fishing regulations.

Yve slides into her aunt's old Toyota, and it's like sliding into bed. 'I'm tired,' she says.

'Well, it's been a big day.' Edna fidgets with her mirrors and the seat, readjusting from her taller son. She looks over at her niece slumped against the window. She would like to tell her, You get used to it. When they leave, you have to give them up as if they're not coming back. And when they do come back, you're happy. And when they don't, well, at least you were ready.

45

She says instead, 'You hear Bea say Sandy took a job at the yard on that schooner?'

Yve rolls her head on the window. 'No.'

'He did. Ten dollars an hour. And no guarantees it'll last more than a month or two.'

'Well, maybe he's not so stupid. John says there's no guarantees of fishing in a month or two.'

'Don't believe it.' Edna throws her arm over the seat and speeds in reverse to Water Street, then whips the wheel around so the car spins out on the gravel. She says, 'I've been on the phone nonstop to Gerry, and he swears a deal'll be cut. Dotty Sayles, you know, from Loften Bay, she says—' Edna stops talking. Her lips hang open the way they do when she is thinking. The car idles in neutral. 'Don't believe it,' she says again.

'Well, it's just what John said.'

'That'll never happen,' Edna says. But she is just saying this. She knows that, in fact, anything can happen. Didn't she put her husband on a boat one day, and didn't he get washed overboard? Didn't she swear up and down she'd never let her son on a boat after that? And didn't she just kiss Walley and send him off on the very same boat that took Abel? Between what is said and what is done lies a vast and troubled sea.

II

Little Susie Taylor—
Haul her away!
said she never had a sailor—
Haul her away!
'til she got harpooned by a whaler!
Haul her away!

4

Out, away from land, the sea turns a richer blue. The wind takes on a damp chill, but in the wheelhouse John is comfortable enough to remove his jacket. He even slides the window open for the fresh air. The green scent of land has disappeared, and the only smells are the ones they carry with them: diesel, mildew, and a fishiness that never washes away. For a while a gull keeps pace, soaring over the aft deck so steadily it looks as though it's tethered to the stern, but later, when John checks again, the bird has flown off.

The rest of the men spend the morning below, sleeping off the party. Dan wakes up briefly around noon and takes the wheel so John can piss and grab a sandwich and warm up his coffee, but then he sends Dan back down. He likes making this part of the trip, the steam out, alone. With the autopilot on, it's fourteen hours of not much beyond checking the chart and watching waves slip past. They are making good time with the westerly wind at their back, and they've got a following sea. The swell has grown a bit since the *Pearl* left Rosaline; now the boat has a pitching gait, lifting up on the crests and dropping down in the troughs. John takes it with bent knees. There's a stool, but he prefers to lean against the cushion more than sit upon it. The engine thrums, the throttle vibrates, his coffee ripples in the mug. He listens to the occasional sideband chatter on the radio and sometimes he slaps

49

a cassette in the box – old rock from his high school days – but often when the music runs out it's a long time before he notices. As soon as they begin fishing, he won't have another moment to himself, except perhaps in his sleep, and even then he'll hear Chris turning and sighing in the bunk overhead.

The sun moves slowly across the sky. By five in the afternoon, it hovers low behind the boat, capping the waves gold. A fiery glare blinds the glass panels of the electronics. John looks up and sees his father on deck, a steaming mug in his hand. The old man takes a few stiff steps aft to piss off the stern ramp. He shakes himself, then heads for the wheelhouse. Coming in, Warren Fitz nods to John. Then he bends over the small shelf that serves as a chart table.

'Dad,' John says. 'Sleep well?'

'Nah.' Fitz glances at the chart. His eyes wander over the screens. He turns around to the quickly setting sun, then gazes forward. He looks as if he is trying to remember something. His face is the color of stone, gray stubble fills the lines around his mouth. The hand that holds his mug trembles. By the end of the week, his hands will have steadied. John's mother used to complain that Fitz was always either at sea or in the bar. He liked to tell her fishing kept him from dying of drink, and drinking kept him from dying of boredom.

'Well, might as well get them up,' Fitz now says to John. He taps the horn twice, lightly. 'Get a set in while there's light.' Though daylight doesn't really matter; they'll set the nets clockaround, every three hours, until they steam back home.

Soon Chris, Dan, and Walley stumble up from the foc's'le and stand about aft. John joins them. They will divide into two-man watches for the rest of the trip, but it's become a tradition that all the men take part in the first set. It's something of a superstition. If they weren't all up first set, they'd feel uneasy.

'Walley, Dan – doors. Chris, net.' John points and the

men go. Short round Walley to port, Dan to starboard, Chris to the drum in the center. Their cheeks are red, the tips of their ears red. Spray polishes their oilskins so the yellow and orange rubber shines. Chris frees the net, while Walley and Dan busy themselves shackling the heavy steel plates to the cables. They motor out with the doors unshackled and the net tied up on the drum so any Coast Guard helicopter could easily see they aren't fishing off-limits waters. Fines for off-limits fishing are steep, but the truth is they follow the regulations out of honesty, not fear. The Banks are large and Coasties are busy, and rarely seen by fishermen who haven't radioed for help.

John, at the control panel, looks over his shoulder to the wheelhouse, waiting for a signal. Fitz gives a wave; it'll be a moment.

'So Chris,' Walley says, 'Kate's quite a dancer.' He has to raise his voice over the engine.

'Is she, now?' Chris says.

'Looked that way to me.'

'Yeah, well.' Chris moonwalks a few steps on the slick deck. 'I taught her everything she knows.'

'It looked to me like she was taking extra lessons. From the captain off that schooner.' Walley glances between Dan and John, but neither man laughs. Fitz is slowing the engine and their eyes are on him. The old man nods, and John opens the hydraulics.

'Here we go!' Chris sends the cod end of the net over the stern ramp, and as the boat drifts forward, the drum unwinds and the great green web streams aft.

John signals to Fitz and the old man starts the boat moving forward faster. The doors sail apart like wings, spreading the mouth of the net open between. John takes over now, paying out the warps. The parallel cables slice the dark water, and the doors disappear beneath the waves. A swatch of white paint rolls by.

'By the mark one!' John yells.

51

Fitz flashes his fingers at John. He wants three shots out.

Another swatch of white rolls off the drum. 'Mark two!'

Chris, done with his job, leans on the taffrail. 'So,' he begins loudly enough for all to hear, 'fishing being how it is, Walley decided to find himself some new work.'

'I did not,' Walley says. He turns to John, his glasses are covered in droplets. He swipes at them with a wet finger. In school they called him Wall-eye because his left pupil rolls around whenever his glasses are off.

Dan says, 'It's a joke, Wal.'

'Mark three!' John calls out, and the net is set. There is nothing to do now but wait. The men pull out cigarettes and move forward, out of the wind.

'So,' Chris starts again, 'Walley goes down to the yard and gets himself a job on the *Shardon Rose*.'

'Shut up, Chris,' Walley says. 'I didn't, John.'

John ignores him. He wants to hear the joke.

Chris goes on. 'And every day he's hauling wood, and spanking planks on that tub of rot.' He stops to get a light from Dan. 'Anyhow, Walley notices the captain wears a glove on his left hand, and every morning at the coffee break he takes off his glove and sniffs his little finger.' Chris demonstrates removing the glove, delicately sniffing. 'And every time he does this, the captain says, "Ah, Fifi." Well, old Wal sees this for about three days in a row and he finally speaks up. He says, "Hey, how come every morning you take off that glove and sniff your finger and say *Ah, Fifi?*" And the captain says, "Because every night I finger my woman." So Wal goes home and thinks about it and the next day ten-o'clock coffee break rolls around and the captain takes off his glove and sniffs his little finger and says, "Ah, Fifi." And old Wal here pushes up his sleeve and runs his nose down the length of his arm and cries, "MABEL!" '

John laughs, not so much because the joke is funny but because of the gleeful look on Chris's face and the hurt look on Walley's. Dan is laughing too.

'That's not funny,' Walley says.

'Sure it is,' Chris says. 'Dan and John are laughing.'

'It's not,' Walley says. His face is suddenly bathed in green. Fitz has hit the running lights. Ahead, the sky is dark. Behind, the red sun widens and flattens as it dips below the horizon.

'You got the deck.' John slaps Dan on a wet shoulder. He will go below, nap for a few hours, get a bite to eat. The men on deck will haul in, dump the catch, set the net, clean and ice what they've caught. In six hours, he and Chris will come back up and take over.

Going below, John is once again conscious of the engine, throttling behind the aft bulkhead of the foc's'le. The low overhead keeps him bowed as he moves about the tiny galley. The plastic curtain dividing the cabin swings back and forth, onions and potatoes sway in their mesh hammocks. Everything else is held in place by bungee cord or catch. The galley smells like meat. On the back corner of the stove, wedged against the fiddles, are two tinfoiled pans. John lifts the foil of one and finds a cold slab of steak. He eats with his fingers, standing. It's dry. The coffee in the pot is cold, but he doesn't want coffee anyhow. He looks in the refrigerator. There's a cooler of red bug juice and a carton of milk. Neither appeals to him. He wants something, but he doesn't know what. He thinks maybe he should want sleep, but he isn't tired. Someone on deck opens the hatch, and a cold wind swirls through. Chris's boots appear on the companionway.

He jumps the last two feet and, landing, announces, 'Walley's a dick.'

'Yeah?' John sits at the table with the steak pan and a hamburger bun. He scrapes up the black bits of fat with a butter knife, then smears the bread.

53

'I should kick his ass. Hoo-wah! Hie! Hie!' Chris makes a few kung fu-style feints with his hands and boot heels. He settles down and sits at the table. 'That's my wife he was talking about up there.'

'She was just dancing.'

'Didn't your mother tell you that dancing leads to fornication? He's accusing her of foreplay with another man.' Chris leans back in his chair and puts his boots up on the table, then immediately pulls them down. He looks at John. 'I'm very on edge. D'you see that? I'm really on edge.'

'Yeah?'

'What are you doing now?'

'What do you mean?' John holds out the bread, the knife as evidence. 'Eating. You should too.'

'What is there?'

John goes back to the stove and checks the other pan Walley left.

'Eggs and beans.' He ladles himself some and sits. The pan's been on the stove a few hours, and now the beans have a dry skin and the eggs are hard. John mashes the mess together, adds hot sauce, and scoops a mouthful up with another piece of bread. 'It's not bad,' he says.

Chris jerks his body like a dog that's just eaten grass and is retching. Then, when John doesn't laugh, he says, 'Just kidding.'

John scoops more eggs and beans to his mouth.

Chris says, 'Are you going to go to sleep on me? 'Cause if you do, I'm gonna crawl out of my skin. Literally.' He pretends to claw his face. 'Crawl right the fuck out.'

'I'm not here to entertain you.'

'I can't sleep. Not one second more. I've been sleeping all day.'

'Well, I'm going to try.'

'Don't leave me hanging.' Chris leans forward in his seat. 'Let's play cards.'

'You want to play cards?'

'No.'

'What do you want then?'

Chris slumps back. He pushes out his lower lip. John swipes his bun around the pan, but there's nothing left.

'Do I have to beg?' Chris says.

'I'm not making you beg.'

'Okay then, how about it?'

'How about what?'

Chris folds his hands together. 'Can I please have my medicine, mister, please?'

'It's not medicine,' John says.

'Puh-lease.'

'You sure?'

'Yes, please. Now, please.'

John reaches into his breast pocket and pulls out a small plastic sandwich bag. Inside are smaller baggies, and in those, still smaller wax purses. John takes his time getting one. His face is expressionless, as if this is just another habitual action like flicking the poke from a flounder or honing a knife. It is. On trips, John holds and doles out Chris's dope. It's a deal they've had for a while now. Left to his own devices, Chris would do up his supply too early on and get sick before they've fished their limit. Once, Chris got so desperate he fouled the gear, and they had to go in early. Fitz nearly threw him off the crew that time. If it wasn't for Kate, Chris would've been gone. After that, John started holding for him. He slides a waxed package over.

'Thanks,' Chris says. He is serious now, even slightly embarrassed.

'Don't let me keep you,' John says.

Chris gets up from the table, clears his throat. He waits a moment more, then ducks through the curtain to the foc's'le.

John hears him settle onto a bunk. He would be sitting on the lower bunk, John's bunk. Chris always

55

says he doesn't like to sit on the upper bunk to shoot because if he relaxes too much he might fall out and hurt himself. John has tried to give him the lower bunk permanently, but Chris says he can't sleep with someone on top of him, so John lets it go. There are some things not worth arguing about, he has learned that much. Chris has developed some strange rituals around his drugs. John read about this in a pamphlet Kate had at her house, how this sort of thing is normal for junkies. Chris's been a junkie a long time now, years. Ever since he spent a season working a dragger out of New Bedford. He'd always wanted to fish. Originally, he'd tried to climb aboard the *Pearl*, but Phil Albin forbid him. Phil told Fitz, If you take my son fishing, I'll kill you myself. So Chris left to fish with strangers. He made a lot of money, but he was lonely. And bored. And a lot of the fishermen down in New Bedford are dopers. Or were back then – John doesn't know how it is now. People don't think about that, but it's true. The older generation goes drinking and the younger folks shoot up. Cash and free time. When Phil Albin heard what his son was into, he hauled him back to Rosaline and tried to beat him clean. Chris ran away. Got Kate pregnant. Married her. Fitz gave him a job on the *Pearl*, which was all he wanted in the first place. So Chris is a junkie. At least Chris and Kate are married and have a house and a kid. At least Chris's never tried crack. It's the crack that makes you crazy. No one ever cleans up off of that. You see them hanging around the park, looking like hell. Chris never looks like that. And he isn't a fool with his needle; he never shares. He isn't going to bring some disease home to Kate.

John sits a moment more, then he walks to the sink with the pan and knife. He washes them both, leaves them in the rack to dry. He looks in the fridge one more time for something, finds nothing. He closes the door and stares at the photos and papers taped to it.

An announcement about a fisheries management meeting later in the month, an ad for a shop that carries parts for the Cummins. The AAA Salmon and Sons calendar. A photo of his mom, another of Kate. Dan's taped up a picture of Susie, there's a photo of Edna Larkin. There's also a photo of Abel Larkin, from before he washed overboard. There's one of Yve. She's in the field behind the high school. Chris took the shot, a bit of his thumb shadows the corner. He wasn't a junkie then. They smoked pot in Walley's basement sometimes, that's all.

Once, when Chris was nodding, John asked him, Why really? and Chris said, Because it makes me feel good. John said, How good? and Chris said, The best good you can imagine. Like you're back in the womb, man; you should try it. John said, I'm kind of afraid to, and Chris said, You should be. Then, when John rolled up his sleeve, Chris shook his head. He said, Man, you'll have to go somewhere else. I wouldn't wish this on anyone.

They're old, the photos on the fridge. The colors have deteriorated.

'I'm ready to sleep,' John calls through the curtain.

'Yeah, baby,' Chris says. 'Come on in.'

John slides the curtain aside, and there is Chris sprawled spread-legged in John's bunk. His works have fallen about him. A plastic line is tied around his upper thigh. He is naked but for a T-shirt. His long johns are bunched around one ankle. His gray cock has shrunken into its nest of dark brown hair. His balls rest on John's sleeping bag. His inner thighs are white as a cake of soap and pocked with small bruises. He shoots only in his crotch now, out of respect for his mother, who saw, last Thanksgiving, as Chris was reaching for the potatoes and his forearm was extending from his pushed-up sleeve, the cranberry-colored needle tracks staining his smooth, pale skin. They all saw her see. The least you could do is not shame your mother in front of company, Phil Albin said. Right there at the table.

'Chris,' John says.

'Mm.'

'Can you get in your own bunk?'

'Mm,' Chris says, but he doesn't move.

John clears the needle, the spoon, the lighter and wad of wet cotton from around Chris's legs. He unties the line. He flips a corner of sleeping bag over Chris, then climbs up into Chris's bunk. He's tired. He sinks into the mattress.

'John?' Chris's voice rises from below.

'Yeah?'

'Thanks, man.'

'No problem,' John says, though he isn't sure what he means. He's half asleep already and his thoughts are broken up with dreams. Something about Chris nodding, and safety, and falling asleep in snow. And a half-remembered conversation in a bar about drowning. How it isn't so bad once you give up. The water fills your lungs and you feel drunk. The engine rumbles behind the bulkhead at his feet. When he rolls over and puts his ear right against the hull, he imagines he can hear the waves slipping past.

5

The radio is on in the kitchen and a piano concerto tinkles through to the living room. Phil Albin snaps his paper at the thin walls – they are cracking from the damp. Every year he must spackle and paint.

'The radio's still on,' he says. Neither his wife nor daughter gets up. 'You can hear it in here.'

Alma glances from her knitting. The room is filled with her handiwork. Lace doilies under all the table lamps and on all the chairs' arms and backs. Needlepoint throw pillows, an embroidery wall-hanging behind the sofa. She goes through craft cycles; last year it was bread-dough ornaments, and the year before crazy-quilt Christmas stockings. Now she is making baby's caps that look like vegetables. She sells them to a boutique in Charlesport for ten dollars each, and they turn around and charge thirty. A basket filled with finished caps sits beside her chair. Purple with an olive stem for eggplant, red for tomato. If she adds little black stitches for seeds, the tomato becomes a strawberry. She ties a final knot and says, 'I was thinking we might all help ourselves to lunch. Edna sent me home with so much food.'

'Fine,' Yve says. She is lounging, still in her night-gown, on the floor before the woodstove and working her way through the Sunday crossword, though it is past nine on a Monday morning.

'There's cold turkey, and you can heat up the green beans . . .' Alma's voice fades.

'Every man for himself, again.' Phil half-directs this last remark at Martin. They've had the boy since Kate dumped him on Alma's lap at the dance. He naps on the worn plaid couch. His lower eyelids are wrinkled and puffed. With his eyes closed, it looks as if they were put on upside down. His broad, flat nose is continually stuffed so that sleeping he breathes open-mouthed. Phil prods his slippered toe into his grandson's ribs. The boy waves at Phil's foot with drowsy inaccuracy. He whimpers a bit, but doesn't roll over or move.

'Don't,' Alma says.

Phil nudges Martin again. 'Lazy as the rest.'

Alma sighs. Her needles click and flash and the yarn loops around her finger, turning the tip white.

Phil snaps his paper, reads aloud. 'Says here: "Restoration Begins on Schooner."' He snorts. 'You see her? A mess.'

Alma nods. Her mouth moves with silent numbers as she casts yellow yarn on her needle. She wants to try making a lemon, but is unsure of what to do for a stem.

'It'd be faster to scuttle her and build new from the keel up,' Phil says. He looks over his paper at his wife. She has pulled her chair near the window to take advantage of the morning light. Bent over her work, her skin hangs loose off her bones, and her half-glasses slip down the bridge of her nose. She lifts her head and catches him watching. A smile flicks across her lips, then disappears.

Phil says, 'Ames's gonna need a lotta lumber.'

'You should give Joe a call,' Alma says.

'I'm not calling him. He should be calling me.'

Yve sits up. 'Dad—'

'You know what I think? I think he's already cut a deal with Service Marine.'

'Why won't you call?' Alma says.

'Why should I? If the restoration's started, then he's already got all the lumber he needs.'

'You don't know that. He could order the paints from you.'

'Mom's right.' Yve sits folded in her flannel night-gown, hugging her knees to her chest so the round caps look like breasts.

'Ahh—' Phil waves them quiet. He turns a few pages of his paper, then folds it sharply, whaps his thigh with it, and tosses it at the sleeping boy. It opens mid-flight, fluttering in pieces around the coffee table. 'Well.' He stands. 'I'm off to the shop. Can't waste another whole morning.'

Alma unravels the row and starts over. The screen door in the kitchen bangs open and shut. A few moments later the outside air winds its way to the back of her neck and chills her. She says to her daughter, 'Why don't you take Martin out?'

'I'm not dressed.'

'Get dressed, then.' Yarn hooks around her finger, twists and hooks around, hooks around. 'We

60

won't be having many more nice days like this.'

'Martin's asleep.'

'He's not.'

Yve looks at her nephew. His breathing is light and even, but his eyes are open. He stares into the middle distance, perhaps at the worn spot in front of the stove, perhaps at her crossword. 'Martin?' Yve crawls to him, trying to intercept his vague eyes. 'Are you awake, little man?'

His pupils dilate and he blinks. Yve waves; he waves back.

'Would you like to go see Mommy at work?' It is nearly ten and Kate won't open the bar till eleven, but she'll be there now, setting up.

Martin nods.

'Good then,' Yve says. They could stop by the ship-yard, too, and see the restoration – since it has begun, as her father said. They might as well. Yve brushes lint from Martin's cheek. 'Would you like that? See Mommy and the boat?'

A few regulars are waiting outside the bar. Men who divide their time between the park, the library, and the Whiskey Wind. Road-map faces, hand tremors, chapped and swollen skin flaking red scales. Yve steps over the legs of one; he sits on the sidewalk, back against the brick and legs stretched out as if all the world's his sofa. His ankles look like bags of water spilling over his shoes. Yve mumbles an apology and hikes Martin higher on her hip. They never seem to have socks, these men, though the Free Store at the SnugHarbor Ladies' Auxiliary has piles for the asking.

Yve raps the glass, then cups her hand around her eye and peers through a gap in the gold letters. The smoky window allows a gray shape behind the bar: Kate, stepping around, then disappearing into the foyer. She opens the door and leans against the frame. She is wearing large sunglasses that flash in the bright sun.

'Yve. Handsome boy,' Kate says. She touches her son's hair a moment.

The man on the ground rocks to his knees. Kate puts her foot in front of his hands and says, 'Not yet, Jimmy. I open in half an hour.'

He looks up, and Yve recognizes him. He used to come into her father's shop all the time. Once he had a dragger named for his daughter, Irene. She moved to Portland to study secretarial skills.

'Hello, Mr. Daly,' Yve says. She hurries in before he can answer.

The bar runs most of the length of the north wall. Its maple has been polished by thousands of sleeves and darkened by tens of thousands of cigarettes. The brass brightwork glows. The bar is nearly as old as the town, made by a shipwright in the whaling days. The grandiose open-faced liquor cabinet is carved in rich scrolls and columns, fleurs-de-lis, and fancywork. It houses a large mirror. Between continents of liver spots, the glass reflects the backs of the pricier bottles. The top-shelf display throws off multicolored spangles – the Chambord, the crème de menthe, all the other candy-colored liqueurs, the caramel brandies and tobacco cognacs. Kate goes back to dusting these. A song is playing on the juke, Rod Stewart singing about young hearts beating free.

Yve lifts Martin onto the bar and steadies his back with her fingertips. She gives him a few straws and napkins to play with, then settles herself on a stool. There are no clocks, and the lights are as low as candles. It is as dark as late afternoon, but Kate keeps her sunglasses on. She moves from the top-shelf bottles to the soccer trophies. The radio wakes up and calls for security. Kate keeps her radios – one in the bar, one at home, one in the car – on at all times. '*Sek-yur-it-tay, sek-yur-it-tay, sek-yur-it-tay; this is the* Lady Day—'

'Why didn't you call?' Yve says.

'Why should I've?' Kate picks her bar mop through the register keys.

'Come on, Kate. We've had Martin since Saturday.' Martin looks up at his name. 'Nothing,' Yve tells him and he goes back to his straws. She whispers to Kate, 'He wouldn't go to sleep. He kept waiting up for you to come get him.'

'Yes, well.' Kate bends to the sink, her head ducked at a strange angle as if her neck is sore.

'Are you okay?'

'I'm fine.' She throws her rag into the sink and goes to the kitchen. Light shines through the service cutout. Yve considers wandering back and apologizing, but she stays sitting, her hand on Martin's back, rising up and down with his breath.

'You want coffee?' Kate calls out. She's moving things loudly, banging drawers open and shut harder than can be good for them.

'I'm fine,' Yve calls back.

'It's making anyhow. You might as well stay for a cup.'

The song on the jukebox ends; there is a little click and whir, and the same tune begins again. Yve is reminded of the video, a bunch of teenagers in a brick alley, dancing on top of a car – *Time is on your side* – something sizzles in the kitchen, and soon the bar is filled with a sweaty, masculine smell.

'Did you have fun at the dance, at least?' Yve calls back to Kate. 'With the captain?'

'What?'

'Did you enjoy the dance?'

'I don't know. It was okay, I guess.'

'You left early,' Yve says.

'Chris came and got me.'

'Really? When was that? I didn't see him.' Yve waits for an answer, but Kate says nothing more. The juke sings on, Martin sails his napkins and straws over the bar. In the kitchen, the coffee burbles. Now Kate is

63

opening cupboards, thumping mugs down on the counter, now the swinging door slams open. Kate comes through, hands full with a tray that holds a tube of soft yellow cheese and a roll of crackers, a plate of sausage, and two mugs of coffee. She stops at the juke and, balancing the tray on her hip, feeds four quarters in the machine and punches the same number four times. Then she ducks behind the bar. She creams the coffees and places them on the rubber-nibbed mat.

'Sorry,' Yve says, before Kate can turn her back again.

'For what?'

'For jumping on you like that.'

'No, you're right; I shouldn't've left him.' Kate turns to the mirror. She touches her eyebrow behind a dark lens, then brushes her bangs over. 'Mommy shouldn't leave you with Auntie and Granma so long,' she says to the mirror. 'He looks fine, though. Better than when he's with me.' She tilts her head and lets the bangs fall over her sunglasses from a new angle. 'Maybe you should keep him. Do you want to stay with Auntie Yve for always? No more Mommy? Bye-bye Mommy?'

Martin's lower lip pokes out.

'Stop it, Kate. You're scaring him.'

Kate nods at the cheese and crackers. 'Why don't you make yourself useful and do the cheese plate?'

Yve cuts the tube and squeezes the soft mess into a bowl. She shapes it a bit with a knife, then points the blade at her eye. 'What happened?'

'This?' Kate laughs. 'It's nothing.'

'Really?'

'I was going to drive Chris – he was throwing my boots out the window for me – I'd walked out in my slippers—' She laughs and starts over. 'It's so stupid. I was going to drive him down to the boat, but I walked out in my slippers, and he was still inside, upstairs – so I yelled up at him to throw my boots out. So he says okay and I'm looking up at the window and

64

it was all dark, and *pow*—' She punches the air. 'Right in the eye. I'm such a shitty catch.' She lifts the glasses and quickly lets them drop back in place. 'Does it look bad?'

'No.' Yve concentrates on smoothing the cheese in the bowl.

'It does, doesn't it?'

'No.'

'Do the sunglasses look dumb?'

'No.' Yve smooths the cheese mound over and over, blurring the knife ridges. She doesn't let Kate catch her eye. Kate turns to the sausage and for a while there is only the snick of her knife on the plastic cutting board.

'I just had this bad headache all Sunday, and I didn't think I could take Martin running around—' The boy looks up and Kate stops talking.

'He was fine. Is fine.' Yve fishes an orange slice from the garnish tray for Martin. 'Call next time, though. Before, you know.' She puts a maraschino cherry in the center of the cheese.

Kate checks her watch and takes her keys from the peg. 'Get him off the bar, will you?'

Yve lifts Martin to the floor and hands him a cracker. He still holds his orange slice and his straws and napkins. He looks among his possessions. Kate pats his head in passing. She swipes herself a cracker.

'That looks like a giant cheese tit. What's the cherry? A nipple?' She laughs and Yve smiles stiffly.

Kate unlocks the door, and the men come in, trailing the outside air. They spread along the bar, a few empty stools politely between. Kate pours without asking, glasses and shots. She weeds a wrinkled bill or plucks a few quarters from the damp piles in front of their coasters. She pulls a pale Harp for Mr. Daly and fortifies it with a finger of whiskey. The liquor sinks through the beer. His hands murmur at the base of the pint. He lowers his lips to the rim, reaching his tongue down into the glass. Kate tops it for him, and he

65

repeats the process until his hands are steady enough to lift without spilling. Once the men are served, Kate stands off, down near the windows, zesting lemons. The oils spray her hair, and the rind curls over her fingers.

'So you'll come by for him tonight?' Yve says. She is gathering up Martin's straws and stuffing them in his overall pockets.

'Yes. Sixish.'

'Sixish,' Martin says.

Yve shows him her wristwatch. 'When the hands are straight up and down like this. Six.' She holds her arms straight over her head.

'Six,' Martin says.

'One two three four five six.'

'Five six.'

Nearly three and he should be counting already, Yve thinks. She picks the boy up for a faster getaway. 'We're going now.'

Kate nods.

'Say bye-bye . . . say bye-bye.' Yve opens and closes her fingers.

Kate is busy watching Mr. Daly pocketing crackers. She says, 'You should get something solid on your stomach, Jimmy. I got the sausage special. Protein.'

'Bye-bye, handsome.' Kate blows her son a kiss.

As soon as they round the corner to Water Street, Yve hears the familiar sounds. She jogs the boy on her hip. 'Shh. Listen, Martin. Hear that?'

Martin looks at Yve. His face is mottled from the big cry that began as soon as the door closed between him and Kate.

'You can't hear if you keep crying.'

He downshifts to hiccups and turns his ear toward the noise. Echoes bounce between the arms of the bay – the wrench of planks crowbarred and splintering from ribs, the clock of wood on wood, mallets driving

trunnels, the long dowels squeaking into new holes, a
tinny transistor playing oldies, an occasional shout,
sawing, cursing, laughter – the men are out and working. Yve hasn't heard these sounds in a while, and she
finds herself smiling. They walk the curve of the
waterfront road, and the sounds become louder. The
echoes close in and finally join their parent sounds,
and then, as Yve and Martin reach the cliff over the
Titus Fish Pier, the schooner comes into view. They
press against the chain-link fence and look down.

She looks flayed. Holes show throughout her hull as
if she's been consumed by some cancer. The working
men are dwarfed by her black bulk. They crawl under
her, they carry things, they pass tools and boards to
more men on the scaffolds surrounding her. Orange
extension cords snake through a scattering of ebony
blasting grit and tangle on the marine railway.

Martin points at the yard.

'You want to go closer?' Yve says.

The boy digs his heels into her sides and bumps up
and down on her hip.

'Let's go closer, then.'

A sign on the fence says *No Trespassing,
Condemned*, but someone has cut a body-sized hole in
the wires. Beyond the land is eaten away. Yve slides
down the sandy cliff with Martin in her lap. She hops
the scree between dry land and the old pier. It has
broken free from the rocky shore and hovers boatless
in the bay, connecting nothing to nothing. The small
sea gurgles and foams over the rocks, filling tide pools,
bobbing mats of blackish kelp and snarls of nylon line
and wood from the rotten pier. Yve moves slowly,
careful of her piggy-backed nephew. A bright red scrap
of something, a balloon, catches the toe of Yve's
sneaker. The wave it rode splashes up her shin and
soaks her socks. Martin squeals, delighted.

'You like that, eh? Me getting wet?'

He laughs again.

The sea has carried off a few feet of rock since the last time Yve came out and the step up to the pier is large now. They walk out to the end.

'Here we go, little man.' She sits cross-legged and settles him into the curve of her skirt. From here, Yve can see faces. She doesn't see the captain, though she looks carefully for him. Most of the workers are Helio Carreiro's Portuguese cousins or the sailors from the transit crew – she recognizes them from the party. Some local men hang by the wayside, their hands in their pockets. These are the ones who haven't given up on finding work yet. Yve recognizes Sandy Hopewell and Mr. Bliss on the starboard scaffold, prising chunks of plank from the hull. Rotten wood overflows the dumpster and litters the ways. A pile of uncut timber waits near the saw shed. The blade rips boards nonstop, and a small old crewman passes the new planks through to his partner – a boy Yve knows as Joe Ames's nephew. Yve tells Martin who the men are and what they are doing.

'The planks are carried to the steam box.' She points to a long, coffinlike construction. At the far end, a coal fire blackens an oil drum, and the water inside boils to a pressurized steam that billows from the seams. A pale sailor feeds the new planks into this steamer. 'So they can bend.' Yve curls Martin's fingers into a hull. She shows him how his finger is like a plank, then points out two Portuguese men spanking the steamed plank into place. 'And that man' – she nods at a fat sailor hanging off the bow in a bosun's chair – 'taps cotton and oakum in between. You know what that does? It keeps the water out.' Rolls of caulk hang from the hull like hair; the man gathers and tucks, his caulking irons ringing with mechanized precision.

'I don't know where the captain is, though.' She wraps her arms around the boy and leans her chin on the crown of his head. 'I wonder what his job is,' she says. 'Maybe we'll see him, would you like that? Want to see the captain?'

Martin nods against her chin.

They watch a long time. The boy refuses to leave for lunch, though the whistle blows twelve and the men disappear up the hill, up Cooper and farther. She could carry Martin screaming home, but he's getting too big for such a long carry, and she isn't very hungry herself. She doesn't mind sitting on the rocks. It isn't quite cold yet, and in the sun she is almost tricked into believing it's still summer. She closes her eyes and watches the veins in her lids till the men come back at one. The whistle blows, she opens her eyes, and the captain is there, on the ways with Helio Carreiro. The two men walk around the hull, inspecting. The captain carries a tape measure on his hip, and a pad and a pen, and every so often he measures and records. He slaps the shoulder of the skinny old man ripping boards under the saw shed, then saunters back to stand beneath the scaffold where Mr. Bliss and Sandy Hopewell work. Arms crossed, head back, he watches them awhile. Sandy looks down, says something, and the captain removes his jacket and tucks it in a lower rung of scaffold. He rolls up his sleeves and unbuttons his shirt at the throat so the collar flaps open. He pulls himself up to the platform easily. He is a full head shorter than Sandy, and half that shorter than Mr. Bliss. The captain takes the older man's mallet, demonstrating stance and grip. When he swings, tendons spring up on his neck and forearms and the plank thocks into place with three blows.

'That's the captain,' Yve says. 'He's the boss.'

The captain sends Mr. Bliss down to hump boards, and for the rest of the afternoon he stays up on the scaffold, working with Sandy. The other men mill about, Martin naps. At half past four, the men put away their tools, and by the five-o'clock whistle the yard is empty.

Martin startles, covers his ears. He has never gotten used to the whistles, though they've been blown every day of his life at eight, noon, one, and five. The fish plant has shut down, but its clock still sets off these four hours, and the town still schedules life around them. Fathers with town jobs go to work at eight. Mothers tell children to come home from play at five. The whistle also blows alarms: fire, storm, fog along with the lighthouses. Fog drives Martin crazy with its incessant siren. When the five-o'clock dies off, he takes his hands from his ears, reaches for Yve's wrist, and flips it over.

'Six?' he asks.

'Five. The whistle blows at five.' She turns her wrist so he can see better. 'See, this is five. The whistle blows. Mommy is at six.'

'Six.'

'We have to go home for Mommy. She won't know to come here.'

He pulls against her hand.

'Come on; the men won't be back again. Not until tomorrow. When the whistle blows tomorrow, they'll come back. We have to go home, now.' She lifts him and he begins squalling. His fists, wet with snot, hit her face and catch in her hair. His feet kick her sides, then slow until he's merely prodding her on, as if she is his horse. His cries change to strangled noises that rise and die in his throat, strange whines and clucks. Halfway up Water she understands. He is the ripsaw and mallets. He is imitating the tearing planks and caulking irons. He wants to see the men working again. Well, don't we all, she thinks, don't we all?

6

They shoot the net, haul it in, shoot the net again. Every three hours, eight times a day, two, three, four days in a row, on Warren Fitz's command. The hauls aren't terrible, but they aren't good either. Fitz keeps a mattress in the wheelhouse because he refuses to go below for rest. He naps an hour in the afternoon, a few hours in the middle of the night, while his son drives. His sleep is fitful; he feels the lightness of the net. He swears there is something in the way it pulls against the boat that reverberates through his bowels. It is as if the bag is tied to his own self, and he can feel its drag. A strain on the warps, a hum on the cables, a certain heaviness in his guts, these would be signs of a good catch. Fitz waits for such signs.

Up at three a.m., alone in the wheelhouse, he waits. His son and Chris are aft, waiting. A wash of watery light bathes the wheelhouse. The Loran and the radar, the GPS, the compass and the fathometer display their findings in glowing greens and golds. The sounder feels along the bottom; peaks and valleys shimmer across its grid. If a large school of cod were to swim within its range, it would paint a luminescent swatch like an oil spill. Fitz mostly watches this instrument, and sees nothing but the rise and fall of the seafloor. There are other boats out there, though the old man can't see them. All he sees is 360 degrees of black water. But he knows the fleet is out there, and the ocean feels very small because of that. It is as if he can sense those other nets scraping the floor clean like so many hands to so many mouths.

He signals his son to get ready to haul in. John goes to the control panel. The warps start coiling around the drums. Before the bag surfaces, Fitz knows it will be a light haul. Still, he watches. The doors surface, the net follows. Fitz visually measures the heft and quality. The haul is bunched down at the cod end. He draws invisible numbers on his thigh with his fingers. He frowns. He swallows a mouthful of the chalky antacid he keeps on the chart shelf. He goes through a bottle a day, because, for the most part, the catch is like this one, small and mixed. If he figures in diesel, and food, and repairs, market price, shares to crew, interest to the bank, if he takes into consideration that the *Pearl* must spend a day in port for every two at sea and is allotted only eighty-eight fishing days each year so that each day fishing must pay for four days not, then it becomes clear he's losing money with each set.

It's been a long time since they've had a pure haul. The net drags along the bottom and scoops up everything, whether they want it or not. Of course they keep whatever they can. Any lobsters of size get rubber-banded around their claws and tossed in a tub of seawater. They'll go to Phil Albin. He's got a nice sideline selling to the tourist crowd, the B&Bs. The odd scallop gets shucked on the spot and eaten raw off the tip of the knife. And restaurants will take things nowadays they used to turn away. Monkfish, for one. There's even a market for dogs now; time was if you pulled up a dog you slit its throat before you threw it overboard, cursing it for being a worthless nuisance. But these new fisheries don't make up the loss. What the men really want are the money fish. The ground-fish: cod, halibut, haddock, flounder. But mostly cod. John is too young to remember, but Warren Fitz remembers when the cod would come up by the brailerful. They'd need four men just to hump the heavy load over the ramp. The net would be swollen like a snake that'd swallowed an egg. The egg would be a big ball of olive bodies. Dull, ugly fish. Beautiful fish. Fat tubes, moneymakers. The men would boom the bag up with straps, open the cinched mouth, and it would vomit its load about their ankles. Up to their knees! They'd wade through the fish, many the size of young children, a few the size of men. Nowadays some cod come up, but they are usually small, and most of the rest of the bag is trash – flopping and dying, swim bladders burst, goo and slime to be hosed overboard with the offal and gurry.

'Dad?' John stands in the door.

'Yeah?' Fitz looks at his son. John is a big man;

where he got his size from, Fitz doesn't know. His neck is thick and his head square and heavy, but his face often looks boyish – brows knit together and eyes round. He looks that way now, twisting his gurry-stained gloves in his hands.

'What is it, John?'

'You want coffee?'

'I'm all right. You can go get yourself some. You don't have to stay on deck.'

'Maybe later.' John steps just inside.

They stand awhile looking out at the oily water. The only reflections are their running lights, the stars and moon are cloud-covered. Fitz feels his son looming in the corner. He doesn't know what John wants, and perhaps John doesn't either. Sometimes, often, John comes into the wheelhouse, stands around saying nothing, then goes back out. The small shack traps the man's silence the way a glass overturned at the water's surface traps air. Fitz clicks on the weather radio and catches the nasal announcer midword: '—cy rain . . . wind picking up out of the south . . .' The announcer, probably bored out of his wits, reads with the inflection all wrong so it's hard to tell where one sentence begins and another ends.

Fitz picks up the transmitter of the VHF and says, 'Where the hell is everybody?'

After a few moments, Sal Liro's voice crackles through. 'This is *Three Marias*.'

Fitz shifts his dead cigar to the other corner of his mouth. John rustles behind him.

'Hey, Sal. You've been awfully quiet,' Fitz says. 'Izzy? Pete? I'm wondering where you all are – you holding out?'

Sal says, 'Iz's out here with me. I can see his lights.'

'Where's that?'

'Gravel Flat. I can't find any fish out here – you?'

'Nothing. We've been all up and around the Lightship and it's weak.'

'I'm thinking if it doesn't pick up I'm heading in. Save the rest of my days for November.' Every trip Israel Titus says he's going to save his days for November, when the weather is worse and fewer men are out and prices are higher. Every November he's out of days. 'Hear from Pete?' he asks.

'Not a word,' Fitz says.

'He's probably got something, the bastard.'

'You think? Pete, you out there? You holding out?'

The radio chirps, then through the static comes Pete Hopewell's voice. '. . . *Lady Bea* . . .'

'How're you doing, Pete?' Fitz smiles.

'Not great.'

'Not great, eh?'

'I got maybe fifty fish all told. I got nothing. I'm pulling up bags of water.'

Fitz winks at John. 'Where've you been?'

'Low Hole. The Baths—'

John leans over his shoulder and Fitz points on the chart.

'I been there.' Sal's voice. 'I didn't see you.'

'There was nothing out here.'

'Tell me about it,' Sal says.

Pete says, 'I'm thinking of coming in early.'

Fitz elbows John. 'If the man was coming in early he'd've said so before now. He'd've been calling in to see where *we* are instead of us calling *him*.' He speaks into the radio, 'Where you now, Pete?'

'Heading out of Celia's Garden.'

'Yeah, how's that?'

'I don't know. I'm not having a lot of luck. I'm not getting any fish – or sleep. Now Sandy's gone, I'm short-handed. Maybe I'll go home, haul his ass off that schooner, and come out again the middle of next week.'

'You hear that, right?' Fitz says to John.

'What?'

'He's trying to change the subject.'

74

'Yeah?'

'He's got something.'

'You think?'

'He's got flounder. The man's got flounder, I bet.'

'How do you know?'

'Celia's Garden. That's the sweet flounder spot.' Fitz hits John in the arm with the back of his hand. 'Get that net in. Go!'

John runs out of the wheelhouse. Fitz watches him yell at Chris, rousing him. He relights his cigar, rings the bell, and in minutes the net is pulled up. He turns the wheel over to John and they are motoring to Celia's Garden.

They get there around dawn. The southern sky is the color of lead, and a black scurf, like metal filings, hangs below the clouds. With the wind rising, the waves have grown pointy whitecaps. Fitz keeps his running lights on. As does Pete Hopewell; the *Lady Bea* is a mile off, motoring out. Fitz looks through the binocs. By the activity on deck, Pete's not a man who's been pulling up bags of water. His nets are tidied on the drum, his crew are busy cleaning. Gulls are thick over the dragger, like flies. So many birds dive-bomb the aft deck Fitz can hear them screeching, even this far off.

'Heading in?' Fitz says over the radio.

'Yeah.'

'Looks like you had some luck.'

'A little. Not much.'

'Try not to flood the market, eh?' He can't resist saying it, though he knows Izzy and Sal are out there listening.

7

Sometimes, mornings, for no clear reason, Phil Albin picks his breakfast off the kitchen table and goes around front to his store. He stands there now, drinking coffee. A handful of children straggle by on their way to school. Toddy Styles comes out in her housedress and slippers for the paper. He calls across, 'Nice weather!' and she nods and shuts the door. The maples across the street are beginning to turn orange and yellow with a few green veins. The shrubs underneath are red. The Jameisons have set a pot of rusty mums on their porch. The Hopewells have hung Indian corn off their door knocker. Halfway through September and there hasn't been a real frost yet. The air still smells like dirt. The rising sun reflects off the white storefront and warms his back. He can still get away with just a sweater, but soon it'll be cold. Soon days'll seem too short. Another few weeks or so.

The door to the old chandlery is padlocked, and Phil won't unlock it. He doesn't spend time in the actual storefront anymore – it's mostly empty. There's no sense in keeping the shelves stocked. He places orders to larger marine supply houses whenever someone needs the odd something. And that doesn't happen often enough to warrant keeping up the appearance of regular business hours. Instead he prefers to rely on the posted sign: *Come Round Back.* An arrow points around back to the barn, which sits directly behind the chandlery. The barn is where Phil spends most of his time. Last June, Joe Ames made an offer for the storefront; he said the museum wanted to restore it to its original condition, make it part of the museum's Maritime Village Tour, but Phil hasn't felt like selling.

He hears the truck before he sees it. A cloud of dust, then a white Ford with antlers on the grill crests the rise where St. Peter crosses Water. Phil watches it pull up, slow, park. The door creaks open and a young man steps out, slams the door. He comes toward Phil with his hand extended.

'Mr. Albin?' The man's voice is loud, as if he has to shout over a distance. Phil nods. The man takes Phil's right hand and pumps it hard twice. 'I'm Wendell Holmes, captain of the *Shardon Rose*.'

'Yes,' Phil says. He tilts his head in the general direction of the yard. 'You're down at Helio's yard. Joe Ames's restoration.'

'That's right. Helio directed me to you, as a matter of fact.'

'He did now, did he?'

'Well, he and Mr. Ames were talking, and I heard the name Albin mentioned—'

'Good man, Helio.'

'He speaks highly of you, too.'

'Ah, he's as good himself. We do different things. I more build small craft.'

'That so?' the captain says.

'Dories. Yawls.' Phil looks into his cooling coffee, then he squints down at the shorter man. 'You want to see the shop?'

'That'd be great,' the captain says, but he's looking back at the house. An upstairs light is on, and someone is moving about inside, shadowy.

'Well, then, I'll give you the dime tour.' Phil leads the captain around the south side of the chandlery, toward the barn first. The two buildings are separated by a thin strip of worn grass. Phil nods at the heavy slats of the barn's double doors. 'This is where I do most of my work.'

'Look at the size of those planks,' the captain says. 'Those must've been some big trees.'

'Yeah. Good wood, that.' Phil pats the door appreciatively. He says, 'Folks're tearing down old barns just to find seasoned wood like this, nowadays.'

'Tell me about it. It's damn hard to find. And Mr. Ames's got us on a tight budget—'

'You know, I might have a few ideas for good cheap lumber.'

'I wish I'd known ahead of time. Mr. Ames already ordered—'

'Yeah, well.' Phil chucks his cold coffee out splat on the cement ramp. 'I'm just saying you should come see me if you run out of what you got.'

'Sure.' The young man looks vaguely bored.

'Well, there's nothing in there,' Phil says suddenly. 'Let me show you around back.' He leads the captain to the waterfront side.

The captain whistles low.

From here, the whole sweep of bay is visible. To the south, the derelict Titus Pier, the fish plant, the Museum Pier, Helio Carreiro's boatyard with the schooner looking small so far off – to the north, the spit of pine and rock. On either side, the twin light-houses. Here, the curve of land gathers and amplifies the constant surge and hush of waves like a hand cupped to an ear.

'The property is almost five acres. Three buildings: house, barn, and chandlery. Worth a lot more'n anyone can offer.'

'Lot of history here, I bet,' Wen says. He is conscious of taking on the old man's clipped speech, and is slightly embarrassed by this artificiality, but the man doesn't seem to notice.

Phil has turned around and is looking at his out-buildings, as if surveying his own property for the first time. A sign on the back of the barn, facing the water, says *Albin's Marina*. 'My grandfather, the first Albin out of Newfoundland, put that up in 1893. He laid the drive.' Phil nods at the gravel-and-shell path that flows from the road down to the cement boat launch. Next to the ramp, the shore, built into a bulwark of railroad ties and fixed with cleats, could provide dockage for a good-sized boat.

'I used to sell a lotta bait, lotta dry goods, diesel. Boats'd pull right up and refuel, buy what they needed.'

'I'm sure that was something to see.'

'Yeah, well, summers we keep the lights on at night

– we still get the occasional yachty. But not so many this time of year. They tend to go on to Charlesport.' Phil turns his back on the bay. Between the house and the chandlery, in a grass alley worn nearly to dirt, sit his finished dories. 'Let me show you something,' he says. But the captain is already heading across the lawn.

'I spend most my time building those.' Phil catches up to him.

Wen strokes the curving planks. Their hulls are filled with water, swelling them watertight. 'Beautiful.'

Phil runs his fingers in the groove the seat would rest in. 'Removable seats so they can nest on deck.'

Wen nods, feels for himself.

'Details—' Phil says. He wants to say something about the geometry of boatbuilding, and the elegance of that geometry. He builds his boats the old way, by eye. His hands can feel a fairline. Instead he says, 'They come with spruce oars – strong and light, spruce. I keep the handles unfinished for grip. All the sharp edges're rounded.' He touches the parts as he comes to them. 'Sole comes up for bailing, copper bottom paint for weeds and barnacles, turp and linseed bath against rain and salt—'

'Museum quality, all right,' Wen says.

'Museum quality.' Phil puts his hands in his pockets, pulls them out. 'You know the dory in the playground over at the museum?'

'Yeah?'

'I made that,' Phil says.

'I'll have to take a look when I get back.'

'It's just like the kind of dory that schooner of yours used to have. Ames didn't show you?'

'We've been pretty busy.'

'Yeah, well.' An uncomfortable mix of pride and anger swirls in Phil Albin's chest. Joe Ames hasn't shown this captain his dory. 'Well,' Phil says.

'So Mr. Ames bought one, but who buys the rest?'

'Oh,' Phil chuckles. 'You hear of Captain Blackbeard's Seafood Bonanza?'

'Yeah – those are your boats?'

Phil nods.

'That's a lot of work for—' Wen stops and gestures vaguely.

'For decoration. That's what Alma – my wife – says. She says I'd make more money if I'd just cut a few corners. Who needs antifouling when they just get cut in half and hung on a wall?'

'She's got a point.'

'Yeah,' Phil says. What he means is, there's a right way to do things and that's the way he does them. It's the way he was taught by his father, who was taught by his father, who was taught by his father, and on back.

'And this keeps you going? Moneywise?' The captain looks incredulous. 'I mean, you got quite a large property to keep up. The taxes alone must be deadly.'

Phil feels his neck and chest warming. 'Small orders come now and then through the chandlery. If you need anything, paint or anything – Hey, that boat of yours is a dory schooner. She'll need some dories. You can check back with Ames and give me a call anytime, I can hold a few of these or make some up special—'

'Well, Mr. Ames is thinking more along the lines of leaving the deck space free for dancing and schmoozing, you know.'

'Ah.' Phil clears his throat. 'Well, anyhow, we do okay. Once in a while a yachty rents out the dock.'

An awkward silence stretches between the two men. The captain digs clods of grass up with the toe of his boot. Phil watches and wonders if this young man realizes it's not his own lawn he's tearing up. He's about to mention that when the captain sticks out his hand and says, 'Well, Mr. Albin. I'd really like to thank you for showing me your place.'

Phil doesn't shake. 'That why you come down? To check out the property? I'm not selling. Ames tell you that? Or he leave that out too?'

Wen drops his hand. He is embarrassed for the man, for putting him through the tour and getting his hopes up about his dories.

'Why're you here?' Phil asks.

'Actually, I came to see your daughter.'

'How do you know my daughter?' The man looks angry and sounds suspicious. Wen decides not to mention that he met her at the dance.

'I don't. I was going to offer her a job.'

'And now you're not going to.'

Wen doesn't know how to answer. He realizes now, after the stupid comments he's made about finances, the offer might be mistaken for charity, and he can tell the old man is proud. And he feels dishonest. He wishes he'd just gotten the girl's number and called her instead of making this all up. He finally says, 'I just realized the job is terrible and the pay is worse. I don't think she'd want it.'

'She's a grown woman. You should ask her yourself, let her decide.'

'I don't know.'

'I'll go in and get her. You wait here.' The man ducks around the corner of the house.

The first thing Phil sees when he gets in the kitchen is his daughter, still in her robe, feeding teaspoons of milky coffee to Martin. His wife stands at the counter rolling dough. He looks between the women and says, 'Jesus, Yve, you're still not dressed?'

Yve ignores him, and Alma doesn't turn. She says, 'Are you walking on my clean floor with your muddy boots? Get on the paper.'

Phil backs up to the square of newspaper just inside the door. His hand is still on the screen, and the door is still open. A wet breeze blows through the kitchen.

Alma says, 'You going to keep that door open?'

'There's someone here to see Yve.'

'Who?'

Alma scurries the few steps to the door; 'Shh, shh! Both of you, shh!' She elbows Phil aside, looks out quickly, then shuts it. Her hand leaves flour on the knob. 'He's right there in the yard.'

'Who?' Yve holds another spoonful out to Martin, teasing him by offering it and pulling back. He bats the air, then her arm, and the coffee slops on the table. She wipes it with a paper napkin.

There's a small window high in the door. Alma rises on her toes to peek through the lace curtain. 'Looks like that captain.'

'What captain?' Yve asks.

'Off the schooner!' Phil says. 'Off the *Shardon*.'

'The *Shardon* captain?' Yve touches her pajamas, her cheeks, her uncombed hair.

'Why would he want to see Yve? How would she know him?' Alma looks at her daughter. 'How do you know him?'

'I don't!' Yve drops the spoon and covers her mouth – she nearly screamed it, for Christ's sake. She chokes on a giggle, then sees her mother's face and stops. 'Mom. Lord. I don't know him.'

'He's here to give her a job,' Phil says.

'You didn't say.'

'I didn't say?'

'No, you didn't,' Alma says.

Yve looks at her mother. 'He didn't say.'

'Well, I'm saying it now!'

'A job?' Yve says. 'What kind of job would he want to give me?'

Her father stands just inside the door, his muddy boots carefully on the paper, his curved hands hanging heavily from his shoulders. Her mother twists her fingers in her apron, wiping off scraps of dough. Something clouds her face. She looks at Yve as if she's finally recognized her, and her daughter isn't who she'd thought. Then she blinks. Says, 'Lord, Yve, put something on. What are you doing still undressed?'

'Come on now, get going.' Phil flaps at her.

'I'm going!' Yve jumps from the table. She runs through the living room, up the stairs, her shoulder grazing the wall and her hand pulling the banister.

Downstairs, her parents listen to her hurried steps, drawers opening and closing, the creak of the bed as she sits to slip on socks.

Alma says to her husband, 'Well, you can't just leave him out there like that. Go offer him coffee.'

Yve finds her father and the captain in the small shop room inside the barn. She stands at the door a moment, holding Martin by the hand, watching their curved backs. Coffee mugs sit by their elbows, and over their heads her father's tools hang neatly on their pegs, inside black-marker outlines. They've got the die cutter down on the bench, and her father is twisting the wings, threading a bolt. Martin frees himself and runs headlong into the back of his grandfather's knees.

'Is that the little man?' Phil says.

Martin giggles and squirms.

'Is that the little man?' Phil turns, spreads his hands as if he's surprised. He grunts lifting Martin onto the workbench, then gives him a few carriage bolts to drive over the paint roads. 'My grandson,' he says to the captain.

'Your daughter's son?'

'My son's son. This is my daughter, Yvette—'

'Yve,' she says.

The captain turns, looks at Yve. He says, 'Yve?' as if her name is in question.

'This is Wendell Holmes, captain of the *Shardon Rose*.'

'Yes, hello.' Yve moves the die cutter out of Martin's reach. She puts out her hand.

For a moment, the captain's eyes are blank, as if he

83

cannot place her. Then he recovers and smiles, shakes, says, 'Pleased to meet you.' His hand is thick and paddlelike, just like John's, but the palm feels different, hard and horny, as if his callus isn't continually softened by water. She lets go before he does. Her father takes her by her elbow and pulls her to his side. It's an awkward pose. She feels as though he's displaying her like a piece of work he's just completed. He gives her arm a little squeeze.

'The captain has a proposition for you, and I think you should consider it.' His voice is loud and smiling. Yve feels the tops of her ears burn. 'Go ahead,' he tells the captain.

The captain looks uncertain.

'He says you won't like it but I told him to ask you himself,' Phil says. 'Tell her.'

Wen leans against the workbench. He kicks the heel of his boot against the other boot's toe, looking down at the result. 'It's cooking.' He feels almost ashamed. He would like to leave, but he can't figure how. The young woman looks at him, open-faced, eager. 'The pay is awful and the hours are bad—'

'What happened to your old cook?' Yve asks. 'The one you sailed in with?'

'He ran off.'

'Why?'

'Ed put the toilet plunger in his stew. Just as a joke. You really don't want this job.'

'How much does it pay?'

'Forty dollars—'

'Day or week?'

'Day. Jesus!' Wen is astounded.

'That's a nice bit of money for Christmas,' Phil says. 'A little pocket change.'

Wen shakes his head. 'But that's for three meals. And you got a huge crew for lunch – all the day-workers. And cleaning and shopping are part of it too. Anyhow—'

'It's fine.'

'I shouldn't've mentioned it. It's terrible.'

'No, it's fine, I'll take it,' Yve says. 'When would you like me?'

The captain takes a moment to answer, as if he didn't expect his offer to get this far. Now that she sees him close up, Yve understands why Mabel Dowd thought him handsome. He isn't really – his eyebrows are too thick and his lips too fleshy, but he has the sort of face that, if you liked his personality, you might find him attractive. 'I can start tomorrow,' Yve prompts. 'When do you want breakfast?'

'Oh no, that won't be necessary. We have cereal.'

'Well then I'll come by afterward. Is eight too early? That way I'll have time to see the place and make lunch.'

'That's fine.' The captain looks defeated.

'Tomorrow, then,' Yve says. 'At eight.'

'Good then!' Phil claps the captain on the shoulder. He steers him out of the small shop, through the dark barn – Yve follows quietly behind, Martin on her hip – and out to the sunlight.

Turpentine wafts from the paint-cleaning station. Phil smiles, says loudly, 'Stop by anytime you need something else. I can do special orders—'

'See you tomorrow,' Yve says.

Wen squints at her. She is definitely not the woman he danced with. He might've been drunk that night, but he's not mistaken now. 'Tomorrow.' He offers his hand to her father, who's still talking.

'—call if you need anything, Captain. Paint, anything. Dockage once she's off the ways—'

Wen pulls his hand free. 'Sure thing.' Then he cuts around the chandlery and trots to his truck. When he looks back in his rearview, he sees the two and the little boy standing out front of the closed store, watching him drive off.

8

Dan, Walley, and Chris gut on the aft deck, their gloves sopping red, blood flecks on their foul-weather gear. Even with the three of them, even though flounder are easy and fast to dress, the waiting fish pile high in the bins. The men's fingers are cold, their hands are sore, their toes are blocks of ice. The weather doesn't help – stinging pellets of icy rain. The seawater freezes to pink slush about their boots.

Down in the hold, John is sweating. With the hatch bolted shut, he's out of the wind, and the bare bulb hovering above his bent back gives off a surprising amount of heat. His foulie overalls are heavy on him, his jacket came off a while ago, his sweater's off. Steam rises from his long john undershirt. He's in a good mood. His father's been hauling in faster than the men on deck can clean. John flips a wire basket of fish dark side down so the flesh will stay white. Then he covers the flat bodies with ice. He works carefully but quickly, spreading the weight so the fish at the bottom won't bruise. Ice, fish blood, and sweat mix together and smell metallic. The week has turned a corner and begun to pay off. The work has a rhythm, and there's something soothing about the monotony. It's like being part of a machine, nothing is required beyond movement. His breath comes in short white puffs. A strand of an unrecognized song runs on a loop through his head, the engine thrums, the shovel bites and scoops and scatters ice – *chash-chet-chash*—

Chunk. The boat bucks. The engine stops. There's a beat of silence, then the engine alarm rings.

In the second it takes him to react, John hears Chris yell, 'Hangdown!' Then he hears footsteps, Dan and Walley running. John rushes up on deck without his oilskin. He skids through the slush to Chris, who stands over the stern ramp looking in the water.

'We got a hangdown,' he tells John.

'Yeah.' John crosses his arms over his chest.

'Where's your jacket?'

John nods toward the hold.

'Might as well go get it. This may take a while.'

But Fitz is waving at John to come to him. He's got the boat in reverse, and he's backing down on the net.

John hurries to the wheelhouse.

'Goddammit, tell them to take up! Take up!' Fitz turns his face over his shoulder as he hollers, as if the men on deck can read his lips.

John slides back through the slush. 'Take up! Take up!'

Chris controls the winches, taking up slack, but Fitz is already shaking his head and yelling something else. He throws the throttle in the opposite direction, and the engine growls forward as whatever is anchoring them pulls them backward. The old man yells and curses, backs and forwards. John runs between the wheelhouse and Chris to relay Fitz's yelling. The old man's trying for a careful balance of taut and slack: taut enough to pull free, slack enough not to lose the net or burn out the engine. No one seems to be getting it right, judging by his red face. He spits brown bits of cigar, thrusts the throttle forward and back. Dan and Walley, with nothing to do, are white-faced and tense. The boat surges, catches, springs back. The engine stalls, the alarm rings. They restart, back down. Chris calls a mark. But the cable coils slowly on the drum.

It goes on like this. The temperature drops, and the icy rain turns to hail. Now John runs back down for his sweater and coat, throws them on over his wet undershirt. His face feels tight and wet. It is frustrating trying to hear what his father and Chris are saying. It is frustrating trying to be heard. The wind loops his voice back, the engine is loud, hail patters his sou'wester. He feels as though he's trapped in a bubble of noise and wet and cold. They back up, take up slack, pull forward, and get nowhere. Whatever

87

they're pulling against is heavy or fixed – rocks maybe, a sunken buoy, an unmarked wreck. Something missed on the sounder. Fitz must have looked away from the green grid – in some forward- or backward-gazing moment he missed whatever they were passing directly over – and this failing on his own part makes him yell even more at John.

'Take up, take up! You didn't tell him to take up soon enough!'

'I told them! You're pulling forward before they get the chance. We're bouncing back and forth. *You're* not going back enough!'

'Don't tell me what I'm doing, boy! Tell him take up now! Now!'

John goes back out to Chris.

'That's it. We're over top of whatever it is. There's no more to take up,' Chris tells him. The warps are thickly cabled on the drums. Chris tries to take up more cable, and the winch labors but doesn't turn. It starts to smoke, and he shuts it off. The net has become an anchor line to whatever is holding them in place.

'We're not going anywhere, John.' Walley stares over from across the deck, eyes blind behind water droplets.

'I know,' John says. 'Chris, come with me.' They slip across the icy deck.

'I said take up!' Fitz yells when the two men enter the wheelhouse.

John doesn't answer.

'Well?' Fitz says.

'We can't,' Chris says. 'We're over the thing already, and it's holding us. It's gonna fuck the winch.'

The old man's nose and cheeks are purple, his forehead is white. He runs his fingers over his lips. The room is small, and the men stand close enough to feel the humidity rising off each other.

'I say we secure her and just haul forward,' Chris

88

says. 'Either the thing – whatever it is – 'll come up or the net'll rip and loose itself.'

'Or snap at the shackle and we lose the net,' John says.

'Or that,' Chris says.

Fitz exhales tobacco and sugared coffee. 'Well, we don't have much choice, do we?'

'Aye-aye, *mon capitaine!*' Chris turns on his heel. He opens the door and the wind takes it, slams it against the small shack. John pushes it shut. It is like pushing against something solid.

They work another quarter of an hour. Or not so much work – the men stand around aft, huddled in their wet gear. They know better than to go below for a cigarette and a hot coffee. Fitz would rant on them for leaving the deck during a hangdown, but they are unable to do much more than watch the humming cables. Fitz is the only one with anything to do. He drives the boat forward, lets it catch and bounce back, then drives the boat forward again. John starts to feel sick from the repetitive motion. More than once, he imagines the fire ax in his hands. He sees himself hefting it and bringing it down on the cables so they snap into wiry fray and the net slips off and they are free. Of course he won't do it. The ax couldn't cut through with the one strong stroke he pictures in his mind. And the net is worth more than just about anything on the boat. Engine, net. All the other fancy equipment they can do without, but not the net.

He thinks of the flounder they aren't catching, lying on the bottom like quarters in a duckpond, waiting to be scooped up. He knows Sal Liro and Israel Titus are out there somewhere, hidden by the icy rain. They radioed as soon as they figured out what Fitz had figured out, that this was the trip to follow Pete to the flounder grounds. Now they're getting all the goods.

'I don't know,' Chris says to John. 'I say it's time to give up. Loose the net from our end.'

89

'No. Not yet.' John pictures the net anchored to the bottom catching fish and letting them rot, and then catching more, letting them rot, catching more, on and on to the benefit of no one. 'Don't say that to my dad yet.'

'Well, he'll come to it on his own soon enough. This is whack.'

John walks aft to the rail and peers in. The boat surges and bounces, surges and bounces. Walley peers at him through his spotted glasses. The lenses magnify his eyes. 'I'm getting cold, John. Can I go down maybe and start lunch?'

'Go ahead.'

Walley heads forward, bracing himself rhythmically for the surge and catch. John watches his shiny orange back stopping and starting. The boat catches, Walley stops, the boat surges, Walley walks, and suddenly, instead of bouncing back, there's an unexpected give. Walley's feet slide out from under him and he goes down hard. Chris starts laughing; John smiles, too. Then he cheers. They are free.

'Let's bring the net in!' John calls to Chris. He takes his place at the winch. The doors break the surface, Chris secures them, and soon the rest of the net limps aboard. They boom it up to get a good look at the damage. Chris parts the dripping chafe gear. The mesh is in bad shape. It's torn from one end to the other, and there are many places where whole sections are missing, as if someone has been at it with a giant razor. He talks to John as he goes. 'See here, that's all gone. And there. And there's a long slice here.'

'How long will it take to mend?'

Chris pulls aside a hank of frayed line. 'It's shredded.'

'How long do you think?' John asks. 'How many hours?'

'Hours nothing.' Chris's hands play down the mangled web. 'It's destroyed.'

'You're kidding me, right?' But John knows Chris isn't kidding, he can see for himself. He looks up to the wheelhouse. Fitz is staring back at them, his face white in the dark glass. 'You tell him, then. You're the net man.'

'Come with me,' Chris says.

'You can go below,' John says to Dan. 'Walley's starting lunch.' Then he goes with Chris to the wheelhouse.

Fitz is waiting for them. He's breathing like a man who's exerted himself. He looks back at the net and not at them as he speaks. He asks Chris, 'How long?'

'It's destroyed.' Chris unsnaps his foulies and gets himself a wet cigarette. He puts the pack on the chart shelf. 'I don't know. I don't think we even have enough line with us to mend it all.'

Fitz picks a mug off the shelf. He swallows cold coffee and winces. He helps himself to one of Chris's cigarettes. Chris holds out his lighter.

'Really, man,' Chris says. 'It's fucked. I mean, if we go back, I'm pretty sure my dad'll front us some line.'

Fitz looks out. Rain dulls the water, shortens the horizon. They could stay, do their best with repairs – but all the while Sal and Izzy and whoever else will fish up the flounder, go in, drive the price down. And there's no guarantee the fish'll be there when they're ready for them. If they leave now, maybe they can beat the crowd. They can repair the net on docked days, and save the days out for fishing.

'Ah, what the hell. Tie that shit up. We'll make tomorrow's auction. Meet Pete for breakfast.' Fitz picks up the radio and says, 'This is the fishing vessel *Pearl* calling the Coast Guard.'

'*This is the Coast Guard Station Group Southwest Harbor we copy*—'

John steps out of the smoky wheelhouse. He leans against the hatch. His father's voice vibrates through. He is giving their current location and their planned route; he is telling the Coasties that their net is damaged; he is promising they will not fish in the off-limit waters they plan to motor across. The old man's voice rises and falls in a familiar cadence. He still has a slight brogue from coming over when he was thirteen. John's mother had an even heavier accent. When John was young, he'd lie in bed and listen to his father and mother through the wall. It helped him relax. Nights his father was out fishing, and the house was quiet, he found sleep hard to come by.

9

The *Shardon Rose* crewhouse is on the other side of town, but Rosaline is small enough to cross in a forty-minute walk. Still, Yve leaves an hour early, just to be safe. She cuts across the Finast parking lot. It rained earlier. The maples along Water Street look bedraggled. The air smells of wet leaves. Her boots make slight sucking sounds on the shiny asphalt. Yve walks past Stewart's Pharmacy – *For All Your Stationary Needs* is painted in white script on the dark window. She finds the misspelling amusing and oddly appropriate. Next door, Orsten's competes for the same slim back-to-school-supplies market. Then Kiernan's Hardware, Woolworth's. The accordion gates in the storefronts are still padlocked. The streets are empty of pedestrians except for one woman on the corner of Pine, stamping her high heels in a fruitless tattoo. Her stockingless legs are goosepimpled with cold; her shiny skirt is too short for the damp chill. On her upper half, she wears a rabbit-fur jacket unzipped to its elasticized waist; beneath that, a red Lycra body suit with a plunging neckline and a scatter of hangnail snags. Women often work this corner, though it's odd she's out so early on a weekday morning. Yve wonders if maybe she just hasn't gone home yet from last night. This one eats a bag of chips – it seems to Yve they are always eating chips, these women, as if it's some kind of code, and maybe it is. A tiny handbag dangles from the wrist that moves mechanically between mouth and chip bag. A car drives past, heading out of town, toward Charlesport. The woman waves. The car continues on. She goes back to her chips and stamping her feet. Yve crosses to the other sidewalk.

Another block down, where Main bisects Center, the Historic Hill District announces itself with a welcome sign: *One foot in the past, one in the future.* Here, too, begins the museum's new Maritime Village Walking Tour. It ambles up and down the steep, cramped streets as a blue line painted on the cobbles. According to the sign, the original settlers of Rosaline built on steep hills rising from the waterfront so they could look out their windows to see the masts of the incoming vessels. Yve looks down to the bay and sees nothing but steely water and white sky and the asphalt roof of the fish plant. The sign is new since she's last bothered to come down here. She takes a wet pamphlet from the plastic sleeve and follows the blue line down Center.

Other cleanup efforts have been made. Planters with mums and colorful cabbages hang in front of the empty stores. Boarded-up windows are painted with curtains and cats. The old streetlights have been replaced with gaslamps. The lampposts are short. If Yve were to reach up her hand and stand on her toes, she could touch the bottom of the wrought-iron poles. The hexagonal lanterns have beveled glass. There was a small war over these lamps in Town Council. Yve's Aunt Edna led the SnugHarbor Ladies' Auxiliary in a protest walkout because the historic lamps were expensive and didn't make the streets any safer after dark. But CARP and the Rosaline Business Associates were ready to pay for them, and since no one else had offered money for anything better, Council went with gas.

Handy maps have been posted on corners with You-Are-Here stars and circled Ps to direct visitors to lots with ample parking. Plastic-laminate signs identify the brick and cedar-shake ruins as counting houses, candleworks, inns, supply shops, and private homes. Each displays a photo of the building in its prime, tells the name, purpose, colorful history. The signs are numbered to correspond to information in the tour pamphlet. At Fisherman Park, a paragraph explains that the bronze Unknown Sailor is a memorial for Those Lost at Sea, and that surviving family members still leave memorial wreaths at its base. Yve crumples the pamphlet and tosses it at the Sailor's furrowed brow. She walks the next few blocks quickly.

15 Cherry is a brick three-story wedged between two other identical brick wrecks. According to its sign, it's the old Mather Clay Warehouse. A mailbox set into the wall says Citizens Assoc. R.P. Beneath the mailbox is a buzzer. Yve buzzes, waits. No one answers. She leans over to look in the window. The interior is dark behind the peach venetian blinds. Clearly no one is home. But the scrap of paper her father gave her says this address. She looks up and down the empty street. From here, it's a straight shot to Carreiro's yard, though it is hidden by the slight rise where Cherry crosses Center. All she sees of the schooner is the masts, rising like two sticks over the bay. The street channels the sounds of the men working, though the eight-o'clock whistle has yet to blow. She wonders if she should go down there, but she doesn't want to seem overeager. She'll wait until the whistle, then count to a hundred and then start walking down, slowly. No, two hundred. Three hundred, that's five minutes. Twice. After the whistle, though. She twines her fingers in the loose fabric of her skirt and wonders if it was the right thing to wear. It's what she always wears, skirts, but the captain said cleaning and maybe he'll think she's dressed up and won't clean. Foolish. He won't even notice.

Down at the fish plant the whistle winds itself up like an air-raid siren. It whoops one long rising, then falling note. On the dying tail end, she sees him cresting the rise on Cherry. She nearly waves, then feels a rush of relief at having not done so. Sweat greases her armpits, between her breasts and shoulder blades. She feels silly standing there early, but then again, she would've felt silly arriving late. Silly. A silly word. She wishes she wasn't so nervous.

The captain limps toward Yve, carrying his left shoulder higher than his right. She hadn't noticed that about him before. She composes her face to the flat, middle-distance stare she remembers from the filleting line. Slit, scrape, slice, pass it on. She hopes it is appropriate to this work, too. Her palms feel slick. She puts her hands in her pockets, then pulls them out again just in time to shake. Standing slightly below her on the hill, he is exactly her height.

'Morning,' he says.

His beard is coming in. She finds herself wondering if he's the sort to grow it for winter. John keeps his year round; he has a weak chin otherwise. She realizes she hasn't spoken yet. She mumbles, 'Good morning,' and feels like a fool. She pulls her hand free and wipes it on her skirt.

'Shall we?' He walks ahead without waiting for her answer. She nods to his back. They turn the corner, their mini-procession of two, then around the corner again to the lot directly behind the three brick buildings. A chain-link fence surrounds the weedy square. Vines tangle its links.

'Do they bloom?' Yve asks.

'What?' He's working at a chain woven between the fence and gate. It's just dummy-locked and wound through and through.

'These are morning glories, I think. Do they bloom?'

'Not since I've here.' He swings the gate open and stands there, holding it. She ducks under his arm and stops. Three mud-colored dogs bound across the yard. The captain barks once, and they freeze; only their noses twitch, sniffing the air as if to catch his scent. He barks again, and they break rank, scuttle away. One pees on a pile of rubble. The bitch has long teats and a hounded look about her.

'Are they yours?' Yve asks, though they are collarless and mangy, and look like no one's.

'No, but they were here first.' He rattles the chain at them. They sidle back more. He shuts the gate and hangs the chain through a few links. 'They don't bite. Me, at least.'

'Okay.' She lets him go first.

They walk over weeds and broken glass. The dogs keep an eye on them, edging closer to the building as they approach.

'Go on, get!' The captain chucks a piece of brick at the larger one. It runs to a shelter of garbage cans, half-ducking and cringing sideways. 'It's this one.' He points to the center building. 'Top floor,' and he begins climbing the fire escape. It's the old-fashioned kind that comes directly to the ground like a grillwork staircase, switching back on itself at every floor. The second-story platform bites into the side of a huge oak whose branches reach through the fire escape's scaffolding.

Yve hesitates. The captain's boots sound like a hammered anvil on the iron steps and the whole structure trembles under his feet.

He looks down at her. 'Just climb on up. It's strong enough.' He shakes the banister. It rattles, and a few oak leaves tumble free. They fall around her upturned face. 'That wasn't so reassuring, huh?' He smiles. 'Really though. I'm a lot heavier than you.'

She climbs, pausing with him on the second-story platform to check between its slats for the dogs that now gather beneath, looking up.

'They won't follow us.' He climbs on ahead.

A twig catches her cardigan. She says, 'It's like you live in a tree house.'

At the top, he's left the steel door open, the door-knob hooked to the fire escape with a bent coat hanger.

He speaks from the inside, his voice echoes as if from a well. 'We don't keep it locked yet, but if we do, you'll get keys.'

She follows his voice into a dark, narrow hall with five doors. One on each wall, including the one they'd come through and another next to that. Then she sees the door on the ceiling. A real door, with a knob, but overhead, like you'd find in a carnival fun house.

'We don't use the CARP entrance downstairs because they can't have all of us trooping through all day. Besides, there's no way to get up here from there anymore.' He takes off his coat, hangs it on a row of books. Yve keeps hers on. The walls are papered with glossy magazine photos of naked women meticulously cut and fitted together as if the hall is a giant jigsaw puzzle of pornography. She strokes the wall and feels the raised scar where two pictures have overlapped. Then she realizes what she's doing and jerks her fingers to her mouth.

'We didn't do that ourselves. They came with the place, kind of a bonus.' He sounds apologetic. He is looking at her strangely again. Yve smiles through her quivering fingertips.

'Anyhow,' he says, 'we take all our clothes off here – I mean, just the outer stuff, to keep the dust down. Don't bother cleaning here much. It's a losing battle.' Yve nods. He turns to the nearest door. 'Don't open that – it's the old elevator that's not there anymore. You'll fall and die.' Yve nods again, but he has his back to her, opening another door. 'The bathroom – sorry—' He shuts it quickly. It looks as though it hasn't been cleaned since they moved in. Perhaps since before. 'This,' the middle door, 'is the living room, but we're using it as a bedroom for Charlie and Hank.'

Yve peeks in. Two stacks of foam mattresses, sheets and blankets twisted on the floor, a snarl of books and clothes between. Someone smokes a pipe, the air smells of cherry tobacco. Two windows open on the street side. The captain points to another door on the inside wall of the living room. 'That door through there goes to Neil's—'

'It's a maze,' she says.

'No, a ring.' He points off the names clockwise, 'Hall, Hank and Charlie's, into Neil's, into mine, into the kitchen – which you can also get to through here.' He swings open the last door at the end of the hall opposite the bathroom to reveal a wedge of kitchen. 'See?'

'Not really.' She tries to repeat the loop in her mind, boxing each room on the compass according to where she knows she entered from, the staircase is on the back side, the north side, so the window she saw that faces the street – the place seems to have turned. It doesn't come out correctly. 'I'll figure it out,' she says. 'Where do the rest of the crew sleep?'

'Up there.' He points to the door in the ceiling. 'The ladder's in the closet. You don't need to clean the attic – I don't even go up there myself. The boys can just throw their sheets down once a week and be grateful.' He smiles, and she smiles back. When he stands, his shoulders seem to be almost on the same plane. He opens the kitchen door. 'Come in,' he says. He has an odd way of opening doors, standing to the side with his hand still on them so she must duck under his arm as she had to before, at the gate. He hasn't showered recently, she can tell that now he has his coat off. His smell is warm, a bit like old books and woodsmoke. She doesn't mind it.

The kitchen is large but old-fashioned. A poor use of space. The counters on either side of the double sink are shallow, and the orange cabinets hang low over them. One wall is given over to a bricked-up fireplace. A black rotary phone and a stack of dog-eared phonebooks crowd the mantel. Already numbers are scribbled on the wall, some in pen, just as on the wall in her father's shop. Jake's Auto. Scrap Metal. J. Deere. Jenny. Yve wonders if that's Jenny Stewart. Dora is up there. She should put her own name up there, see how long it takes him to notice. No, she would never. Underneath, near enough the mantel to be convenient to the phone, squats an overstuffed sofa, its green velvet worn and stained. It looks odd, living-room furniture in the kitchen.

He gestures to a doorless pantry sunk into the wall. Inside are sacks of dry goods; beans, pasta, rice. 'We got the leftover ship stores. They're old; you'll have to check them.'

She pushes the packages around a bit, taking stock. Tins of canned fish and a flat of condensed milk. Another two flats of ramen. Fifty-pound buckets of flour, sugar, cocoa, and cornstarch—

'We could thicken the sea,' she says.

He smiles. 'Paul was a bit strange. He didn't even eat his own food. You eat your own food, don't you?'

'Yes.' She unrolls a bag of oatmeal and a tiny moth flies out.

'Flour worms don't hurt,' he says. 'We don't have much of a budget.'

'I can sift them out.' She's done it before. 'But if you don't mind me asking – I mean, you aren't sailing anymore, you could take turns cooking, or just get one of the guys—' She trails off, afraid he'll take her advice. He's leaning against the mantel, looking at her quizzically.

'I'm sorry,' she says.

'No, you're right. I think I've made a mistake.'

'Oh, I didn't mean that at all. I really want this job, I really do.' To show him, she starts clearing the dishes from the card table in the center of the room, putting away the remains of a cold breakfast, depositing cereal bowls in the already full sinks. 'I'm an idiot. I mean, it's clear you haven't had time to do much.' She moves around him, opening the cabinets, the refrigerator. She runs water in the sink and talks over it. 'I can have this clean in no time, and I noticed you need milk, I can run down to the store—'

'Yve—'

She turns the water off and turns to face him. His eyes are brown as pennies, and the color fills nearly all the orb like the eyes of the dogs below. His pupils disappear in all the brown.

'Albin,' he says. 'Yvette Albin. You have a sister named Kate, don't you?'

'In-law, only. Sister-in-law. Oh—' She suddenly understands. Her stomach pitches. This job was never meant for her. 'You have made a mistake, haven't you?' she says. 'You wanted Kate.' With her coat still on she feels overheated. 'I'm sorry.'

'No, I'm sorry,' he says. 'I heard Helio say Albin and didn't realize.'

'Kate's married to my brother, Chris Albin. I should tell you they're still together.' She blushes, saying something so filled with assumption.

'I see.'

'I'm sorry.'

'For what?' A spot on the counter catches his eye. When he looks away, she feels as if he'd been holding her by the shoulders and has just now released her.

'She has a job at the Whiskey Wind. She's day bartender there, if you want to see her.'

'No, I don't think so.' He works at the Formica with his nail. His lips draw a hard line. 'We didn't have time to clean.'

'It's fine,' she says. 'That's why I'm here.'

'I could send someone up to help. Rob maybe.' He chips at the counter. His low shoulder shrugs.

'No, really. I'd rather work alone.'

He smiles and wipes his thumbnail on his thigh. 'I don't want you scared off.'

'I'm not.'

'You haven't seen my bedroom yet.'

She smiles. 'Maybe another day.'

'Maybe,' he says. 'I'm sure you'll do fine.'

'I'm sure I will.'

'Good, good.' He claps his hands once. 'Lunch at twelve?'

'Twelve.' She holds her hand out for a goodbye shake. 'Captain.'

'Wen,' he says.

She thinks for a moment that he's asking the question. 'Yes, Wen,' she finally repeats. They shake. His shirt is stretched at the throat, and black hairs curl over the neckline like a breaking wave.

'We'll be looking forward to it.' He backs himself out. She hears the steel door shut, his feet pummeling the fire escape. She folds her coat on the sofa and goes to the window over the sink. From here she can see him crossing the yard, throwing bricks at the dogs. He loops the chain through the gate, trots half a block, and disappears around the corner. She breathes for what seems to be the first time this morning. She watches a little while more, the dogs circling. They look up as if they sense her.

By quarter of, Yve has the dishes done, a shopping list made, a pot of navy bean soup on the stove, and egg salad in the fridge. That worries her a bit, beans and eggs together like that in one meal, but that was really all they had quantity of, eggs and beans. There were hardly any vegetables – just a few limp carrots and one celery stalk, practically rubber, some withered onions – no fruit at all. In her nervousness, she peppered the flavorless broth too early on, and now it is too hot. She puts the soup on the table, then back on the stove so it will stay warm, then back on the table again. Leaves the coffee on the stove – that surely needs to stay hot. She wonders if she should try to set out bowls or simply stack them. Where will they all eat? She wipes her hands on her skirt. Then remembers the egg salad. And bread. There are no tomatoes, or lettuce. No pickles even. Nothing green – not her fault. Do they use plates? There is no room really; maybe soup back on the stove? Make room for plates? She whirls about, sets the soup back on the stove for once and for all. Her heart pounds.

At exactly twelve, they arrive. The noon whistle is wailing as they climb the fire escape. At least there'll be no sneaking up. She can hear them coming even with all the windows closed – a stampede of boots tramping up the iron steps, half of the slats loose. They ring and rattle and shout at each other. The outside door bangs open. They are in the hall now, loud as their climb up the fire escape. All talking at once, English and Portuguese, stripping overalls, sweatshirts, hats, dropping shoes, hanging coats on hooks, covering the naked girls, and when the hooks are full, throwing the rest on the floor in a dusty heap. She scurries to the kitchen door to shut it against the dirt.

But then they are tromping through anyhow, filing past the stove in a crowd. The Carreiro cousins shout Portuguese as if they are shouting over power tools still and are not right behind each other, lips practically at ears in an otherwise quiet kitchen. Her father's friends come through, Mr. Bliss, Len Snelling. Sandy Hopewell nods hello. Their hair and shoulders are sawdust-lightened, their rusty hands balance sandwiches across their steaming bowls of soup. Then, finally the transit crew crowd in. Two old men, one fat, one thin; two young men, one wiry, one loose; an uptight yachty, a nervous college kid – they don't seem to see her. She feels as if she's left the room even as she stands there against the sink, the heels of her hands pressed against the counter, holding her head above the flood of men. The windows fog with their loud talk and the heat streaming off their backs. They file through the kitchen in one door and out the

102

other, settling in the other room. ~~~~~ kitchen is empty and quiet again. ~~~~~ the captain. Wen.

She checks the level of the soup. There ~~~~ Steps on the fire escape. That would be ~~~~ smooths her hand on her hair, down the front ~~~ blouse. There are two sandwiches left; she shou~~ made more. The door opens. He's in the hall peeli~~ off his outerwear. She runs back to the sink, leans ~~~ there.

'Yve,' he says. He goes straight to the stove and ladles himself soup. Then he takes the last two sandwiches and sits at the table. He straddles the chair; feet planted, legs spread.

'Well, Yve, how'd it go?'

She looks at the empty sandwich plate. 'I'm afraid I didn't make enough.'

'There'll never be enough.' He talks with his mouth full, but tucks the food away in his cheek like a wad of tobacco so it can't be seen on his tongue. 'You just make what you think is right and dictate the ration when they come through. They'll take as much as they can and leave nothing for the next guy unless you tell them what's what. You meet the crew?'

'No, not really.'

'Introduce yourself next time.'

'Yes.'

'You'll be fine.' He blows on his spoon. 'Hope you're half as spicy as this soup.'

She says, 'There's too much pepper.' It comes out a whisper.

'Warms the cockles of my heart.' Wen makes a big show of eating his soup, licking his lips and patting his stomach, helping himself to seconds.

He is making fun of her somehow. Heat rises up her chest, her neck, her face. She wants to go into the living room, where her father's friends are. She could sit next to Sandy Hopewell and ask about his mother

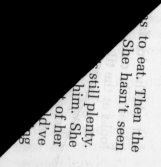

gry at him for taking this
her place at the sink. She
toes. His eyes are on her,

n the windowsill, wings
t. Yve turns at the sudden
move. She is upright. She
vich platter. And now the
ugh, helping themselves to
opping dirty plates in the

'Say hello to Yve, ... ew cook.' Wen names them
as they drop their dishes in for her to wash. He introduces her to his crew, and the names fly through her
head. The yachty's named Neil; Rob Ames, Joe Ames's
nephew; Hank – the fat caulker that Dora Schultz liked
at the dance. The other old man, the thin one, is
Charlie. Yve gives him a smile, and the old man smiles
back with an added wink that doesn't bother her in the
least. Then comes Ed, the wiry one – a black-haired,
watch-capped bosun. He whispers in the ear of the
loosely slouching blond. This sailor comes forward
and introduces himself without Wen's help. His voice
is a liquor-soaked drawl. He says, 'Jefferson, Able-
bodied Seaman,' as if this is a description of his
virility and not a Coast Guard ticket. The black-haired,
watch-capped bosun, Ed, laughs as Yve shakes
Jefferson's limp hand.

'Yve'll be making our meals and cleaning up around
here, so let's try not to scare her off right away,' Wen
says. 'That means you Ed, Jefferson, hands to yourselves – and *that* only in the attic.' They laugh, and
Yve feels heat rise in her face again. They are all looking at her. She begins washing their dishes just to have
a reason to turn her back.

And once her back is turned, they seem to forget
about her. They settle on the sofa and at the kitchen
table with mugs of coffee, cigarettes are lit. Charlie

lights his pipe, and cherry smoke fills the room. They begin talking about the ship; rotted futtocks, leaking bilges. Removing the engine. Their words run over her like water. Now and then, a day-hire man comes in from the living room, drops his plate in the sink and picks up a mug from the cabinet over her left shoulder, helps himself to coffee, exchanges words with Wen or not, goes back out. A few, her father's friends, some of the Carreiros, say thank you, say they appreciate it. She wishes these men would stay in the kitchen, but it seems the kitchen belongs to the transit crew and there's some unspoken rule that the day hires are to have their coffee in the living room or hall. They leave their mugs on the sills and against the walls, and head for the yard before the one-o'clock whistle.

Wen is the last to leave. He eats a third helping of soup. He finishes the pot and brings it to the sink. She feels him standing close behind her.

'Don't be nervous.' His voice curls in her ear. His chest brushes her shoulder as he lowers the pot into the sink.

'I'm not.' She swallows and her tongue peels from her dry palate. 'I'll need money for shopping. Supper'll be simple tonight, I'm afraid. There's not much and I'll be at the store awhile. It's quite a walk.'

'No prob.' He steps back. His knuckles wrinkle against the front pocket of his jeans. He hands her keys on a leather loop. 'Use my truck. The white Ford with antlers. It's down at the yard. You can't miss it.' Then he pulls two hundreds from his wallet. A slip of paper with the words *KATE ALBIN – Whiskey Wind, day??* sits in the foremost plastic pocket.

Seeing the slip, Yve feels a click, a settling in like a tooth in a groove. She is reminded of her place in things, and that makes her feel suddenly easier.

'I'll get a receipt,' she says. She looks into his eyes easily, and sees that he saw her see.

'Of course,' he says.

105

She folds the bills into her own pocket. They are wrinkled and soft, like skin. 'I have dishes,' she says.

'Of course.' He gathers his cigarettes and lighter off the table. 'Catch you later.'

'Yes.' She doesn't have to turn away from the sink to say goodbye; she has work. She fills the dirty pot with hot water. Steam rises on the windows. She shuts the water, steam disappears. Her nerves are gone like that. Click, gone. It's a relief, really. She couldn't've gone on with those kinds of jitters. She isn't that young anymore. She scrubs the pot. Really puts her back into it. She feels calmer now, really. Like herself again. Still.

10

There used to be an auction in Rosaline. When that closed down the men took their fish to the auction in Charlesport. Then that closed. Now the fishermen deal directly with the Charlesport processing plants, and the price is generally set before they've arrived with their catch. When the older ones talk, they romanticize the auctions. They recall times when a buyer held out for their catch, or bought it despite a bad market, because a relationship had grown up over time. The bidders were your neighbors. You knew who you were dealing with. You could appeal to them as one man to another. Now, with the new system, there is no room for bargaining. If flounder is a $1.70 a pound at Burgess Seafood Inc., it's likely to be the same at Sea-Town. The different facilities advertise in the local papers: *Premium Prices Paid for All Species! Your One-Stop Unloading Facility! It's Monkfish Liver Season Once Again!!!* – but a man can go up and down the line of docks and find that if City Fish isn't buying monkfish liver today, no one is. The buyers shrug and say the markets are global now and difficult to understand; the prices are set by suits who have no more interest in fish than they do in any of the other commodities they buy or sell, and that is that. It isn't personal. Nevertheless, the habit of taking things personally is hard for the fishermen, especially the older ones, to break. Fitz, like the other captains, has developed loyalties based on imagined favors, and he always sells his catch to AAA Salmon and Sons. Every Christmas, AAA Salmon and Sons sends him a calendar.

After the men tie up to the Salmon Pier, Fitz releases them. Today the docks are full. Boats wait to unload their catch, and word is the price for cod is high and flounder low. Cod gets priority. It will take a couple hours before their catch is dealt with. Since there is nothing for the crew to do while they wait, they pile out into the streets of Charlesport. It is a beautiful morning. The sky is a clear, high blue, and the air smells like incipient autumn even though there are few trees near the wharves. The men head directly downtown. There's a breakfast spot they've been going to for the last couple of months, the Golden Egg, where the waitresses are pretty in a tired sort of way. Walley likes to think one of them likes him. Her name is Monica and she works Saturdays and today is Saturday. He bounces along on his toes.

Downtown, the streets are lined with boutiques, and even though most don't interest the men – chocolates, designer clothing, scented candles – there are still some windows that entice them to slow. John stops at the REI window. The display is different every time they come into town, and there is always something John wants: a kayak, snowshoes, a Filson hat. Today the dummy holds a fly rod. He looks lifelike, propped against the corner of his cabin, at the edge of a lake. The display seems to be offering a certain kind of life along with the objects. John was taught to believe freshwater fishers are wimps. Catch and release is lazy and weak, but he doesn't feel that way looking at this display – if only he had a cabin in the woods, he'd catch himself some fish – his thoughts materialize as pictures instead of words. Something squeezes in his chest. Walley offers to go ahead and secure a table. No, John says, he's coming, but he walks slowly.

Most of the piers downtown are taken up by charter boats, and the men spend a few moments looking them over. Sandwich boards advertise the various services: sportfishing, whale watching, sunset cocktail cruises. They find fault with this one and admire that one, they talk about money. How much to buy and how much to keep in good repair. How much a man could expect to make.

'What do you think of that?' Chris nods at a boat advertising fishing for blues.

John reads the sign and whistles. 'Imagine paying that to fish,' he says, as if he can't understand it at all. They nod, laugh a bit; hands go in pockets and come out.

'People pay money for some pretty stupid shit,' Chris says.

Walley says, 'Take you all day, and maybe you catch something.'

'Lot of money in it though,' Chris says to John. 'I was talking to the captain a couple months ago. He said it's not bad. You just load up a case of beer and make sure the tourists don't fall overboard. You just go out and fuck around and come home in time for supper.'

'What's he make?' John asks.

'Don't know,' Chris says.

'How many days can you go out?' John asks. 'Is there any kind of limit?'

'Dunno.'

'So what do you know?' Dan asks, laughing. John laughs, too.

'Not much, I guess.' Chris walks to the end of the pier and spits into the water. John stops laughing, and Dan stops, too.

'Are we going to eat or what?' Walley says. The restaurant is right across the street.

At the Golden Egg the breakfasts are big and the benches around the booths have high backs, giving a sense of privacy to each table. Chris talks all through breakfast about a man he knows who is farming salmon. He pushes his food around his plate, speaking quickly and drawing descriptions in the air. The fish aren't caught, they're grown in cages and are fed fish chow like pets. They have to put something in the feed so the flesh will turn pink. When the time is right they get corralled and slaughtered like cattle. They're bled to death in a salt-ice slurry, so they die refrigerator-fresh. They're packaged the same day. 'And the crazy thing – this guy was telling me – is that people prefer farmed salmon. They actually like their fish farmed, but then they want their chickens free-range. What's that about?' He laughs and pushes his uneaten breakfast away.

The rest have cleaned their plates. John waves to the waitress. She refills their coffee and the men lean back as if they plan to sit a long time; the check is paid and a ten-dollar bill sits under the ashtray as a tip so she won't hurry them. It's one of the few restaurants where they can still smoke. Chris lights himself a cigarette. The conversation rolls back around to money, and John allows they probably haven't done well with their catch.

Walley asks, 'How much, do you think?'

John shrugs. 'Pete came in before us, and apparently everyone's been bringing flounder all week.'

'Yeah, but how much?'

'Try and guess, Wal,' Chris says.

'Well I don't know,' Walley says. He pushes his glasses up his nose. 'Maybe the price was good.'

'No one wants what everyone's got,' Dan says.

Walley looks into his Coke. He puts his finger over the tip of the straw and traps the liquid up, then releases his finger and lets the brown liquid dribble back. 'We haven't done well in a long time.'

'No, we haven't,' John says. 'And we won't anytime soon.' He shakes a couple packets of sugar down and pours them into his coffee. 'I understand they're hiring at the yard.'

'I don't want that,' Walley says.

'Really,' John says.

'Why would anyone want a yard job,' Walley says.

'Things aren't gonna get better,' John says.

'How do you know that? You don't know that,' Walley says morosely.

'Christ, Wal.' Chris hits the table softly and the ash falls from his cigarette. John clears his throat. The waitress comes by with more coffee.

Dan takes the last cigarette from Chris's pack and crushes the Cellophane.

'They don't grow on trees,' Chris says.

'What?' Dan says.

'I'm just saying, if you're gonna quit, quit; if you aren't, start buying your own.'

Dan takes the cigarette from between his lips and holds it out to Chris. Chris waves him off.

'It just adds up is all,' Chris says. 'That pack costs like five U.S. in Canada.'

'That doesn't sound right. That sound right to you?' Dan addresses John. John shrugs. He doesn't care one way or the other. He smokes rarely.

'It's true,' Chris says. 'Taxes. Cigarettes and booze. Canada taxes the shit out of them.'

'You buy your cigarettes in Canada?' Dan says.

'I'm just saying if I did. If you think about it, five dollars divided by twenty – that's like twenty-five cents.'

'I owe you a quarter.'

'Shut up.' Chris fixes his coffee with milk and sugar. He stirs awhile and then puts his spoon down. 'I was talking to a friend of mine—'

'You're always talking to a friend,' Dan says.

Chris ignores him. 'He was saying taxes are so high you can make good money just running cigarettes and booze over the border.'

'What's good money?' Dan says.

'I don't know,' Chris says.

'You never know anything.'

'Think about it though,' Chris says. 'If you're just over the border, you know, just one guy in a skiff. Even if you just make a couple hundred bucks—'

'We're not right over the border,' Dan says. 'And we aren't driving a skiff.'

'I wasn't saying for us.'

'Then why are you talking?'

'For knowledge. For edification.'

Dan drags his cigarette. 'We don't need edification from you.'

'Wal does. He needs all the edification he can get, don't you, Wal?'

'No I don't.'

'What do you know, Wal? You know what I'm talking about? What am I talking about? Come on, Wal, what am I talking about? You don't know.'

'Shut up, Chris,' Walley says. 'I do so.'

'What am I talking about?'

Walley turns crimson.

'He's just talking out of his ass, Walley,' Dan says.

'Of course I am,' Chris says. 'But let's just say I wasn't. There're other things to move, worth more than cigarettes. We could double our money. Little import, export.'

'I can't believe we're even talking about this,' Dan says.

'We're not,' John says.

'Yet,' Chris says.

'What *are* you talking about?' Walley asks. Chris writes a word on a napkin and turns it toward him. Walley reads, then crumples it quickly into the ashtray.

111

'That's no way to destroy evidence. Eat it – eat it!' Chris shoves the napkin at Walley's mouth.

'Leave me the fuck alone.'

'Leave him alone,' John says. 'Drop it now.'

Chris looks affronted. 'I wasn't saying for me, I was just saying, you know, I can see how these things happen. Like for Walley maybe.'

'For Walley what? He's living with his mother still.'

'I wouldn't do it anyhow.' Walley drops his voice to a whisper. 'We could lose our boat.'

'Not *our* boat,' Chris says. '*We* don't have a boat.'

'If it was mine, though, I wouldn't.'

'Well then.' Chris turns to Dan. 'How about you? If you had a boat.'

'I don't.'

'But if you did. Think about it. You got the mortgage and the kid—'

'So do you.'

'But Kate's got a good job,' Chris says.

'Susan's got a good job,' Dan answers.

'What if she lost it, though?'

'Still never.'

'I don't know,' Chris says. 'She might think different. You don't know what goes through a woman's head when her kid's hungry.'

'You're so full of shit.' Dan pushes Chris's shoulder and Chris smiles and then laughs; he pushes Dan back and Dan laughs. Walley smiles – he tries to get himself laughing, but he missed the joke.

'Anyway, we're not in that kind of trouble, yet,' John says.

Dan's smile straightens out. He looks between Chris and John. 'I thought we were joking. We were joking, right?'

'Yeah,' John says. 'I'm sorry. I wasn't really listening.'

'Shit,' Dan says. 'I thought you were serious.' He smiles and shakes his head.

112

'No. Of course not.' John's coffee cup is empty again. He signals the waitress.

11

'*Security, security, security, this is the fishing vessel Pearl—*'

When the security call comes over the radio, the women stop what they are doing to listen. Working late at the SnugHarbor Ladies' Auxiliary, Edna Larkin stops stuffing envelopes. Susan Furlong, pacing her tiny bedroom, hangs up on her mother-in-law. At the crewhouse, Yve rushes in off the fire escape – she was scraping the dinner plates for the dogs – to the kitchen, where they keep the VHF. The captain is sitting on the sofa, smoking and drinking a beer. It is just after six, they are done with dinner. He laughs at Yve and says, 'You can go down if you want, leave the dishes for tomorrow.'

'I don't come in tomorrow,' she says. 'It's Sunday.'

'We'll do them.' He waves her off. 'Go on.'

She smiles and ducks her head. She throws her apron on its hook and runs down to the museum. Her feet slap the pavement, and the air is cool in her mouth. The sky is the color of a plum, the sea is nearly black. The water surges and burbles under the pier. Susan Furlong and Edna Larkin are there already. Susan's pickup is parked under the streetlight, and the two women lean against the fender drinking diet Cokes.

'Hey,' Yve says.

'Hey,' they say. 'Hey.' Edna passes her soda to Yve. Yve takes a sip and catches her breath. She tries to lean against the truck, but she is too happy. It's been six days, nearly a week, since she's seen John. She can't wait to tell him about her new job. All week she's been telling him the stories in her mind. She walks circles

113

between the truck and the end of the pier, until she sees the red, green, and white of their running lights.

Though she hears the call come over the bar's radio, Kate doesn't go down to the pier. She finishes her shift, turns the bar over to Dora, and, as usual, pulls herself a pint of Guinness and goes down to the basement office to reconcile the day's receipts. She puts the money in the safe, she counts and rubber-bands her tips. She sits smoking and finishing her pint, flipping through *The Tides* – she reads the Coast Guard reports and the fish landings; she reads the piece about a lobsterman missing and presumed drowned, though she already heard from Dennis Pelletier when he came in with the mail that they found the body, one Emil Kronenhall. There is an ad on the last page announcing the public hearing on the proposed amendments to the fishing regulations that exhorts Fishers to Show Up and Be Heard! She reads the whole paper, ads and all, even the recipe, Halibut in Tarragon, then she reads the business cards Dora's pinned to the wall: Solveigs Propeller Service and Supply, Rosaline Check Cashing, Trio Saluti Boat Settlements: *Nós Falamos Português*. The words slip under her eyes. She thinks if he wants to come home, he'll get there on his own. He knows the address, and he has a key. When her beer is finished, she leaves the glass and puts on her coat. She goes out the back way.

She walks home slowly, stopping by the Albins' to pick up Martin. Alma invites her to stay for supper; John Fitz is already there, barbecuing out back with Phil, and Yve is laying the table on the enclosed porch – it would be easy enough to throw an extra burger on, Alma says, lay another plate. No, no, Kate says, she has to get home. Chris must be home by now, waiting for her, she says. Of course, Alma says, her fingers pressed against her lips. Kate puts Martin on her hip and shrugs his bag onto her shoulder. The boy has to kiss everyone goodbye; he's in a kissy phase. When Kate leans him in to kiss his grandma, Alma hugs them both and presses her cheek to Kate's.

Back home, Kate boils spaghetti for Martin and gets a can of beer for herself. She feeds the boy, gives him a bath, tucks him in, and reads him a story. She goes into the kitchen for another beer, then into the living room to watch some TV. She drinks and watches. Eventually *The Late Show* comes on. During the monologue, she gets up for another beer, then she wanders into the bathroom. She finds herself in front of the mirror. She watches her hand touch her cheek. When has Chris last gone to see his parents? He never visits them, he and Phil fight, they can't even talk politely nowadays. Kate and Alma keep the family together through Martin. Not even through Yve. Yve won't talk to Chris. Of course, Yve thinks in sides; she thinks she's being a help, a support, but it makes things harder, not easier. Watching what she says to Yve all the time is hard. She never remembers to tell the good parts, only the bad. What should she say? We laughed so hard, or he brought me coffee in bed, or he stayed home all last week without going out once, or we were watching the TV, and he got up before the commercial to get me a beer. Her eye's gone down. He probably thinks she's still angry, that's why he's not here. She wishes he would come home. She wishes he was here right now. Wanting him feels like a bubble in her heart. The idea of a bubble in her heart seizes her, and she starts breathing hard. It could pop, then she'd die. She could die. She rushes from the bathroom, through the living room, to the hall. She puts her hand on her jacket to pull it from the hanger, and she stops. She stands there a moment. She'd promised herself never again – but no, he'd be here if they hadn't fought – she snaps back, rushes again. Up the stairs, grab the boy and a blanket around him, off with the TV, on with the jacket, one-armed, shift the whining child, other

115

arm and door and key. The boy whimpers against her shoulder. She joggles him as she trots to the car.

'Trot trot to Boston, trot trot to Lynn, if the horses go too fast we all fall—' Into the car with him. She skitters to the other side.

'Shh now, honey, put your head on Mommy's lap, there's a boy.' She strokes Martin to sleep and backs the car from the dirt driveway. She hits the brake. Martin rolls forward in the seat, but she catches him. She should put him in the car seat, she knows, but then he'll really wake and start to cry.

'There's a boy, there's a boy, gonna go see Daddy? See Daddy?' She knows where to go, can drive it cross-eyed. The streets are empty. Trot trot.

She drives quickly and the wheels squeal around the corners. Two years ago November, she drove this same way the first time. Up and down through the old part of town. Is that a nursery rhyme? Up and down town? She tries it aloud for Martin, Up and downtown, there'saboy. She had a photo of Chris and she stopped everyone she saw and showed the picture, until finally he came out of the yellow Victorian on Maple and Pine and yelled at her to stop doing that, she was scaring people. He ran out in his socks. Air came from his mouth in clouds, it was that cold, but they had it out right there in the street. She said, I have to know where you go, don't I? What if something happened? How could I find you? He asked her what she thought she was doing, and she said, I'm taking you home. You have to come home sometime. He said, I'm not coming home, and she said, Then I'm going in with you. I want to see where you go. She kept yelling it, I want to see where you go! I want to see where! until he took her in and introduced her to Dina and Rea, the two dykes who ran the shooting gallery. She met other people too, but most of them are gone now, and new ones have come and gone and come and gone again since then. She watched them shoot and nod – hands cupped on legs

116

falling open – she didn't shoot then and never will. She doesn't see the attraction. She's afraid of needles, afraid of losing Martin. That first time, when she went out and came back with pizza, the dykes said, You're all right, you can come back anytime.

She turns onto Pine. Martin rolls on the seat, but her hand is there to catch him and press him back. The neighborhood's changed. They've boarded the windows with tin sheets on which someone has painted cats and houseplants, as if that fools anyone. And the new streetlights, the old-fashioned kind. Trying to clean up this section of town, and so what do they do? Bring in weak gaslamps because of history. She parks the car under the dim orange light and trot-trots up the wooden stairs. Knock knock, who's there? No one yet. She shifts from foot to foot and wonders if coming for him was a bad idea.

In a marriage, what do they say? Compromise. Those articles. 101 Tips from Leading Experts. That support group with a whole book of different suggestions. Those women circled in aluminum chairs passing tissues. Change the things you can. Accept the things you can't. Let him find his own bottom, work on yourself. She doesn't know if that's the answer. He comes home more often now, and when he doesn't, at least she knows where to find him. Sometimes she picks him up in the morning and takes him out to the Blue Moon Diner on the highway for a big breakfast. Then she drives him back to the dykes' house, if that's where he wants to be, and she goes to work. Sometimes, if he doesn't come home for a few days, she brings him clean clothes. It isn't always that bad. Sometimes, often, he comes home on his own. He does. She told John where to find him in case he misses the boat, but Chris never misses the boat. Someone is moving in the house. A light comes on and feet pad downstairs. The walls are so thin you can hear everything inside from outside. They must get cold.

Beginning of last winter, she took a batch of second-hand coats from the SnugHarbor Coat Drive and brought them to the house and handed them around. She likes Dina sometimes, at least more than Rea. Dina is the tiny one, the light one. Rea is big and dark and frightens Martin. Rea broke Dina's collarbone, but Dina said it was an accident. Kate said, I know how that is, and Dina laughed. Dry like a cough. Dina is the one who answers the door now, and Kate is glad.

'Hey, *mamacita*,' Dina says. She comes halfway out the door and pulls it half shut behind her. 'How're you? How's the baby?'

'Okay, he's okay.' Kate looks over her shoulder. She's left Martin asleep in the running car. The streetlamp makes a halo around it.

'You okay, *mami?* You don't look so hot,' Dina says. Her skinny fingers light on Kate's wrist.

'I'm fine,' Kate says. 'Can you get Chris?'

Dina doesn't answer. She doesn't look too good herself.

'Can you get Chris?'

'You know what time it is?' Dina says.

'Can you get him?'

'Hold on.' She disappears inside a few moments, and Kate stands on the porch. Every few seconds she looks at the haloed car. Dew is settling on everything. The porch railings gleam. Dina comes back. 'You wanna come in?'

'Get him to come out,' Kate says. 'I got the baby.'

Dina goes away and there are voices and then Chris comes. He's barefoot and bare-chested and looks as if he's just woken up. He stands on the doorjamb, door wide open behind.

'What are you doing here, Kate?' he says. 'You know what time it is?'

'Martin wouldn't sleep without you. He saw John at the Albins', and he kept asking, Where's Daddy? Where's Daddy?'

118

Chris crosses his arms over his chest and looks down at her.

'He did, really,' she says. 'Where's Daddy?'

'Come on, Kate, go home.' He rubs his eyes.

'He won't go to sleep. He's in the car awake.'

'Please, Kate, I'm tired. Okay? I'm tired. Go home, and I'll see you tomorrow.'

'He won't go to sleep,' she says again, and the backs of her eyes prickle.

'Kate, please.' He sounds annoyed. 'You're drunk. Go home, okay?'

'No! I'm not going! You're coming!' She punches out at him, but her fist bounces off his chest without force. 'You can't not come!' She windmills her arms and hits him again. He grabs her wrists and holds her hands down against her thighs. She starts crying. She turns her head to let her hair cover her face, because he keeps a tight hold on her hands.

He watches her cry until she quiets. Then he says, 'Are you done?'

She nods.

'If I let you go, are you gonna hit me?'

'No-oh.' Her voice catches on phlegm.

He lets her hands go. 'Okay?' he asks.

She nods, hiccups. She feels ashamed. Her red face and her clumsy body. Her ugly red voice.

'I'm sorry.'

'Oh Kate, Katekatekate.' He rubs her shoulder blades, and she starts crying again. He lets her lean her forehead against his chest, and she coughs herself calm. He pulls back a little so he can catch her eye. 'You really want me to come home?'

She nods.

'And the little man?' he says, smiling.

'He wants you to come home, too.'

'Okay, then. Okay.' He pushes her off him. 'Let me get my stuff.'

* * *

119

She drives slowly and carefully. Chris sits beside her in the front seat with Martin asleep on his lap. When they get home, he carries the boy upstairs. Kate puts his duffel at the bottom of the stairs to be carried up if he wants, or not. She sits at the kitchen table with two beers in front of her, one for Chris.

He comes down and sits across from her. He's smiling, and she thinks he probably feels smug about her going all the way out there and lying like that to get him to come home. It's his mother's fault. All the time, when he was young, his mother was at him. So handsome, my angel boy, look at that face – just look at it. He's spoiled. He probably feels like a big man about now. Thinking these bitter things against him is like building a wall. If she builds herself up against him, why should he want to come home? She's the one making herself lonely and hateful. She feels blamed and sad and angry at once and he's said nothing yet, nothing. She feels crazy.

He lifts his beer, toasting her.

She says, 'You lose all our money?'

'No.' His smile goes away. He reaches in his pocket for an envelope, which he throws across the table at her.

'That it?' She counts and says, 'Don't fuck with me. I'll call John and ask how much he gave you.'

He goes into another pocket and comes up with a thin roll of smaller bills. She adds these to the envelope and waits.

'That's it, Kate.' He spreads his empty hands. 'I spent the rest.'

'Jesus, how'd you do that already?'

'I owed some.'

She sucks her back teeth. He looks at her, and she can see he's thinking: Bitch. But he makes her be that way; she has to do all the counting and keeping track, so of course she's a bitch. She looks away from him. Her face feels hot, and the backs of her eyes sting again. She closes them. She will not cry. She wants him to feel bad, see it's his fault, be punished some. With her eyes closed, she says, 'You know your dad was barbecuing. Probably the last barbecue of the season, soon it'll be too cold. John was over there, and your mom invited us, me anyway—'

'But you had to decline on my account.'

She doesn't answer, because she wanted him to say something like that, but not that. Sarcastic bastard. Anyhow, it isn't really true. She could've stayed. No, she couldn't. She didn't want to be the only half-a-couple sitting there, the only one not paired, because Martin doesn't count – he belongs to everyone, really. And her mother-in-law would be sitting there pitying, and Yve would be judging, and John would be red with guilt for not dragging Chris off the boat with him. So yes she declined on his account.

She opens her eyes, and he is looking back at her.

'I just want us to be normal,' she says.

'I know. I'm sorry, Kate. I really am.'

She sighs.

'Are you angry still?'

'No.'

'You should be.'

'I guess,' she says.

He pulls the tab from his beer. He flips it on the table, spinning it between his thumb and forefinger.

'Are you hungry?' she says. She gets up and opens the fridge. 'We got some spaghetti and pizza—'

'Let's barbecue,' he says.

'—no, it's old, forget it.' She throws a curdled slice in the trash. 'What?'

'Let's barbecue. Last of the season.' He gets up. 'I'll start the grill.' He goes into the garage, and she hears him banging around. She hears him wheel the grill out and down the slate side path into the backyard. She hears coals and then smells the oily smell of the lighter fluid, then the smoke. She stands on her toes and looks out the kitchen window at him. He has an apron on and a lobster-shaped oven mitt. The apron is an old jokey one his dad gave him a long time ago: *Barbecuers Do It Medium Well.* He lifts his tongs hello.

She opens the window and whispers through the screen, 'Do you know what time it is?'

He looks at his watch under the lobster mitt. 'Quarter to two. No wonder I'm hungry.'

She shakes her head. 'You're crazy. We don't even have meat.'

'So stick the spaghetti in some foil. And get out here with a couple beers.'

She goes back to the fridge. The corner of her mouth ticks upward, and she frowns on purpose, but it is also sort of a smile. She pulls out the Tupperware, gets the foil, dumps the lump of noodles into the foil and adds canned sauce. She collects the foil package, bread, butter, and beers onto a tray and goes barefoot into the backyard. The moon is full, high, and white. The dew is cold on her feet.

'It's not that warm,' she says. She puts the tray on the plastic table. He is sitting in one of the plastic chairs, feet stretched toward the barbecue, waiting for the flames to die back.

'It's warm by the fire.' He pats his leg.

She frowns and feels oddly shy. She bends to light the citronella candle, though it's too late in the year for bugs. The lemony mediciny scent reminds her of summer. 'This is retarded,' she says.

'You're retarded.' He looks at her fondly. 'Come here.'

'Why?'

'Just come here,' he says. He holds his hand out.

She lets him pull her onto his lap. He rocks her back and forth a bit.

'Am I too heavy?' She half rises off him.

'Never. But get me a beer while you're up.'

She leans over for the beers, and he grabs her hips

122

and pulls her back, onto his lap. He kisses her on the mouth. His lips and tongue are cold and fizzy, they taste like beer and aluminum can. It is past two and they are the only ones awake.

She says, 'Watch it. The spaghetti's gonna burn.'

'Just let me take care of that,' he says. 'Don't you worry about a thing.'

'That'll be the day,' she says. But she doesn't get up. It is warmer there in his lap, and she doesn't want to put her bare feet back down on the cold grass.

III

Now when I was a little boy, or so me mother told
    me—
Way haul away, we'll haul away, Joe!
that if I did not kiss the girls, my lips would grow
    moldy.
Way haul away, we'll haul away, Joe!

12

The coffee has perked, the tea water boiled, the sugar is dished, and the icy creamer sweats onto the chrome shelf of the service window. Tidy fortresses of apple spice loaf and molasses oatbread sit on doilies. The napkins are folded in triangles and spread like a fan. The stainless-steel forks and spoons have been organized into their proper plastic trays. There is nothing left for the SnugHarbor Ladies' Auxiliary to do. They have come to the Seamen's Fellowship Hall straight from church. They wear their best florals beneath their aprons, their dress coats perfume the coat rack in the entranceway. Their square, sturdy purses, filled with useful items like sewing kits and Band-Aids, nail files and rubber bands, are tucked in the dishware shelves. The women stand in tight formation, looking out the kitchen service window into the crowded hall as if, with their coffeecakes and safety pins, they might hold the line against chaos.

The hall itself is packed with folding chairs and fishermen. More men stand along the back wall. They are here for the National Marine Fisheries Service Informational Meeting, to hear the new regulations. For weeks the papers have been following the proposed legislation. Fishers and their wives have received notices, sent letters, drawn up petitions, contacted their representatives, done all they could to forestall further regulations, but it has still come to this. Every man in the region seems here, up from Charlesport and down from Bardot, but the women watch only their own. Edna Larkin watches her son, Walley. Susan Furlong and her mother-in-law, Joan, watch Dan. Mabel Dowd watches her father, Reverend Dowd, pulling at the loose skin over his collar, and she pulls at her own loose skin. Leaving the house this morning for service, the Reverend told his daughter that he thought he should be at the Fisheries Service meeting to give spiritual guidance, but so far he stands off by himself near the flags. Bea Hopewell divides her attentions between husband and son on opposite sides of the room, Pete by the windows and Sandy by the door. Mrs. Bliss waits for Mr. Bliss, who hovers near Sandy Hopewell and the knot of Portuguese workers from Helio Carreiro's shipyard. A thin aisle separates the men who are restoring the schooner from the other fishermen. Now that all the yard jobs are filled, feelings have changed about their desirability. When the fishermen bother to talk about the *Shardon Rose* at all, they mutter about low pay, and temporary scablike labor, though there is no strike and no one to strike against.

Yve's father stands near the yardworkers. He's talking with Joe Ames, near the double doors that are open to the noon sun, Martin upon his shoulders. The boy squints against the light. Joe Ames will be even less liked if today's news is bad, as it most certainly will be. A man with money coming in, or even the possibility of money, is easily despised by one with no hope of new income. A line is being drawn, and Joe Ames – with his museum and his schooner, his talk of tourism – is on the wrong side of it, surely. Yve's father, too, straddles it dangerously. He should walk away from Joe; it doesn't matter if the line makes no sense, drawn on emotional points and not facts. Her father should go sit with John and them. Go sit with John and them, Yve thinks.

John sits with her brother and the other *Pearl* crew. They take up a whole row of aluminum chairs: John, Fitz, Chris, Dan, and Walley. They balance uneaten cakes on napkins on their knees. Coffee cools in their hands. Amazing, how her father can be in the same room as Chris and pretend he isn't. Yve would like to be sitting next to John herself. She wishes his arm were around her. Her shoulders feel uncomfortably naked.

'Look.' Susan Furlong nudges Yve with her hip. 'Master Bates is here to keep the peace.'

Officers Jack Hagerty and Richard Bates stand at either side of the stage. Jack Hagerty talks with Sal Liro, but Dick Bates talks to no one. He stands like a sentinel, arms folded across his thin chest, legs spread in a wide stance, and instead of his regular beige deputy hat, he wears a white helmet. His billy club is tucked under his arm.

'What's he expecting?' Edna Larkin says.

'Bad news,' Bea Hopewell says.

'When isn't it?' says Joan Furlong.

'Dear God,' Edna says. 'He's dressed for riot.'

Yve went to school with Dick Bates. They picked on him for his unfortunate name, and the pleasure he now takes in being the law doesn't surprise her. Dick Bates seems to enjoy hauling men out of the bar or off the street for public drunkenness, fighting, lewd behavior. Whereas Jack Hagerty – once the goalie of the Whiskey Winds, second son of a lobsterman, well liked – rarely makes an arrest.

The doors behind the stage open, and the talk in the room hushes for a moment, then becomes louder. Their council representative, Gerry Thomas, and another man step up to the podium.

'I don't envy him,' Edna says. 'Ger.'

'No,' says Bea Hopewell. 'That other one either.'

Edna sucks her back teeth.

The other man is from State Fisheries. He wears a

gray suit – right off, that sets him apart. His groomed hair, his wan hands loosening his tie and unbuttoning the top button of his cream-colored shirt. He clears his throat; his clean-shaven, poreless cheeks quiver like the delicate globes of moon jellies. He is very young. His premature baldness makes him look younger, as if he is still a baby without his first head of hair, dressed in a suit and shoved out on the stage to act the man. Clearly they've been sent a low-level flunky, and that only compounds the insult. Gerry Thomas is older, near sixty, a big man with leathery skin. He wears dress pants and loafers, but he doesn't wear a tie and his button-down shirt is open at the neck and rolled at the cuffs. He used to fish himself.

Bea clicks her tongue. 'I don't see the mayor.'

'You won't, either; Barrett's smarter than that. He's not a man to lose votes,' Edna says. She touches the small of Yve's back. 'Lord, I wish they'd just get on with it.'

'Me too, hon,' Bea says. She flurries her hands off her hips as if it is all already over and done with, no sense even staying to listen. 'It's gonna kill Pete. Put him right in his grave.' Hearing herself, she looks horrified, and she presses her angel collar pin to her lips.

The talk in the room grows louder. They've read the papers, listened to the radio. They've all got theories of what the new regulations mean – all different inter-pretations, and none of them good. That's why they won't let the Fisheries man begin; as if by filling the room with their words instead of his, they make it not so. Make it as if the papers aren't already pushed across bureaucratic desks. He has the podium now, the Fisheries man, his hand up for silence.

'Please, gentlemen. Please—' Gerry Thomas steps to the microphone.

Yve rises to her toes. She feels insubstantial, like sugar stirred through tea. She wants her mother here, but her mother went straight home after Mass with a headache and apologies. Kate, too, is missing. She and Dora are at the Wind, preparing for an after-meeting rush.

'We don't want to keep you from your Sunday dinners any longer.' Gerry Thomas half-smiles. His lips stick to his teeth. 'Can we please begin?' The Fisheries man and he wait a few moments for silence that doesn't come. Gerry speaks into the mike again. 'As some of you may know—' He holds up his hands, and there is a lull. 'As some of you may know, the newest amendment framework is calling for a trip limit of one hundred pounds cod—'

'One hundred! That's no more'n by-catch!' a man from the back wall hollers. The room settles a bit to hear better. The man who hollered looks surprised at the quieting room. Emboldened, he steps away from the wall and takes his hat off and holds it balled in his fist while he points at the man in the suit. 'I catch more cod'n that going for pollack, and you want me to throw everything after a hundred back? You call that management? You call that management?' He struggles for something else to say. A couple men nod, but he has nothing more. 'Fuck your by-catch!' he says. 'Fuck your hundred!'

The women murmur among themselves. The man is right: at a hundred-pound limit, cod will become no more than by-catch – the incidental, accidental species caught in pursuit of another. A hundred-pound limit will, for all intents and purposes, shut the cod fishery down. The room gets loud again.

'Ger looks like he wants to be anywhere but,' Susan says.

'This won't earn him my vote.' Joan Furlong sounds bitter.

Yve wants to say something vicious, too. It has to be somebody's fault they are all here. It would be good to have someone to blame. If a man is at fault, then things can be remedied. Just form a protest, sign petitions, vote him out of office.

'Come on now, gentlemen,' Gerry Thomas starts again. 'You and I know that limit's bullshit and I'm fighting for a seven-hundred-pound—'

'That's bullshit too! Seven hundred ain't shit!'

Gerry Thomas's cheeks shake. 'Gentlemen. Gentlemen.'

Warren Fitz stands. He hooks his cigar from between his lips and points it like a sixth finger. His temper shows red and white on his skin. John remains sitting in the chair beside him. He is nearly as tall sitting as his father is standing, yet his wrinkled brow and beard-pulling make him seem small.

'We all know what this meeting's about.' Fitz barks down the other voices. 'Goddamn get on with it.'

There's a scraping of chairs and one or two coughs.

'Thank you.' The Fisheries man takes the microphone.

Fitz remains standing. The rest keep to their seats or keep their backs pressed to the walls.

'As you know, we've been doing studies for the last few years regarding the decline of groundfish on the Bank.' The Fisheries man speaks clearly, his education cutting his pronunciation with razor precision. 'Cod, haddock, flounder, et cetera; and we've done our best to keep you posted on our findings. But our methods have been, at best, inexact and—'

'Get on with it!' Fitz bellows again. A few voices echo him.

'We've done our best to regulate . . .' The young man looks around, and his words stall. 'We've done our best . . .'

'Goddamn regulations, what's the long and short of it, man?' Fitz's cigar draws a red exclamation. More shift in their seats and give barks of approval. Across the hall, Phil Albin shakes his head. They've already heard so many regulations – harvest levels, net size, limits to days out, off-limit species, undersized

132

caught and thrown back dead. What is one thing more?

'The suggested hundred-pound limit—' starts the Fisheries man.

'By-catch! That's bullshit! By-catch!'

'You take the food off my table!'

The Fisheries man fingers his tie. It was a mistake to wear it; they'd strangle him with it if they could. He clears his throat again. He looks about himself like a man lost and trying to get his bearings. Gerry Thomas says something in his ear. Recognition flickers, sparks him back up.

'We are prepared to offer you a package. Qualifying forms are available at your Fish Lumpers Local, the SnugHarbor Fishers' Aid House here in Rosaline, or you can contact the National Marine Fisheries Service attention Emergency Buyback Package—'

'What emergency?' Pete Hopewell now stands. 'What emergency? What buyback?'

The Fisheries man falters. Gerry Thomas takes over. 'The details are explained in the brochures you hopefully found in your seats. If you didn't get one, or you need one in Spanish or Portuguese, you can come up after the question-and-answer period for a copy.'

Pete shakes his pamphlet. 'It says here we scuttle our boats. Why the hell would you buy our boats and then have us sink them? What kind of package is that?'

'Shut up and let the man talk,' Sandy yells across the room at his father. Bea closes her eyes.

'Get on with it!'

'Please, gentlemen. If you'll quiet please,' the Fisheries man says. 'The upshot of it is this: it looks as though we have no choice but to close six thousand square miles of the Bank—'

A roar, like a wave, slams the stage. It crashes, burbles about the room, clatters like washed stones rolling back out.

'Oh God, oh Lord help us—' Bea Hopewell grabs Mabel Dowd's forearm.

The Fisheries man leans into the microphone. '. . . biologically bankrupt! If you look at the areas in red on the back of your information brochures, chart 9 C . . .'

'What's that?' Fitz holds his hand to his ear as if he is deaf.

The Fisheries man brings his lips even closer to the mike, as if he really believes he hasn't been heard. 'Until more studies show an increase . . .'

'Studies my ass!'

'Fuck your studies!'

The hall erupts. Chairs scrape and fall to the floor. Men shout, shove. Hands and fists wave about, hats swipe off heads and are put back on in frustration. The women surge forward, and Yve's hips are crushed against the metal lip of the service window. Joan Furlong clutches her daughter-in-law. Bea Hopewell is white, her lips are whiter.

'Christ, it's the end,' Edna whispers. She reaches for Yve and pulls her in.

Yve looks out over her aunt's shoulder. Gerry Thomas stands beside the Fisheries man, hands raised as if he is Moses and able to part turbulent waters. His mouth is moving, but his words drown under the din. Officer Jack Hagerty blocks an enraged Sal Liro from the stage, talking the big man down with the sort of gestures one would use to quiet a wild horse. Officer Dick Bates slaps his billy club against the palm of his hand and looks at the men as if they are not his neighbors.

John remains seated, his elbows propped on his knees and his face in his hands. Chris is rubbing circles into John's back, the same way Yve would, if she, not her brother, were sitting beside him. It is hot in the kitchen, and some of the women have started to cry. The room smells of perfumed sweat and coffee, and Yve, smothered in Edna's bosom, feels sick.

'Edna, I've got to – I have to – excuse me.' Yve frees herself, but more women block the door. She hikes her skirt and climbs over the service counter only to find herself trapped by the shoal of angry men.

'You take the food from my children's mouth! You take the food!' a Portuguese protester cries over and over until his voice breaks.

The Fisheries man stands his ground a full minute, adjusts his tie again and again. Finally he removes it completely, rolls it into a ball, and stuffs it in his pocket. He waits a few seconds more, then exits the stage. The men let him go. They are done with him and his NMFS studies, his regulations. They don't want the details; the details are meaningless. They have the brochures. Their own council representative. They'll get the details anyhow from the Legal Notices section of *The Tides*. At least there is a paper with a fisherman's interests at heart. No need to listen to government flunkies. Suits. They'll go to the Wind and hear it from each other. From the TV. At least there they can get a drink.

Yve pushes through the crowd to John. He doesn't raise his face from his palms.

'Yve—' Chris says.

She crouches in front of John, shakes him by both shoulders. 'Come on, honey. Come on, John.' He does not move. She slips her fingers around his; they are thick and dry, like wood. 'John, please.' She pries his hands from his face.

'Yve,' Chris says. He touches her arm. As she waves him off, he tries to catch hold of her hand. 'How's Kate? Is she okay?'

'Why don't you go ask her yourself?' she barks at him. Then in a softer voice she says, 'Come on, John, honey. Come on.'

Chris disappears from the corner of her eye. She wonders for a moment about her brother, what he really wanted, then she turns back to John. 'Come on, John. Everyone's going.' She pulls John to his feet. He doesn't seem able to help.

'Come on, honey. John, you have to help a little.' She moves him to the door. They'll go buy a pint. He'll talk eventually, if she's quiet long enough. She'll be quiet. She'll listen and nod and play the girl. She'll tell him how he's going to be fine, just fine. She'll make it all better; she'll kiss him well again. She leads him from the room by his hand and he drags along behind, as if he were her child.

John lets Yve lead him. His hand finds the back of her neck and he falls a half-step behind, his eyes on her swift-moving calves and her heels skimming the sidewalk. The walk goes from cement to brick, and the road beside from asphalt to cobble as they move deeper into the old section. By the time they arrive, the Whiskey Wind is packed. The crowd spills out the doors and onto the street. Yve pushes into the tight press on the walk; it parts briefly, then closes around them like water parting around rock. They swim up to and through the doors and find a small island of air near the palm that stands in the foyer corner. Its pot is filled with cigarette butts, and a Heineken bottle leans against its trunk. Yve turns, presses herself against John, presses him back between the coats piled on the hooks. She kisses him quickly. Too quickly for him to wake enough to kiss her back. She pulls away and gives him a look. Then she is towing him again, farther in.

Both Dora and Kate work the bar, where the men stand three deep. Kate barely looks up at the opening door. She is by the taps, serving the crew off the *Shardon Rose*. John figures they staked the choice spots early in the day, while the rest of the town was at the meeting. Kate's hair falls over one eye when she leans in to hear something the captain says. She crushes her breasts into a deep cleavage between her folded and leaned-on arms and makes this seem like a natural and necessary action. She has always had an

136

easy, flirty manner, John thinks. Now her head falls back suddenly in a deep belly laugh, she flips her hair off her long white neck and exposes a handful of fine throat. She is fun; her life is fun, she seems to be saying. No fishing means more drinking means more money for her – men will always drink.

'I didn't know they were such good friends,' John says to Yve.

'They're not.'

'Chris is probably right behind us.'

'Probably not,' Yve says, but she stands on her toes and waves to get Kate's attention. Kate waves back and mouths, *I'll call you*, and holds her hand to her head with a pinky and thumb extended in a phone shape. She blows kisses that set her lips in a perfect bow. The captain leans back on his stool.

'She likes to make trouble,' John says.

'She's just working,' Yve says. 'Come on, where're we sitting?'

John looks out over the sea of heads. Everyone is there. All the men from the meeting, all their wives. The older ones, still in their Sunday dresses, sit at tables on the dining side of the etched-glass dividers. They hold on to their beers instead of leaving them be on the coaster; they warm them in their wrinkled hands, wedding bands ticking against the glass. Thick ankles crossed, thick-heeled shoes, thick wool skirts. They sit heavily and fussily at the same time, like nervous hens. They cluck to each other, their jowls shaking. They remind John of how his mother was. Don't want the men at sea, don't want them home. Now they must be patient, wait out the drunk. The younger women wait outside with their babies, the babyless ones stand around the bar.

He looks at the back of Yve's neatly braided hair and thinks, Don't be like them. He means any of them; old, young, he doesn't care. He cups her neck and swears to himself he won't be his father if she won't be his mother. He feels weak and sentimental. We could be more than that – he wants to say it aloud, but it isn't the sort of thing he normally says, and he thinks he'd embarrass himself, so he hesitates. And anyhow, if she read his mind and suddenly turned and asked, What then? What are you thinking we'd be instead? – he wouldn't have an answer. He doesn't know what else is there to be.

They wade farther in and bits of conversation separate from the matted mass. Sentences, like strands of seaweed, bob about and touch John's ears. The talk is loud and constant. *A hundred! I caught more'n that in one set. You should've seen it when I was a boy. Like this they were. Like this. Remember, Bill? Remember? You don't know. You're too young.* The old men coddle their years of fishing experience like their precious balls. John feels suddenly angry at them, as if this is all their fault. If they hadn't taken so much before, there'd be fish now. But he recognizes the hypocrisy in such thinking. He would have fished the same, if he'd been born thirty years earlier. His anger deflates to a peevish frustration. He would like to kick something. He would like to spit, but he does neither. He looks about for his father.

At the front of the bar, at the starboard circular booth, Warren Fitz is holding court. Sal Liro, Izzy Titus, Pete Hopewell, Dan Furlong, and Walley Larkin sit in the leather banquette. Walley looks morose. Others have pulled up chairs around John's father: Harley Swain, Morgan and Marty Jameison. They've got a few pitchers on the table and shots all around.

John leans in to Yve. 'Let's not go over there, okay? Let's just go somewhere else.'

'How about there?' She points with her chin to the far end of the bar.

John looks around. Yve's father is there, near the kitchen. Martin sits on his shoulders, piggybacked, his head in the blue smoke cloud. Phil Albin moves between groups, grasping a shoulder in sympathy, slapping a back and shaking his head with a grim laugh. The man nods like a politician. What is he up to? Securing his place in an insecure future. Now shaking hands with the *Shardon*'s captain, now with Joe Ames, who may need dories for his toy schooner, now with Matt Preston. Preston majored in marine affairs at some fancy Rhode Island school and has ever since been lobbying hard for Rosaline to convert to fish farming. Phil Albin would stand to gain. They'd need pens for the fish, a protected area of bay like the bit off Albin's property. As if fishing and farming are the same. Preston even thinks they should gather kelp. Harvest it like a crop. Hoe it off the beach, maybe. Here's his chance. Desperate men, desperate measures. Farmer Fitz. That'd be the day.

Yve pulls his arm. 'Okay, John? Can we go over there?'

John shakes his head. Yve gives him a little shove with her shoulder. 'Then you find a place that makes you happy, and I'll get the drinks.' She swivels off in an exaggerated hip-swinging walk. She is trying to get a smile out of him. He feels lamed. He looks about for seats. That much he can do. Find seats. He looks to the fishermen table again. A mistake. His father smiles and waves him over.

Outside, the sun sinks, shrivels, and reddens. Shadows lengthen. Wives begin to give up and go home, and the place starts to empty. Around the booth, talk turns from boats to fish to money back to boats, around and around again. They refer to the pamphlets at first and then forget them and set their drinks down upon them. Dinner becomes supper before they take a break from drinking to order some fries and onion rings, something to put on their stomachs. John orders a burger, but he finds he has no appetite for it and can only eat half. Yve picks at his cooling plate. She chatters on about her new job and all the men who work there. She points them out with a fry so John will know who is who, but the names only skim his ears.

'You're not listening.'

'I am.' He dips his index to the thin head on his Guinness. It doesn't peak – that's the fault of the pitcher. If Kate was pulling it directly from the tap it would peak nicely like the top of a meringue pie. Kate pours a nice Guinness.

'Okay, so what did I say?'

'I don't know.' He takes a sip. He is getting drunk. The foam ladders a bit, but not like it should. It should make a line with each sip. He takes another and checks and feels a bit disappointed.

Beneath the table, Yve squeezes his hand. He shifts his fingers in hers to break the sweaty stick.

'I'll shut up now,' she says.

'You don't have to. I'm sorry. What were you saying?'

'Nothing important.' She laughs a bit and looks about the table with bright twists of her head. 'Remember this song?' she says abruptly. A song is ending on the juke. He hadn't noticed it before, but now the chorus is on repeat and fade and he remembers it as a song that used to play on the radio often.

'I've always liked it,' she says. 'It's so happy. Isn't it?' Her gaze lights on John and her eyes hurt him. He looks away. The music says *da da da dum, dedum dedeedee*. He gets lost listening. When he looks back, she is smiling and talking to his father. The old man laughs loudly at something she says. John wishes he'd asked Yve the name of the song while it was on, but now it has faded.

'Marry her soon or I will,' Fitz says to John. He has his arm around Yve's shoulder. He's been drinking steadily all afternoon. He's been putting down shots like a machine built for that purpose. An occasional pint of beer for lubrication. His empty glasses line

140

up in front of him. His cigar stubs gum the ashtray.

'You think she'd have you?' Sal Liro says.

Dan Furlong cocks his head at John. 'He's just a knockoff, Yve. You should go for the original.'

John opens his hands as if to say, I can't stop her. Another song comes on, but it isn't one he cares for. He wants to hold the prior song in his mind, to fix it there, so he can sing it later. What were the words? *I am –* something something something – *I'm your instrument of joy –* The song that's playing keeps breaking through and insisting on itself; John moves his tongue against the roof of his mouth to keep his own song going.

'Ah, he's a dirty old fart,' Sal says.

'Come on now, I'm like her second father. Right, love?' Warren Fitz mugs at Sal and winks, hugging Yve in close and kissing her. She turns her face to John so all Fitz gets is her cheek, but the old man gives her a squeeze anyhow.

John watches them as if from a great distance. He thinks, I will hum it to her later, she'll remember. She's good at those things. She was the one who pointed it out to him in the first place. He remembers now. That summer, between her junior and senior year, she was working the fillet line, and smelled of fish no matter what she washed with. He worked on his father's boat, and was rarely in town. Once, when he was driving her home from her shift, the song came over his truck radio, and she knew all the words. She wanted them to have a song, something to remind them of themselves when they were apart. It seemed important to her for a moment, then when he claimed he'd never heard it before, so how could it mean something to him, she'd laughed. He sees the memory as if it is encased in a bubble. They are in the old Ford without the air-conditioning, with the American flag stuffed in the broken dash to prevent fumes from coming through. It is early August. She is thin, he can circle her upper arm with his thumb and forefinger. She wears a white dress with little flowers, and as she reaches toward the radio to turn it up, her collarbone presses against her skin till it stands out like a handle. She says something like *I love this* or *Listen! Listen!* and then she sings *dadadadum dedum dedeedum* – no, he's lost that last note. He tilts his head and squints. The bar comes back into focus, but he feels as though he is looking down a long tube. He has missed something. The men are chewing The Package again. It has grown capital letters in the course of the afternoon.

'Twenty-five million for the whole region? What'll that be per?' Sal Liro says.

'Yeah, yeah, but they're still fishing off Rhode Island; monk, squid, butterfish—' Pete Hopewell counts on his fingers.

Sal reaches for an onion ring. Takes a bite, winces at its coldness, and throws it back in the basket. 'Come on now, Pete. What're you gonna do? Motor out four days and fight the locals for a handful of garbage?'

'—fluke—'

'Is going down in the market. I don't like it any better'n you.'

'All I'm saying,' Dan puts in like he's been saying something all along, 'all I'm saying is we used to be like the cowboys. You know? That kind of respect.'

Izzy nods. 'We just want to fish, is that so bad?'

'Nothing,' Walley says, still answering Liro's earlier question. His face droops like a hound's, his shoulders droop. Even his vagrant eye has headed south, keeping a watch on his pint.

'I should sink the damn tub; I'd get more from insurance,' Sal says.

Fitz looks up. His eyes are red and slanting. His jaw is slack. It takes him a moment to focus, then he smiles. 'Just do me a favor.'

'What?'

'Just do me a favor, would you?'

'What?'

'Sink her somewhere else. I don't want you clogging the channel with your piece of shit.' Fitz laughs and Liro joins him.

Marty Jameison comes back from the bar with another pitcher. Everyone slides around and Izzy is pushed off the other end.

'Izzy, where you going? Where you going?' Fitz waves a rubbery hand.

Izzy shrugs.

'You going somewhere?'

'No.' He looks at the table, swaying. 'Got nowhere to go.' His lip starts to quiver.

'Oh come here, come here.' Sal slides over and the crowd scrunches to make room.

Izzy perches next to the big man. 'I just wanna fish. Is that so bad?'

'I know, I know.' Sal pushes a beer at him.

'I just wanna fish!'

'Well, they're not leaving us many options,' Walley complains softly. 'Like they're trying to kill us. Get us up against the wall, then—' He jabs and twists the air.

'Goddamn suits!' A pint, Fitz's, cracks down on the table. Shot glasses jump and a forgotten cigarette tumbles from the ashtray. For a moment, there's a little scramble. Yve brushes embers from her skirt, Sal sops spills up with used napkins. Walley starts to giggle, but then looks at the others and stops before much noise gets out. His eye spins a wild circuit before settling back on his pint.

Fitz weaves in his seat. 'Urchins. Market for that. Japs'll eat anything.'

'So you know the first thing about catching urchins?' Liro says.

'How about that Icelander company? I heard,' Fitz mumbles, 'they wanna reopen the cannery. Herring.'

'Different nets.'

143

'Sword, then.' The old man's jaw works slowly. He looks like a toy, winding down.

'You got the gear?'

'Got tuna gear. Last summer.'

'Think sword is doing better?' Sal says. 'There ain't none out there.'

'Fish've hid before,' Fitz says.

'They're not hiding,' Sal says. 'There ain't none left to hide.'

The men look between Sal and Fitz. Fitz points a shaky finger at the big man. 'Don't start that. Don't.'

'Well it's true!'

'Don't.'

Sal lowers his voice. 'It's true.'

Fitz stands.

'Sorry, Warren,' Sal says. 'Sit down. Okay? Sit down. Lemme buy you a drink.'

Fitz ignores him. His hands pat his various pockets, then locate his half-glasses dangling on his chest, the earpiece through a button hole. He fumbles them to his nose. 'What do I owe here?' He searches the table, hands crawling like a blind man's. He throws his glasses. 'Damn things!' John puts them in his own pocket.

Fitz wobbles to Sal. 'Where'sa goddamn tab?'

'Don't worry about it, Warren. I got it,' Sal says.

'What? Show me the goddamn tab.' Fitz searches his pockets for his wallet.

Sal shoos his hands at him. 'Your money's no good here. I got it.'

'Pay my own goddamn tab.'

'That's enough, Warren,' Sal says.

'S'pose a mean, eh? What the hell?'

'Sit down.' He pulls Fitz down to the banquette, but Fitz keeps going, sliding with momentum. His head bounces off the table and his body slides under.

'Shit, Dad!' John reaches across Yve's lap and grabs a floppy arm. Yve twists, tries to help, succeeds only in pulling Fitz's shirt from his pants.

She stops helping suddenly. She looks at John, eyes wide, and says, 'John? Can you—'

John makes a bridge with his arms. She ducks under and out of the booth. She stands by, her hands held stiffly away from her body. She looks ill.

Sal and John struggle the old man to his feet. Fitz's trousers are a darker brown in the crotch and thighs. He stinks of urine and beer.

'Oh Lord.' Yve tucks her nose in her sleeve. Sal turns his head away and lets the old man go. John can't hold his father alone, and Fitz sinks again to his knees.

'Shit, Sal,' John says. He looks from man to man. They all stand away, like they're afraid of a puddle on the seat. No one steps up. They look sheepish. 'Christ, Walley. I'm too drunk to hold him all myself.'

Walley bites his lip. He points his thumb at the Men's and takes his beer with him.

John looks around for Dan, but he's gone to the bar with their empty glasses. The *Shardon* crew boys are all staring, Kate's staring too.

Dora comes around from the bar, wiping her hands. She gets close and says, 'Oh Jesus, John. Can't you get him up?'

'He's heavy as hell.'

'Oh Christ. He's pissed himself,' Dora says. 'Can we get some help here? Wen?' She hits the captain of the *Shardon Rose* on the arm, and John wishes she hadn't. The captain takes it as an order. He swivels on his stool, slides off slowly. He smiles as if this is part of the local fun, and he's glad to finally join in.

'Now what's the problem here? How can I help?' He doesn't wait for an answer. He glides into the booth, to the other side of Fitz, and gets a grip in the old man's armpit. Fitz chuckles. He swats the air about his head, as if he's shooing flies.

'Find your sea legs, man!' the captain says. 'Two-six!' Together John and he wrestle Fitz standing. The captain flips the old man's arm around John's neck. 'There's an old salt, an old sour. There's a dirty dog.' He keeps the cheerful banter going, finds Fitz's cap, and slaps it on his head.

'Dirty dog!' Fitz says.

'That's right, matey!' The captain winks at John. 'I think it's time you got Captain Courageous home.' He slaps John on the shoulder. 'Lead on, brave man.'

John limps Fitz to the door. He looks over his shoulder to Yve. 'I'll be back in a bit,' he says.

Yve looks back at him, but the door's already closing. The fishermen have wandered off. Kate comes over to their empty table with a glass of soda water and a bar mop. She scrubs at the seat where John's father had been. Yve gathers up glasses and pamphlets. She stuffs a napkin in the dirty ashtray.

'Where we going?'

John doesn't answer. He's having a hard enough time unlocking the door with one hand and holding his father up with the other.

Fitz gets his feet under him and starts to wander off. John grabs him by the shirt-tail and the old man's legs give way. He knocks the keys from John's hands, and when John bends for them, the old man falls across his back, keeping him bent.

'Now, you're doing that on purpose, Dad. Stand or I'll drop you.'

He finally gets the door, and they fall into the house, arms wrapped around each other like wrestling bears. Their landing rattles china in the dining-room cabinet. John drags Fitz to the sofa and thumps him onto the cushions. He turns on the reading lamp, and a buttery circle lights his father's face. The old man's eyes are nearly shut. A white crust has dried in the corners of his mouth, a trickle of the same down his chin. John clenches the cuff of his sleeve in his fist and wipes the face roughly. Fitz smiles, swats at John's cleaning hand. Then he gives up and sighs. John gives up too, removes the old man's cap, and places it on the coffee table where he can see it first thing when he wakes.

'Johnny—' His father doesn't continue out loud. His lips move a bit more but no words come out.

John unlaces the shoes, wiggles them free. The old man's socks are dirty and smell, and John pulls these off too. His big-toe nails are ridged and black, his toes are purple and white.

'Dad, I'm getting the bottle. Don't fall asleep yet.'

He goes to the toilet and fetches the johnny bottle from next to the seat. Its white enamel is chipped a bit and tin shows through at the handle and the blue lip. When he gets back, his father is trying to unbutton his trousers.

'I got you.' John bats the thick fingers out of the way. He kneels by his father and unbuttons his trousers and fishes through the shorts and pulls him out. He guides him into the bottle. Waits, head turned away. Nothing happens.

'Come on now.' He peeks to check.

Fitz has fallen asleep. His chin rests on his chest, his hand loose on the cushions.

'Dad!' John shakes him good. The reading light jumps and Fitz opens an eye.

'Piss. Now. No accidents.' John shakes him again for good measure. He gives a shake every few seconds until a weak stream hisses into the bottle and warms it against John's knuckles. The urine smells like aspirin.

'There you go.' John tucks his father back in and swings his legs onto the sofa. One-handed, he pulls the afghan up.

'Johnny—?'

'Yeah, Dad.'

The old man's hand reaches blindly to pat John's shoulder. 'You're a good boy. Have I told you what a good boy you are?'

147

'Yeah, I'm a good boy.' The bottle is warm in his hand. He places it carefully on the coffee table.

'Don't leave me alone, promise – promise?'

'I'm just gonna go back for Yve, okay? To walk her home.'

'No. C'mere, c'mere.' The hand waves the air.

'No, I got to go.'

'Please—' Fitz stretches his arms out. 'What're we gonna do? What're we gonna do?'

'You're going to sleep.'

The old man's crying now. 'We're not gonna make it.'

'Yeah we will. Go to sleep.'

'Let me die. I wanna die.'

'You're not gonna die,' John says because he's not; that will never be John's luck.

He pulls on John's sleeves, crying. 'Please, Johnny. Don't leave me. I'm gonna die.'

'You're not dying, all right?'

The old man's sobs become coughs, and he leans forward in John's arms, choking. John thumps his back. He spits up on John's sleeve. When he's done, John lays him against the cushions. The old man pants heavily, then snores lightly. John pulls off his own shirt, careful to keep the gob from his face. It is brown and thick, like drying ketchup.

Yve sweeps Kate's lipstick across her mouth. She's had quite a few beers, but she didn't feel them until she tried to walk to the head and the floor went woozy on her.

'You look *mahvelous*,' Kate says. She's sitting cross-legged on the tiles. She's also been drinking. The sailors have been buying since John and the other fishers left.

Yve fishes a compact from Kate's fringed purse. She puckers, pats her cheeks. She stares at herself in the mirror. 'I should wear makeup more often.'

'You should drink more often is what you should do,' Kate says. She gets up with great difficulty, clutching the sink. Her reflection bobs beside Yve's. 'Give me my lipstick.'

Beer is working on Yve's emotions, and she loves Kate. Loves Kate, has always loved Kate, will always love her, even when she can't stand her. Something foggy forms in her mind, something about the intimacy between two women, the things they know about each other, but that's not it exactly. Nothing is anything exactly.

Kate slowly redraws her lips. She talks with only her tongue. 'What are you looking at, dirty girl?'

'Nothing. I should go. I have to make breakfast in the morning.'

'What's it like?'

'What?'

'Being there when they wake up. What's it like?'

'Oh, I don't know.'

Kate finishes, kisses the air. 'The captain, what's he like?'

Yve thinks. Wen wandering through the kitchen, shirtless, barelegged, barefoot, in boxers of ridiculous fabrics – alligators wearing reindeer horns, red noses, and jingle bells, fried-egg platters and coffee cups with angel wings – she generally tries to keep her back turned; she tries to anticipate his entrance and to find something in the sink that needs attention, or an item in the refrigerator to search for as he passes through to the bathroom. He never closes the door. His urine hits the toilet water for what seems like forever, before he trickles off and lets loose a long fart. She tries to make noise to cover this – rattle a pot, run water. The others laugh at her embarrassment.

'Come on, what's it like?'

'You just want stories of men in their underwear, dirty girl.' Yve turns and the room tilts. 'I should go home.'

'Oh, one more, come on. If you leave it's just me and Jenny Stewart and I can't stand her and Dora'll make me work.'

They hold each other up and, arms linked, wobble back to the booth the sailors took over after the fishermen left. Yve and Kate slide in. Jenny Stewart is already sitting there, mooning at Rob Ames. The guys have taken to calling him Peg Boy. They've got a pool going on when he'll lose his cherry. Thinking about it makes Yve giggle.

'Hey Cookie.' Hank, the caulker, leans across the table. 'You're up mighty late on a school night. We still getting breakfast tomorrow?'

Yve smiles. Tomorrow feels far away.

'God, I hate this song,' Ed, the bosun, moans. The lenses of his glasses are greasy with fingerprints, and he smells like diesel.

'Dance with me,' Jefferson says.

'Get away from me, you fag.'

'I just want to be inside you,' Jefferson says, and they all laugh.

The jukebox song wails like a barroom drunk about a piano man with too much talent for a small-town bar. Jefferson pulls Ed to his feet, drags him through a limping waltz. Ed starts howling. He looks tiny in Jefferson's arms as Jefferson flings him about like a rag doll.

Drinks arrive again. They are running out of table surface. Kate gets a bus tub to clear glasses. Dora follows, fisting two pitchers in each hand.

'I love a strong woman,' Hank says. 'Allow me.' He relieves Dora of half her burden. Kate raises her eyebrows and purses her lips at Yve.

'Sit a bit.' Wen maneuvers Kate to his lap.

'Remember, I'm a married woman.'

'How can I forget?'

'Yve was telling me stories about you in the bathroom.'

150

'Nothing bad, I hope.' The captain's big arms wrap Kate's waist and make it look small. His wrists press up against her full breasts. She sits easily. Her white back is a wall to Yve. Yve lays her chin on the table, so she has some view of the proceedings.

Jefferson is rocking Ed in his arms now, like a baby. The old sailmaker, Charlie, sings along, swinging his beer in time. Even Neil, the uptight first mate, joins in, but Peg Boy Rob only has eyes for Jenny. She'd come in for dinner with her parents, then come over to say hello, then stayed for a drink. Her smile looks as if it comes from a can. Empathy for all hopeless lovers cracks open Yve's chest. She can no longer balance on her chin, the weight of emotion tips her, and she must lay her cheek on the cool slate.

Wen ducks his head behind Kate's back and whispers in Yve's available ear, 'How are you doing?'

She gropes for her beer and tilts it. It's still mostly full. She sloshes it in the glass, a line of minute bubbles thread to the surface. John hasn't come back for her. Her father is gone. It's late. She has to make breakfast in a few hours. 'I think I should go,' she says. Her lips feel swollen and fat from the slate pressing up against her face.

Kate scrunches around. She pouts at Yve. 'You never stay for the fun.'

'It's a school night,' she says. Hank laughs. 'Really, I should go,' she says.

'Poop.' Kate hops off Wen's lap. Her skirt is a series of wrinkled moons now. She pulls him to his feet so Yve can slide out.

Yve finds standing makes her head swim. She wipes her hands down the front of her blouse and waits for the red haze to clear. Conversation has stopped for her.

'Well, goodbye then.' She half-waves to the men – an aborted little gesture. She'll be feeding them in a few hours.

'You'll let Wen walk you, okay?' Kate gives her a big

squeezing hug. 'I don't like you going home by your-self. Walk her, okay?' she tells Wen.

'What about you?'

'Dora'll drive me later.' Kate slaps Yve's butt. 'Go on now.'

Outside, the cold almost fools Yve into sobriety. She doesn't feel so tired. The captain doesn't seem drunk at all. The rising moon fades the stars and casts long blue shadows. They are walking up Water, Yve shuffling through the oak leaves piled in the gutters – they break over her feet in shushing waves. She can think of nothing to say. Her head is filled with helium, and she listens to the noise of leaves. It is an awkward thing, this walking under the moon with a man who isn't John. It shouldn't mean a thing. She could make conversation: the new regulations, work, Kate – So, do you still want to sleep with my sister-in-law? – but she discards every sentence half formed. She tells herself she doesn't need to make conversation, it isn't her job to entertain him. He is simply walking her home, for safety's sake, and it is irrelevant whether he enjoys her conversationally or not. He probably isn't even think-ing about it. He probably isn't thinking much at all. He's probably just drunk, just listening to some song go around in his head. She knows this much about men. There was a time when she was trying to under-stand John. They'd have such long silences, so she took to asking him what he was thinking, demanding a quick response to trick him into revealing something about his mind, maybe something he didn't even know himself. She'd say suddenly, 'What are you thinking? Right now? What?' He'd look puzzled, then say something like 'That tree over there – the moon.' She'd probe – was he thinking anything special about it? No, just that it is there. Sometimes how it may be useful, such as 'That tree's branch – your dad could make a knee from it.' She eventually gave up asking. She imagined his thoughts to be a simple list of

152

observations; *tree, moon, leaves, knee*. Without even aesthetic judgments – not 'graceful tree', 'rising moon', 'shushing leaves', 'good knee'. Just: tree, knee, moon, leaves. She suspects most men think this way, empirically. She listens to their talk; *that's some fish, lotta cod, not enough by half*. Numbers and measures and money. Weather and repairs. Things that to her seem without emotion. Cold things. Metallic things. Perhaps this is what gives them the confidence for such prolonged silences. They never even think to ask the thoughts of the woman next to them, assuming instead that she too is simply experiencing and observing. Weighing the world by the same criterion: its use. Making grocery and chore lists. Men don't take into account the constant small judgments and adjustments women have been trained to make every moment of every day—

'You're awfully quiet,' Wen says.

She laughs.

'Why are you laughing?'

'Because you caught me.' She turns and walks backward a bit, sort of a half-skip, so she can face him. 'I was just looking at the trees, the moon, the leaves,' she says. She laughs again, and he smiles back at her as if he's a bit puzzled, but charmed. She closes her laugh to a smile and raises her eyebrows in a way that makes her feel mysterious. She hopes she looks mysterious. And playful, maybe. Maybe this is the beers she's feeling. Maybe that is her excuse. She feels young and flirtatious, skipping backward like this, and she likes that feeling.

'They're pretty,' he says.

'Yes. Exactly.' She stops skipping back. Blocks him from walking farther. 'Do you know John Fitz?'

'Yes; the one with the pissed father.'

'Exactly. He's my boyfriend.'

'I figured.'

'Oh, did you, now? Smart man.' She turns and

walks beside him. 'John never asks what I'm thinking.'

Her small betrayal shines between them like a coin.

'Well he should.'

'Why?'

'Because you're a thoughtful woman.'

She stops walking and he stops beside her. The moment feels dangerous and heady, like the running of a finger through flame on a dare. He taps her forehead lightly.

'Thinking all the time,' he says. 'I see you thinking when you're washing the dishes. Your back is turned, but I know you're listening and thinking.'

'Do you, now? And what am I thinking?' She walks on again, and he follows.

'Deep thoughts. I'm sure you'll tell me someday.'

'Will I?'

'Maybe.'

They are passing the yard now. The *Shardon Rose* squats between her scaffolds like a woman hunkering down in her skirts. Wen says, 'You don't mind if I check on her before I take you home?'

'No. Fine.' Yve pulls her hair elastic off and scratches her hair free, running her fingers through the strands and letting the wind cool her scalp. Her hair and clothes smell like cigarettes. 'What's she like inside?'

'You mean you haven't seen her?'

'Not the inside.'

'That's terrible.'

'I'm always up at the house. Washing dishes, thinking deeply, you know.'

'That's terrible,' he says again. 'Let me give you the dime tour.'

'I'd like that.'

He smiles at her and she smiles back.

'Go on up,' he says.

He makes her climb the ladder to the catwalk first. Air blows up her skirt, cold on her thighs. He watches from below. She wonders where his eyes are. Is it all shadows from his point of view or can he see? She waits for him at the top. It seems very high up, very exposed. Like standing on a cliff. You never realize how tall boats are until they're out of water. They're like icebergs, mostly hidden. She can't help looking down. Watching him climb. Below, the red and green lights that mark the channel flicker in the bay. Buoy bells, three haphazard notes, clang with the odd chop. The swell bobs the light, rings the bells, then slaps up and under the piers with a hollow pop and a fizzing retreat. The surf rushes over the marine railway, gurgles around the schooner's supports, then hisses away. Nothing betrays the sea's newly diagnosed emptiness. Fish, no fish, the black, foam-marbled waters swell and roll with the same random waves.

Wen steps onto the catwalk, sending a slight ripple down its length. 'I know it doesn't look like we've done much, but you'll see below. We've completely gutted her.'

He crosses the gangway, suspended high above the ways between schooner and scaffold. His hips are narrow. His left shoulder is higher, and his gait leans slightly in that direction. He waits on the deck, holding his hand out. She takes his offered hand. He helps her aboard, and she lets him as if she hasn't been on a boat a thousand times before. Then she lets him keep her hand. She tries to empty her head like a blown Easter egg, tries to not have thoughts or pictures of him with Kate on his lap. Her palm presses his; his fingers curl around hers. Sensitivity increases in her palm and fingers, called up by the dry warmth of his skin. She can feel the grain of each fingerprint and callus and how each differs. She can count the fine hairs on the back of his hand. In the hollow space where their palms curve away from each other's, air pools and swirls like a warming current. She feels all this and marvels at the minutiae of these sensations with a divided mind – half feeling his hand, half commenting on the wrongness of it.

He leads slightly, negotiating shadowy obstacles. The deck is covered with cardboard and tarps that crinkle beneath their feet. Midships, he stops and feels around inside the companionway. He pulls out a flashlight. Its beam quivers as he shines it along docklines, chafe gear. Up and down the length of the schooner. Checking for vandalism perhaps, maybe for nothing. Maybe just to draw out their walk. She keeps her mind empty, lets her consciousness curl in the warm air between their palms. She follows him. One circuit around the tarpaulined deck. It is dusty and their feet leave ghost prints. Everything is fine and in place.

They stop once more at the midships break. He shines his light at nothing in particular. He says, 'We're restoring her to her original state – except for the dories and fishing gear. Since she was a working boat, there won't be a lot of brass or shine. She'll be pretty enough when she's done, though. The deck'll stay black – I was on this yachty rig a while back – *she* was bright. Lots of polish. We holystoned the decks every morning, till they were white as this.' He turns her hand over and strokes his finger down her forearm.

She pulls her hand from his and holds her own against where he stroked, as if that place now bleeds. 'I should go.'

He acts as though he hasn't heard her. He climbs down the middle companionway. Perhaps she said it too quietly. Perhaps she only thought it.

'Watch your head,' he's saying. 'I've got you.' He holds the light between his teeth and puts his hands gently on her hips. She looks down and is momentarily blinded by the flashlight shining up. He spits it into his hand. 'Sorry.'

She blinks away red spots.

They are in a large empty hold. He flashes the light around the hollow space. Blackened wood and rusted iron; low dewy beams. It's cold and damp and close. Yve keeps her hand on the shallow overhead, marking available space. It feels like an underground cave, only they are not underground at all. They are high above ground, midair in fact. In a schooner supported on shores. They are deep in a bowl hovering in midair – here and there, where a plank is absent, she can see a slice of sky. He shines his light forward and the space extends freely to the bow, interrupted only where the masts drive through the deck to the exposed keelson, which they stand upon. It's been recently painted with a red primer and looks raw, like a skinned backbone. Frames rise up and out from it like ribs.

'Is it safe?' She taps her heel on the boards beneath her feet.

'Keep to the frames,' he says. He jumps a few ribs forward. 'This here, the old saltbox, will become the main cabin, with bunks on either side and a dining table in the center.' He draws the plan with the light. 'Ames thinks we can get twenty guests a week for windjammers.' He shines the beam around and names imaginary rooms. 'Captain's quarters, galley – we'll need a cook again, come spring, if you're interested – bosun's locker, engine room – getting a new engine next week, so the Cummins guy may stop by for lunch.'

His light catches crystals deep in the cracked planks. He brushes his finger along a crack and touches its whitened tip to her lips. 'Still salty.'

'Yes.' Her answer tastes salty.

He pries a soft splinter from a nearby joint. 'Think we'll ever get it together?'

'Perhaps,' she says. He means the boat, restoring it.

He crumbles the splinter and tosses it over his shoulder, as if for luck or making a wish. 'You don't trust me much,' he says.

The salt is still on her lips, but she does not lick them.

157

'Do you, Yve? Trust me?' He looks at her and doesn't say anything else. She doesn't either. If she says nothing she knows that in a few moments more he'll stroke the air near her cheek, then pick up a strand of her hair and crush it between his fingers as he did the splinter.

She turns to a slice in the hull, her eye caught by glowing white. A pale gull hovers, then dives from view. 'Have you given Kate this tour?' she says.

His throat bobs with silent laughter. 'You're good,' he says. 'What a good friend. A good girlfriend. Good sister.'

'People talk . . . someone gets hurt . . .'

'You're worried I'm a home-wrecker?'

'Are you?' she asks. Because he is a wrecker of things, she sees this clearly now. He has found something weak in her and has smashed it. A shard now pierces her breast.

'Maybe. Them that go down to the sea in ships.' He rides his hand on imaginary waves. 'We break hearts.'

'John doesn't.'

He raises his brows in a mock *oh*.

She puts her hand on her chest. 'He's a good man.' Her heart pounds beneath her fingers. Here, her heart. She feels foolish. But what she says is true.

He takes her hand away and presses it to his own sternum. Then lays his own palm between her breasts.

'Am I a good man, Yve? What do you feel there?'

She feels her heart beat against his palm, and his against hers. The rhythms are different. She confuses her heart with his. She pulls her hand back.

'I should walk you home now,' he says.

'Yes, you should.' She feels as though she has been stabbed. His intruding palm has pushed the broken piece deeper and now blood fills her stomach. She is ill from it. 'Yes, you should.'

But they stand there a while longer. Then he walks her home. Without touching, in silence.

13

John wakes up late. He went back to the Wind and Yve was already gone, the place was dark, and he didn't get home till nearly four. Now it is half past nine. His head throbs as if he's been beaten. His mouth tastes of ash, and his eyes feel peeled. His father slumps at the kitchen table drinking a glass of Alka-Seltzer. He has his books out, his box of receipts, his calculator. The room smells sour.

'That's got to hurt this early in the morning.' John gets himself a glass of tap water and sits opposite the old man.

Fitz pushes the box of antacid over. He waits for John to flip the tabs in, and for the fizz to start, and for John to take a sip. He says, 'It's got to be done sometime.'

'Now though?'

'Sometime.' Fitz picks up a slip of yellow paper and puts it back down. 'You know how much Phil is charging for that line? I'm half a mind to go to Service Marine.'

'Service won't give you credit, and you wouldn't do that to Phil.'

'He's gonna put us over the edge.'

'Is he asking for the money now?' John waits for Fitz to say nothing. 'Of course he isn't. God, my head's killing me.'

'There's coffee.'

John gets up and gets himself a cup. He stirs in milk and sugar, then carries the spoon to the sink. There are a couple of spoons and coffee mugs with hard brown crusts in the bottom.

'What're your plans?' Fitz says.

159

'For what?'

'Today. You gonna work that net?'

'It's gonna rain this afternoon. I figured I'd look at the stuffing box, do the net when Chris is around.' John sits again. 'You?'

Fitz spreads his hands at the paper mess.

'Huh,' John says. The coffee tastes good. A square of pale sun hits the table right where John's forearm rests. They get the morning sun in the kitchen. His mother always said an east-facing kitchen was best for waking up to. Except on the shortest winter days, she could make breakfast without the lights on, from the sun shining through the windows. She liked bright things. Her tea towels – neither he nor his father uses tea towels, so the ones she last used still hang beside the sink – are bright reds and blues. The everyday plates are every kind of color – red, green, yellow. She would buy them mismatched at garage sales and flea markets.

'Stuffing box leaking?' Fitz says.

'What?'

'She leaking? The stuffing box?'

'I noticed a lot of water last trip.'

'Oh yeah?' Fitz glances to his books. He turns a few pages one way, then back the other way. He turns them forward again, picks up a pen, puts it down.

'How's it look?' John says.

'Bad.'

John half-laughs. 'When isn't it?'

'You really want to know what I think?'

'Do I?' John says. 'Do you want to tell me?'

Fitz looks over his glasses at him. 'I don't think you want to hear it.'

'Look at yourself.' John pulls a long face. 'That's why you shouldn't do those things first thing in the morning.'

The old man looks toward the window. His hand trembles near his mouth.

'Come on, Dad.'

Fitz waves him off.

'You just had a bad night.' John leans back in his chair. He snags a bottle of Bushmills from the counter. 'Hair of the dog,' he says, and he pours a nip in his coffee. 'There's nothing different between yesterday and today, and you weren't like this yesterday.' He pushes the mug toward his father.

Fitz ignores it. 'There's everything different.'

'The closings might not happen. Ger'll fight for us.'

'Gerry Thomas is stalling, but it'll go through first of the year. They did it up north, they'll do it here.'

'So that's next year,' John says. 'We'll worry next year.'

'That's two months.'

'Three. And it's likely we'll be grandfathered in.'

'They'll still close spots.'

'There're other spots to fish.'

'Less spots mean more men in them.'

'Some'll take the buyback.'

Fitz shakes his head. He scratches the two-day beard on his chin and throat with the back of his hand.

'Some will,' John says.

'We might have to ourselves.'

'You're not serious,' John says. He pushes the mug at his father again. 'Drink your coffee.'

Fitz takes a swallow, grits his teeth. He reaches for the bottle and pours a bit more. He drinks and says, 'You want to take a look?'

'No,' John says. 'No. Yes.'

Fitz spins the binder so it faces John. The old man's handwriting covers the pages: pen, pencil, Sharpie marker. Numbers and names are crossed out and written over, arrows connect this entry to that, a few are circled. Between pages are slips of paper, business cards, lists. A phone number is scribbled across one ledger page, and another has its top half torn out. John's head hurts. He rubs crust from his eyes. The mess angers him.

161

'What am I supposed to be seeing here?' he says. He spins the ledger back. 'It's useless. You can't find shit in there.'

'You can't 'cause you don't want to.' Fitz flips pages quickly, one tears. He curses and keeps flipping. 'You want me to do every goddamn thing.' He stops and points. 'There!'

'What?'

'There, goddammit!' He grabs John by the back of the head and holds his nose to the page. 'There.'

John bats his father's hand away and sits up. He reads the page slowly, the numbers with the minus signs before them and the numbers with the pluses. His coffee cools. He takes his time. Two mortgages are outgoing and fish is incoming, and there is a large discrepancy between. There are repairs, and diesel, and the shares of the crew. There is money to the museum for dockage. He refigures.

'So? This is one month only,' he finally says.

'I can show you every one is just like that,' Fitz says.

John looks out the window. The light is cooler and more diffuse. The sky is white and the sun is a small white ball behind clouds. He gets up and goes to the sink and finds another mug and washes it out. He pours himself more coffee, milk, stirs sugar. He feels his father watching him. He turns. Fitz is writing in the book.

'What do you want me to say?' John says. 'What do you want me to do?'

'I don't know.' Fitz doesn't look up. He punches a few numbers into the calculator, writes again.

John watches him a few moments. He waits for him to say something more. The clock over the window hums. It is getting late.

'The morning's half gone,' John says.

Fitz doesn't answer.

'I'm going to fix the stuffing box.'

Fitz nods at his book.

'Okay then,' John says.

By the time John gets to the *Pearl* it is raining softly. Most of the fleet is in; the men didn't go out yesterday because of the meeting and few were in any shape to leave this morning. There is no wind and the rain falls straight down. The docklines sag, the museum's banners sag. A yellow schoolbus idles in the parking lot, the driver reading a paper in her seat, the children presumably inside on a class trip. The bus is from Fenland County District, a richer community an hour south. John hates that the bus is idling. It stinks and it is wasteful. He wants to go up to the driver and tell her that. She should go into the museum lobby if she wants to read her paper somewhere heated. He gives her a dirty look as he passes, but she doesn't see him, and he's not the sort of man to bang on her door and say something. He is in a bad mood going below, and the high water in the bilge doesn't make him any happier.

The boat rocks a bit. Small waves clap the hull. He lifts the hatch and lays his cheek on the cold sole and shines his flashlight along the shaft to the stuffing box. Water ripples over the shaft. It gurgles under his ear. Leaning way over, shoulder on the sole frame, head in the bilge, he looks farther back. His breath mists. He touches a few things, for no real reason. The driveshaft is covered with rime and rust and too much water. He sits up quickly and dizzies himself. He waits for the black sparkles in the corners of his eyes to clear, then he takes the sump pump from its shelf in the engine room and gets it going.

He works a few hours without noticing the time. Tufts of rotten packing crowd around his legs like wet mice. Water flows in and the pump sucks and belches and water rumbles up the ribbed hose and out the hatch, back to the bay where it will line up to creep back in. It is a losing battle. The boat is too old. She

163

needs to be hauled out. He stuffs new packing in, shines his light up and down, waits for more water. There should be a little but not too much. One drop every second or so. His head aches. He pulls and repacks. Pulls and repacks. The pump gargles and chokes; there is no more water. A miracle. He turns it off and pulls it from the bilge. He sits a few moments and nothing happens. Then, slowly, the packing darkens and water trickles back in. The trickle becomes a spout. He pokes about and the spout grows to the size of a woman's little finger. He drops the pump back in. He starts it up. It rumbles and whines and he lies back on the sole and closes his aching eyes. He lies there a few minutes, a few minutes more. His head throbs along with the rumbling pump. He imagines the boat filling with water. He pictures her scuttled. He tries to imagine what he would do. He tries to imagine not having a boat. He feels about for the roll of packing. He holds it up to his eyes. It is near gone. He throws the useless end bit across the sole and sits up to watch where it lands. It bounces under Walley's bunk. He'll have to run over to Phil Albin's now for another roll.

He doesn't want to see Phil. He doesn't want to have a conversation with him about Chris or Yve or the new regulations for that matter. The man makes him uncomfortable. When he shakes John's hand his face is a strange mix of warmth, respect, and disapproval. The families have known each other forever. Phil and the old man were friends a long time. Phil and Alma were the first people after John's own parents to see him when he was born. John was in Alma's kitchen as much as his mom's growing up. He's Martin's godfather. Things change. Now when John visits, he and Phil have little to say to each other besides sports and weather, and John doesn't follow sports closely when he's out fishing. He goes to rub his eyes, smells the bilgewater, and drops his hands to his lap. He will leave the pump to work and cross his fingers it won't flood or burn out before he gets back.

Outside, the rain has become a fine mist. The children are out of the museum and back in the idling bus. Their heads bob in the windows; they are eating their sack lunches. The noon whistle is just winding up to blow. John puts his hands over his ears, and he stops walking till the whistle winds down.

He stops by Carreiro's yard instead of Phil's. The *Shardon* is coming along quickly. The scaffolds are gathered around the midsection now and the bow is striped with new boards. They are so green they look gold compared to the blackened hull. A few holes show where rotten planks have been pulled and not yet replaced, and someone has begun scraping off the old bottom paint. Rust has been chipped from the dolphin striker and chains and hawseholes; red primer speckles the metal.

John waves at Sandy Hopewell. The man's strolling from the shiploft, wiping his hands on a rag.

'She's really coming along,' John says.

Sandy walks over before answering. He gives John's hand a shake; he smells citrusy, like Fast Orange hand cleaner.

'Yeah, he works us hard,' Sandy says.

John nods at the empty scaffolds. 'Looks like you're the only one working.'

'Lunch.' Sandy looks up the road toward the crewhouse.

'Don't let me keep you.'

'I bring my own.'

John laughs. 'I didn't think Yve was that bad a cook.'

'She's fine. I just like the break.'

John wonders what kind of men you need a break from, if you're only working an eight-hour day. His question must show in his face, because Sandy adds, 'They're not bad. There's just a lot of them.' He clears his throat. 'And I'm staying there now, you know.'

'No I didn't,' John says absently. He is thinking of Yve up there with the lot of them. 'You see Yve today?'

'Yeah. She was there for breakfast.'

'She made it to work okay then.'

Sandy smiles. 'She looked a little green.'

John laughs.

'Everyone looked hurt,' Sandy says. 'I guess I missed a big night.' He left after the meeting, never made it to the bar.

'Guess so,' John says. 'I missed a lot myself, though I was there for most of it.'

'How late'd it go?'

'Till two? Three? I left early 'cause of the old man—' John shakes his head, smile fading. 'Anyhow, I'm glad to hear she made it home in one piece.'

'Yve? She was fine. Wen got her home.'

'Who?'

'The captain.'

John nods. 'Huh.'

'You know him?'

'We met last night. I didn't catch his name.' Wen the captain, thinks John. The captain Wen. He looks at Sandy. 'You think this million-dollar project can spare a buck's worth of packing? Stuffing box.'

'I may be able to help you there.' Sandy disappears into the henhouse.

The sea is dulled by the fine rain, but the sky is lighter east. It will clear by evening. Sandy comes back out with a spool, tosses it to John.

'That'll do.'

'Good.'

'So. Well.' John pockets the oakum. 'Thanks.'

'Want to take a look around?' Sandy asks.

They take a stroll around the schooner. John kicks a broken clamshell. Gulls drop them on the ways to get at the meat. He wants to ask Sandy about his view on The Package. Will they take it or won't they. It's a hard topic to raise, tied as it is to so many other personal things. Money, debt. Fathers. Boats.

'So,' John says again. They've come back around to the starboard side.

'We'll be done by Thanksgiving, I think,' Sandy says. 'Wen wants her painted before snow. Joe Ames doesn't want to be paying to keep her on the ways all winter.' He looks north to the Museum Pier, where their fathers' draggers pull against their lines.

'What'll that mean?' John says, though he knows.

Sandy answers anyhow. 'Ames's making noise about kicking the fleet off the pier. He'll be wanting it for the *Shardon*. His pier, his boat, he says.'

John takes a breath in and holds it.

'Sucks, right?' Sandy says. He looks like a guilty man.

'Yeah.' John exhales. 'Ah well.' He slaps Sandy on the back. 'It can't be official yet. We got nothing in the mail but bills.'

'I guess.' After a moment Sandy adds, 'If you need a little extra, I bet there're jobs. I could ask Wen. And Helio likes you.' He brightens as he speaks. 'It'd be good to have more of us around. It'd make Yve happy.'

John frowns.

'They'll need more men for painting,' Sandy goes on. 'One week, Christmas money. There's no way they'll finish without more help.'

'Ah well. Seems like a good reason not to work.'

'I guess.' Sandy hunches his shoulders.

'I wouldn't worry about it, Sand. This schooner isn't what's gonna break us. We got bigger problems.'

Sandy toes a wet splinter from the ways. 'Your dad taking The Package?'

'Not if I got anything to say.' John's surprised to hear himself say this. 'The old man doesn't want to either. I don't know. You?'

'I don't know. I haven't really talked to my dad. It's not up to me anyhow, it's up to him. And I bet he'd rather die first.'

'I know how he feels,' John says. 'Bastards. They want to shut us down.'

'The Great Gray They.'

'The government.'

'It isn't the government's fault,' Sandy says. 'They should've done this years ago.'

'What're you saying?'

Sandy faces him. The mist has gathered on his sweater and in his hair in droplets. He swipes at his wet face. 'We have to take some responsibility.'

'For what?'

'For the fact the fish are all but gone.'

'That's not our fault. And they aren't gone.'

'I suppose they're hiding. Whose fault is that?'

John ticks off the guilty. 'Factory trawlers, foreigners coming in over the boundary, Magnuson Act opportunists – everyone and their cousin got a dragger after—'

'You want to blame someone,' Sandy says, 'blame our parents. You and me, we'll never have our own boats. You know that, don't you? It's over. Fishing's over. Maybe it'll limp along five more years. Ten, maybe. But they fucked it up good. And they fucked us up. There's gonna be nothing left for us, 'cause they fucking took it all already!' He restrains himself, finishes quietly. 'I wish they'd just take the fucking Package and quit banging their rattles.'

John stares at him. 'I guess a man learns a lot about economics working a yard job.'

'Christ, John.' Sandy shakes his head. He goes to the far end of the ways. John wants to go after him. He wants to say, I know what you mean. All this big talk is foolish. Who is he fooling? The boats are called draggers, that's the point. Drag nets along the bottom and everything up and down the food chain tumbles in: plants, rocks, small fish after the larger fish have plugged up the regulation net holes. They have their Furuno fish-finders and no fish can hide. They have dragged the bottom bare. They have left behind acres and acres of barren sand. Short of a total moratorium, short of a miracle, the fish won't come back. He'd go after Sandy, but he doesn't want Sandy to be right. But Sandy is right. What is wrong started going wrong a long time ago, and now the only answer is to stop. But he won't. Most won't. Still. He doesn't know. He doesn't know. He walks to the end of the ways and looks out over the blurred water.

'I bet we will,' John says. 'Take it, in the end. I mean, what else is there?'

Sandy steps back from a wave. 'I got a postcard from Todd,' he says. Todd is Sandy's older brother, who left home to get a boat of his own. Now he fishes salmon out west. 'He says we should break out of here and head for Alaska next summer. There're a lot of fish up there still.' He takes a step back. The tide is coming in.

'Save your pennies,' John says.

'Why do you think I'm here?'

'Smart man.' John tosses the spool of oakum in the air and catches it. He tucks it back in his pocket before it gets wet. 'I gotta go. I got a pump running. See you.'

'Yeah,' says Sandy.

Yve feels better by the time dinner is over. The morning was rough. She felt as though she was still drunk all through breakfast and cleanup. But the men were half in the bag themselves, and they didn't seem to care about much more than coffee and aspirins. Wen didn't come out to eat breakfast at all. He just had Jefferson bring him coffee. She sent along some toast, and he said thanks and patted her on her back on his way out the door. Thanks, I appreciate it, he said. He said the same again after lunch. He smiled and winked. He is always thanking her and that doesn't really mean anything – she is very good at her job. She smiles to herself now as she clears the table of the dinner dishes. The apartment is spotless, the laundry is done, the dry ingredients for tomorrow's muffins are already mixed. Last Thursday, she lined all the shelves and drawers with fresh contact paper. White with little ivies. Tonight, she made a roast turkey supper so elaborate the place smells like Thanksgiving already. She just has a few plates to wash now, the walk home, then the night stretches long and blank as a sheet of unwritten paper.

Charlie lights his pipe. Cherry smoke mixes in with all the other good smells. The men are talking about whores. Dishes slip under her sponge. Outside, the sky is purple, it is getting dark earlier and earlier now. She can see her pale reflection in the darkened window, and she wonders how she looks. It's hard to tell. Her hair is wisped around her face from dishwater steam, her cheeks are probably red. She wonders, Am I pretty? The thought feels strange. It feels as though something inside her has been disconnected and rehooked up wrong. She has spent the day trying to not think about the captain. Her palm itches as if it feels his there.

Behind her, Wen is telling a story. '—so we see the *Mary Day* about a half mile off, and our captain is friends with their captain, right? And they got this one-up-man thing going on. So our old man says we're gonna play a joke—'

She wonders if he is looking at her. Bending to scrub a pot, she becomes aware of her hips, and how the heavy wool of her skirt moves over the back of her thighs.

'We get the mate done up in this kind of bra thing – we stuff two of those dust masks with socks, and we make him a wig out of a mop, you know? He gets up on deck, nancing around – it's kind of foggy so they can't really see – and we convince them he's this whore we bought in the Philippines for three hundred U.S. And their captain's all on the horn trying to bargain a trade! He's like, We'll give you five hundred and shit!'

The men laugh. They always laugh at his stories.

'Oh, but no—' The laughter quiets. 'That was nothing. Me and some of the guys on the *Sandy Dee* – this gorgeous yacht I was transiting for this rich asshole from the fucking Marshalls to New Orleans. Anyhow, we did get this Marshallese gal, not a whore, just some chick, to come with us.' He pauses and she feels as though he is talking to her. He wants to shock her. He wants to see if she'll react, turn around, admit she is listening. She rinses her hands and gets the tinfoil from the bottom drawer, crouching carefully, her knees sideways instead of bending the broad of her backside to him. She goes over for the carcass. She lifts the pan carefully. The men rest their forearms casually on the table. They don't shift for her; she must slide between their shoulders and spread knees and lift the turkey high over their heads while they go on talking as if she is not moving around them.

'Anyhow, by the end of the trip the whole crew was scratching and crying—'

Ed starts singing. '*You can tell by the smell that she isn't feeling well—*'

She takes the pan to the counter and rips tinfoil sheets, covering the song. She can't stand there doing nothing, because if she has nothing to do then she must go home. They often tell stories at the end of the day. Wen has the most, it seems. Or he tells the most, or she listens most to him. Once he worked on a factory trawler and was out for months, fishing and flash-freezing right on board. It was like a floating jailhouse; you didn't see women for months at a time. The men got brutal. He slept with an iron bar in his bunk. Once he was on a long-liner, out weeks for sword or tuna. Once he captained a ship that went down in white squall in the middle of the night. He jumped into the raging sea with just a flashlight and a man in a helicopter basket scooped him out. He has dead mates. She's heard the tale of the first *Pride*, of how the

171

ocean poured down the galley companionway and slammed the cook who was the size of a 49er against the bulkhead and broke three of his ribs, but he still swam out and is alive today, but goes to sea no more. He tells stories of fighting, drinking, swearing, and fucking. Injuries are his specialty – bloody and detailed; hands smashed in hatch covers, severed fingers preserved in salt ice, a dislocated shoulder set by a bunkmate, deep gashes sewn with dental floss and a match-burnt needle. A face ripped open by a sudden pitch into a line drum; the man held down and foaming while his broken teeth are capped with West System. But they put in extra hardener, he said, so it'd set faster, and you have to remember it's a heat re-action (he explained that for the benefit of whom? Yve supposed herself, though she knows all about West System from her father's shop), and so the man's mouth burned and smoked and all they had for the pain was two aspirin and the cook's wine. What happened to him? Was he poisoned? Did he die of in-fection? She couldn't bring herself to ask. She will sometime, though. She will ask him when the other laughing men aren't around and he'll probably tell her. John would never tell her. He says such things are too ugly the first time around, why would you want to relive them? Besides, he says, she doesn't need to know.

John walks the length of the northern spit, up to the light and back, with a forty-ounce beer he picked up at Garenelli's. The stuffing box is repaired and the rain has stopped. The moon shows behind the parting clouds. Though it's cold and damp, he doesn't want to go home, and he doesn't want to go to the Wind, where he's sure to find his father. He doesn't want to be inside at all. Along the shore, the rocks are slick and black. He catches spray when the waves break. The beer is icy in his ungloved hands – he has to keep switching from one to the other. He drinks too fast and is almost relieved when the beer is gone, so he doesn't have the pain of holding it anymore. He shatters the bottle on the rocks. Let the waves make more sea-glass for tourists to pick up on the beach. He puts his stiff hands in his pockets. His head feels swollen with the quick drink.

He decides he feels good enough to swing by the crewhouse, but by the time he gets there Yve has already left for home. Though the captain, Wen, invites him in for a beer and a card game, something doesn't feel right without her there. He begs off. Thanks the captain for last night's help. Buys a six-pack on the way to Albin's.

Yve comes to the door. 'Hey,' she says. She stands in the doorway, neither asking him in nor coming out.

'Hey,' he says. 'Sorry about last night.'

'It's fine. I got home okay.'

The smell of her mother's meat loaf and coffee and something sweet wafts out at him, and he realizes he is hungry. 'D'you eat already?'

She shrugs. 'I'm not really hungry. I'm sick of food by the end of the day.'

'Oh,' he says. He thinks a moment. He remembers the bag of beers in his hand. 'You want to go for a drink?'

'Ugh. The thought of it after last night.' She wraps her cardigan tighter around her chest.

'How about an ice cream or something?'

'I don't know. I've got Martin.' She looks back into the house.

'Where's Kate?'

'Working double. She says it's a madhouse.'

'Huh,' John says. He can imagine all the men waking this morning and starting over. 'What about your mom?'

'She's had him in the house all day. With the rain. She's beat, and I said I'd take over.'

173

'So bring him along.'

'Who said we're going anywhere?'

'I don't know. The rain's stopped. We can take him for a walk. Tire him out.'

She leans back into the house and speaks into the family room. 'Martin, you want to go outside a bit? Uncle John's here. You want to go out with Uncle John?'

Yve pulls Martin along by a hank of old line. She's got one end and Martin's got the other, and he's singing behind in a breathy voice, '*Heave away – haul away.*' It's the only line he seems to know, but he sings it over and over with steady interest. John, walking a step or two ahead, looks back at the boy.

'You're a strong one,' John says.

'What're you gonna be for Halloween, Martin?' Yve says. 'A pirate? Show us the pirate.' The cheery rise and fall of her voice is automatic. Her smile, too, is here and gone.

Martin swashes an imaginary buckler. 'Yar! Yar-be-dar!'

'That's a good pirate! Pretty scary!'

John looks at Yve's frozen profile, the wedge of blue-and-white eye over her sharp-boned cheek. She has had nothing to say to him all the walk so far. She speaks to the boy, he speaks to the boy, as if Martin is their sole juncture and without him they'd walk in opposite directions. John figures she is still angry at being left last night. It sometimes takes her a while to warm back up, he's gotten used to it. It is after dark, and they are the only ones on the street. Under the streetlamp the pavement shines from the earlier rain. They come to the corner of Pine and Maple.

'You want to go up to Fisherman Park?' John offers. 'He likes the swings there.'

Yve shakes her head. 'There's always broken glass. And just the other day Susan Furlong found a needle

174

stuck in the bottom of Danny's sneaker. He must've gotten it running around. They were lucky he didn't get it in his hand or eye or worse.'

John wonders what is worse than a needle in the eye, but he doesn't think Yve would find the question funny.

'Susan checked his foot carefully, and apparently it didn't go through, but imagine if it had.'

'Imagine.'

'It's getting really bad,' Yve says, as if he is somehow disagreeing. 'My mom won't even take him there in the day anymore. All those bums sleeping on the benches, and the sandbox always smelling like a toilet—'

'You're right. You're right. Bad suggestion,' John says. 'Let's just go to the museum.' He means the playground on the north side; the museum isn't open at this hour.

'You want to go to the museum, Martin?' Yve says. The boy nods and heaves and hauls away.

The Children's Discovery Center is not a real playground. Just a small fenced-in yard kids can run around in, with some child-sized displays they can pretend with. It's open all the time; there's only a latch on the gate. Yve heads straight for the dory. She sits in the prow and pats the seat beside her, smiling. She chirps to Martin, 'You want to play rowing boats? We can pretend we're fishing!'

The boy doesn't say anything. He's been told about this dory many times. His grandfather made it, and so he is expected to play in it, but it isn't his favorite. He offers the dropped end of his rope to John. When John takes it and gives a little tug, Martin looks up at him, surprised.

'It's okay,' John says. 'We can play with whatever you want, Martin.'

'Go ahead.' Yve waves them off.

Martin pulls John to the capstan. This is his favorite,

175

and John taught him. Now John sings while he pushes the big, clanky machine with the wooden bat: *'Haul on the bowline, the bully bully bowline, Haul!'* Martin tries to sing along. He knows *bully bully* and *Haul!* so he says them over. John places the bat in the holes, and Martin tries to help, though he can't reach the heavy stick. He joins in on the last *Haul!* and the machine clanks around a few more pawls, then stops. His uncle isn't pushing it anymore.

John has wandered back to Yve. 'A person could do some damage with that bat. Break a few ribs,' he says.

Yve nods. She's watching Martin struggle with the capstan. Small waves dimple the lead-colored bay. The crests are silver where the moon shines on the water. John sits on the cold bench opposite Yve.

'How about it?' He tilts his head at the Museum Pier, indicating the *Pearl*. 'We could duck below.' He's joking, but she clucks her tongue as if she is disgusted with him.

'We have Martin.'

'We always have Martin.' He tries to take her hand, but they are mittened and tucked between her thighs. He gives up easily.

'We don't.'

'Don't we?' John says. The boy totters about unsteadily; the muddy yard has strange peaks and valleys that give him trouble. From the capstan, to the figurehead, to the lighthouse – his second favorite. He clangs the bell as if there's an emergency.

'No.'

The boy punches the button that sounds the foghorn – for some reason this foghorn doesn't scare him like the big ones. He sounds it again and again. The light-house should light, but it doesn't. Either the bulb is out or it's been turned off for the season.

'Okay, then, but you're always working,' John says.

'I'm not the one gone for days at a time,' she says, but quietly.

John pulls the oars from under their feet. He thinks, How women pick up where they left off, days later, like they're picking up knitting. Then he thinks that's worth remembering. He'll tell it to Chris and Chris will laugh in agreement.

'Well,' he says, 'I don't like you working for those sailors.'

'Why not?'

'They're rough,' he says, feeling childish.

She rolls her eyes. 'Where'd you get that?'

'Sandy.'

'Please,' she says. 'They're perfectly normal. They're just a bunch of guys. I bet you're the same with my brother and them.'

'Other people've said so too. Helio, Mr. Bliss.' They would say that, if he asked, John is sure.

'One of us has to earn.'

'So you're taking the high road. So they are a bit rough.'

Her face gets hard. 'I'm not taking the high road. I'm taking the reality road. Adults earn money and move out of their parents' houses.'

'What do you think I want to do?'

'I don't know, John.'

'What do you want me to do? First you don't want me going out, and now you seem to hate having me around.'

'I'm just not—' She stops and thinks. 'I'm just not so happy with the way things are.' She looks at him a long time. He sets the oars carefully in their locks.

'What things?'

'I just want to get away sometimes.' She scrapes forward on her seat as though she'd launch the dory with her shift of weight. 'I want different things.'

'What things?'

'I don't know. I don't even know! That's how stupid it is. We don't go anywhere, and we don't do anything. Other people go places and have exciting lives—'

'Okay, I'll take you far away.' He rows the oars against the air.

'I mean it, John.'

'Okay, where'll we go?' He's still joking, though she isn't.

'Anywhere. Not here.' She looks down at her trapped hands. 'We should go somewhere by ourselves. We'd get along better.'

'We get along all right.' As soon as he says it, he sees it isn't the right thing to say. Her face goes sour.

'Do we?'

'Yeah, we do.'

'Why don't you do something about it, then?'

He knows what she means. He doesn't want to talk about getting married right now. He isn't in the mood, and he doesn't see the point. They never get anywhere on that topic, and they never will till he has more money, and he never will have more money, and so it goes.

'You know I care about you,' he says instead.

'Why?'

'I just do.' He just wants to be with her and for it to be nice.

'Well don't.'

He brings his face close to hers. She looks up and away from him. He moves to catch her eye and she won't let him.

'Why?'

'Because I'm a terrible person!' She suddenly falls forward, clutching his neck. She burrows her face into his shoulder.

'What's this about?'

'You know how you say Kate wants to make trouble?' Her voice is muffled against his sweater. 'Sometimes *I* want to. Sometimes I hate everyone and I want to ruin things!' She pushes off him roughly, as if he, unwelcome, had clutched her.

178

'You're just upset from yesterday. Everyone is. Everyone's fucked up.'

'Maybe.' She sighs. 'But don't you feel like it gets old sometimes?'

'What?'

'This . . . this . . .' She opens her mittened palms to the sky. 'I want to go forward and you want to – I don't know what you want – but we just stay put. It's stagnant. Don't you feel that?'

'No.' He says this quickly, before he can feel it or not.

'I feel stuck. Don't you feel that? Tell me you do, too, or maybe I'm crazy.'

'I don't.'

'Haven't you ever thought of what it would be like to be with just me for the rest of your life? It's horrible. You don't get to be with anyone else ever again. Doesn't that idea kill you?'

'No.' He looks over his shoulder. Martin is a shadow in the sandbox. He pokes a stick again and again into the wet sand, and the sound is like scratching. 'Is there someone else you want to be with?'

'No.' She doesn't even try to sound convincing.

'We've never made any promises. You can go anytime you want,' he says, knowing he's being cruel.

'You're a real bastard.'

'You're the one who brought it up.'

'Only because I feel so old! Sometimes I feel like I've already had all the life I'm going to get and I just want to scream.' She says *scream* as if she is screaming.

'Don't do that.'

'No, it's true, John. I feel like I'm at the end of everything. I'm past the end. I'm living in the last little bit after the end. Like – like—' She is stuck on the idea and he doesn't want her to go on. He feels sick; he's gone too long without eating.

'—like that blue dot on the TV after you turn off the set, that small blip – I'm that. I'm there.'

179

'God, Yve, you're fucking depressing me.'

'Sorry.' She tucks her hands back under her thighs.

He looks at her hunched in her frumpy overcoat, her woolen hat and scarf, and thinks of how unfair he is. He could put his arm around her and tell her pretty things about herself, and make her feel like something special, but even as he moves to do this, he stops, because he also wants to punish her. For what? He doesn't know exactly. Perhaps for getting old, and being as she is, and being part and proof and witness to his own stagnant life.

'I'm sorry,' she says again. She slides forward until she can lay her cheek on his knees. He puts his hand on her back and wishes he could give her everything she wants, and feels bad because he knows he won't even try. He pushes her up and looks at her white face. She looks horribly, miserably serious. Most of all, he wants her to stop looking so.

'*I am the fountain of affection, I'm the instrument of joy*—' He puts his right hand over his heart as he sings. '*To keep the good times rolling I'm the boy, I'm your boy*—'

'Shut up,' she says.

He ignores her, adds more warbles to his notes, bobbing his head in a pantomime of sincerity. '*Oh the world could be our oyster, just put your trust in me. We'll keep the good times rolling, wait and see, wait and see*—'

'Stop, John. I'm serious.'

He stops. 'You want to keep complaining?'

'Not really.'

There is a small break, and he thinks, I should kiss her, but he hesitates, and she is talking again.

'I'm just tired of waiting for you. Everything takes so long. Everything's so hard for us. I just want to feel young and pretty again—'

He kneels forward on the floorboards so his face is under hers. 'You are. Young and pretty – you are.'

'But I'm not.'

'You are to me.'

She pushes his face away. Her mitten smells of wet wool. He sits next to her on the narrow bench. He runs one finger up her arm, up over her collar. He hooks his finger against the bone. He is surprised to find he wants her. Her thigh presses against him through their many layers of clothes; he takes her hand through the mitten.

'Come on, Yve. You know everything'll be okay. You know that, don't you?'

'I guess.'

He leans in for a kiss.

She makes a space for him in her mouth. Her lips taste like salt. He takes them between his teeth and feels their ragged edges with his tongue. Their exhalations show as silver mist. They breathe in synch, and it feels very intimate, their chests rising and falling together. Their mouths go still. They sit a long while doing nothing. He thinks maybe she's fallen asleep so he opens his eyes, then she opens one eye. He brings his eye close and pretends to look inside her, as if through a peephole.

'I see you,' he says.

'Don't.' She shuts her eye.

14

Down at the SnugHarbor House, John – his father's books in a cardboard box on his lap – waits for Peter Gusek to be free. The man is always busy. He used to be a loan officer for Fleet Bank. In retirement, he's volunteered his Wednesday afternoons to advise fishermen on their finances. Edna Larkin pulled strings to get John a meeting so quickly: apparently there's a waiting list a mile long – she says, at least. But her son works for the Fitzes and so John has been bumped up.

Mr. Gusek is a small round man with a pink-and-white complexion and soft banker's hands. He wears a cardigan and a tie and smells sweet. Right now he bends over the books of Burgess Harper. John knows Burgess by sight, but they've exchanged maybe ten words in all John's life. Burgess is a lobsterman, and of a different generation, and he keeps a different schedule. He tends to go home at night.

The table next to John's chair has a pamphlet rack, and in the pockets sit pamphlets in English and Portuguese. John thumbs through: Family Planning; HIV/SIDA – imagine being seen pulling that one out, its purpose across the front in big red letters; HEAP; WIC – John wonders is everything an initial? Career Counseling at CCC – Charlesport Community College; Does Someone You Know Have a Problem with Alcohol? John takes this one out. There's a test of fourteen questions on the last page. Do you drink in the morning? Do you drink every day? Do you tell yourself you aren't going to drink and then find yourself drinking anyhow? Do you sometimes forget what happened while you were drinking? At the bottom it says, If you answered two or more of these questions yes, you might have a problem with alcohol. John wonders who could possibly not answer two or more of these questions yes. Even Yve would answer two or more of these questions yes, he thinks. Even his mother would have. He puts the pamphlet back.

He has dressed up a little for this meeting with Mr. Gusek. He wears chinos and a gray sweater that Yve gave him last Christmas, and his black three-hole Doc Martens with new white socks. His hands feel too large without something in them. He cracks his knuckles and looks about the room. The SnugHarbor House is the bottom floor of an old triple-decker. The office where John now waits was once the living room/dining room, the kitchen has become a Free Pantry, and the rest of the space – the bedrooms and such –

182

have become the Free Store and are piled with clothes, dishes, and scraps of furniture you can take away for nothing, or a little donation if you're proud.

'How's your father?' Edna sinks into the chair beside John. She was on the phone when he came in and only nodded hello.

'Fine.'

The chair sighs as she leans closer. Her fingers, on John's forearm, are fat and shiny. 'How are you doing?' She emphasizes *you*.

'Fine.'

She clicks her tongue as if she doesn't believe him.

'We're doing okay. Really, Edna.'

She looks at him sternly. 'You going to be around for Thanksgiving?'

'We'll see.' His father has a plan of saving their last days for around the holidays, so there'll be less competition and higher prices.

'You know I don't like you boys out in that weather,' she says.

Burgess Harper now stands and shakes Mr. Gusek's hand. He leaves without nodding to John or Edna, and his passing stirs the pamphlets on the table.

'Okay then, I'll leave you to Mr. Gusek. He'll take care of you. Won't you, Peter?' Edna winks at John. She is one of the few women who can wink without it meaning anything.

John waits a moment more while Mr. Gusek organizes his desk. When he's done tidying, he looks up at John and smiles, and John comes forward with his cardboard box.

'Hello—' The man consults his blotter; it is a calendar and John sees his name in a box near the bottom. 'Mr. Fitz.' Mr. Gusek half stands, extending his hand.

'Hello, sir.' They shake, sit.

The old banker continues to smile pleasantly. His hands rest on his desk, fingers loosely entwined. After a moment, he says, 'Now, what are we here for?'

'Oh yeah. Sorry. I have this.' John puts the box on the desk. The other man doesn't do anything, so John takes the books out for him. He finds the most recent. 'This is this year – my father's been doing them and I'm trying to see – well, I'm wondering what our options are. Here are the bank statements—' John shows the papers in the front-cover pocket. 'Most recent on top. These are our outstanding loans; we've been making payments up till July and then we missed some – here—' He shuffles pages forward and back and finds his hands trembling slightly. He feels as if he is at the bank, and this man is judging his loan eligibility.

Mr. Gusek takes the book gently from John. 'Let me just look a few moments, do you mind?'

'No. Fine. You go ahead.' John sits back. He is too hot in his sweater, but he doesn't want to take it off because he wears only a T-shirt underneath.

'It might take a while,' Mr. Gusek says.

'Okay, then. You take your time.'

'Would you like to help yourself to coffee?'

'No thanks. I'm fine.'

Still, after a few moments, John wishes he had something to do. He watches Mr. Gusek poring over the scribbled pages, and he kicks himself for not looking in the books before, for leaving it up to the old man. He thinks what he would have done if he'd known earlier. He could've insisted they go to a skeleton crew, split things three ways instead of five. They could've checked out more fisheries. Perhaps they could've upgraded their product, gotten an on-board flash freezer; maybe they could've just worked harder to be first in with fresher product, or gone out for fewer but longer trips. He goes around and around it. They have less than thirty days left, and there is no way now to make up the year, he is sure that is what the banker will say.

'What do you think?' he asks Mr. Gusek.

'Well.' The man leans forward. 'What are you hoping to hear?'

'I'm hoping to hear we won't need The Package.'

'You say your father's been keeping track of the money.'

'Yes sir.'

'Does he know you're here?'

'No sir.'

'Aha,' the man says, and John takes a sudden dislike to him.

'What do you mean, aha?'

'Has he let you see the figures? Have you looked at them together?'

'Sort of.'

The man gives John a grandfatherly look – a small, closed-mouthed smile and a tilted head and hunched shoulders.

'Look,' John says, 'I know it's bad—'

'I think the two of you need to sit down and talk. There are certain factors—'

'That's why I'm here. I'm just trying to find out if there's some kind of loophole or something.'

The man straightens his smile away. He starts closing John's books and putting them in the box. 'To be frank, I'm surprised you haven't gotten a foreclosure notice already. You're in default. You have a mortgage on the house and another on the boat, and at this moment it doesn't look like you're carrying either one.'

'So you're saying it's The Package.'

'It would clear your debt.'

'Yeah, but what would we have after?'

The man gives a conciliatory frown.

'We wouldn't have anything after,' John says.

'You can strip the vessel before you turn it over and sell anything of value. Nets, electronics—'

'Yeah, us and everyone else. And who'll be buying that shit? Forget it.' John snatches his box off the table. He is shaking.

'Have you given any thought to what you'll do if the closings go through? If you don't take advantage of the buyback now, you may not be able to later. I think the closings will pressure a lot of men into taking the money, and from what I understand it's strictly a first-come-first-serve deal.' The man speaks quietly, politely. He speaks as if he is truly concerned. He looks up at John, who is surprised to find himself already standing, looming over the desk like a thug. Edna, at her desk, is watching, and John is suddenly ashamed, and angered at being ashamed.

'Thank you for your time,' he says. He jerks his head at Edna and goes out. For a moment, he's disoriented. He doesn't know which way to walk. He looks up and down the block, and everything appears foreign. The black oaks against the white sky, the brick buildings, the blank windows. In this part of town all the storefronts are closed, and cars rarely drive the streets. He walks three blocks before he remembers that he drove his truck, and he must turn around and go back for it.

15

'She just wants to be knocked up,' Chris says of Yve casually, as if it is as simple as anything else one does, as simple as netting. He and John sit on the aft deck, under the cold sun, the net boomed up and draped about them, casting diamond shadows across their faces and hands. It smells of chum and damp, and the web is cold and wet. Every so often John has to shake his fingers out to get his blood going again. He doesn't much like netting. He isn't fast at it, like Chris. Chris works the stiff yellow line his father fronted them easily – after a few passages his fingers have memorized the mesh size and his repairs are even and swift. Chris learned to make net from his father as soon as he was old enough to hold a mesh stick.

'I don't know,' John says.

'What don't you know? You get a kid in my sister's arms, and she's all cooing and cuddling and boo-boo-boo—' He holds his netting needle like a baby, rocking and billing at it as if it's a newborn.

'I'm not sure I'm ready.'

'For what, man? What are you waiting for?'

John takes a long pull off his Old E. 'Money.'

'You don't need money to have a kid.'

John gives him an incredulous look, and Chris gives it back.

'Hello, Social Services,' Chris says, making a phone of his fingers. 'I met this Newfie guy – they haven't fished up there for fucking ever – and he was saying he gets all his dollars from having kids. They hook up with their cousins, trade the kids, and collect for foster care! No one even checks!'

He hitches the needle through a few more knots, then he looks up at John smiling, as if proud of the brilliance of this plan. John gives no expression back, and Chris, shrugging, bends again to his work. The sun weaves in and out of the clouds, their shadows shorten, then pass behind them and lengthen. They knot their way down the net, stopping every so often to tie up another section, or wind a repaired piece on the drum. Chris makes another run to Garenelli's for more beer and cigarettes. He's having a good day. His timing has been good, and he is clear and lucid, without the bone-grinding, head-slamming pain that comes on with a jones. He is a good man to work with when he's like this. The afternoon reminds John of why he and Chris are friends still. Every so often, Chris lets fly with some half-baked theory or plan. They gossip about who's fucking whom, and who's been kicked out by whom. John tells him how Sandy Hopewell's moved out from his parents' house, and how Jenny Stewart is making moves on Joe Ames's nephew, and Chris rewards him with raised eyebrows and an appreciative *Hoho!* The spool of line thins, the repaired net thickens on the drum. By the five-o'clock whistle, the setting sun has shot the ashy bay with color.

John says, 'It's going to be too dark to work soon. Another hour.'

'If it's money—'

'There's other things,' John says, though he'd be hard pressed to articulate what.

'Well, it's just that I've been recently offered some stellar opportunities in the financial department.'

'Good for you.'

'Unfortunately, I'm a boatless man.'

'I'm not interested,' John says.

Chris frowns, nods his head. He finishes the length of line he is on with a final bend, then secures the end with a splice. He waits for John to come to a stopping point, and together they bundle the repaired net back in place. Then they sit back down to appreciate the sunset, their beers, another cigarette. Even John takes one, though he doesn't generally like to smoke – it makes him light-headed and dizzy.

'I just have a problem with making money off others' misfortunes,' John says, feeling sage for getting off such a mouthful so smoothly. Sometimes, when he drinks exactly the right amount, he becomes agile in word and thought, and he's feeling confident in that department now, and ready to take Chris on.

'Whose misfortune? Who said anything about misfortune?'

John shifts uncomfortably. 'You know.'

'I don't. Explain.'

'Well, for instance, the families suffer.'

'Like *my* family, you mean.' Chris draws himself up. 'They "suffer," if you want to be so patronizing about it, whether I get a piece of the action or not. At least if I'm moving it, instead of just using it, their "suffering" is alleviated by some serious cash. And it's gonna get moved, and I'm gonna use, whether I do the moving or not. Make money or lose money. Carrot, stick. I'm motivated.'

'Good for you.'

'I know what your problem is. You feel you're on some kind of high ground. Like this has something to do with morality. You don't want to be responsible for riding the Evil Horse into our clean community. John, man, it's already here. Proof positive.' Chris points to himself. 'And you're already involved. By the mere fact that you employ me, hold my shit for me, wipe my leaky nose, and tuck my scabby ass into bed, you've got the powdery taint.'

'That's just us.'

'That's what I'm saying! It's just us. Friends and family making their choices, making money or spending it. Free will, free market. The real crime, the real moral fuck, is when someone on the outside comes in and tells you you can't make money anymore. When they take away your right to make money for your family. You want criminal? You want immoral? I'll give you criminal immorality.' He holds up a proclaiming finger. 'Tuna.'

'That's got nothing to do with it.'

'That's got everything to do with it. You need me to remind you?'

John doesn't need Chris's help remembering. The tuna sticks in his mind like a raised scar. Last July, the groundfish situation being what it was, Fitz had this grand idea to go out for tuna. So they took a second mortgage to buy the gear – Fitz convinced the loan officer at Fleet it would be an investment – found a decent price, converted the *Pearl*, and set off. Unfortunately, they weren't the only ones. But they didn't know that at first, or didn't pay attention. They were too high on the idea of a new fishery. A few days out, they caught their first tuna: ninety-four inches and just over six hundred pounds – at $15.08 a pound they made over nine thousand dollars on that one fish. John had never seen anything like it. These Japanese buyers came right down to the dock and outbid each other, and the next day their fish was sushi halfway around the world. They went out again, and caught their second – five inches longer and a hundred pounds less. A long, lean fish, dragging a hook and line from some other boat – its caudal fin was chafed and scarred as if it'd been dragging that line awhile. It must've taken a lot of energy to drag that hook and line around. It was certainly weakened by the burden. It was eating, but dying slowly anyhow. When they cut the second one open the pollack they'd used for bait was nearly digested and its stomach was otherwise empty. It wasn't such a great fish, so they put it on ice while they looked around a little more. The next day they were called in. Some quota was filled and the whole fishery was shut down – they were ordered to dump what they had. Even though the fish was dead and iced, overboard it went. And not just the fish off their boat – a whole fleet of tuna boats, dumping bodies. The waste was sickening. John actually felt sick in his soul. The steam home was like dying. For the first time he envied Chris. He asked for a hit, and Chris refused him. When John got home, he drank for an entire week, until Yve hauled him off the bar stool and forced him to sober up. They're still paying off the loan, and though Fitz placed an ad in the classified of *National Fisherman*, no one wants the gear.

'But at least we were fishing,' John says.

'Sure. One whole fish.'

Chris picks the butts off the deck and drops them in an empty bottle, he gathers the bottles, the mesh sticks, and needles. He stands and cracks his bones. He's beginning to ache, and he doesn't want to argue anymore.

'It'd kill my father,' John says.

'It'd save your father. He's completely paralyzed.

190

He can't do fuck-all. He wants you to do something.'

'He'd never go for it.'

'Don't tell him.'

'I'd have to tell him. It's his boat.'

'So tell him, then. Just talk to him. We'll do whatever he says — I bet he says yes.'

From Water Street comes the sound of children laughing, and they both turn to look. A group of kids, eight or nine years old, three boys and a girl, trip up the sidewalk. Costumes poke from under their winter jackets: a princess skirt, a cowboy's fringed chap and spurs. They carry plastic pumpkins for their candy. A woman wearing a quilted plaid shirt under an orange hunting vest grabs the two nearests' hands and hurries them along.

'I just want to fish,' John says, as if this excuses him.

Chris looks down at him. 'You've got a boat. People want to give you money for using your boat. You're gonna lose this opportunity when the moratorium rolls around. Every boat on the water'll be suspect then. Take advantage while you still can. Come January ain't nobody fishing.'

IV

Oh sing that we boys may never be—
Leave her, Johnny, leave her!
in a hungry bitch the like of she!
And it's time for us to leave her!

16

Kate pours Burgess Harper his fourth whiskey and knocks the bar with her knuckles. On the house. Dora has a fourth-drink buyback policy. Tomas is owed one next. It gets confusing when they start buying each other rounds, and the coasters pile up marking the purchased but yet unpoured drinks. It's like a competition, who can buy the most drinks. One-upmanship even when they're broke. The lunch rush hasn't cleared. It is mid-November and most of the fishers have used their days. Now they take all the stools and most of the tables. The booths at the window brim over; Sal and Izzy and Pete and the two Jameisons; John and Warren Fitz; Chris, Kate's beloved husband. If it weren't for the bar, she'd never see him. He hasn't been home in days. That isn't entirely true. He stopped by while she was at work; his clothes drawer was open when she got back. Water runs cold over her hands, the glass washer whirs. Sopped up to her elbows, cold every time the door opens – they keep coming in and none leave. Kate pulls beers and makes change. Hands wet the bills, make them stick together. On one screen football murmurs, muted weather on the other. The radio is silent. Some old man tells a story – Jimmy Daly – talking to the air. Outside a siren. When Chris gets back from this next trip, she'll tell him he has to make some kind of choice, she just can't take it anymore.

The door opens, and Edna Larkin bundles through, bringing more cold with her. She stands by the taps and makes a general announcement. 'How about giving an old lady a seat?'

Burgess gets off his stool and takes his drink with him.

'Edna.' Kate dries her hands on her apron.

'How you doing, love? You hanging in?' Edna settles herself; her purse, her scarf, and a cardboard box of photocopied handbills pile upon the bar. 'How's the boy?'

'A pain. It'd be nice to have some help.'

'Alma not baby-sitting?'

'No, she is.'

Edna looks puzzled a moment. Then she tilts her head to the fishermen. 'Oh, you mean him.'

Kate puts a glass of Harp in front of Edna, and the woman pats her arm.

'Ah love, I know. But you can't fault them, they have to work.'

Kate pulls her arm back. 'Whatever.' She moves down the bar for refills. She collects the coasters, the bills and coins, pours and knuckles the bar for Tomas's shot. Pee Wee calls 'Order up!' and she gets a cheeseburger for Sal Liro, then takes her time going around the tables filling a bus tub with dirties. Edna perches on her stool, waiting. When Kate gets back she whispers, 'You hear about the Jameisons?'

Kate shakes her head.

'They're scuttling the *M&M*. They'll lose the house otherwise, says Peter Gusek. Maude locked herself in the bedroom and wouldn't come out till Morgan promised to go through with it.'

'Smart lady.'

Edna clucks. 'I don't see how keeping the house'll help if he can't work.'

'At least they won't be homeless. That's what the

bank wants. I saw it on *60 Minutes*. They come into crappy neighborhoods and give all these big loans and then when you're at your lowest, *pfft!*' Kate shafts the air. 'Foreclosure. Get all the houses for dirt. Waterfront property. Turn around and sell it for millions.'

Sal Liro bellies up with two handfuls of empties, a finger sunk in each so they clink.

'You're not giving up on us, are you, Sal?' Edna asks him.

'Fuck no.'

Kate takes the glasses, and he licks his fingers. 'Again?'

'Yeah.' He bobs his chin at the poster taped to the mirror over the register. It says: *Thanksgiving Holly-Day Kickoff!* The picture shows a pen-and-ink drawing of the *Shardon Rose* with holly boughs decorating her masts. She sails above Old English text: *Kick off the Holiday Season with the Rosaline Maritime Museum As We Welcome Our Newest Exhibit Home!* What is not advertised is that the Shardon's new home is the fishing fleet's old home. It's what the men have been talking about all morning.

'Dora going in for that shit?' Sal asks Kate.

'I don't know.' Kate tips the Guinness tap and half-fills a fresh pint. She sets it on the rubber-nibbed mat and starts another. 'She doesn't tell me anything.'

The big man turns to Edna. 'Barrett sent me one of those, you believe that?'

'He sent everyone one. He asked if my ladies would help with decorations!'

'I hope you told him where to stick it.'

'Disgusting.' Edna means the mayor, not Sal. Mayor Barrett had the nerve to tell her it was her civic duty as a community leader. Of course she hung up on him. Now she tells Sal and Kate, 'He said he wants a "Harbor of a Thousand Lights" and a tree on every dragger! The lobstermen can get away with big wreaths, he said, as long as there are red bows.'

197

Sal snorts. '"Come See the Fleet Kicked Off the Pier." That's what it should say.'

'That's a good one,' Edna says. 'Maybe Bea can work it in. She's making signs.'

'Yeah, tell her that.' Sal watches Kate top the pints. 'You need a tray?'

'Nah.' He peels a few bills off a roll. Kate rings his sale and comes back with the change. 'Kickoff,' he says again. 'We'll kick their asses from here to high heaven.' He sounds tired.

'Cheap bastard,' Kate says, dropping two quarters in her cup.

'He's got nothing coming in,' Edna says.

'He's got enough for beer. Fifty cents more wouldn't put him over the edge.' She picks a red flyer from Edna's stack, doesn't read it. 'You want me to put this in the window?'

'Yes. And leave some by the door. And maybe put stacks along the bar. I want everyone to have one.'

Kate reads the flyer now. Another one of Edna's exhortations: *Fishermen Unite! Fight, Fight, Fight! Our Town, Our Waterfront, Our Pier!*

'Actually, it's Joe Ames's pier.'

'It was ours before it was his,' Edna insists.

'When does he want them off?'

'End of the month,' Edna says. 'But they won't go. I mean, they'll go into the harbor if the Coast Guard makes them, but they'll block the channel. They won't let that schooner through.'

'That'll be something to see.'

Edna shakes a small fist. 'We really have to take a stand.'

'Go for it.'

'I'm serious.' Edna looks disappointed. 'We're really getting squeezed. First the regulations, now this.'

'I'm sorry. I'll personally see to it that everyone here gets one.'

'TV'll be there,' Edna says. 'We need bodies, you know, with the signs and all that.'

Kate puts the flyer back. 'Oh Edna, I don't know. It's Thanksgiving. It's the only day I'll have off all month. Alma wants us over for dinner, and I promised Martin we could watch the parade. He's so excited. They're gonna have Santa, and he really wants to see the boat go in.'

Edna raises her eyebrows, and that is enough to make Kate's complaints burst forth. 'Come on, Edna, I can't. It's been so busy. I'm so tired when I get home I can barely pay attention to him. And the only time I ever see Chris is here. And it's not like we ever get to talk, because I'm so fucking busy. It's been insane. They're waiting at the door when I get here, they stay forever, and they never tip. It's like I'm running a day care.' She glares over Edna's shoulder at the men around the booths as if they've gotten louder and yells, 'Hey quiet down! This isn't a day care!'

Edna ticks softly, shaking her head. She sips her drink. Her fingers rest lightly on her stack of flyers. They don't understand, these girls, they just don't. They only see the immediate, the next problem in line, the next desire. This town will be nothing without fishing, she is positive of that. Without a working waterfront, it will be nothing. Sometimes Edna feels she is fighting a lonely battle, a lonely battle. She watches Kate busying herself with a case of bottled beers. She stabs them into the ice as if she couldn't care less should one break. So angry, Kate is. Edna can't blame her, but it doesn't do any good to be so angry if you don't redirect that energy toward a good fight. They have to support the men. It is the least a woman can do. Behind her, the men have settled down. Then something happens in the football game, and a soft roar rises from the booths. As Edna and Kate both look toward the fishers, Chris extricates himself from the crowd.

'Get him whatever he wants, will you?' Kate says. Before Edna can answer, she ducks under the service end of the bar and goes to the juke. In the machine, pink and blue disco lights flash on a twirling CD, splash out from the plastic bubble, and color her hands and face. Here, her back is turned to the room. A strange, electric energy thrills up and down it, as if her spine is an antenna, feeling for Chris. She pretends to be scanning the selections, idly flipping the cards back and forth, but she already knows what she'll play. She is stalling. She doesn't want to be at the bar. She doesn't want to serve Chris as if he is not her husband, as if he is just another guy getting another pitcher for his boys. She doesn't want to hear whatever it is he has to say, even if it is just 'More beer.' Something about that thought feels familiar, and suddenly she remembers the party, back at the end of the summer, when the *Shardon* had just come in and they all first saw the new sailors, and Jenny Stewart said something about 'More peas,' and they teased her. And Kate danced with the captain, and shocked them all. She smiles now, remembering. The captain comes in every so often, but nothing has ever come of it. It was just a lark, just a flirt. She is a married woman. She feeds a dollar into the juke, and presses the letter and numbers for her song four times. There's a little whir, then the opening beats begin.

From the front booth, Sal Liro hollers, 'Come on, Kate, enough already. You're killing us!'

She doesn't turn from the machine.

'You played that like twenty fucking times already!'

'If you don't like it,' she yells back, 'get out!' Behind her, the room quiets down. She hears clearly the scrape of a chair, and the massive bulk of Sal rising.

'I'm going,' he says, as if this is a threat he'll willingly take back. He waits a few moments, but she doesn't give him a reason to stay. 'Okay, then. I'm outta here.'

She listens to the door open, and, too late, she yells, 'Pay for your goddamn burger!' The door shushes shut. 'Cheap bastard.' She is sure he will pay for the burger another day, he's honest like that, but she will get stiffed the tip. They never tip on tabs. She turns to go back to the bar, and Chris stands before her.

'Hey, baby.' His hands reach for her upper arms, his lips dart for her cheek.

She lets him kiss her. She waits for him to say or do something more. He stands there, as if he has only just left her this morning and this is a casual meeting. She bugs her eyes out at him. 'What?'

'What do you mean, what?'

'What do you want?'

'Let's go for a walk.'

'I got to work.' Kate looks to the bar. Edna has stationed herself behind it, and is happily pulling a pint for Tito Faluti, talking his ear off while he waits.

'Come on.' Chris leads her into the kitchen. He nods hello to Pee Wee, who nods back from his perch on a couple of empty crates. The oily kitchen heat clings to Kate's skin like plastic wrap. They go out the back way, onto the small square of cement Dora calls the loading dock, though it is no more than a step up from the alley. The door shuts and suddenly Kate is cold in her thin knit top. She folds her arms across her breasts.

'You cold?' Chris asks.

'No.'

'You want my jacket?'

'No.'

'Sure?'

She shakes her head no. Chris steps off the landing to lean against the dumpster. He finds himself a cigarette, lights it, draws a bit, then hands it to Kate. She smokes, hands it back. Rod Stewart bleeds faintly through the back door.

'I'm missing my songs.'

201

'So miss them.' He hands her the cigarette again. 'Let's go somewhere.'

'And who'll watch the bar?'

'Edna. I'll get your coat and tell her to hang tight. Dora'll be in soon enough.'

Kate shakes her head. The smoke streams from between her lips in a sinuous wave, and she shortens her focus to follow it.

'Come on. We'll go get Martin and take him out down the point.'

She ticks her tongue. He shoves his hands in his pockets and walks a frustrated little circuit around the alley, kicking things as he goes: dumpster, pallets, the clanking service doors to the cellar. He stops in front of her. 'Come on, Kate. I just want to—'

'We have to talk about Thanksgiving,' she says. 'Your mom wants to know what our plans are.'

Chris makes a deflated sigh.

'Will you even be back?'

'I don't know. It's not up to me.'

'She's inviting the Fitzes. If they're back, you're back. And Edna and Walley – though it seems Edna's got other plans.'

'I can't make any promises,' Chris says. 'It's not up to me.'

'Well, how long can you guys be gone? You can't be gone that long.'

'It's not up to me.' He squints at her. 'What did my dad say?'

'About what?'

'Thanksgiving. Me coming.'

'Oh. Nothing.' She taps her heels on the cement. The air smells like cold. Like shaved ice, like – Kate doesn't know. She wants to go in. 'I'm cold.'

'Let me get your coat.'

'No. I'm going in.' She puts her hand on the kitchen door and stops. 'When you get back, we're gonna have to talk.' She stops herself short of adding,

Okay? 'We're gonna have to talk,' she says again.

Chris nods.

'I can't keep living like this,' she says. 'You'll have to make a choice.'

'I know,' he says. He watches her push the door. A warm eddy of meat and fries swirls from the kitchen. 'For what it's worth,' he says, 'I do love you.'

'Yeah,' she says. He stands beside the dumpster, his knuckles pooching through the ratty pockets of his jacket, his eyes squinting against the wintry sun. She doesn't know how to answer him. He rarely says such things. 'Well, I'll see you,' she finally says.

'Yeah, see you.' He touches the air above his head like a tipped hat.

Paper turkeys, the orange-and-brown silhouettes of children's hands, decorate a cardboard oak taped to the inside of the Finast window. Each one represents a dollar donated to the SnugHarbor Thanksgiving Fund. Tuesday before the big day, Edna Larkin and her SnugHarbor Ladies' Auxiliary will tally the donations and load Abel's old truck with turkeys and canned yams and deliver them to needy families. After Thanksgiving the oak will be replaced with a cardboard evergreen and paper ornaments will replace the turkeys, and the SnugHarbor Ladies will use that money for cheap Christmas presents. They'll go again around the town spreading holiday cheer. They're always collecting and redistributing. Though this year the cardboard tree, like the oaks and maples outside, is mostly bare. Fall is nearly over. Yve feels a prick of guilt. She's been too busy to help her aunt. Nor has she gone to see Kate – falling behind in all her duties. Fall and she's falling behind in her duties. Fall and she's falling in . . . say something enough times and it stops making sense . . . fall fall fall falderol, if the pony goes too fast we all fall iiiiinnn—

She drifts through the produce aisle. Special on old

Halloween candy near the apples. Caramels and popsicle sticks. A stack of unpurchased black-and-orange foil-wrapped chocolates. Every day's getting shorter and darker. October went so quickly, November will too, December. That happens when you work. You wait for the holidays, then they tumble one after another too quickly to enjoy. Turkeys replace the ghosts, then Santas replace the turkeys, then here comes the confetti and horns and silly hats. Watch the ball drop. Then the long blank of January, February, March. Her job'll be over then – but maybe in the spring – the captain said they might need a cook for the season then. She throws a few bags of candy in her cart – Wen likes chocolates with almonds. She's very good at her job – shopping on a limited budget. For instance, at Mass last Sunday, Susan Furlong tipped her off that chicken was going on sale, so here she is with five in her cart. She'll freeze some and bake some – serve them for dinner – then they'll see leftovers in soup and sandwiches. She finds it funny getting paid to do what her mother's done free all her life.

Her hands squeeze and count, selecting apples, cucumbers. It's been a couple weeks, and Wen hasn't mentioned their walk home. Still, she feels it at odd times. It reminds her of when she was a child, and her mother tied balloons to her wrist whenever they went into Charlesport so as not to lose her in the crowd. The balloons lifted Yve's wrist and changed her move-ments, made some lighter and some more inconvenient. The walk home with Wen has become just like that. It pulls at her and changes everything. Her regular movements, her body, her thoughts – some feel lighter, some get tugged in odd directions.

The lettuce sprinklers come on, misting her. She doesn't know how long she's been standing there with the romaine in her hand. She shakes her head and almost laughs, then looks about uneasily. She's alone. It's still early afternoon, so the supermarket is relatively empty. That's why she comes right after lunch, to beat the crowd. She sees her cart is full. She wheels it over to the only open checkout aisle and flips through a *Woman's Day* while she waits. Susan Furlong's busy with an older man and his package of bologna.

'Hey, Susan,' Yve says, when it's her turn.

Susan nods. She keeps her eyes down, grabbing and weighing a plastic bag of apples. She sends them down the aluminum counter and a few roll out. Yve scurries around to bag.

'How're you?'

'As well as can be expected.' Susan runs onions through, celery, carrots.

'Well, I guess that's the case for us all, eh?'

'For some.'

Her tone catches Yve off guard. She waits for Susan's deprecating laugh, but it doesn't come. Susan scans the produce with increasing speed, and the vegetables pile up before Yve can bag them. She punches the numbers with blows that shake the register. The pasta comes next – shells, elbow, linguini – tossed down the shoot with sounds like little explosions. A can of tomatoes hurls into a package of spirals.

'Jeez, Sus, hold on!' Yve looks up and Susan is pale and trembling. 'Are you okay?'

Susan swivels her head as if looking for an escape route. The day manager sits behind the customer service desk reading a newspaper and an older woman stands in line holding a roll of toilet paper and a yogurt. 'You can take that to customer service if you're paying cash,' Susan tells her. When the woman is gone, she slumps against the checkout counter.

'What is going on?' Yve whispers, a little more fiercely than she means to.

Susan takes a few moments. The groceries lie where they are and neither woman moves to bag or check things through. Finally Susan says, 'I can't believe you.'

'What?' Yve gets a fizzy feeling in her stomach.

'I can't believe you didn't tell me. I thought we were friends.'

Susan won't look her in her face. Yve wonders what exactly does she think she knows, and how did she find out, and who else might know. These concerns fill her lungs like a rush of forced air, and she has trouble catching her breath. Of course, she knows there've been bad feelings toward the schooner crew for a while now, toward Wen especially, but really, those feelings are just displaced frustrations. She'd like to explain to Susan that Wen and his boys have nothing to do with the regulations, or the dock for that matter – that's all Joe Ames's doing – they're workingmen just like everyone else—

'John's letting Dan go,' Susan says. 'He came by last night.'

For a second, Yve's so surprised she doesn't know what to say. Susan watches her with pink-rimmed eyes, waiting for some kind of reply. Yve manages to blurt, 'That can't be.'

'Why not? Think about it. He's in trouble, and something has to give. Last hired, first fired.' Her words come out in little chokes. 'I don't know why I'm crying about this now. I wasn't crying before.'

'Oh, honey.' As Yve comes around the counter, Susan's tears brim over. She crosses her arms and looks away. Yve stops, suddenly unsure of whether or not a reassuring arm would be welcome. It is the sort of thing her aunt would do naturally, reach out and hug another woman. Instead, Yve settles for touching the conveyor belt near Susan's hip. She feels terrible and awkward and guilty, though she's done nothing wrong. Or has she? Has she done something wrong? The black rubber skims under her fingers, then stops at the metal suture.

Another woman, this one with a bloody package of kidneys, comes up.

'Go to the service desk,' Yve says.

206

The kidney woman walks away, hesitates, and turns back. Yve jerks her head and she scurries off.

'I'm sorry.' Susan shakes her head. 'You're the first person I've told. I guess that's why I'm like this.' She blots her eyes with her checkout apron. 'I mean, it's not like they won't all be out of work in a couple months.'

'Oh God,' Yve says. 'You want to get me going, now?' They laugh little choking laughs. Yve coughs and frowns. 'Really, Sus. I'm so sorry.'

'Not your fault.'

'What'll you do?'

'I don't know. I've got this – maybe Dan can pick something up.'

'You should have him stop by the yard. They need painters. I can talk to Wen.' Yve feels odd using the captain's first name to Susan.

'Dan'd be too proud to work for that—' Susan's hands spring to her mouth. 'I'm sorry, I didn't mean—'

'It's okay.'

'It's just that—'

'It's okay.' The uncomfortable silence spreads between them like a stain. 'Well!' Yve clears her throat. 'I just don't understand it, I mean about Dan. John never said anything to me.'

'He didn't?'

'Nope.' She keeps her tone bright, light. 'That man's a mystery. He never tells me anything. Then again I hardly ever see him anymore.' She hears herself chattering, and, though embarrassed, can't seem to stop. 'It feels like I haven't seen him in ages. He's always in the bar and I'm always working—'

'You know he's going out, right?'

'Well.' Yve laughs feebly. 'I figured he had to be soon. He's got days still. His father always saves them for the worst weather—'

Susan starts checking through groceries, slower now. She slips the chickens into white plastic bags

207

before putting them in the brown paper sacks. 'When's the last time you two spoke?'

'I don't know. A couple days ago?' Yve thinks about it and realizes it's been more than that. They went to the playground with Martin ages ago. She's been spending her weekends baby-sitting the boy and getting a jump on her baking. She hasn't thought to call John, and he hasn't called her.

'Yve, they're going out really soon,' Susan says. 'Walley and Chris were in here this morning, getting a load of food.'

'But that doesn't mean they're going out tonight.'

'Chris said they were.' Susan runs Yve's coupons under the scanner and the tape clicks through, subtracting.

'He said tonight?' Yve tries to remember if she knows something about this. Were there any messages? Did her mother say? She comes up blank. 'That doesn't sound right.'

'Sixty-two seventy-three.'

Yve counts her money from the red plastic petty cash envelope.

'I thought Chris said tonight.' Susan rings change. 'Maybe I didn't hear right. I was so pissed when he said it, like he was flaunting it or something. Not Walley so much, he could barely look at me.'

Yve tucks the receipt and the bills away. She folds the envelope into her purse. That John hasn't called her, or come to see her, and that he is going out tonight, makes no sense.

'That makes no sense.'

'Tell me what does these days.'

Yve stares blankly at the woman. The groceries are in the cart. She should now wheel them to Wen's pickup and load them in. She should get back to the crewhouse and get going on dinner. They will have chicken and scalloped potatoes, peas and pearl onions. 'Chris said tonight?'

'Swear to God, Yve.' Susan crosses her heart. 'Or else I'm crazy – and I might be.'

'No, that's okay. I mean, I'm sure you heard right. Maybe Chris said it wrong,' Yve says. She feels strange and vague. 'Maybe we're both crazy. Sometimes I think that's their goal, to make us crazy.' She laughs an awkward half-laugh and Susan smiles sympathetically. Yve is suddenly, horribly aware of her own self-centeredness. 'Oh God, Susan, I'm so so sorry. Are you sure you're going to be okay? Is there anything I can do? Do you want me to call my aunt?'

'Don't you dare,' Susan says. 'The day your aunt lands on my porch with a casserole is the day I kill myself.'

Back at the crewhouse, Yve unpacks the groceries. She reheats the lunch coffee and makes herself a bitter cup, sits on the kitchen sofa with it. She sits a long while. Squares of afternoon sun track across the floor, then climb the wall. She forgets to turn on the radio. Usually she likes the radio, the afternoon programs. A dog in the yard barks and she startles. The clock over the sink says 4:10. She jumps up. Dinner. A flurry of movement gets the chickens in the oven and the potatoes washed, but when she sits at the table to peel them, she falls back into a stupor. She moves as if in slow motion. Every so often she wakes herself up, realizes she's been motionless a few moments, thinking. She keeps coming back to the same thing. What Susan said doesn't make sense. John not telling her he's going out fishing tonight. Him letting Dan go and not calling to talk about it. She has always known everything about John, and he about her. She flashes on Wen, walking with him, listening to him, and she winces. She shuts down that thought and goes back to the potatoes. Peels curl in long ribbons over the back of her hand, between her spread knees, and into the refuse bowl between her feet. The longer the peels

209

the longer your years of marital bliss, her mother always says.

John is going fishing. How was she supposed to find out? A message through her mother? A note? What could his excuse for not telling her possibly be? Perhaps he'd say he meant to see her, but she's been so busy with her new job. Hadn't he come around the other night and hadn't he gotten nothing for it but an argument? Hasn't she been cold and distant? He's probably still angry about that; he's probably found some way to turn it around, off himself. Still, he could've come by. He could've walked her home any evening, and they could've talked. She was home all weekend. And if he paid better attention to her, maybe she wouldn't look elsewhere – she shuts this thought down, too. She has done nothing wrong. She was drunk, and she's done nothing wrong, though she could have. But she didn't. But she could've. But she didn't, and that's what matters. But John. Going out without goodbye, when they never know what might happen, when she never knows if she'll see him again. And especially since the last time they saw each other they fought. She'll end up like her Aunt Edna, throwing the wreaths in the water, wailing about how she sent him off with harsh words – Cancel, cancel. Yve crosses herself and sends the unlucky, unwelcome image up to God. Of course, she has to go see him now. If anything were to happen, that awful last conversation is what she'd remember. She scallops the potatoes, makes a salad and dressing, washes the prep dishes, sets the table, then writes a note and props it between the salt and pepper shakers:

Dinner in the oven, salad in the fridge, back in the a.m., went home sick.

Yve.

She rattles down the fire escape, trots past the dogs.

Halfway to Water she realizes she is wearing her apron and, still jogging, she unties it and balls it into her bag. When she sees the *Pearl* at the Museum Pier, relief hits her so hard she bends over, gasping. She straightens up and walks around with her hands on her hips, getting her breath back. Banners advertising the Holly-Day Festival festoon the museum's front door, complete with picture of *Shardon Rose* tied to an otherwise empty pier. For now, the pier is crowded with the fishing fleet. Pete Hopewell's *Lady Bea* is in, as is Sal Liro's *Three Marias*, and Israel Titus's *Lizzie*. The tide is out and the boats sit way below the boards. Yve climbs halfway down the ladder, then a wave lifts *Lady Bea*, and she stops. *Lady Bea* bobs, her bowline pulls and her aftline loosens, then her aftline pulls and her bowline ducks to the water, then this forward line draws tight and wrings out a few drops red as the low sun. Yve waits till things settle before making the jump.

'John?' she calls out, feeling a bit silly. Skirt in hand, she steps across the decks of *Lady Bea*. 'John?' she calls again, from the rail of *Three Marias*.

'Yvette?'

'Oh Jesus.' She turns. Sal Liro, up from below, looks apologetic. 'You scared me,' she says. He gives her a hand down.

'John and them are probably still at the Wind.' Whiskey and beer coat his breath.

'You were just there?'

'I left a couple hours ago.'

'Oh. Okay. Thanks.' She starts off, and he follows. Sal helps her jump back to *Lady Bea*, then he scrambles his big self over to help her to the pier. He stands on the *Bea*, looking up expectantly.

'Thanks again,' she says.

'No problem,' he says. He keeps staring up at her.

'Well, goodbye,' she says.

Sal leans his forearms on the rail. 'I was wondering.'

He pauses casually, as if he has just been struck by a fleeting fancy, and thought he might run it by her, or anyone for that matter, whoever happened by.

'Yes?'

'Your father isn't buying now, is he?'

'I wouldn't know.' She knows her father isn't – he can't afford more inventory when there are no buyers – but she doesn't want to say no for him.

'Well, 'cause I been thinking. I got a few extras I might want to off-load. Survival suits, EPIRB, radio, you know.' He squints and visors his eyes with his hand, so she cannot read his expression. 'Her engine is still clean; it'll run forever. And the winches are new last season.'

'I don't know, Mr. Liro. Have you tried Service Marine?'

'Ahh—' He waves his hand. 'I hate those bastards.'

'But they're big. They could probably give a good price. Better than my dad could.'

Liro shakes his head. 'They aren't taking any more secondhand, they say. They don't have room.'

'Oh. Well. I don't know.'

'Okay then.' Sal nods. 'I guess you want to catch up with John.'

'Yes.'

'Tell your dad I'll be calling him.'

'Sure.'

She goes a little way down the pier. When she turns, he is still standing there, looking at nothing in particular.

A wary man inside the Whiskey Wind can keep a sharp lookout through the storefront window, and by the miracle of the shaded glass, see someone on the street clearly before that approaching someone can clearly see him. Add to that the approaching someone's handicap of coming from bright afternoon light into a dark smoky bar, and a man sitting in the Wind has a moment to collect himself before the attack. So

212

Israel Titus sees Yvette Albin, and knows what is coming early enough to warn John, who sits at the bar waiting for Kate to finish topping his pint, that his girlfriend is on her way and she looks angry.

'Hoho!' Warren Fitz winks at his son. 'Just like your mother!' Izzy and Walley laugh, but cut their laughs short as Yve storms through the inner door.

John stands to head her off.

'I can't believe you!' She starts right in with the side of her fist to his chest. 'When were you going to tell me?'

'What?' he says, though he means Which. Which thing is she angry about.

'How can you leave without seeing me? You never leave without seeing me. You know that.'

All the men at the booth twist in their seats; Jimmy Daly has swung around on his bar stool. Kate conveniently disappears into the kitchen. She's not one to take sides.

Yve doesn't sound angry so much as peeved. John tries to put his arms around her.

'Don't you touch me.' She bats his hands away. 'Don't, don't—'

He touches her anyhow. 'I was going to come around tonight. I was going to pick you up at work and take you out. We won't be leaving till three—'

She breaks his hold and takes a step back. 'Why didn't you call this weekend? You could've told me before.'

'I didn't know before. It was kind of sudden.' As soon as he says it, he knows he has caught himself in something. She looks at him from the corner of her eye.

'You knew last night. I just saw Susan at the Finast.'

'Okay. Fine. You're right.' He lets his hands drop, and he makes like he is going back to the men.

'What's that about, anyhow? They're our friends, you know.' Her voice gets louder. 'She was crying, right there in the checkout line.'

213

'Calm down. Okay? Can you calm down?' He takes her upper arm. She wrenches away, he realizes he is a little too drunk. He takes a moment to calm himself. 'Let's go for a drive.'

'Why?'

'We need to talk. I'm sorry. I should have called. I'm a jerk.'

She visibly softens.

He drives her to his house. Once in the truck, she hardens back up. She gets out of the truck without his help and stands by the hedge while he unlocks. Inside, he offers her a beer, and she nods. He gets beers for the both of them. They sit at the kitchen table. It is still littered with ledgers and papers, and John has to put some on the floor so she has a place for her drink.

'Did you eat?' he asks.

She shakes her head.

'I could make something.' He doesn't know what they have, but he is sure there is something.

She says nothing. She sits there with her hard face.

'Listen, Yve, you want me to let go of Walley? Or Chris? I'm sorry for Dan and Susan, but someone's got to go, and that's just reality.' He waits for a response. Walley is her cousin, Chris is her brother. She should give him some credit for looking after her family. He tells her this. 'You should give me some credit for looking after your family. How about I don't? How about I let them both go and I just take care of me? How about just me and my father go out and screw everyone?'

She sits with her hard face turned to the window, her beer untouched. He reaches across the table with both hands and pulls on her sleeves. Reluctantly, she allows him her hands. He holds them on the table, and the bills and receipts are dry beneath his wrists. He gives a little squeeze, and she glances at him.

'Listen, Yve. I know you think I'm an asshole right now.' She gives him a wry look. He smiles back. 'Okay.

214

I am an asshole. But I've been over the books, and we're in a lot of trouble.'

'Then take the buyback. I just saw Sal Liro. He sounds like he's taking it. You could strip Pearl and my father could sell everything. He couldn't buy it outright, but he could work on consignment. You could get a lot for the engine, the electronics—'

He shakes his head. 'You can't get anything right now, and you know that. Everyone wants to sell, no one wants to buy.' She opens her mouth as if she might speak, but he cuts her off. 'The Package'll barely cover our debts. If we took it now, we'd basically have to take the scuttling money and hand it to the bank and have nothing left over. We just need to get a little something extra before we give her up. We've got a couple months and a couple ideas, and if things go right, I'll have a little something extra—'

'But you are taking The Package.'

'Yeah.'

'Thanks for consulting me.'

'I didn't realize I had to.'

'Bastard.' She pulls her hands free of his.

'Oh come on, Yve. I don't mean it like that.'

'How else could you possibly mean it?'

He sighs. 'I know you've been waiting a long time.' She rolls her eyes. He wants to prove she is wrong for agreeing he's an asshole, so he speaks without thinking. 'If things work out, maybe next year we can get our own place.'

'Are you asking me to marry you?'

He doesn't answer quickly enough.

'I see.' She stands and takes her beer with her into the living room. He hears her footsteps on the stairs.

When he gets to his room, she is standing before the window, unbuttoning her dress.

'What are you doing?'

She keeps unbuttoning. She shrugs her dress from her shoulders, and it falls to the floor. She steps out of

215

the ring of material. She lets her slip go, her panties, her bra. Naked, she says, 'You're going out tonight, right?'

'Yeah.'

'I'm saying goodbye then.' She lies on the bed.

He picks her clothes off the floor and folds them on the chair. She stays on top of the quilt, one leg bent and the other straight, her arms flung above her head as if she is comfortable, though he can see she is cold.

'Get under the covers,' he says.

He undresses and gets in with her. It is a narrow bed – his childhood bed, with the plaid comforter and the beer-can airplanes flying overhead from nylon strings. She shifts and rolls to make room.

'You really want to marry me?' He touches her hair.

'Yes.'

'Just because you want to get married, or because it's me asking?'

When she doesn't answer, he kneels over her. He has the intention of making it a joke, sort of peering in her face as he often does until she laughs and pushes at him, but as soon as he straddles her, he gets hard. He tries to catch her eye, but her gaze hovers somewhere about his chin. He lowers himself down, so his face is inches from hers. She turns the slightest tick away. She doesn't seem to want to be kissed, so he goes for her breasts and her belly. Her skin smells like a kitchen, like onions and oil and cinnamon and bread. She lies quietly beneath him, letting him do all the work. He doesn't mind; it is easy enough. He knows her body as well as his own. They have lain beside each other their whole lives – their mothers put them in the same carriages and cribs, and as kids they began touching each other soon as they touched themselves. When she's ready, he moves back up and inside. Her eyes are closed, and her head is still turned slightly. He kisses the corner of her mouth. He tries again, and she turns her head farther. She lies beneath him as if

216

out of duty. He thrusts hard to get her attention. Her breasts bounce, but otherwise she doesn't respond. He grabs her hips and stabs at her again, quickly and deeply, and she cries out and wrinkles her brow as if he has hurt her, but she doesn't open her eyes. He does it again, and she gasps. He wants her to say something, say Stop, say You're hurting me. Instead she arches her back and raises her hips to meet him. He hesitates. She puts her hands on his buttocks and rocks her pelvis up. He pushes away and out of her. She opens her eyes. He comes, shuddering, on her stomach.

'I'm sorry,' he says even as it pulses out. 'I'm sorry.'

'It's okay.'

He snatches up his T-shirt to catch the mess. He wipes them both down. 'Sorry. It's been a while.'

'It's okay,' she says again, but she sounds disappointed. He reaches down to bring her off and she pushes his hand away.

'Don't bother.'

'It's not a bother.' But the moment is past, and he feels like a fool.

She gets up and starts dressing. He knows as soon as she is dressed she will leave and he won't see her again until he gets back. They haven't turned on the lights and the setting sun washes her shoulders gold. She looks pretty.

'Yve?'

'What?'

He doesn't know what he plans to say. He wants to give her something, some kind of gift. He says, 'We're not fishing this trip out.'

She stops buttoning.

'That's why I let Dan go.'

'Really.' She sinks to the chair. Her dress gapes and her stomach folds beneath her bra.

'I didn't want to involve him. I don't think he would've wanted to be involved.' He sits up and gathers the quilt around him. She looks at him,

217

waiting. He turns the light on the nightstand on. 'We're going to import something. From Canada. Not Canada actually. Miquelon – it's still French—'

'I know Miquelon,' she says. 'What are you saying? What are you going to get?'

He has never actually said the word aloud. He rarely even thinks the word – if he has to think of it he thinks pictures – a baggie with white powder, or Chris's needle – and now he isn't sure if he should say heroin or dope or smack. Heroin sounds ridiculously clinical, but dope and smack make him feel as if he is posing as a tough.

'Drugs,' he finally says.

She doesn't move at all. She doesn't seem to be breathing.

'Yve?' He crouches in front of her and rests his chin on her knee. She puts her hand on his head but it is an absentminded gesture. 'Are you okay?' he asks.

'No.' She stands. She bends for the rest of her clothes, then stops. 'Asshole!' She grabs her shoes, her cardigan. She moves as far from him as is possible in the small room, and turns her body away, as if by hiding her quivering breasts she might somehow protect herself.

He stands also. 'Yve—'

'Just . . . just . . .' She holds a shoe out in warning.

'Come on.'

'Drugs?' She glares at him. 'Since when do you run drugs?'

He spreads his hands and steps nearer. She is hopping on one foot, trying to put her shoe on. She gives up and slaps him about the head with it.

'Yve, stop. Calm down.'

She throws the shoe and gets him in the eye. For a moment he tears up and can't see. Through the blur, he reaches for where she was. He manages to catch her in a hug. 'Are you going to calm down?'

She stops struggling and says, calmly, 'I want to go home.'

He holds her a moment more. His eyes clear. He blinks at her.

'Take me home.'

'Okay,' he says. He lets her go. She stands by the door while he dresses himself.

In the car, she tells herself she will not look at him. Then she broadens it: she will not look at him ever again, he may as well be dead, they may as well break up if he's going to do this. Her vengeful thoughts feel ridiculous and petty, like the thoughts of a child, and she wishes she were a different sort of woman, a high-minded, intelligent sort who could coldly shut him out with a few choice words, and then never look back. But he has seen everything: he has seen how her family can't even talk, can't even sit together at a meal; he knows what her brother was like – charming, funny, handsome, their mother's favorite – and what he is like now, and how his deterioration is the background noise of all Sunday barbecues and holiday dinners and birthday parties and Kodak moments, like a buzzing clock or a high-pitched whine in all their ears. John has always been there. He knows everything. He should understand. How could he not understand? He is already like the closest member of her family, even without marriage. If they split up it would be, for her, like losing another brother. He is that, to her. But if he runs dope, John will be proving something terrible about how little Yve is to him. She is not sure exactly what she means by this – words fail, and as she gropes for a way to explain it, all she finds is a dreadful sense of gross misunderstanding, as if the scale by which she'd weighed their relationship, the actual units of measurement were horribly inaccurate. Beyond inaccurate; wholly inappropriate. She'd been foolishly figuring in so many teaspoons, when she should have been sounding fathoms, or triangulating their position by the stars.

John takes High Street, where the houses are really

run-down. He doesn't want to pass any of his neighbors on the road. He is shaking, not with anger so much as adrenaline and cold. Yve shivers also. He cranks the heat, but only cold air blows, and he shuts it off. He grips the french-hitched steering wheel hard enough to print the sennit pattern in his palms. He shifts violently. The miniature monkey's fist on the rearview hits the windshield.

'You gonna talk to me?' John asks her.

She faces forward, so he gets only her closed profile. Her eye is a dark hole and her mouth draws down.

'I'm leaving tonight whether you do or not,' he says. 'Fine then,' he says, after a while. They drive up High, past the boarded houses and fenced lots with their rusting refrigerators and rotting sofas, everything edged in twilight blue. They drive past the burnt-out social club for Portuguese fishers, where someone has grafitti'd in red the ambiguous words *Town Plot*. Past the cemetery, past the neon cross, past the dump, into the beginnings of the next residential section.

A stray makes a feint at the road. John sees its movement only, slams the brakes. Gravel sprays. The mutt freezes at the curb, paw raised, nose turned toward the skidding truck. They lurch to a stop, and Yve's forehead hits the dash. The dog minces across the road.

'You okay?' John scratches the back of her neck. He feels like shit.

She lifts her head and turns her awful face to him. 'How can you?'

Though they're in the middle of the road, he turns the car off.

'You have to be crazy,' she says. 'That's the only answer. How long have you been planning this?'

'I knew it was a possibility for a while.'

'When did you decide? I can't believe – you never mentioned—'

He makes himself look at her, though it is difficult. 'I didn't think it'd come to this. But it has. We need the money.' She opens her mouth, but he cuts her off. 'This job came up suddenly. You see now why I had to let Dan go?'

'Oh, this reeks of my brother.'

John opens his hands slightly.

'But you.' She shakes her head. 'I mean, you've seen what it's done to my family. Kate, Martin, everyone. How can *you*?'

'I'm not doing anything to anyone. And if we don't do it, someone else will. So this way we're just getting some of the money.' For some reason, he can't make the argument sound convincing. They were Chris's words originally, and he wishes Chris were here to explain.

'I can't believe your father agreed.'

As it turns out, Fitz was surprisingly docile. When John tried to tell him, he murmured, Do what you have to, I don't want to know.

'My father didn't have any better ideas,' John says.

'How can you, though? How can *you*?'

'How can't I?'

'Oh please. That's just bullshit and you know it.'

'Is it? Do I have a lot of choices?'

She doesn't answer, and she stiffens as if it would be beneath her to do so. He doesn't want to defend himself against her stiffness; it would be like running headfirst into a wall. She always wins when he tries to get her with words. She's too good at stonewalling. With her silence, she can force him to take his finest ideas – finest in the sense of most fragile, filamentous, delicate; ideas so tenuous they exist only in a suspension of image and sensation – and mash them into ugly clumsy words too thick for anyone to credit. He wishes he could just open her head and pour his pictures in. When he imagines smuggling – not the actual actions of smuggling so much as the idea of it, the making of the decision to do it, the being the sort of person who does it – he pictures himself surfing

221

barefoot on top of an amazing tattoo-blue wave, with an ornate break of curling white froth, like one he once saw inked on the back of a Japanese lumper in Charlesport.

She would laugh if he said any of this. In words it sounds ham-handed and doltish, even to John now that he's given it too much thought. He hates how she, by just sitting there, can take things from him.

'At least I'm doing something,' he says.

'It reeks of my brother.'

'It was also my idea.'

'He wrecks everything.'

'It was also my idea,' John says, though he doesn't exactly remember how. Of course it started with Chris, but John did make the decision to involve himself. When? Back in the coffee shop in Charlesport? Earlier? Holding for Chris, monitoring his onboard use, that was John's own decision. He's been involved a long time. He's no innocent patsy, he would like to tell Yve. And with drugs, any amount, you lose your boat if the Coasties board you.

She looks at him looking at her. She looks at his eyes. She can read nothing there. It seems she rarely looks into his eyes, despite their years of intimacy. She has always felt (oddly, awkwardly) that to look so pointedly at him is generally rude, an invasion of privacy. Now, looking at him so pointedly feels like an attack. She wants to ask him, What are you thinking, right now? Has he thought of the danger of it, of the dangerous sort of people he will surely be meeting? She doesn't want to voice these concerns, because first and foremost, she must remain angry. Anger is her only power with John, and if she relents and shows a softer, worried side, he will know he has won. For his own safety, she can't let him win. She tells herself she must stay angry so he won't go through with this foolishness. Still, she hears herself asking, 'And if something goes wrong?'

222

'We won't get caught. We're no one. If they were any good at catching people—' He is about to say *your brother wouldn't be a junkie*, but then he sees how this contradicts his earlier point. 'We'll only do it once,' he says. 'Three times tops. We'll get enough money—'

She tries to open her door, but it sticks.

'I wanted to tell you. But Chris said not to tell anyone. He hasn't even told Kate. So don't you go around talking.' He hears his own harsh tone and softens. 'At least I told you.'

'Thanks a lot.'

He starts the car again, begins driving. She gets the door open. She peers down at the blurred gravel. 'Come on, Yve,' he says. 'Shut the door. I'll take you home.'

She jumps out and slams the door and starts walking. He leans across the seat and rolls down her window. He drives slowly beside her.

'You shouldn't've told me,' she says. 'Why'd you even bother?' She walks gingerly, looking at the road. She has begun crying. Her lips curl back from her teeth and her sobs are wet. He considers reminding her how upset she was before when he hadn't told her he was letting Dan go. Now she's upset because he is telling her something.

'I'm doing this for us,' he says.

She stops walking. She stares at him as if he has said the worst possible thing.

'Get in the car at least. You don't have a coat.'

She looks at him leaning over to open the door.

'Come on,' he says gently. 'You're being ridiculous.'

She gets in and sits with her hands folded in her lap.

17

Yve fetches the stockpot from the pantry, lifts it to the sink. She turns on the radio. After dinner, Wen likes to hear the news. NPR, *All Things Considered*. A special report on logging begins and Wen hushes the crew. Hank moves to the sofa to call Dora. He makes plans to meet her at the Wind. Ed and Jefferson leave to pick up beer at Garenelli's before they close; they take orders and money from the others. On the radio, the news-caster tells of some loggers who were illegally marking extra trees for cutting, and how the Parks Department caught them by examining the paint markings forensically. Yve goes to the fridge, fills her apron with vegetables, carries them to the sink. Then back for the platter with the chicken carcasses from last night's dinner. The men didn't burn them, apparently. They finished dinner fine without her. John is gone now, has been gone at least sixteen hours, maybe more. She is aware of this, even as she tells herself she does not care. She does not care, she does not care. Neil gets up from the table and heads to his inner sanctum and his studies of Chapman; Rob goes to the attic to practice the song he's been writing about Jenny Stewart, though the girl in the song is named Penny. Something about 'shining' and 'bright' rhymes with 'pining' and 'night.' Yve washes carrots and celery, puts them whole into the stockpot.

The logging story finishes and behind her, at the table, Wen and Charlie resume talking work. They need to get their hands on a solid curve of oak to replace a rotten knee.

'You might check with my father.' Yve pins bay leaves to an onion with a clove.

Wen nods. 'That's an idea.' Then he's talking to Charlie again. 'We can't really move on that aft section till it's in place. And we need to get painting before the cold really sets in. Before snow.'

Early November and they're already on snow. Yve runs water into the pot, over the vegetables and empty carcasses. Bits of fat and meat shear from the bones; the water rises up and floats the cheesecloth bundle of spices. She turns off the tap and grease eyes coalesce on the surface. Looking out the window over the sink, she can just make out the dogs below; no scraps for them tonight. The men need soup tomorrow, and chicken bones would splinter in the dogs' mouths. She puts the stockpot on the stove to simmer, then she goes back to the endless dishes. The men talk on and she doesn't try to listen.

'All right then,' Wen says. Charlie removes his pipe and belches loudly. Two chairs scrape back; two men stand, stretch, pop their knees and spines. Hank puts his feet up on Charlie's vacated chair.

'How about tonight, Yve?' Wen touches the small of her back, startling her. The plate she was washing slips from her soapy hands and breaks on the drain.

'Sorry.' He removes his hand. 'I was just—'

'It's okay,' she says, though when she picks up the broken halves she clucks her tongue. She holds them together, checking the fit. A clean break; it can be glued. She turns to show him, and has to lean against the sink, so as not to touch him. He is crowding the small space between the sink and the table. 'Excuse me,' she says.

He steps back, knocking over a chair. 'I was just asking when was a good time to see your father.' He rights the chair and leans on it.

'Oh. Anytime.'

'Tonight?'

'Whenever.' She doesn't know what to do with the plate. 'Sorry,' she says. 'I could glue it.'

Wen shrugs. 'It's not mine. Some CARP castoff, I bet.'

'Oh.' She lays the halves gently on the sideboard and turns back to the sink, feeling through the suds for splinters.

'Really, it's no prob.' He reaches over her shoulders, and for a moment she doesn't understand what he is trying to do. His elbows press briefly down against her collarbones for leverage, his chest presses against her back, and he grunts. He is trying to open the window.

'Let me.' She slams the corners with the heels of her hands and pushes it up. Cold air rushes in.

He steps aside, cocks his arm, and sails half the plate out the window. The break makes a satisfying sound. A moon-shadowed dog skitters sideways, its snout turned over its shoulder, tail tucked in. Wen smiles at her and hands her the other half. He wants her to throw the plate out the window. She bends her elbow, makes a feint to throw. He catches her wrist.

'Not like that – like this.' He changes her position. 'You throw like a girl.'

'I am a girl.'

'That's no excuse.'

She feels as though she is skipping backward again, facing him, down the dark street. She feels her expression change to match this sensation. Her cheeks soften, the pinch between her brows loosens. It's how he looks at her that makes her weight shift and her hips thrust out, makes her breath expand her chest and lengthen her waist. She'd thought she'd forgotten such tricks, but here they are, rising unbidden from some deep hiding place.

She throws the plate with a sideways flick. It sails like a Frisbee and shatters below.

'Good one!' He slaps her on the back, then doesn't remove his hand.

She grins. It was a good throw. 'I should've started throwing plates long ago.'

'Everyone should throw plates.'

'Yes,' she laughs.

'Shall we? Tonight? Go see your father?'

She could still take the pot off the stove. It's barely heated. She could put it in the fridge, there's room. She could make the stock tomorrow, while breakfast's cooking.

'Yes.'

He gives her one more pat. 'Good, good.' His hand

drops from her shoulder. 'Good, good.' He goes to the hall and gets their coats.

The main section of the barn is dark, but the light is on in her father's small shop. He is in there, talking with Sal Liro. At first Yve can't quite catch their words. Then her father's voice rises. 'I can't, Sal. You know I can't. Things are bad right now—'

Yve knocks the door gently, pushing it open. The two men stand at the workbench, leaning over some papers. They look up, surprised. Sal recovers himself first. He folds the papers into the bib pocket of his overalls.

'Mr. Liro, Dad,' Yve says.

'Yve,' Phil says.

Sal Liro nods once, straightening up. He cocks his head at a strange angle, as if making an effort to not see Yve and the captain. He doesn't meet her eyes. His jaw is tight. He balls his hands and crosses his arms, hiding his large fists in his armpits.

'Dad, Wen's here,' Yve says, despite the obviousness of Wen's presence.

Phil comes forward, hand extended. Wen steps slightly in to meet him. Between the paint shelves, the woodstove, the table saw and workbench, it seems there are suddenly too many people in the small shop, and Yve feels that she is the one too many.

'What can I do you for?' her father says.

'I'm in the market for a knee.'

Sal Liro clears his throat, fingers the papers in his pocket. His eyes dart between the captain and Phil.

'Sorry.' Wen turns to Sal and holds out his hand. 'I'm Wendell Holmes. Captain. Off *Shardon Rose*.' His voice raises politely at the end of his introduction, as if this is all still in question, as if it is all still news, who he is.

Sal steps back, avoiding Wen's hand. His retreat creaks the shop floor. But it is not a retreat so much as a shift of weight, a gathering up of himself into himself. He seems for a moment to hover like a boulder balanced on the edge of a cliff. Yve sees what is coming and steps out of the big man's way. Sal lurches forward. He brushes past her. His shoulder slams Wen's shoulder and Wen stumbles, pushed through the shop door and back into the barn.

'Excuse me,' Wen says. He sounds girlish; and Yve winces for him. Then, just as quickly, her embarrassment takes a half-step toward pity, then another toward guilty alliance.

Sal Liro bangs the barn door shut. The whole front wall rattles, shaking dust from the eaves. Wen stares at the door a few moments, his hand still extended. He turns to Phil Albin, the insulted hand flipped over, begging explanation.

'Don't mind Sal.' Phil steps from the shop into the barn. He shuts the shop door, after Yve. 'It isn't personal. He's got a lot on his plate. He can't afford to get rid of his boat and he can't afford not to.'

'He wants my father to buy some of his equipment,' Yve says.

'Or dock his *Three Marias*,' Phil says. 'Till he decides what to do. Apparently Ames is kicking the fleet off the pier soon' – he nods at Wen – 'to make room for your schooner.'

'Not my schooner.'

'No, of course not,' Phil says. 'But Sal isn't a man for details. He thinks town money should've gone to fixing the Fish Pier instead of the *Shardon*. You captain the *Shardon*. Therefore, you represent the problem.'

'I guess I should lay low.' Wen chuckles like a man with no intention of laying low. 'He's a big guy.'

'As should I, maybe. If Joe kicks them off, Fitz has our dock. That's what I had to tell Sal. Family first.'

'We've only got room for one,' Yve explains. 'And my brother works on Fitz's boat. And my cousin, too.'

'Ah,' Wen says. 'That's bad news for Sal.'

'Yes, bad news.' Phil looks absentminded a moment. Then he catches himself. 'You came for a knee.' He ushers Wen farther into the barn, his hand resting on the shorter man's shoulder. From behind they look like father and son. They walk the length of the barn, turning over forked logs with the toes of their boots. Phil grunts, upends a joint of heavy oak. 'If that's too small, I don't have anything else here that'll do.'

Wen pulls a length of yellow metal tape from the measure strapped to his belt, figures all the angles. 'This'll fit fine.' He smiles at Yve, and she feels as though she's suddenly stepped into a bright room.

'All right then.' Phil rocks on his heels once.

Yve glances from her father to Wen. They stand there, the two of them, looking at the jumble of shadows between. He will leave now. If Yve does nothing, Wen will leave.

'I'll go get us some pie,' she says.

Between the barn and the house, Yve fiddles, one-handed, with the plastic sheeting behind the paint-cleaning station – a corner has come loose and she is trying to press the tack back into the old loose hole, trying to make it catch. In her other hand, she holds the dirty pie plates. Wen leans on the stack of nesting dories, watching. Her father is inside the barn, closing up the shop.

'Thanks for bringing me over,' Wen says. 'I've got a good feeling about that knee.'

'Good. I'm glad my father could help.'

'And that pie was good.'

'Yes. My mom made it.' She thinks they might as well be saying nothing. They are simply holding space with these words, marking a circle for something to happen in.

Her father comes out and latches the barn doors. Her heart jumps as if she's been caught at some mischief, but her father just nods good night to both of them and goes into the house. The screen door slaps shut.

'How's the job working out?' Wen says.

Yve looks across the dark alley at him. She tries to see him clearly, but the dark blurs his face.

'Fine. It's good to have something to do.'

'Well, we like having you around.'

'Oh,' she says. She doesn't know how else to reply. He is watching her. She can feel his eyes rolling like two ball bearings over her skin. Her inarticulate shyness feels as prominent and foreign as the plates in her hand. She could throw the plates — they could laugh again about thrown plates! — then she realizes she can't throw her mother's plates and laugh. Not here, where her mother's house looks over her shoulder. She turns quickly. The kitchen light flicks off. A few seconds later, the upstairs light of her parents' bedroom comes on behind the heavy curtains.

'My parents.' She points up with her chin. 'I should go in now.'

'Yeah, long day. Early start tomorrow.' He continues standing there. So does she. He trails his fingers through the top dory, rippling the reflected moon. It must be icy water now. Soon her father will drain the boats and tip them over, tarpaulin them for the season.

'Knock knock,' Wen says.

'Who's there?'

'John.'

'John who?'

'John the Baptist.' He flicks water from his fingertips. The drops burn her cheeks and she gasps from the cold.

'I should splash you back!'

'But you won't.'

'How do you know?'

'You don't do such naughty things.' He looks mischievous.

230

'You're right. Oh, well. Good night.' She turns as if she will actually walk into the house.

'I bet you wish you did, though.'

She pretends this is enough to make her stop walking. She comes back and leans on the opposite side of the dory stack. 'How do you know?'

'I know many things.'

'Like.' She dips one finger in the water and sends rings through the slender moon.

He becomes serious. 'Like you're angry at John.'

'Am I? Why, do you suppose?'

'For him going fishing.'

'And other things. I don't really feel like going into it, with you. Ask Kate if you really want to know.' As far as she knows, Kate knows nothing. She only says Kate's name as payback for his bringing up John's. She thinks about this instinctual revenge for half a second, how it springs from emotion more than thought. She has no words for this behavior. She can pretend she doesn't understand its origin; she can pretend one hand doesn't know what the other does. It is as if she has two minds. One surrounds and hides the other, like a shell hides an egg. She can choose to look only at the outer mind, the shell. And for the most part, this is what she's been doing. All day at work, at home with her parents, she's been looking at the smooth clean shell. Simple, solid, white shell, innocent shell, protective shell. She has been pretending there is no inside, no fecund membrane where things have been developing. But Wen sees inside her little shell. To him, she is hopelessly transparent. It is exciting and nauseating at once, knowing this. It is like the thrilling, sickening moment at the top of a roller coaster, when you see the inevitable drop and know there is nothing you can do to prevent it, and you know you cavalierly volunteered for this thing that now frightens you, and you wish that you hadn't and you wish it would happen already, be over and

231

done with, even as your stomach flips in anticipation.

She says, 'We had a fight before he left. He made some bad decisions.'

Wen shrugs. 'Men do what they do.' Then he splashes her.

'Oh!' She drops her plates on the soft grass – they clatter without breaking – and she lunges for the dory. Close now, she can see his eyes easily. He is just beginning to laugh and open his mouth in disbelief. She cups an icy handful of water and throws it at him. It catches him full in the face. He splashes her back, wetting the front of her blouse and cardigan.

'Bastard!' She tosses armfuls at him, wetting herself up to the armpit, showering his hair. He douses her head, she opens her mouth to shriek, and he slams it shut with cold water. Cold water forces down her throat and into her lungs like a thousand tiny fish-hooks. She gasps and laughs and nearly screams – but he catches her from behind, his hand over her open mouth, her back pressed to his stomach, his arm tight around her chest.

'Shh, don't scream. You'll wake everyone up,' he whispers. Heat transfers where he touches her, from his skin to his clothes to her clothes to her skin. 'You want to wake your parents up?'

She shakes her head no against his hand. She doesn't want them to come down and see the two of them wet and trembling. And the way he holds her. He laughs silently against her. She's laughing too, breathlessly, open-mouthed and tasting his palm wet from stagnant, oak-steeped water. Their bodies hook together in silent laughter. His chest and stomach rise and fall against her jerking back. They make small rocking movements.

A shudder twitches through her.

'Cold?'

She nods. His hand still covers her mouth.

'You want to go inside? I bet the stove is still warm. We won't turn on the lights.'

She nods again.

'I'll let you go if you promise no splashing.'

She nods. He lets her go. She unlatches the barn door and catches a wet slap of water square in the back. He pushes her in and slams the door behind them.

'Got you!'

'No fair. Absolutely no fair.' She sprints the length of the barn and tries to shut him from the small shop, but he wrestles the door free and traps her inside with him.

'Sh-sh-sh.' He laughs through his fingers.

The room is still warm. Four squares of pale moonlight spill across the floor and workbench. A branch waves back and forth outside the window. Small hairs stand up off Yve's wet arms. They turn dark, silver, dark, silver, with the shadow of the branch and the moon.

Wen crouches in front of the stove and she sits on the workbench, dangling her feet like a child. From her high seat, she gets a good view of his uneven shoulders under his wet shirt. He feeds the coals. They crackle, catch.

He says, 'You are an evil man, Wendell Holmes.'

She swings her legs. 'Are you? And how is that?'

'Well,' he stands, 'I wouldn't be here right now if I wasn't.' The stove door clangs shut.

'Is that so?'

'That's so.' He steps to the bench and leans against it so it hits him exactly where his pelvis meets his thighs.

She holds her hands out to him and he pulls her to the edge of the bench. She lets him spread her legs with his hipbones; she places her hands on his belt. He puts his arms lightly around her. A finger of steam rises from the open collar of his wet shirt.

She feels as if she is spinning, like a child twirling till she falls on the grass. 'When I was a child—' she begins.

He puts his hand over her mouth and brings his face close to hers. 'When I was a child.' He breathes the words on her cheek. His breath smells of apples and cinnamon and coffee. 'When I was a child, I was so evil, I turned streetlamps off just by walking beneath them.' He lets her mouth go.

She feels dizzy. 'Is that so?'

'That's so.' He strokes his hands down her arms, cups her elbows like breasts and raises her hands off his belt. Folds her hands back into her own lap. 'I'm telling you this for your own good.'

'My own good,' she repeats.

'Yes.'

The word falls past her, barely touching, settles in the sawdust beneath her spread feet. It makes no impression. 'What good? I'm very bad, myself.' She pulls the elastic from her braid and shakes her hair loose. Her breasts lift in response to her hands.

He grabs her hands and keeps them over her head, both in one large fist, bound together at the wrist. 'That so?'

She looks down. She gives the slightest nod, sends the smallest shiver out. The air shifts, becomes liquid, then solid, and each molecule in the room – the wood imprinting the backs of her thighs, the smoke from the stove, the warming air itself – rotates slightly and locks into a firm, hard place.

He bows his head. He lets her hands go and he kisses her and she lets him. His mouth is deep and round, reminding her of a cave. She's never been kissed by anyone but John, who holds his mouth politely small. Still, after a while it's not so difficult, not so strange.

Alma Albin sits at the kitchen table working a cross-word Yve started and abandoned more than a month ago. She doesn't enjoy crosswords. She struggles and wrestles with them, pale words sketched in the margins, not yet committed to, others written, erased and rewritten, until the letters cut holes in the thin paper. Still, she can never leave well enough alone. She can't just discard the puzzle as too hard and accept that another will arrive next Sunday, with equal but different challenges. She sees each one as needing completion. She often falls behind, and they stack up on the kitchen table.

The spring of the screen door whines open, then cold air comes, then her daughter's voice. 'I thought you'd be asleep.'

Alma doesn't look up. 'Your father came in hours ago.'

'Not hours.' A pause. 'We were talking.'

Alma finally raises her head. The clock says 11:10. 'It's past eleven.'

The kitchen is cold. The wool robe Alma wears is stiff. It was originally her father's, Yve's grandfather's. Yve has no grandparents now. They all died when she was young. Accident, Alzheimer's; accident, grief. The accidents the men's; Alzheimer's and grief the women's. The robe is large. Alma's hands look tiny, peeping from the open cuffs. Her ankles look frail and purple. She's an old woman herself, now.

Her daughter, not so young either, keeps her cardigan buttoned. She hugs it to herself; it is dark in spots, wet. The air coming off Yve smells a mix of woodsmoke and the iron-filing scent of an approaching cold front.

'Storm coming,' Alma says. 'Did you look at the moon?'

'No.'

'Bet it won't stay long.'

'No, probably not.'

'Just because it storms a bit here doesn't mean it'll be bad where John is.' Her chafed hands fidget on the table. Her fingers find a familiar groove, the blackened curve from a pan set down too hot. 'He'll have different weather, or maybe he'll have it after us. Which way is the wind?' She looks to the window, but it is black.

'Tea?' Yve half-offers.

Alma traces the groove again. The table is pushed against the wall now that only three of them eat there, not four. They are together, Chris and John, on the same boat, under the same weather. Talking about John is talking about her son, but her daughter won't oblige her. One of Alma's greatest sorrows is that her children don't get along. 'The kettle's on the stove,' she says, 'though the water's probably boiled away. I forgot it.'

'Would you like more then?'

A mug sits at Alma's elbow. 'Please. This is cold.' She holds the mug to her daughter, who doesn't reach for it. 'Go ahead, dump it.' Alma waves the mug a bit.

Yve goes to the sink to refill the kettle. Water foams from the tap and drums against the stainless steel. Then a twist of gas, and a match is struck. Alma has the sensation of waiting for explosion, but there's only the usual whiff of sulfur and small blue-orange flame. The heating kettle hums. Mugs clatter down from the cabinet. Then comes the faint lemon-and-grass scent of chamomile. Her daughter leans against the counter and presses the sharp Formica edge into the heels of her hands. She is daydreaming of something, of the captain, surely. Alma would tell her daughter: Stop now, you will only lose if you play that hand. We make our beds and we must lie in them – but there seems to be no way to get to that conversation.

The kettle whistles and Yve rouses herself to pour. 'I can't stay up much longer,' she says. 'I have work tomorrow.' She sits down and places the mugs on the table. She smiles vaguely. Her lips are red.

'Where are the pie plates?' Alma asks sharply.

Yve hesitates, looks down.

'Why are you wet?'

'Am I wet?'

'Your sweater is.'

They both wait for an answer.

'Oh.' Yve sips her tea. 'The dories.'

Alma pushes the crossword away.

'Wen told a joke and splashed me. We were just fooling around.'

'I see.'

'Well.' Yve stands, mug in hand. 'Good night.'

'What were you talking about this late? Without your father? Didn't he come to see your father?'

'Work. Things. I don't know.'

'What do you want me to think?'

Yve looks affronted. 'Nothing. There's nothing to think. And it's not your business.'

'People will think things, though. They probably already are.' Alma looks toward the blank windows. 'Do you know what people are saying about those men?'

'Should I care? Dad doesn't care. Their money's good as anyone else's.'

'You don't know anything, Yve. You think you do, but you don't. You're very lucky to have John. You know the saying "Plenty of fish in the sea"?'

Yve nods.

'Well, there aren't.'

'I know.'

'No, you don't.'

Yve sits back down. 'John's not a fish, Mom.' She smiles at her own feeble joke, and Alma allows a thin smile back.

'He's a good catch.'

'I haven't caught him yet.' Yve stands again. 'Let's go up, Mom. I'm really tired.'

Alma stands too. The moment is lost. They creak up the stairs together. A wedge of light shows Phil is still awake behind the closed bedroom door. His nightstand radio plays soft jazz.

Nearly at the top, Yve says, ''Night, Mom. Wen expects me at seven.'

Alma recognizes the pleasure her daughter takes in

saying his unnecessary name. She was young herself once. 'What's going on with you two?'

'Nothing.'

She pulls on her daughter's sleeve.

'I'm not talking to you about this, Mom.'

'Are you sleeping with him?'

'No! Oh Lord – we just—' Yve searches the dark stairwell for some elusive words. There are none worth saying. She gives up and starts back up the stairs.

'Don't walk away while I'm speaking—' Alma doesn't release her daughter's sleeve, though Yve tugs against her. Tea slops over, scalding Yve's ankle.

'I'm not talking to you about this!'

'You think you're something, don't you?' Alma says. 'You think that sailor'll stay here for you? He won't. His sort doesn't. And don't think you can go running back—'

'Is everything okay?' Phil pops from the bedroom, a rectangle of light spreads down the stairs.

Alma can see her daughter well now and Yve looks like a cat in a corner. She whispers so her husband can't hear. 'Well? You think you'll still have John to run to when this is over?'

'You're crazy,' Yve hisses back. 'I don't even have John now. You think it's so simple. You think maybe I could just get pregnant, right? Maybe I could just do like Kate—'

Alma slaps the words from her mouth.

Phil is calling again, asking if anyone is hurt.

Alma digs her fingers into Yve's arm, so the nails will leave half-moons. She calls up to her husband. 'No one's hurt. It's just tea. I'll clean it.'

18

Chris is a fetal lump in the bunk, the sleeping bag over his head. John balls his fist and thumps the ceiling beside Chris's ear.

'No,' Chris says.

'Yes.'

'Shit.'

'Yes, shit. You said you wanted a half hour, and it's been two wholes.'

Chris moans. He stretches, shudders, and unzips the bag. He rolls onto his hands, then knees, then he climbs down and stands before John in his gray long underwear, swaying a bit with the slight roll.

'Fuck,' he says. His bottom lip quivers. He licks it. 'My mouth tastes like ass.'

John ducks back into the galley. He pours himself a cup of coffee and sits down. Chris scuffs in. He goes for the coffee also and dumps three spoons of sugar in half a cup. He sits opposite.

'I'm thinking I could eat something.' He says this like it is a peace offering. 'You want cereal?'

John shakes his head.

Chris gets up and pours himself a bowl of cornflakes and one for John anyhow. 'Take, eat,' Chris says.

When the bowl is in front of him, John pours milk and starts eating. He lifts the spoon to his mouth mechanically and stares at the table. He is still angry at Chris for the way things went with his father. John had started the steam out as usual. A few hours later, he had Chris set the net so they'd have some fish in the hold. In case anyone asked what they were doing, they could say fishing. Of course, Fitz woke the second he heard the net, and he stalked into the wheelhouse, bellowing something like Where the hell are we and what the hell are you thinking? About then, Chris came in.

The old man turned on him. 'Who told you to set the net? You never do first set without my say-so. Where the hell's everyone? Why didn't you wake me?'

Chris looked at Fitz evenly. Eyes on Fitz, he said to John, 'I thought you were going to take care of this.'

John didn't answer right away. His father was right:

239

traditionally, superstitiously, first set was the group of them, on Fitz's order. And he didn't like Chris's tone, as if the old man was an annoying child come sleepily downstairs, in the middle of his parents' dinner party, to be handled quickly and quietly, shuffled back to his bedroom with a pat on his pajama bottoms and an extra glass of water.

'I thought you told him,' Chris said.

'Told me what?' Fitz said. 'What didn't you tell me?'

'Did you tell him or not, John?'

John looked past his father, out at the cables slicing the water. There was little wind, and no white curl beyond their wake. The sea undulated like a sluggish oil, and the water was the color of mercury spilled from a broken thermometer.

'Come on, Dad. You know what we're doing.'

Fitz stared hard at the floor.

Chris lit a cigarette. 'Are we clear?'

'Dad? We clear?'

Fitz shook his head once.

'Come on, Dad. We discussed this.' They had discussed it, after a fashion. They'd been out all day at the Wind, tying one on, and while they were walking home, John mentioned the possibility. Fitz had mumbled, 'Do what you have to, I don't want to know.' But he understood, and John knew he understood, and he hadn't said no, so John had told Chris to go ahead and make the contact. 'You didn't say no to this before.'

'Well, I've changed my goddamn mind.'

John looked to Chris. Chris smoked casually, like a man waiting for a bus he didn't really need to catch. 'He can't do that,' he finally said.

'Like hell I can't. It's my boat.' Fitz made for the wheel.

'John—' Chris warned.

John, embarrassed, pushed his father off with one arm. The old man stumbled back, then surprised John with a roundhouse punch to the jaw.

'Jesus!' John licked his lip and tasted blood in the corner. He touched his chin tenderly. 'Jesus.'

Fitz bobbled by the door, dukes half up. 'Come on, son.'

'I'm not gonna fight you. You want to go back, we'll go back.' John turned the wheel slightly, just for show. Chris reached out and stopped him.

'We're committed, John.'

John jutted his sore chin at Fitz. 'He doesn't want to. It's his boat.'

Chris ticked his tongue like a disapproving old aunt. 'You do realize what these people are like, don't you? They don't like welchers. It's a matter of trust. They took on a certain amount of risk just asking us to do this job. They don't know us from Adam. Now if we don't come through, they'll think we played them. They'll get angry.'

'Fine,' Fitz said. 'Let them get angry.'

'They won't get angry at you,' Chris said. 'No one gives a shit about you. John and I have been kind enough to keep your name out of things. As far as the big men are concerned, John is the captain of this little jaunt. So if anything about this doesn't go down, he's the one they'll come for. I think that was quite the filial sacrifice on his part, don't you? You wouldn't want to see your son hurt, now, would you?'

John said, 'No one's getting hurt.'

Chris pointed to him and said, 'You don't know your ass from your elbow.' To Fitz, he said, 'As far as they're concerned, you're just some drunk. You don't have any control. You're about as relevant as Walley.'

That shut the old man up. Chris told them from here on in, he'd be making the decisions and he'd give them information on a strictly need-to-know basis. Now Fitz is in his bunk, refusing to drive, and Walley has the wheel. They have given up on the charade of fishing, and with a few hundred pounds of mixed garbage in the hold, they have pulled up the nets and secured them.

In retrospect, John sees he should have handled things much differently, yet he can't figure out what he should have done. He has been going over it in his mind, and he's come to the conclusion that he let Chris take over due to a lack of fluency on his own part. It is as if when the decisions were being made, he became voiceless. If he had more of an affinity with words, he could have come up with something convincing. He could have convinced his father of one thing, or Chris of another. Or perhaps he never would have listened to Chris in the first place. He is too easily bowled over by arguments. But then again, he has never been very verbal. He has always been more capable with his hands. It seems he has used more language in the last few days than he has in his whole life, yet here he still is.

Chris spoons sugar on top of his cornflakes. He spoons and spoons until the sugar makes a little cone. The milk creeps up, changing the cone from white to clear.

'Check that,' he says.

Together they watch to see how far the milk gets before Chris sticks his spoon in, straight through the sugar. It sounds like sand between his teeth. After two bites he puts his spoon down. 'Is it cold out?'

'Yeah,' John says. 'Dress warm.'

Chris smiles as though what John said has touched him. 'You still worry about me.'

'I don't worry about you at all.'

'Okay, you don't.' Chris lights himself a cigarette. 'You're still pissed.'

'You were an asshole to my father.'

Chris carries their bowls to the sink. There, he says, 'Let me tell you something about your father – A: he's a drunk; B: if he wasn't okay with this, we wouldn't be here.'

'You don't know anything.'

'I know more than you, apparently.' Washing takes two hands, so Chris has to keep the butt tucked in the

242

corner of his mouth. He squints against the smoke and speaks in a close-lipped fashion. 'I know you hate me right now.'

'I don't hate you,' John says, though at the moment he does hate Chris a little.

'In your mind, or maybe even out loud, you have a need to vilify me. And that's what you should do – I'm not denying you that one bit. Go right ahead, buddy, lay the blame on me. I'll be the scapegoat. I'll be the sacrificial lamb. In hard times someone has to make the hard choices, and it's just natural that that person isn't liked by those he has to make the hard choices for. It's okay. I'll take the blame and you take the benefits. But remember, I do this for you.'

The radio in the wheelhouse crackles. A man's voice comes on. At first John can't make it out, and he gets up to hear better. A moment later, Walley sticks his head down the companionway.

'We're being hailed. I don't know who it is.'

'You see him?' John doesn't wait for an answer. He runs up to the wheelhouse to look for himself. The radar shows a blip directly ahead, though the boat is not yet visible through the binocs. Walley hovers over his shoulder. The radio squawks again, *Bonjour, 'allo, 'allo*. Something more follows. Though he took French in high school, John is at a loss. He can't tell where one word ends and another begins.

'What's he saying?' Walley asks.

'How the hell should I know?'

'Shouldn't we answer?' Before John can decide, Walley speaks into the radio. 'Hello? Hello? Hello? This is the fishing vessel *Pearl*.' He looks at John worriedly, as if he is afraid he is doing the wrong thing even as he continues. 'We don't speak French,' he yells into the transmitter.

There is a moment of silence, then the man says, 'Yes, hello. We will meet with you. You keep coming.' His English is very bad.

'Are these the people we're supposed to meet?' Walley asks.

'I don't know. We'll see.' He pushes Walley away from the wheel. 'Get Chris.'

Chris comes up, and all three of them look out. The sky is gray, and the shallow waves shimmer like silver scales. Eventually a black spot appears on the horizon. They watch it grow, turn white, and take on the shape of a cutter.

'Are these the people we're supposed to meet?' John asks Chris.

He takes the binoculars from John. After a while he says, 'I don't know.'

'Aren't you supposed to know?' John says.

'We were supposed to meet them in a certain spot.'

'Is this the spot?'

Chris hesitates. During the planning stages, Chris was vague on specifics. When John pressed him for details, he reiterated his belief that the less John knew, the less he could accidentally tell. He'd told John ignorance was safety. He said the meet would be about a half day from Miquelon, and they are, in fact, about a half day off.

'Well, is this the spot?' John asks.

'Sort of.' Chris consults the chart. He points to a position a couple of hours south. 'That's more the spot.'

'We're past there.' John hits the chart, and Walley jumps.

'Chill, chill,' Chris says.

John lowers his voice. 'When were you going to mention it?'

'I didn't realize where we were, man. I was sleeping.' He gives John a withering look. 'You were supposed to wake me up.'

'When were we supposed to be there?' Walley asks.

'About now.'

'So these may be the people,' Walley suggests.

'Maybe,' Chris says, looking through the binocs again. 'We'll see.'

John stares at him. It comes to him that he has given his life over to this man. He has given all their lives over to this man who hasn't enough sense to worry about his own skin, much less anyone else's. A man without enough sense to set an alarm clock. He considers laying Chris out. But they are in the middle of nowhere, in foreign waters, heading toward who knows what, and Chris is the only one with any information.

'I can't believe you,' John says. 'I can't believe this whole fucking thing.'

'John, man,' Chris says, 'these things are generally much more casual than you're making them out to be. Half the time people don't show, and the other half the time they're late.' Chris gives this a few moments to sink in, but John is not appeased. Either things are dangerous or not, either they are casual or not. He doesn't know which story to believe.

Walley is squinting through the binocs. 'They look sort of official.'

'What does that mean?' Chris says.

'Maybe they're Coasties.'

'Do you even know what Miquelonian Coasties look like? They probably don't even have them,' Chris tells Walley. 'Listen to me, John. We're in great shape. Think about it. Luck is on our side. If we had picked up back there, we'd be heading straight for that boat with weight on board. It's much better this way, don't you think? If they're the meet, good. If they're some kind of official, we're clean. Am I right?'

'You're an asshole.'

'We'll see about that too,' Chris says. He lights himself a fresh cigarette.

John keeps track of the cutter through the binoculars. Her decks are clear of any fishing gear and her paint is fresh. As she gets even closer, John can see, on the front of the hull, some kind of insignia, like a seal, or the symbol on a medallion. It has been painted over, or maybe has faded from the sun and sea.

'They look official,' Walley says again, quietly.

John gives Chris a chance to look through the binoculars. Then he says, 'Are these or aren't these the people we're supposed to meet?'

'I don't know, John. Do you want me to get on the radio and ask? Hey, are you the drug dealers we're supposed to meet, or some kind of border patrol? We're wondering whether we're supposed to get some heroin from you or not.'

'You should go below,' John tells him.

'What the fuck.'

'You're high as a kite.'

'I'm not high. I just fucking woke up.'

'What if they are border patrol?' Walley says.

Chris waves him away. 'Jesus, Wal, you're a pain in my ass. You're a fucking old woman, you know that?'

'But we have fish,' Walley says.

'Fish aren't illegal.'

'Depends on where they're from,' Walley says. 'We're not in legal waters.'

'Our net's on deck. Our doors are off. We got them on the legal side. We're clear,' Chris says.

'We can't prove that,' Walley says. 'It's not like the fish have U.S. stamped on them.' He pushes his glasses up his nose. 'And anyhow, wouldn't bringing fish over the border be illegal import? If they want to give us trouble they could.'

'So we get fined. Just shut the fuck up. Try to be cool,' Chris says.

Chris looks cool. John thinks too cool. He looks artificially cool, and John is convinced Chris is still high. And if these men are officials, and they board the *Pearl*, there is more here than fish. There is Chris's stash. He seems to have forgotten all about it, perhaps because it isn't in his pocket, it's in John's. As soon as he gets aboard, Chris stops taking responsibility for his own habit. They are trusting this man who can't even remember his own habit.

'Where are your works?' John asks him.

'Secured.'

'Where are they?'

'They're secure, all right?'

'What the fuck does secure mean?'

'Secure means secure. Don't worry about it.'

'I want you to get rid of them.'

'No fucking way.'

'Get them up here and get them overboard now.' John keeps his face stern. When Chris doesn't move he adds, 'I'm throwing your shit over.' He grabs a U-bolt from the junk shelf.

'No way.'

'Yes way. Walley—' John makes a break for the starboard rail, leaving the wheel to Walley.

'No way!' Chris chases John. 'No way!'

John pulls the bag of dope from his pocket and Chris grabs for it. John jerks it away and turns his back. He keeps the bag close to his chest and he jumps from side to side, while Chris feints and reaches. Chris says, 'Come on, man. Not funny. Gimme.'

The foreign boat is about a half mile off now. If they are looking through binoculars they can see Chris and John scuffling on deck. Perhaps they can even see that the scuffle is over a small package. John twists from Chris's grip and lets the bag, weighted with the U-bolt, drop. The rattling engine covers the splash. For a second John feels as if he's finally won a long and tiresome game.

'I'll kill you,' Chris says sadly.

Walley, who peeks from the door of the wheelhouse, looks from Chris to John and back to Chris. 'He had to, Chris. In case they're Coasties.'

Chris moans, 'They're not fucking Coasties.' He looks as if he is about to cry.

'What if they are?'

'Walley,' John says, 'get back in there and drive.'

A quarter mile off, the white cutter swings around and drives toward them at an intersecting angle. When she is close enough for them to see the faces of the two men aboard, the one on deck speaks his terrible English through a megaphone. 'Slow yourselfs. We are coming along the side of you.'

He wears an expensive jacket made of red water-proof material with white rubber zippers and a removable lining. Back home it is the sort of foulie gear yachties wear. But on his head is a black watch cap and on his feet are rubber boots, and his face is the weathered brown of a fisher. The other man, in the wheelhouse, is similarly dressed. The man with the megaphone doesn't show a badge, but he moves his jacket in such a way as to reveal a leather halter around his shoulder and ribcage. Though John doesn't see a gun, he is convinced this man, and probably the other, has one.

'Get my dad,' John says to Walley. He takes the wheel and slows her. Fitz and Walley come up just as the cutter lets three fenders, like white lozenges, over the side. The two boats throttle down and bump gently together. John lets Walley take the wheel again, and he walks to the rail with Chris. Fitz stands a little bit off, as if he isn't interested in the proceedings. But John knows he is listening. The man who spoke through the megaphone asks to see their passports. John collects their wallets and passes them over.

'We only have driver's licenses,' he explains.

The man takes his time looking at their wallets, then he passes them back. 'You realize you are far from home?' He speaks only to John.

'Yes.'

'You are in French waters now.'

'Yes,' John says.

'Some people thinks this is Canada. But we're in

France here.' The man laughs and looks at his friend at the wheel, who can't possibly hear him.

'Yes,' John says.

'Where are you going?'

John decides truth is best. He answers, 'Miquelon.'

'For what purpose?' the man asks.

'To visit a friend,' Chris interrupts. The man glances sharply at him, then turns back to John.

'You have been fishing? If we come aboard we will find fish?'

'Yes,' John says. 'But we got them in U.S. waters.'

'And you are going to Miquelon to sell these fish?'

John isn't sure what the correct answer would be. Would it be better to pretend they are simply selling fish? He doesn't know if there is a market in Miquelon, though there must be. But would that be illegal importation? He looks to his father, but the old man doesn't help him out. He reminds himself that technically they've done nothing wrong yet, and these men may not be officials.

'No,' John says.

'They will be no good by the time you get home.'

'They keep okay on the ice.'

The man shakes his head. 'I don't understand. Why fish on the way here if you do not sell them here? I would fish on the way home, no? Then the fish would be fresh.'

'It's not a lot of fish.'

'Still it seems a waste, no? To fish, then to go somewhere you will not sell them.'

'We had a sudden change of plans,' Chris says.

'Ah.' The man gasps as if he suddenly understands. 'Well. We will take you in, yes? We will escort you?'

They are still a number of hours from Miquelon, and it was never part of the plan for them to land there. John looks at Chris, and Chris nods imperceptibly.

'We will escort you,' the man says, climbing aboard. It is not a question.

The man drives the *Pearl* and his partner keeps pace in the cutter. Four, then five hours pass. The sun climbs overhead, then sinks to port. Walley and Chris sit on the lazarette drinking coffee and Fitz stands at the starboard rail. At some point John tries to approach his father, but the man moves forward, so John leaves him alone. He can't sit comfortably as Chris and Walley do, with the gunman driving his father's boat. Still, he is afraid to enter the wheelhouse and do something about it. Likewise he is afraid to go below. He finds himself wandering the deck, looking out at the glowing water.

They come upon Miquelon as if by accident. It rises from the sea suddenly; like money dropped in the road, it seems a careless mistake. The French passed through, then forgot this land. Walley and Chris join John by the rail. At first the island is just a blue hump; as they get closer the blue shades into grays and browns, then shifts again to dull yellows and pale rippling greens – dry grass blowing over rock is what they see when they get close enough.

'Wow,' Walley says.

The barrenness shocks John, too. Miquelon has no trees. He is used to land looking more like land. With some protection. Trees and bends in the roads to keep the eye from going on and on as it does at sea. Land is supposed to relieve you of that endless kind of vision. But Miquelon may as well be the ocean for all its openness. He can't help shaking his head.

'Some crazy-ass shit, right?' Chris says.

They round a bend and a house comes into view, then another. Then a street of houses. They are small and vinyl-sided, but the siding looks new, as do the roofs and windows. The lawns are well kept and the treeless yards are decorated with sculptures: plaster geese and gnomes, ceramic deer and cement swans with holes in their backs for sprays of artificially bright ivies and geraniums; wood cutouts of women

250

bent over, their old-fashioned knickers peeking from under red polka-dot dresses. Plastic squirrels are nailed to the new roofs. Butterflies the size of dogs fly up the walls. Pinwheel daisies spin in the flower beds, protecting rows of fabric roses from aluminum crows.

Not everything is false. The expensive trucks and vintage motorcycles that sit on the freshly tarred driveways are real, as are the boats alongside the private docks. Some are refashioned draggers, but many have nothing to do with commercial fishing: cigarette boats and cabin cruisers, sportfishers, a brand-new Boston Whaler.

'Those are like a thousand dollars a foot,' Walley says. 'I saw a twenty-foot one for twenty thousand.'

'You did not, you retard. They cost a fuck load more'n that.'

They pass a house with a fleet of Triumphs in an open garage.

'That can't be cheap,' Walley says.

Around another point the houses clot into a small town. John reads the French signs as they pass – *poste, boulangerie, patisserie, pharmacie, tabac* – all clustered where two roads cross at a fountain. On the public pier the boats are again impressive, especially considering there has been a moratorium on fishing here for over five years.

A man waits for them at the dock. Their escort directs John to toss him the docklines, and the man catches them casually, throwing the loops over the bollards almost without looking. The cutter ties up behind. They are directed to step off the boat, the man who caught their docklines comes forward smiling.

'*Bonjour, bonjour!*' He takes John by the elbow and shakes his hand vigorously. He shakes hands all around and looks genuinely happy to see them, as if they are long-lost cousins finally come home to the bosom of family.

'This is Mr. LaFortune,' their escort says.

251

'Sylvain.' The man taps himself on the chest.

John wonders if he is the boss, and if he is the person they were supposed to meet, or if he is some kind of town official, like a French equivalent of sheriff. Maybe he is the harbormaster. Maybe they are to go through customs. He is a large, healthy-looking man, anywhere between forty and seventy. He wears no uniform – just a thick sweater and worn canvas jeans. His gloves look new, and his boots were expensive once. His hair is not slicked back like a gangster's – it is hidden under an amateurishly knit cap, the type made by a wife or daughter as a gift. He has no gold teeth or jewelry, nor does he show a badge. No gun bulges his waistband.

'John Fitz,' John says. He introduces them all, and when he gets to his father he says, 'Warren Fitz, my father.'

'*Votre père?*' Sylvain LaFortune nods and widens his eyes. He pumps Fitz's hand again. '*Bonjour, mon vieux.*' He keeps the old man's hand long after he's done shaking it.

A dark-haired teenager stands behind LaFortune and he puts his arm around the boy's shoulder and pulls him forward. 'C'est mon fils, Mathieu. *Il est agé de quatorze ans.*'

John translates to his father that this is his fourteen-year-old son and his name is Mathieu. LaFortune says something else; he beams at Fitz, nodding, as if prompting Fitz to respond. Fitz looks at John, but John has reached the end of his French. LaFortune apparently wants Fitz to shake his son's hand, which Fitz does sullenly.

'Mathieu,' LaFortune says, expectantly.

'Mathieu,' Fitz repeats. Mat-chu. Like achoo.

The pier is otherwise desolate, as is the town. The emptiness worries John. Everything here is too new and quiet. It is as if the trucks and boats and lawn ornaments have only recently appeared on this tiny

252

island, moments before the *Pearl* pulled up. They seem to have arrived a bit ahead of their cue. The stage crew, in their hurry to disappear into the wings, have forgotten items. Trees, birds, people. Gum on the sidewalk, trash in the barrels. LaFortune looks over John's shoulder as if reading the lips of some hidden prompter, and when John turns, their escort is gone. He must have climbed back into the cutter, but the swiftness with which he vanished makes it feel, to John, as if he dropped off the pier.

Somehow the day has passed. The fat orange sun is sinking, turning the sea purple and gold. LaFortune, through gestures and his son's interpretation, invites them to his house for supper. *À dîner chez LaFortune.* This, too, is not a question. They follow the man and his dark son through the empty town and up the empty road.

LaFortune lives at the end. Just past his house is a red-and-white *arrêt* sign, then the asphalt fades to a trail of broken shells. Farther up the scrubby bluff it becomes a dirt track and finally, at the peak, just a worn line in the tall grasses. He takes them all the way up – it is only another ten minutes, he says – to show his view. That's how Mathieu translates it, for the view. LaFortune talks the whole time, directing his comments to Fitz, who bumps along behind him, head down. They stop at the crest of the small hill, Fitz huffing around his cigar hard enough to worry John, Walley huddled near Chris as if for protection from the wind or something more sinister – his left eye has taken what looks like permanent roost in its upper outside corner.

The wind at the top is deadly. As far as the eye can see, there is nothing to break it. It's a straight shot to the sea. The wind whips up from the waves; first the spray bursts over the granite, then the grass bows and ripples, then they are smacked in the face and their eyes tear.

LaFortune sweeps his arm, pointing out things faster than Mathieu can translate. John only catches a name or two, enough to know they are missing things. The Frenchman points out St. John's, New York, Paris. Nothing anyone can see, just their directions. From here you have to take the existence of the rest of the world on faith.

'What's he saying?' Fitz asks John.

'Nothing, just that we're a far ways from everything.'

Walley whispers, 'Is he the right guy?'

Chris hushes him.

'*Ça ressemble à un grand chemin, non? Une route.*' LaFortune pantomimes stepping off the cliff and walking over the water. Mathieu translates, a big highway, and John sees he means the reflection of the setting sun on the waves. It looks like a molten road.

'I can't understand a damn word he's saying,' Fitz complains.

LaFortune jabbers on, pointing this way, that way. He spreads his hands, makes shapes with his fingers.

'What's he saying now?'

John doesn't answer. He lets Mathieu translate.

'He says the French they used to get their salt cod from here and St. Pierre.' Mathieu and his father go on about the territory, its history and value, the two-hundred-mile limit.

Half-remembered lesson phrases bubble to the surface of John's mind. One pops and *Où est le petit chien?* fills his mouth and it is all he can do to not burst forth with it. *Le petit chien est sur le bateau, sur la mer, sur ma tête.* Absurdist garbles. He remembers studying in the library with Yve. She was two grades behind him, but they had the same French class. She was the better student. He'd get bored studying, and grab her around the waist and try to pull her between the stacks.

Mathieu now says, 'We have not fished in five years.' He holds up five fingers.

'Ahh.' Fitz nods. He glances at John, but John cannot read his father's expression. The old man looks small in the open landscape.

LaFortune spreads his arms out and looks expectantly at Fitz. '*C'est magnifique, non?*'

Fitz spreads his arms also. 'It's a rock, old man. You live on a goddamn rock.' He shouts his words. He nods as if they are in agreement.

John looks at Mathieu. The boy picks up a stone and throws it into the sea.

'Shut up,' Chris says. 'Tell your dad to shut up.'

'Dad, shh.'

'A rock! You know rock?' Fitz keeps shouting and nodding.

'I know rock.' LaFortune smiles slowly. He lifts his brow – *Aha! Et voilà! Je comprends tout.* He looks at them one by one. He says in careful English, 'You should be more careful, eh? Who hears what you say, you never know. *Tu comprends?*'

Fitz looks defiant, and John worries his father might hit the Frenchman.

'I'm sure he didn't mean anything,' John begins.

LaFortune holds his finger up. John closes his mouth. He can feel Walley panicking behind him, but he doesn't turn. The grass is pink from the setting sun. LaFortune pulls up his sweater, one hand scratching his hairy belly. He starts laughing. Mathieu laughs too. They take their time about it, laughing themselves out. Finally, LaFortune punches John in the shoulder.

'You, don't tell your father to shh, eh?' He winks. 'We go eat now.'

LaFortune places Fitz at the head of the table and himself at the foot. John finds himself with Chris beside him, across from Mathieu and Walley. Walley looks pale and he drinks his wine before the toast. *À la tienne.*

It's a table of only men. Madame LaFortune doesn't

sit; she serves from the kitchen. She is a short round woman, her movements bustling as if each thing she does is important. Her upper arms waggle when she carries the stewpot high in front of her ample bosoms. They are like a shelf, those breasts, and her cardigan buttons tightly across. She totters on thick-heeled shoes. Her hair is thin and purplish and she wears a full face of colorful makeup. Her legs are thick, her rump is round as a sofa cushion. LaFortune grabs a handful as she passes and squeezes.

'*C'est bon ça eh?*' LaFortune raises his glass. 'When she was young—'

He seems to enjoy their company. He sends a different wine around with every course, and around again whenever glasses are empty. Fitz's cheeks grow warm. Madame LaFortune's food – monkfish stew, bread, green salad, cheese and apples sliced on a plate – is good enough to make him think of Pearl and her cooking. LaFortune stands and makes toasts: to business, to partnership, to family, to new friends. Fitz begins to get a drunk on. Despite the accent, old man LaFortune reminds him of other fishermen. They talk, with their sons as intercessors, of fishing and the shame of not fishing and the need to do other things to keep body and soul together. If the situation were different, Fitz could see himself buying this Frenchman a beer. As the meal slows, LaFortune wanders away from the table, glass in hand, roaming the living and dining rooms. He names and explains his furniture. The bureau, imported from France, a wedding gift. Actual French Provincial. *Bien sûr.* The credenza – from Montreal.

'Here we go!' The Frenchman hunches his big shoulders conspiratorially, scurries to a large armoire, and opens it. Heavy doors pull back, revealing the stereo, the TV. *Voilà!* The entertainment center! It is situated perfectly between the living and dining rooms for viewing while dining. He turns both on, the stereo and the TV, and returns to his chair with three remotes. He demonstrates them all, pressing buttons and changing stations, volume, CDs, before finally resting with a black-and-white rerun of *I Love Lucy* in Italian and an oompah band on the stereo.

'All the latest,' he says. 'I have a—' He turns to his son, '*Comment dit-on*?'

'Satellite dish.'

'Exactly. In the back. Five hundred channels.' He pops up, two-steps to the living-room window, feet keeping time with the tuba. Oom-pah, oompah-pah. He pulls back the lace curtains so they too can see.

'It's too dark.' He frowns. 'Come, I show you the garage.' Fitz is strong-armed from his chair. John follows. Walley and Chris stay at the table with the son, watching Lucy and Ricky argue.

To get to the garage, they pass through the kitchen. Madame LaFortune sits at the small table, smoking and nodding her head at the TV on the counter. Twists of toilet paper wind between her toes and she holds her legs stiffly in front of her, her heels balanced on the tile. Purple nail polish sits on the table. On the TV a blond woman speaks very fast French.

The garage houses the washer, the dryer, the extra freezer. LaFortune opens their doors, then fiddles with the knobs to show their special features. Water rushes into the washer, the dryer spins, the freezer hums. He translates the price of everything into dollars U.S. Sometimes he holds up his fingers to show the numbers. He has them sit in the Mercedes, Fitz in front, John in back. He raises and lowers windows with buttons, hits a lever hidden under the dash and the trunk sighs open. He turns on the radio. Digital numbers scroll in blue on the tiny screen. He presses another button and Fitz's seat becomes warm. It feels strange, as if he's pissed himself. Fitz says 'Hoho!' and nearly jumps out.

'That's something, eh?' LaFortune's pride is obvious.

He seems surprised by his own good luck. Not to fault him for it, Fitz thinks he would probably act the same with such a car.

LaFortune tells John to pass forward a small polished box he finds in the backseat. 'Cuban. The best.' He hands a cigar to Fitz. Fitz runs it under his nose – a rich mix of chocolate and leather – before he pockets it.

'You will like that.' LaFortune pats Fitz on the knee.

'Be hard not to.'

'Come.' LaFortune takes them out the automatic door and into the front yard. The wind has picked up, and the moon looks small and far away. John folds his arms around himself; his hands are cold. He wonders about Chris and Walley alone with Mathieu in the dining room. What are they getting into?

LaFortune points out his mailbox, the marble walk. The grass is short, sharp, and brown. It crunches beneath John's boots like breaking plastic. He must watch his feet carefully: the lawn, like all those on the short street, is littered with gnomes and mushrooms and other figures. On top of the chain-link fences that divide the properties, windmilling geegaws whir and spin. The wind shifts and a wooden milkmaid on the fence behind John clacks into a new position. Her arms milk with a furious passion and the cow's tail whips around. Her clack is followed by the chop of a lumberjack in the next yard, then by a dog wagging, a goose flying, a couple dancing. They clack down the lines of fencing. John follows the wind through all the yards and shifting wooden figures – clackclackclack, like an invisible factory line. The wind amusing itself.

LaFortune has run out of things to show. He stops over a circle of dirt with some thorny shrubs. His roses. 'Louis had the same at Versailles. Only the best.'

'Versailles?' Fitz says.

'Versailles.' LaFortune's finger pierces the air. 'The best.'

258

'The best.'

John squints through the twilight at his father.

LaFortune takes them back through the front door, this time ringing the bell. It plays the first notes of the *Marseillaise*.

From the living room, if he leans a bit, John can catch a glimpse of the dining-room table. Walley, Chris, and Mathieu are still there, watching the TV. Ricky still yells at Lucy, but the oompah band on the stereo has been replaced by a French news station.

'Good boys.' LaFortune wanders to a built-in hutch near the stairs. It houses a collection of music boxes. 'You like this?'

John nods out of politeness.

'Listen. *Écoutez.*' LaFortune winds them all. Porcelain monkeys and crying children in rainy bubbles, ballerinas, mirrored boxes. He does a little dance with a china clown in one hand and a carousel in the other, prancing to the mix of tinkling music. Fitz bobs his head, smiling. The tunes clash with each other, with the French newscaster, with Lucy Ricardo crying.

LaFortune puts the carousel on its shelf. He's remembered something. He lifts up his sweater. 'And this belt! Cardin! Pierre Cardin!' He laughs, and Fitz laughs with him.

Finally the music boxes wind down, one at a time; the laughing slows, stops. By contrast, the house seems quiet, with only the two TVs and the stereo. LaFortune puts the clown back on the shelf. He searches the room, then his eyes light on the mantel.

'Here. This is the best.'

The crowded shelf is lined with pictures of the family standing in front of their house, in front of their boat, in front of the Eiffel Tower. There is a girl in them all, a daughter John figures, an older sister to Mathieu. LaFortune selects a picture of the girl alone. It's nicely matted and framed, the type taken in a professional studio with soft lights. Someone has retouched the skin and the lips with a pinkish shade. She looks pretty. John would ask who she is, but she clearly isn't here and you never know with photos on mantels. She could be dead.

'My daughter, Sélène. *Très jolie, eh?*'

'*Oui,*' John says.

LaFortune slaps him on the shoulder. Grabs hold and shakes, a bit hard for all his friendly laughing. 'She is not for you, my man.' He lets John go, roughly. 'She is at university, in Paris. Very busy girl, very smart. She studies law international.' His eyes dart over the photo. 'No fisherman for her.'

'University in Paris. That must cost a lot,' Fitz says.

He wants to talk the cost of things more. It becomes clear to John that this was the best way, after all, to convince his father. He wonders if LaFortune knows what he is doing, then he figures he must. After all, LaFortune must need them. Or he would not go to all this effort. Perhaps this is the typical first meeting, a sort of pep rally. Or perhaps he just likes company. Maybe he is tired of his neighbors. Maybe he can't impress them with his purchases, because they, also smugglers, are rich in things. John and Fitz may just be fresh meat. It doesn't matter. John thinks his father and LaFortune are not so different. Fitz wears the Cuban cigar in his breast pocket like a medal. He'll let it go stale and smoke it in the Wind before he'll smoke it here where no one from back home can see.

LaFortune puts the photo back on the mantel. 'No. University is free. So our children won't have to stay on this rock.' He exhales sharply, as if he's trying to laugh, but has run out of steam. 'So!' He claps his hands. The noise seems overly loud. Someone has turned off the radio.

'We should be thinking about going soon,' John says.

Mathieu gets up and turns off the TV manually. Chris stares at the receding blue dot, then black screen. Walley, freed, looks around for John, anyone.

LaFortune frowns, tips his head like a puppy trying to understand human words. '*Mais non.* You will stay tonight and leave in the morning. We still have discussion, preparation. And Marie is making for you a special breakfast. Her brioche is very good. You cannot miss it, she would be insulted.'

19

Lying in bed, Yve presses her ear to the wall. Her father's bedside radio clicks, then comes on. Her parents sigh and shift. The bedsprings creak. Her mother makes the most noise, as if waking is yet another burden to be borne, and she wants it known by all that she is bearing it. Yve listens to her mother get up, find her robe and her slippers. She waits for the groan of the stairs – her mother going down to the kitchen – before getting up herself. Her father is still in bed, propped half up, eyes half closed. She pictures his hand twitching on the bedclothes as the news weaves in and out of his fitful dreams.

Yve dresses in the dark. Wool stockings, a long-john undershirt, a turtleneck. She pulls on her Irish knit sweater – it smells of beef stock and onions – then she slides her heavy tartan skirt underneath. She listens at the door: water in the kettle, the cabinet opened and shut – her mother is making coffee. She dashes across the hall to the bathroom and locks the door behind her. Downstairs, Alma has one ear cocked to the ceiling, tracking her daughter's flurry of movement.

Yve brushes her teeth carefully. She washes her face. She considers her reflection, touching her lips. They feel full – when she presses her fingertips to them, an image of Wen shivers through her. When she removes her fingers, her mouth feels as though something is missing.

Behind the closed bathroom door, she listens again

for her mother. Alma's slippers whisper on the stairs, shuffle across the hall, pause in front of the bathroom door. Yve listens to her mother listening. The door thins and becomes a membrane, and they listen for each other's heartbeats. Yve thinks of Wen kissing her. Alma moves away. The bedroom door opens and shuts. A soft complaint, weight on the bed, a coffee cup is placed on her father's nightstand. Yve scoots through the hall, runs down the stairs, and grabs her coat on the way out.

The bay is black, the streets are empty. The gaslamps shine on nothing. The air smells thick and damp, like wet leaves. The chill goes right through her. As her mother warned, it will rain sometime today, and she's forgotten an umbrella. Her boots slap the cobbles, and the sound ripples out and echoes against the blank-faced buildings. Rounding the corner to Cherry, she hears the rush, roar, wind of a truck. A white Ford pickup, with antlers on the grill, crosses the street and disappears. That would be Wen, up early also and leaving before breakfast.

20

Fitz got the bed in Mathieu's room – Mathieu slept on the living-room sofa – and the rest of them spent the night on cots in LaFortune's basement. Walley slept easily, but Chris claimed he was ill, and he woke John often. Sometime around three, he began to hallucinate. John took him outside so he wouldn't wake the rest. They sat on the back step and the cement was cold, and John put his arm around Chris's shoulder and rubbed his back to keep him warm. Chris smoked all his cigarettes. After breakfast, Chris vomited quietly in the basement toilet. He told John he'd meet them at the boat, he needed more cigarettes, but LaFortune said no, they all go to the boats together. He gave John a carton of Marlboros for Chris, and told him they could have more if they wished – he has cases in his garage.

Now, down at the harbor, great plumes of fog lift off the water and obscure the open sea beyond, as if someone has drawn a curtain around the island. Nevertheless, the town is awake and bustling. At first this worries John – so many men on the docks, women and children waiting in the square for hellos or good-byes. But no one seems to notice their small party, and LaFortune is casual about sending them off, taking his time and joking as if he is reluctant to let them go now that he's finally gotten to know them. He points out his *Marie Deux*, a luxurious party boat. He pretends to be humble about her, but her topside gleams with brass and brightwork. She obviously has no purpose but pleasure.

'That had to cost a pretty penny,' Fitz says, but his voice is dark, as if the admission was solicited against his will.

LaFortune shrugs. The original Marie, his wife, beams as if she is the boat and the boat is she. Something catches the Frenchman's eye, and he nods to his son. '*Eh! Qu'est-ce que c'est—?*'

A group of teens has just gotten in. They've caught a shark and now are shouting curses and laughing through the off-loading as if it's all a big joke, they never meant to get the fish, but now there she is to be dealt with. They wave to Mathieu and he goes over. Slapping hands and backs takes a few moments, then he helps guide the laden net to the pier. They flip the dark body onto a dolly and wrestle the net out from under. The shark flops in that heavy way of dead meat, stiff and flaccid at once.

'So you know where to go?' LaFortune asks Fitz.

John looks at Chris. His skin is pasty, and he holds his body as if his bones are broken.

'Sure,' Chris says. LaFortune ignores him.

'Sure,' John says.

'I'm talking to your father,' LaFortune says.

'Sure,' Fitz says, miserably, because he doesn't. None of them do, except for Chris, who will tell them on a need-to-know basis only. Fitz can scarcely recall the drunken fun of last night, and now he feels hungover, but that isn't the problem, he's been hungover before. He feels something else he doesn't have a name for. His chest feels like an open pit.

A collective shout rises from the other pier. They all look over at the shark. The boys are poking at it, opening its mouth for a gander at the teeth.

'Maybe we should not do business today,' LaFortune says. He is watching his son. Mathieu has his knife out and he is cutting at the shark's jaw. The other boys bend over him, giving advice.

'Why not?' John says.

'Your friend is sick.'

'Who's sick?' Walley asks.

'That one.' LaFortune nods at Chris.

'You're not sick,' John tells Chris.

'I'm not sick.'

'*Putain. Il est un drogué, a junkie.*'

'He's not a junkie,' John says.

'Maybe you're right, old man,' Fitz says. 'Maybe we should call it quits.'

LaFortune turns slowly away from the shark and looks to Fitz. 'This is my family business; you understand that?'

John waits for his father to respond. He waits and finally Fitz nods.

'I have no room for mistakes. This is not a boy's game, *comprenez?*'

'Comprendo,' Fitz says.

'You don't start this kind of thing and not finish,' LaFortune tells him. He frowns.

Fitz doesn't answer. He looks down the pier again, at the man's son. The boys have the shark free of the net and now they trundle it on a dolly down the pier, one steering in front, one in back, the others gathered around to keep it from bouncing off. The wheels clatter on the uneven boards. The snout is red, as is the gash in its side. They've taken the teeth; they've also sliced off the fin, and now a boy holds it over his head like a hat to get a few laughs. Another snatches it and places it on his bent back, rushing toward a crowd of schoolgirls standing on the shore. They screech and giggle and run away.

'I have a certain job to do,' LaFortune says. 'My boss – the big boss – says these people are coming, and I meet you. He says this is a nice family. I have you in my house. Now it seems this was a bad idea.'

Fitz touches the cigar in his pocket. He wonders what will happen if they don't do the job. He supposes LaFortune will have them hurt, or worse. He looks at his son; he is sure John can see his cowardice.

'I can handle my boys, as long as you handle yours,' Fitz says.

'I can handle mine.'

'We're committed,' Fitz says. 'We said we'd do this thing, and we'll do it.'

'You are sure?'

'I'm sure.'

Somehow this does it. All is smoothed out, LaFortune is smiling, and the wife is coming forward with two loaves of bread. She hands them to Fitz. The warm loaves are wrapped in brown grocery-sack paper.

'*Goûtez avant*—' Madame LaFortune makes motions with her hands and then looks to her husband.

LaFortune smiles. 'She says: eat up before tomorrow. Her bread is so good, you cannot bring it into Canada.' He chuckles. 'No, you will have no trouble, I promise.' He claps Fitz's back and shakes his hand. 'Come. It's time.'

The Frenchman keeps his arm around Fitz as they

walk to the truck together. The goons are there, in the bed, and they hand six jerry jugs off to the boys. They are red plastic, they say H_2O in marker on the side, and they slosh heavily with water, as they should. John, Walley, and Chris carry them to the Pearl. John lifts the last one at LaFortune.

'*Comme un petit saucisson.*' The old man shapes sausages, a string of condoms, in the air.

Fitz takes the wheel and the others stand by docklines. He starts the engine.

'It will be fine, you will be fine. We never have a problem yet,' LaFortune calls cheerily, then becomes serious. He raises his finger to Chris. '*Touche pas la marchandise, eh?*'

'*Oui-oui,*' Chris says. 'Aye-aye.'

LaFortune laughs and does a little dance. He throws their lines and stands there waving. Mathieu comes over and waves, Madame waves. The LaFortunes all wave, all smiling.

They motor past the mists, and the sea turns the dimpled green of tarnished copper. Copper sea, tin sky, an aluminum tang to the air. Fitz turns the wheel over to John so he can disappear belowdeck and into sleep. Chris naps on the lazarette; he seems a little better after drinking a bottle of Nyquil. Walley rigs a line with one lure. It is illegal to fish here, but he wants a shark, wants some shark teeth. He says no one is around, and John lets him do it because in all their trip they've seen no one but LaFortune's men. When nothing immediately bites, Walley goes below to fry up some real French toast with Madame's bread. He brings John a plate smothered with Cool Whip and syrup. John eats it standing at the wheel. He leaves the door open despite the cold. The way he feels is too big for close spaces. It doesn't fit in his body, his relief at getting off the island. It keeps bubbling up, and he smiles at Walley.

'I'ma buy me a big truck, like that one LaFortune had,' Walley tells him.

'You aren't getting that much.'

'What do you think it's worth? What we have. How much is it worth?'

'What we get for it. Thirty thousand.'

'No, but I mean how much is it really worth?'

John thinks about it. He doesn't know how much they are carrying. He is afraid to look in the jugs, in case there is some way the men on the other side can tell they've been opened. Perhaps LaFortune has etched a minute mark on the cap and the neck, perhaps he has done some trick with a hair. But, he thinks, if there are just ten condoms in each (each jug could easily carry ten condoms and still feel convincingly filled with water), and there are six jugs – so that's sixty – and let's say (how many ounces does a condom hold?) four ounces per condom times sixty is two hundred forty ounces and there are sixteen ounces in a pound is two-forty divided by sixteen is – he has to stop and use a pen – fifteen pounds. Two point two pounds is one kilo, so just round up to sixteen and divide by two is eight kilos and Chris was telling him once of a man carrying six-point-six kilos pure in a false briefcase and when he was caught it was valued at over ten million dollars street value—

'A lot, Walley. It's worth a lot.' There is no way LaFortune would let them have so much, John thinks. But then he thinks, ten pounds is a sack of flour. Five kilos is a sack of flour. Eight kilos isn't much more. You could carry eight kilos in a small backpack. And he has no idea what a normal weight to carry would be.

'A lot thousands, or tens of thousands?' Walley wants to know.

'I don't know.'

'Hundreds of thousands?'

'I don't want to think about it.'

'A million? I bet it's worth at least a million,' Walley says.

'It's worth what we're paid for it. Like anything else.'

'If other people turn around and sell it for a lot more, we should get more.'

'Don't be greedy.'

'If it's worth a million we should try to get more.'

'How are we gonna get more?'

'I don't know.' Walley pushes his glasses up. 'I just think we should.'

'What are you gonna do about it? You got any ideas?' He waits for Walley to answer. He is suddenly annoyed. 'Get out of here, Walley. Go catch your shark.'

Chris has left the lazarette, and Walley goes there now to sit and watch his line slice the water into silver wrinkles. He still thinks they should get more. Later, when Chris is feeling better, Walley plans to ask him if he has any ideas on the matter.

21

Yve has no idea how the morning passes. What she feeds the crew for breakfast, what she says to them. Wen isn't there. She doesn't know if she should be relieved or ashamed. They only kissed. He touched her through her shirt – that's all. That's all. Perhaps he's disappointed with her. Too much? Too little? She doesn't know what to call his absence. After the men go down to the yard, she starts cleaning their rooms. At one point, she turns on the gas for tea and forgets to light a match. She wanders into the living room to vacuum. Some time later, about to light the oven for bread, she sees the one odd knob and realizes what she's almost done. It shocks her awake. She begins to sweat under all her layers. She throws the matches from her hand and runs to open the windows and door. The dogs look up at her, expecting a treat. She waves newspapers about like worried wings, hurrying the gas out the window. Then she turns the heat up, afraid the crew will come home for lunch and feel the cold and suspect she's losing her mind. She herself suspects as much.

The men storm in for lunch with their loud talk and laughter. She expects Wen to come with the crew, but they arrive in pairs without him. She holds back a bowl of chicken soup and two tuna sandwiches. Then, finally, she wraps the sandwiches in tinfoil and she gives them to Charlie to take down to the yard, just in case.

He says, not unkindly, 'Wen went to Charlesport early. To pick up paint from Service Marine.' He places the sandwiches carefully on the table.

'Well, if he comes back hungry, send him up,' she says.

Hank winks, but Charlie says, 'Will do.'

The men exit as a mob. She watches from the fire escape, their foreshortened bodies and gesturing arms. The sky is green. It will rain soon. She should go in, but she doesn't want to. She wants to wait on the porch until he comes up. She is sure he will come up eventually. He is probably down at the yard now, getting her message from Charlie. Then she worries that standing there might somehow jinx things; she has to turn away for him to arrive. 'When will you get here?' she says aloud. 'When?' She likes the way that feels in her mouth. 'When Wen?'

The wind picks up and the oak slaps its branches against the railing. This new wind is a cold wind, coming strangely out of the west. She can feel the pressure change; the bottom drops out of the sky, and the air becomes an empty bowl to catch the coming storm. Her hair whips her face. The door fights the bent hanger. It wants to slam closed. She goes inside, lets it. The rain hits: at first a few drops, then a sheet of sound rattles west to east across the roof, before settling like a thing squatting on the slates.

He won't be coming up now. Even if he is down at the yard. If he's still in Charlesport, he might not even try driving. She sits at the table and eats his cold soup. She is nauseated with waiting.

The rain comes fast and hard, sluicing down the plate glass window and sopping the bar mop Kate wedged against the front door. It doesn't matter if she blocks it, the men who are already in the bar will stay here, the men who considered spending the afternoon drinking will now stay home to do it. These guys, these guys – so tough out on the ocean, act as though they're made of sugar on land, won't set foot out in the rain. Not many are here: Sal Liro and Izzy Titus; Jimmy Daly, of course, by himself at the far end. Kate settles in for a long, boring, unprofitable afternoon. Maybe there is an old movie on. She scans the channels, finds little of interest, puts it back on the football. The rain makes a steady drum. Occasionally a car whooshes by, loud through the puddles. It is dark outside. Purple almost. She likes a good rain now and then, when she isn't worried for Chris and them. She isn't worried. On the weather channel, the rain is shown going up the coast first, then heading out. The men don't have it where they are, yet. And it isn't bad; it is nothing to fear. The weatherman talks silently, tracing the swirling clouds with a swirling hand.

'Whatta you gotta do to get a drink around here? Kate?'

Kate glances from the TV. Sal Liro, red in the face, waves her over. 'You know how it works, Sal. Get off your fat ass.' But even as she says that, she ducks under the service end of the bar and comes over to the booth. There is nothing else to do. 'What can I get you?'

Sal circles his hand over the table. They are drinking shots and beer. Kate clears a few of the dirtier glasses, then comes back with the bottle and a fresh pitcher. The two men are quiet while she pours.

'I'll get it,' Israel Titus says. He puts some money on the table and Sal puts some money on the table, and they both push the other's away until the piles end up mixed in the middle. Still, Izzy touches what he thinks is his own when Kate goes for a couple of bills.

'Take it outta here.'

'Nah, Iz—' Sal protests.

'I won't hear it, Sal.'

'I'll get the next.'

'We'll see.' Izzy throws another dollar on Kate's tray. As she is ringing the sale, the door opens a few inches, then sticks on the bar mop. She turns. She can just see a dark figure through the window. It tries the door again, but the rag catches.

'Someone's at the door,' Sal says. 'Looks stuck.'

'Yeah, yeah.' Kate comes back around from the bar. 'You could get up yourself, every so often.' She grunts a little, bending. When she straightens, she comes face to face with the captain. 'Sorry. I was trying to keep the water out.' She shows the sopping rag. 'Come on in.'

'How are you?' He smiles at her, nods to the two fishers at the booth. He recognizes the big one as Sal Liro, and figures Sal recognizes him too, from the childish way he averts his eyes. Wen decides he will not make anything of it. He takes his favorite stool in front of the taps. There is only one other man at the far end of the bar. Wen says Hey, but the man hunches closer around his beer.

Kate pulls Wen a pint of Bass. 'That's Jimmy. Don't mind him.'

Wen looks to the dark kitchen. 'Pee Wee here?'

'I sent him home. But I can handle a burger.'

'I'll have a burger then.'

'I'll be right back.'

In the kitchen, the grill is cold, and so is the fry oil. 'Sorry,' Kate calls through the service window. 'He shut it all down. It'll take a while to get it going.'

'Don't worry about it then.'

271

'I can make you a sandwich.' She looks in the cold station. 'We got turkey, tuna, or—' She takes the Saran off a plate of meat. 'I think this is ham.'

'Turkey.'

Kate fixes him a turkey sandwich, and on the side she puts a tomato ring and a leaf of lettuce, little paper cups of mustard and mayo, a handful of chips, and a pickle. She gets together silverware and a napkin. She hasn't seen much of the captain. Sometimes he or his boys come in at night, but she works days, and nights she has no desire to hang at the bar.

'Looks rockin'.' Wen rubs his hands together.

'Good,' she says. 'Enjoy.' But he doesn't pick up his sandwich. He gazes at her with the open expression of a customer who wouldn't mind a conversation. Though she doesn't feel so much like chatting, she says, 'I thought you were supposed to be at work.'

'Yeah. I should be. I was coming back from Charlesport – getting paint – and this started.' He looks at the ceiling with his palms up. Kate looks at the ceiling also. It is pressed tin, painted white. 'Thought I might get in out of the wet.'

'Ah. Yeah.' The wet, Kate thinks. Looks rockin'. How weird. He gives her his attention a moment more, but she says nothing, so he turns to his plate. The bar seems overly quiet. She wishes the juke would start up as it does every so often, advertising its presence with a random song. She'd put a song on, but Sal would protest. Now the captain is spreading his mayonnaise. He holds the top triangle of bread delicately, and he brings the knife carefully to the edge of crust, as if he must cover every bit with a uniform layer of mayo. Then he does the same to the other half. He doesn't touch the mustard. Why did she ever dance with him? Sit on his lap? To flirt, to shock. A bit of rebellion, a little nostalgia. Nothing more than that, surely. He catches her watching him eat, and he smiles.

'Can I get you anything else?'

272

'This is fine.'

'Okay, then.' She goes to Jimmy Daly's end and pours him another glass of Harp. Then she wanders back over to Sal and Izzy.

'This place is going to the dogs,' Sal says. He glances toward the taps.

'Come on, now,' says Izzy.

'It is, Iz. You know? I'm telling you. Going to hell in a handbasket.'

'What's his problem?' Kate asks Izzy. She half sits, half leans on the other, empty booth. The rain is falling straight down. The gutters rush with white water. Fallen leaves have blocked the drain holes, and rain sheets the road. Funny how rain in the midafternoon makes it feel like night.

'The pier is the killing blow.' Sal shakes his head. 'Back in the old country—'

Iz jerks his thumb at the big man. 'He's off to the races.'

'No, Iz, no. I'm just saying, back in the old country a man did what he had to to protect his own, right? You didn't just roll over. You didn't just—' He rolls his hand over in the air. 'You didn't let the bastards beat you.'

Kate nods at him. 'Settle down.'

Sal settles down. He stares at the table like a man with a violent picture in his mind.

'Back in the old country—' Kate snorts. Sal came over when he was six months old. He wouldn't know the old country if it came up and hit him in the face.

'Nah, Kate, come on.' Sal looks contrite. 'I'm just saying it's bad, you know? I went to Albin's, you know, to try to rent the berth off him. I said, Take all the equipment free, and give me the dock. He'd get everything, she's loaded. You can sell it for whatever you get, I said. I was gonna strip her down to nothing. I just want to keep the boat and the net. Wasn't good enough for him. He coulda had two for the space of one, Iz woulda rafted alongside.'

273

'Phil's got enough problems,' Kate says. 'Okay? Give him a break.'

'I don't grudge Fitz the space. He's damn lucky, is all. But what about the rest of us? Where the hell're we supposed to go?' He sends this last bit in the captain's direction.

'Don't make trouble,' Kate says. 'You make trouble, I'll call Maria. I'll tell her to come drag your sorry ass home.'

'He's not making trouble,' Israel says.

'I'm not making trouble. Other people maybe are making trouble, though.' Sal nods at the captain's back. Then he leans at Kate, whispering conspiratorially. 'They're taking over. They're taking our dock now; they'll take more later. They're gonna squeeze us out, if we don't do nothing.'

'What are you gonna do? You guys.' Kate's hand jabbers the air. 'Talktalktalktalktalk.'

'I'm just saying.'

'I'm sick of hearing it.' Kate gets up and goes back to the bar with their dirty glasses.

The captain's plate is empty of everything but the lettuce and mustard, so she clears it and drops the check. He fishes his wallet from his front pocket. She's never liked a man who carries his wallet in his front pocket. As he puts the bills down, he says, 'You busy later?'

She ticks her tongue. 'I'm always busy.'

'Ah, well. I suppose I should get busy too. I should probably work through the night, make up for today.' He lifts himself from the stool like a man climbing from a horse. He looks a little sheepish, and Kate feels suddenly sorry for him. He probably knows he is unliked; he's probably just lonely.

'I got a kid,' she explains.

'Yeah.' The captain looks down at his boots. 'Well. If you ever want to bring him down to the yard, show him the boat—'

'Yeah,' she says. 'Sure.'

*   *   *

Dora is late coming in, so Kate is late leaving. By the time she gets to the Albins', the rain has slowed to a dying drizzle, and the clouds are breaking up. Low in the west, a few hazy stars are beginning to show. Yve is already home. She comes to the door holding Martin's hand.

'He'll be ready in a minute,' she says. 'Come in.'

Kate goes to the kitchen to chat with Alma, while Yve dresses Martin in his foulies. He looks a little like Paddington Bear in his yellow outfit and sou'wester, and he knows it. He has the book. His boots are green, with molded rubber frog's eyes on the toes.

Kate comes back out. 'Why don't you come over tonight? We could get a video.'

'Yeah, sure. I'll just tell my mom.'

'I already told her. Come on. It's stopped raining.'

The wet streets look as if they've been coated with Vaseline. Yve and Kate each hold Martin by a hand, and he toddles between. Whenever they come to a puddle, they lift him up, and he lifts his frog-booted feet, and they all go *wheeee!* It delights him, and he deliberately pulls toward puddles.

'Your captain was in for dinner,' Kate says.

'Really?'

'Yeah. Doesn't like your cooking anymore, I guess. Pee Wee went home; the place was dead. I made him a sandwich.'

'Huh,' Yve says.

Kate looks at her sideways.

'I just mean I thought they were hurrying to finish, you know, so it's odd he'd take the time . . .' Yve trails off. She makes a show of suddenly being very interested in a puddle Martin is about to splash through.

'He just came in to get out of the wet. He said my sandwich was rockin'.' Yve doesn't respond, so Kate continues, 'He wanted to know if I could go out later, but I said no, so he made like he was planning to work through the night, anyhow.'

'He asked you out?'

'Yeah, so? He likes a good time just as much as anyone else.' They both pause to get a better grip on Martin, then they lift and wheeee.

'What's that supposed to mean?'

Kate purses her lips and gives Yve a sly look. She means nothing, of course, but a perverse part of her likes to bait Yve, likes to make Yve believe she is worse than she is. It feels like some kind of power.

Yve stops walking. Kate stops walking, also. Martin spies a puddle a few yards ahead, and he pulls against their hands. Yve lets go. He stumbles a little, swings into his mother's knee. He starts to cry. Yve bends to pick him up. He buries his face in the familiar crook of her neck; she smells of beef and onions and soap.

'John's right,' Yve says. 'You do like to make trouble.'

Kate rolls her eyes, laughing. 'Oh now, what's *that* supposed to mean?'

'Nothing.'

'Come on, Yve. I was just kidding.'

'Of course. So was I.' Yve starts walking. Kate watches her small back and her stiff steps. Her boots scuff the street and Martin prods her hips with his heels. She makes no sign of slowing. She walks as if she'd walk all the way to Garenelli's on her own, then let herself into Kate's house to watch a video without her. It is irritating, her calm voice, her walking off. If she is angry she should just yell, Kate thinks. She trots a few steps to catch up.

'Come on, Yve. What?'

'Nothing.'

'You think I'm fooling around with him? In all my free time?'

'No.' She sounds pained. 'I shouldn't've said anything. I'm sorry. Let's just drop it.'

276

They walk a block in silence. Yve puts Martin down. She lets him walk without her hand, there are no cars to worry about. They pass a house brilliantly lit. Through the lace curtains, they can see everything. The man – fifty-something, solidly built in a tired, meaty way – tips back in his reclining chair, watching a real-life cop show on the tube. His wife sits on the sofa, talking on the phone. A multicolor afghan covers the back of the sofa; a TV tray with remote control, cigarettes, lighter, and TV guide waits beside the man's chair. He looks like a laborer – a bricklayer maybe, or a framer. She is probably a housewife, or perhaps she has a quiet job: cashier at the Woolworth's, housekeeper at a hotel along the interstate. The room is cluttered with decorative objects: shamrock-pattern china plates in the cupboard, bronze praying hands on the mantel, crystal teddy bears and lighthouses and schooners on a three-tiered corner shelf. Then they are past, and the next two houses are dark on the first floors.

'Are you into him?' Kate asks Yve. 'Is that it?'

Yve doesn't answer.

'You are, aren't you?' She waits for a rise from Yve, but none comes. 'Well, I don't want him. You can have him.' As she says this, she realizes she couldn't have him anyhow. Having him would require being free to have him, wouldn't it? Being without Chris, being without Martin? Suddenly Kate is annoyed with Yve – free Yve, unencumbered Yve. 'Why don't you just go for it if you like him so damn much?'

'Because I don't.'

'Yeah you do. Admit it.'

Yve shakes her head. Though she already looks wounded, Kate can't help pushing. 'You know what your problem is? You think you don't deserve anything. You act like the world is some kind of pie and all the pieces have already been passed out. You're just cringing around, sniffing for crumbs.'

'He asked you out.'

'So? He's just lonely. And he knows I'm married. You could have him in a heartbeat.'

'No, Kate,' Yve says wearily, 'I couldn't. You could.'

'Oh, come on.'

'Come on nothing, Kate. I wish you would just . . .' Yve pats the air between them. 'Just drop it.'

'You've got low self-esteem, missy. You've got to snap out of it.'

They have reached Kate's house. Yve steps aside to let Kate and Martin through the gate. She stays at the curb while they go up the walk.

'Well?' Kate turns at the porch. 'Are you coming?'

Yve looks about helplessly. It is already nearly nine. They forgot to stop for a video, and now it seems silly to mention it. What Kate said has left a bad taste in Yve's mouth. She thinks of how right Kate might be. She has low self-esteem. She has low self-esteem and she does believe all the slices of pie have gone to others first. Kate got breasts first, men notice her first, and she is married and she has a house of her own. And she has Martin. Yve cried the day Kate told her, 'I'm pregnant.' She cried for weeks. For nearly a year, she cried every time she got her period. Kate has always outstripped her in all things feminine, and Yve has always felt, by comparison, not fully female. If Kate is a woman, then what is she? She feels like some sort of third sex. A shriveled, genderless thing. She knows Kate's life is hard, she knows, and yet she is jealous of her. She is petty and jealous and she knows it. She would like to be better than she is, but she isn't, and it pains her. So many ridiculous things pain her. She is ridiculous. 'I should just go home. It's late.'

'Are you sure?'

'Yes. I guess.'

'Okay, then.' Kate looks at her quizzically. 'See you.'

'Yeah, see you.' Yve smiles, rises on her toes a little,

waves a little. She waits as Kate pushes Martin in, shuts the door.

22

'John!' Walley thrusts his head in the wheelhouse. 'I think you should get down here!'

'I'm driving,' John says. The sky is still clear, but they are heading into the waves, and there is warning of weather. Nothing too bad, but he doesn't like leaving the helm in such situations.

'I really think you should come down.' Walley sounds desperate.

'You want to drive?'

Walley comes all the way in. He takes the wheel. 'You should go now, John.' The way he stresses now, John hurries below in five steps.

His father is already there, wearing his long johns as if he's just woken up. The engine-room door swings open with the slight pitch and roll, and the noise of the Cummins is deafening. Water sloshes about the sole. Chris screams, and an empty jerry jug flies into the foc's'le.

'He's lost it,' Fitz says. He holds his hands out, and he bends slightly at the knee, as if he is prepared to make some kind of move. His socks are dark with water.

'What's this about, Chris?' John yells. The heavy door slams shut. John dogs it open. In the engine room, the water is deeper. Another jerry jug skates by on its side, its nozzle off. Three more, also opened, float about. Chris kneels with the last, struggling to untwist the cap. His brow is furrowed and his lips are pulled away from his teeth, and John, though he can't hear him over the engine, realizes he is crying.

Chris gets the last jug open. He looks in, then looks at John, aghast. 'They're all empty!' He turns the jug

279

upside down and water pours from the spout. 'Fuck! Fuck! Fuck!' He bangs the jug on the sole, then casts it away.

John ducks his head and crouches in. Water slops about his ankles. The engine room is small — more a cubbyhole than a room — and with the two men beside the Cummins, it is tight. He takes Chris by the arms and he shakes him. 'What's this about, you stupid bastard? What the hell are you doing?' He has to put his lips against Chris's ear to be heard over the engine.

'I'm sick, John. I'm really sick.'

Fitz stands in the door, looking on.

'We weren't supposed to open them,' John yells. His words disappear as if into a hole.

Chris breaks John's grasp and slaps the water with his hands. 'It doesn't fucking matter, does it? They're empty!'

The engine vibrates in John's chest and the water vibrates along the edges of his boots. Chris's pants are wet and his teeth are chattering. 'Come on,' John hollers. He lifts Chris up and walks him out into the foc's'le. It is a relief to close the watertight door and cut the noise. He sits Chris on his bunk. Chris clutches his elbows, shivering. He pulls John's sleeping bag over his shoulders.

'I'm really sick, man.'

'No you're not.'

Fitz leans on the bunk. 'What's his problem?'

'I'm gonna die!'

'No you're not,' John says.

'I'm gonna die!' Chris bends over, rocking. 'I'm gonna die! I'm gonna die!'

'Can't you make him shut up?' Fitz asks.

'He's jonesing.'

'Can't you give him something?'

'We don't have anything. I threw it overboard.'

'I'm dying!'

Fitz puts his face near Chris's. 'Shut up!'

280

'You're trying to kill me!' Chris wails.

The boat rises at a strange angle, then slams down as if dropped into a pit. Foam churns past the porthole. 'What the fuck're you doing up there, Walley?' John bangs the overhead. The boat straightens out. 'That's why he was going for the jugs.'

'But they're empty.' Fitz turns around and surveys the mess Chris has made. His wet socks slop through the sheen of water. He lifts his hands in the air. 'I don't understand.'

'I don't know. Maybe it's some kind of test.' John thinks if it is, then they've probably failed. He'll have Walley fill the jugs back up with water, but if the caps were marked, or the water was weighed, they're screwed. 'Maybe they were testing us.'

Chris covers his face and groans.

'Do we have that crap or not?' Fitz demands.

'I don't know.'

'Well, were they gonna pay us for water? That doesn't make sense.'

'I don't know,' John says. 'You're right. It doesn't makes sense.' Why would LaFortune and his men go through so much for water? They wouldn't. But then again, why should LaFortune trust them with anything of value? He looks out the porthole. It is like looking into a washing machine, the endless variations of water swirling against the glass. Amazing how many colors a colorless thing can take on.

'Maybe LaFortune doesn't trust us, and so he told us it was one place and put it another.' As John says this, it strikes him that this must be the case. Why else would he have them escorted in? Why else would he have kept them overnight? He was making time for his men to hide the package somewhere on the *Pearl*.

John jumps up just as Chris does and they both skid through the water to the galley. Chris sticks his foot out – John goes down and catches his jaw on the fire extinguisher. The pain is blinding. The tank falls from

281

the wall and white foam sprays about the cabin until Fitz throws a blanket over it. He helps John to his feet, and they slosh to the galley.

The boat shifts and clots of dry chem float over the sole. In the galley, Chris has already torn Madame LaFortune's bread apart. Now he has the cabinets open, and he pulls cartons and cans from the shelves, and hurls them to the floor. He pops the lid off the cocoa and shakes a brown cloud out.

'Come on, Chris, you're making a mess.'

He looks at John and says, 'It has to be somewhere.' He reaches for the cornstarch.

'Come on, Chris.' John approaches him as he would a strange dog, hands out, low and nonthreatening. 'You got to calm down.' He steps nearer, slowly, gently.

Suddenly, Fitz jumps. They wrestle and heave – Chris is wiry and pumped, but Fitz is a fireplug and angry as hell. The two men fall against the stove and knock a fiddle loose. It clatters behind the fridge. As Chris bends, groping for the iron bar, Fitz kicks him in the ribs. Chris lands on his stomach, and Fitz puts his knee on his back to hold him there. He leans in, unnecessarily hard. Chris pulls the soleboards with his hands as if he would swim away. He turns his gaze, pleading, to John.

'Get a line,' Fitz says. He wheezes, but he keeps Chris pressed to the sole. He glares at John. 'Dammit! Now, boy!'

John gets a line from the locker on deck. The wind is cold where his clothes are wet. He glances at Walley in the wheelhouse. The man looks worriedly down at John, then back out.

Together, John and Fitz wrestle Chris to John's bunk. Chris struggles, kicking and trying to bite. He catches Fitz in the neck once, causing the old man to sit down hard in the water. This makes John angry enough to regain control. He kneels on Chris's shins and restrains his arms while Fitz ties him. When they are done, Chris lies spread-eagle on his back, panting.

'Traitor!' Chris spits at John.

Fitz leans over to catch his breath. 'Don't give me that look,' he tells John. 'It's not such a big deal.' He gasps some more, wheezes into a small laugh. 'We did the same thing to Abel once. He used to booze it up like you wouldn't believe – you think I'm bad. This was before you were born, when I was still working for Liro. He used to bring a certain amount out, you know – enough to keep himself even but not really out of it. Anyhow, this one time we were out longer than usual and he got the DTs and started raging around, tearing up the place, so Sal tied him to his bunk. We thought Edna'd kill us.' Fitz shakes his head, chuckling. 'But she was glad. He was so embarrassed after, he took the pledge.' He pats John on the shoulder. 'I'm taking over. Walley can't drive for shit.'

'Send him down to clean.'

When his father's gone, John sits on the bed next to Chris. 'You're gonna be okay.'

'Fuck you.' Chris's lips are white and he shivers still.

John pulls the sleeping bag over him and tucks it around. He finds a hat for Chris's head, and socks for his feet. Then he puts another pair of socks on Chris's hands, as mittens. 'Better?' he asks. But Walley is down now, and Chris turns his face to the wall.

23

Yve takes her time walking home from Kate's. She turns their conversation over in her mind. She thinks of the captain in her father's barn. She resolves to go directly home, stop thinking of him at all. Maybe she'll see him tomorrow. She considers stopping down at the yard, just to see if he's there. Her parents don't expect her – she was going to watch a video and be back late.

She tells herself to just go home already, he's clearly avoiding her. He clearly doesn't want to see her. Go home. Go home. Still, when she gets home, she finds herself sneaking in. The TV is on in her parents' room. No one calls down to her; they have not heard her. She searches her mother's refrigerator, packs a brown bag with foil-wrapped leftovers, and fills a Thermos with tea.

The after-rain damp casts halos around the street-lamps and the worklights in the yard. It's been a while since Yve has stopped down. She always stays up at the crewhouse. The *Shardon Rose* has moved along. No surprise. Every day the men swarm her hull like ants; by each evening whistle, more hull has been fitted with new wood. The lumber pile is gone now, and Hank's caulking materials dangle between the new planks like torn lace. The bosun's chair hangs in front of his last worked spot, at the very stern. Hank's belly has receded too, as if he's caulked the schooner with his own flesh. He complains Yve doesn't feed them enough, but as Wen told her the first day, they eat whatever she puts out until there is nothing left. No one can feed those men enough.

She goes down to the ways. Light shines through the remaining chinks in the hull. Wen must be working inside. The nearly completed boat rises over her like a monolith, a pyramid – neither of these words is quite right, but the bulk reminds Yve of something huge and primal: monumental in both the colossal and the memorial senses of the word. She feels a little hitch of adrenaline from the seeming danger of walking beneath this wood behemoth. So much of a boat hides underwater. She toes a brace and wonders, What if? She knows the old ways are secure, but what if? What if she really kicked this brace? What if she tripped all the shores and stood beneath looking up as the schooner swayed, tipped, toppled? Instead, she climbs the ladder to the catwalk and gangway, and jumps onto the deck. Surely he hears her land. He must hear her walking on the plastic. He is beneath her, in the main cabin and probably hungry. He only had a sandwich for lunch, he skipped dinner. She pictures him under her, listening and waiting. If she leaves now, it will seem strange. He'll wonder why she came, walked around above him, and left. If she stays, though, something will happen. She should go straight home, call Kate, say she changed her mind, maybe rent a video, and go over – but here she is, on the deck, in the damp. His dinner, which she holds under her coat to keep dry, is warm against her stomach. She stops at the top of the companionway. She's brought dinner. That's reason enough. He's probably hungry. She will just see how things stand.

He's waiting for her at the bottom of the companionway, looking up. He holds a palm sander in one hand. He doesn't seem surprised.

'Hello there, Yve.'

'Wen.'

'Are you coming down?'

She climbs down to the space that will become the galley. For now, belowdecks is still open and without bulkheads. She balances on a new frame. The incomplete sole opens into rectangular pits, revealing bilge and ballast – iron scraps, old shackles, broken chain – between the framework. Wen crosses in front of her, nearer than necessary. At a tool bench made from an overturned crate, he riffles through squares of sandpaper. His hair falls forward in his eyes so she can't see them.

'Have you eaten? You weren't up for dinner—'

'I thought I'd do a little work on that knee.'

'—or lunch, or breakfast. I thought you might be hungry.' Her throat feels dry. 'I brought you something.'

'What do you have there?' He doesn't turn to look for himself: instead, he selects a piece of paper and lays it against the sander pad, scoring it with his fingernail.

'Tea. Sandwich – meat loaf. My mother's.'

'Tea sounds good.' He tears the paper at the score against the edge of the crate. It makes a quick, violent sound. He clamps this new square in place and she pours tea for two, places his on the crate. She leans nearby, holding her own mug and watching him through the steam.

'Cheers.' He drinks, flinches. 'Hot, hot, hot.' The cup is placed to the side to cool. He pulls a paper-cloth dust mask over his nose and mouth, pinching the metal closed on the bridge of his sharp nose. He hands Yve one. She covers her face, then covers their tea with spare bits of sandpaper. The sander hums over the knee. Dustballs jump on the bend, the vibration blurs through her ribs. It feels odd and unpleasant.

She shouts over the sander, 'Looks like it fits perfectly.'

Wen nods.

'I'll tell my father. He'll be glad to hear it.' Her breath, trapped in the mask, cycles back to her nose as tea-scented moisture. There is nothing more worth saying over the noise of the sander. She feels foolish, waiting there. She has brought his food, now she should go. He has given her no reason to wait, but she does.

He finally turns the sander off, and it shudders itself still. Dust settles back on the crate, the sole frames, the knee. A fine softness coats her skin. He pushes the mask up on his forehead. She shakes hers off completely, remembers the tea that still needs drinking.

'I'm afraid it's cold by now.' She hands a mug to Wen and can't remember whose was whose.

He puts his down without drinking. She holds on to hers. The ceramic has grown cool. He tacks the dust from the knee with a turpentine-moistened cloth, then puts the cloth down and looks at her a long time. The turpentine wash evaporates and the wood goes light and dry again. There is sawdust in his eyebrows and on his lashes. Around his mouth is a clean, dust-free circle. He tucks a loose hair behind her ear. His fingers smell of turpentine.

'Pretty earrings. They're so small, I can hardly get my pinky through.' He strokes her earlobe and the tiny gold hoop pierced there.

'Try.'

'Do you want me to?'

Her breath wavers audibly, and she knows he hears it. He watches her closely, his gaze flicking from her eyes, to her mouth, to her eyes again. She steps back, into the bilge. Her foot rolls on an iron sash weight, and she barks her shin on the frame.

'Ah, the tension—' He laughs, now that the tension's broken. Leaning against the companionway, he no longer touches her. She wants him to touch her so terribly it feels like a wire slicing through her ribs. Now, while she is bent over, rubbing her shin, she wants him to put his hand on her shoulder.

He does. 'This won't be a problem, will it?'

She straightens up, smooths her blouse. 'No. Nothing's a problem.'

He gives her a moment more. Then he hooks his arm around her head. It feels awkward and gentle at the same time, as if he is trying not to touch her with his dirty hand. His tongue is long and wet in her mouth. He offers it like something she should suck, so she does, sucks his tongue like a stick of candy, all the time thinking, How odd. How odd. He didn't kiss this way last night. There wasn't all this tongue and saliva. He palms her breasts and lifts her shirt. The lace on her bra looks gray, and she wishes she'd worn a different one.

'You okay?' he says.

She nods. Her mind keeps running, How odd.

He lifts her up the companionway, bracing her

against a middle rung. He lifts her skirt, pulls her tights down, her underpants – and the air is cold and damp on her legs. She tastes sawdust, tea, smells turpentine and sweat. His beard burns her chin. He is different from John in every way, his cock is rubbery – short and unbelievably thick. It feels like a wedge driven with a mallet. While he thrusts, pistonlike, he talks. At first she can't understand, his mouth is buried in her neck, then she realizes he is saying, You're so tight. You're so tight. She blushes. She wonders if she's supposed to say something back, and the thought of it makes her want to giggle. Her back bounces against the ladder, and it hurts where her sweater has bunched up. Despite all this, she finds herself thrusting back and clutching at him with her legs.

'Christ, I'm building, I'm building—'

Listening to him monitor his progress so, she is mortified. She nearly pushes him away, but at that moment he makes a noise like choking, and his whole body quakes, and he ejaculates inside her.

She freezes. No one has ever – who else but John could have? and he always, always pulls out – no one has ever come inside her. It feels warm, like oil spreading upward.

'Oh God—' Wen falls against her. 'You've got such a nice pussy.' He kisses her neck, her ear.

'Jesus, shh.' She pats his back awkwardly. She pats his hair. 'Shh.' She wants him to stop talking about everything. She wants to bring her legs down. She wants to stand up and adjust herself.

Wen pulls away and helps her off the ladder. He looks at her fondly as she rearranges her clothes and rebraids her hair. If he were John, she'd say, What are you looking at? and he'd say something like Nothing, or Not much.

'Are you okay?' he asks.

She feels the odd sensation of his semen dropping inside her. 'Yes,' she says. 'I'm fine.'

He turns back to the palm sander and his dust mask. He looks at the tinfoiled dinner packages and puts the tools down. 'Thanks for bringing dinner by,' he says. 'I appreciate it.'

She has no idea how to take this. She wonders if it is his way of making a friendly joke. 'Of course,' she says. He doesn't kiss her again. He seems to be waiting for her to leave so he can get back to work.

Halfway up the companionway, her head and shoulders in the damp night air, she feels his fingers grip her ankles and stop her climb. He presses his forehead into the backs of her knees briefly. Then he releases her calves with a friendly tap and lets her climb up and out.

24

'I got you more soup,' Walley says to Chris.

'I don't want more soup.'

'It'll make you feel better.'

'Soup will not make me feel better.'

Walley sits on his own bunk across from Chris. The cabin is small enough that, so sitting, his knees press against the side of Chris's mattress. He balances the bowl on his thighs and takes a spoonful and tries to get Chris to sip. 'Come on. It's the chicken noodle and I put bread in it like you like.'

Chris turns his face away. His pale cheek is red from the red night light.

'If he doesn't want it, don't give it to him,' John says from the bunk above. He's been trying to sleep a little, while his father finally drives, but Chris has kept him awake with his complaints and threats. The boat slams into a trough. They are heading directly into the waves, and the westerly wind is slowing their trip.

'If you keep making me smell that soup, I'm gonna puke.'

'Get rid of the soup, Wal,' John says.

He listens to Walley shuffle back to the galley. A lid opens and settles back on a pot. Then he shuffles back. His sleeping bag whistles on the mattress, and his body settles into his bunk. After a few moments, Walley whispers to Chris, 'Where do you think they put it?'

'How the hell should I know,' Chris says in a normal voice. 'If someone let me go – ' he bangs his ass on the bunk so John's bunk shakes also – 'I bet I could find it.'

John flips his head over the side and looks down at Chris. Chris glares back at him. All his clothes are piled around him; they've made a nest of sweaters and long johns because he was shaking before and nothing seemed to warm him. He has a bowl beside him, so he can turn his mouth to it when he retches.

'We don't want to find it,' John tells them both. 'It's bad enough we already looked.' He just wants to meet this person, whoever he is, and let him take the package, and go. Whoever it is must know where to look. They are to meet a lobsterman. As John sees it, they'll hand the refilled jugs over innocently, and the lobsterman will board them and get what he wants from wherever it is, if it's even there at all, and then go. They'll drive safely away, and he'll do whatever he's supposed to do, sink it in a trap, stuff it in lobster tails, who knows? John doesn't care. They'll get the money later, from Dina and Rea at the house on Pine Street. Dina and Rea are nice enough ladies, even though they run a shooting gallery. And lobstermen are respectable people. Americans, locals, not crazy Frenchmen. Probably just another desperate fisher, probably a family man. Maybe a lobsterman and his son. But nothing has gone as Chris promised. They weren't supposed to have landed on the Miquelon end. And their escort there had a gun. And they were made to spend the night with crazy LaFortune. And the jugs he gave them are empty.

'Where are we supposed to meet the guy?' John asks now.

Chris purses his lips. It is the only defiant gesture he can make with his hands and legs tied to the bunk posts.

'Come on, Chris. Need-to-know time.'

Chris doesn't answer.

'They'll hunt us down if we don't show,' John coaxes. They are still far from home, so he tells himself he isn't very worried yet. Chris should be as worried as he. Every few hours he gives Chris their coordinates, figuring Chris will panic if they pass the next meeting point, and make them go back. He can't hold out forever.

'You're not getting untied till you tell,' John says.

No answer.

'Don't you have to piss? You need to take a leak?' John waits. 'Fine. You better not piss my mattress, then.' He turns out the red light and his eyes adjust to the dark grays. If he was in his own bunk, overhead would be his clock with its green numbers ticking off the wait, and a picture of Yve. He wouldn't be able to see it well in this light, but he has it memorized, and he knows what the shadows and lights represent. There is her hair, there her eyes, her cheek, her mouth. She partially covers her lips with her fingers – she has always been shy about laughing with her mouth open. He wonders what she is doing now. He wonders how long it will take for her to come around this time. For the first time since he began this trip he worries that this has, perhaps, been the final straw for her. Every time he leaves, there's some kind of new damage. Every time he comes back, it's harder to patch things up. Each patch is weaker, stitched as it is to other patches. On her bad days, Yve picks at all the rough spots – remember this time? and that time? and that other time? Because for her, what has been stitched together is never again whole. No fresh start. When they get home, he will go straight to Charlesport and put a down payment on a ring. It's just a thought, not an action – he might never get around to it – but it's a nice enough thought to fall asleep to. Maybe he'll get Kate to come shopping with him. She'd know better than he what Yve would like. The boat rises and falls on the waves, and the engine fades to a pool of white noise at the base of his skull. He will get her something nice, and he will take her out to dinner, and he will drop the ring into her glass and she will drink it and it will catch in her throat like a fishhook and she'll cough like she is coughing now—

'John!'

John claws up from sleep. He sits up too quickly and bangs his head, then remembers he is in the upper bunk, not his own. A white light stabs through the cabin, though it is still night, and they aren't supposed to use it. The portholes go black.

'John!' Walley shouts. 'There's something wrong with Chris! I don't think he's faking!'

John scrambles free of his bag. Landing on the sole, his feet get pins and needles. Chris thrashes silently in the bunk. His eyes pop and his mouth opens and he screams without sound; he arches his back – rising up on his elbows and heels and the crown of his head as if he will launch himself from the mattress – then, caught by the lines, he falls back. He arches and falls again. He looks at John, frightened by his own actions. Then his eyes glaze over and he goes back to his work of flopping and gaping.

'He's having some kind of seizure,' John says.

'He was puking, then he started this – this—' Walley peers at John. He doesn't have his eyeglasses on and his eyes appear small.

'Untie him.' John goes for his hands first. As he works, Chris bucks and the line jerks from John. In his thrashing, the knots have pulled tighter.

'Hold him down, so I can get this!' John says, but

Walley runs up the companionway, calling to Fitz that they must radio for help.

Now Chris shakes his head from side to side, vigorously denying this turn of events. Something frees, and vomit bursts from his mouth. He gasps, chokes, sucks air in. The gurgle stops suddenly; like a cork in the neck of a bottle, something has stopped his inhalation. His red face grimaces, and he raises his head, pantomimes choking. John gets one of his hands, the one on the outside, free. Chris claws at his throat. Now John reaches across his chest to get his other hand loose, and he can hear the struggle in his esophagus as Chris heaves soup from his stomach, and then breathes it into his lungs. Rasping, churning, mucoidal gasps. It strikes John that Chris is drowning.

John frees his hand and sits him up and pounds on his back. Chris leans forward, grabbing air. John slides behind him to do the maneuver he's seen on TV and on the poster at the Wind. As he hugs Chris around the ribs and he squeezes him, he knows he must be doing it wrong. Chris's back is wet and cold with sweat, and he smells terrible. John turns his head to breathe and squeezes him again. Chris jerks in his arms as if he is sobbing. Somewhere, a thousand miles away, Walley and Fitz are fighting in the wheelhouse, and no one is driving the boat. For this emergency, they have turned away from home and throttled down; now they bob like a gull on the waves.

'You're gonna be fine. Walley's calling the Coast Guard.' John works to free Chris's feet. Overhead Walley and Fitz scuffle. Something new is wrong with Chris; his freed heels drum the mattress.

'A helicopter's coming, you'll be fine. Walley's calling right now.' John stands him up. Bent-headed, he walks Chris around the cabin. Chris bucks and shudders, quivers and subsides.

'Help's on the way,' John assures him, though he knows if Chris can still hear him, he can also hear Fitz denying Walley the radio, because the shit's still on board somewhere. He can hear Walley saying, But he's choking, and he can hear Fitz yelling that the Coasties won't get here in time and he won't lose his boat for a dead man. 'Hello? Hello?' calls Walley. 'This is the fishing vessel—'

Over their heads the radio smashes and bits of plastic fall like rain.

John pumps Chris like a bellows. He lays him on the sole and tries to sweep his mouth clear. He tries to breathe into him, but his breath only fills Chris's cheeks before leaking out his blue lips. John drags him up the companionway and out onto the deck, where Chris is white under the pale moon. The clouds are rolling in and the waves are rolling in, and Chris's arms and feet swing limply. John begs him to come on, now, walk with me. Come on now. He hugs him and kicks Chris's feet forward, then he spins him around so Chris lays his cheek on John's shoulder like a waltzing lover. In this way, crying, John holds him; and he wonders why the rain still doesn't come. He thinks: If only we had rain, instead of this terrible wind, Chris would wake up.

V

Oh the losing of those fine young men,
grieved the captain sore—
but the losing of that great whale-fish,
grieved the captain ten times more, brave boys,
grieved the captain ten times more!

25

The red nun off starboard, the green can to port, the twin lighthouses gold in the low sun. They are home. John's eyes burn. He paces the deck near the bowline. Walley hunkers aft. Fitz is in the wheelhouse; the window hides him behind a wash of coppery reflection.

As they motor past the yard, John looks out of habit. The *Shardon Rose* is farther along than he expected – the planking is complete and there's a coat of paint on her already. They've been gone over a week, enough time for that much work to have been completed. Still, he's surprised. He'd almost expected to come back and find time had flowed otherwise in their absence. He feels as though the past few days have occurred in a parallel universe. It reminds him of a movie he saw as a child of a man who rocketed around the sun – the trip was supposed to take six weeks, but instead he landed back on Earth in three. Everything looked the same, and people seemed to know him, but there was something slightly wrong. He had trouble reading, his wife seemed odd, and the heads of his department questioned why he had abandoned his mission early. The astronaut protested, I haven't! I did as I was told! I headed out on the course you set and here I am as you see me! As it turned out, he'd landed on Earth's mirrored twin, unknown to the true Earth because it had always been hidden by the sun. He couldn't

297

convince the mirror NASA of this, he couldn't convince them to send him home. John can't remember the movie's end, except that it upset him, and he was too young to have the word 'despair' to describe the astronaut's final emotion. In the past few days, since Chris's death, John has slept as much as possible, but his rest has been fitful and he's startled awake. He's lain in Chris's bunk – he wasn't about to go back to his own, where Chris had been – exhausted, as though he's been swimming through silt.

In Helio Carreiro's boatyard, most of the men sweep giraffe-necked rollers of paint over the schooner, their faces hidden behind fume masks, their hair tucked into hats and handkerchiefs. Joe Ames must be rushing the project for a reason – money most likely. It's almost too late in the season for paint to dry well. Other details are being attended to. A young man is shellacking the cabin, another paints deck boxes. Another man works on the anchor while two others slush the chain. They dip their gloves into metal tubs and run lanolin over the links. They too are covered with rags and masks, unrecognizable as the others. Then Sandy Hopewell turns and lifts his mask from his face. He waves a grease-heavy glove and John nods back.

A few seconds more and they are close to the Museum Pier. Fitz throttles down. The Pearl makes a lazy swing toward the rest of the fleet. Pete Hopewell waits on the dock. He's got a cardboard sign around his neck that has flipped in the wind so John can't read it.

Pete puts his hands to his mouth and hollers, 'Didn't hear you radio!'

The engine is loud, and the man must repeat himself several times before they understand. Fitz keeps the dragger steady, one hand on the wheel and the other to his ear. Finally he hollers, 'Didn't. Radio's broke.'

Pete yells something and points to the sign on his

298

chest, then to the draggers. John squints against the
western glare. At first he can see nothing different. The
boats are docked in their usual spots. Then he notices
the painted sheets hung from their rails: *PIERS for
FISH! Not TOURISTS!* At a card table in front of the
museum's closed door, Bea Hopewell sits on a folding
chair, her mittened hands folded in her lap, a
pompomed hat on her curls, her fleece-topped boots
crossed at the ankles. A Thermos steams in front of
her. Edna Larkin stands beside her with a sandwich
board similar to Pete's around her neck. She holds
handbills, but there are no passersby to hand them to.
The museum isn't open weekdays off season, except
to school groups. She waves and calls, 'How're you
boys?'

Pete walks out on the pier and Fitz quiets the engine
to hear him better. Pete says, '*Shardon*'s coming off the
ways. Ames's kicking us out.' He visors his eyes with
his hand and squints up at Fitz, who nods once: he's
heard.

'Where're we supposed to dock?' John asks Pete.

'You may as well go along to Phil's; he's holding it
for you. Had a hard time of it too – Liro's been leaning
on him.'

'What're you gonna do?' John asks.

Pete shrugs. 'Damned if I know.' He looks back up at
the wheelhouse. 'See you at the Wind later, Warren?'

Fitz nods and gives the thumbs-up. He puts her in
reverse, and as they back out of the blinding sun,
Walley jumps from the rail to the dock.

'Worm and parcel with the lay; turn and serve the
other way.' Wen weaves tarred marline through Yve's
toes. His head lies on her thigh. She plays with his
long hair as he plays with the line. His room smells of
sex – sweaty, warm, and sour. His bed is a mattress
from the schooner, and he uses a sleeping bag instead
of blankets and sheets, and she thinks that maybe all

299

men are like this: if not for women, they'd be perfectly happy camping through their lives. She was less surprised this time when he began talking at her during it. He lay on his back, while she sat astride him, facing his feet. He kept his hands on her waist, and he talked about her ass, and its shape, and how he couldn't hold back. She had to bite her lip to keep from laughing. Even so, when it was over she fell sideways, her belly fluttering as if it had its own pulse.

He spins on his shoulder and brings his face up to hers. He offers her the marline. 'What do you smell?'

'I don't know. Creosote?'

'Nah!' He takes a big whiff. 'That's the best smell in the world.' He looks at her as if she were crazy to not answer so. 'Someday I'm going to bottle it, sell it as cologne. I'll call it *Served* for men, and *Seized* for women.'

'You're disgusting.'

He opens his mouth and hands in innocent protest. Then he grabs her and rolls her onto him, and she feels him getting hard again. The doorbell rings. They both freeze, then scramble for clothes. He's the first dressed and to the door. His muffled voice travels back to her from the hall. Walley Larkin answers and Yve hurries out, still pulling on her sweater.

Walley stares at her from the fire escape, as if he is surprised to find her here after all. He looks a wreck.

'My God, Walley, what is it?' she asks.

Wen turns at the horror in her voice. He takes a step toward her, but she brushes past.

'Is it John?'

Walley takes off his glasses and rubs his eyes. He puts them back on. The lenses are filthy. 'You should come home.'

She hears what Walley says, and she is aware of the urgency of his words, just as she is aware of the rectangle of pinking clouds behind his head, of the cold air blowing in and rustling unseen papers throughout the apartment, of the garlicky odor of tomato sauce simmering on the stove, of Wen standing, warm and solid, behind her. She is aware of all this as if the moment has stretched, taffylike, to allow so much room for the noting of minutiae. It is amazing to her how many mundanities hold her enthralled, and how slow she is to break free.

'Is it John? Oh God, please say it isn't—'

'What's going on, Yve?' Wen asks. 'Who is this guy? Who are you?'

'I have to go,' Yve tells him. Then, somehow, she's struggling with her coat, she can't find the sleeve and she stabs at the fabric, frustrated. She takes it off and throws it on the floor. 'Jesus, Walley, just tell me!'

'It's your brother, it's Chris.' Walley starts trembling. 'I'm so sorry, I'm so sorry.' He pushes his fingers into his eyes. 'I'm sorry,' he says, over and over. 'I'm sorry. I'm so, so sorry.'

By the time Walley and Yve arrive, the *Pearl* is tied up, and the lawn between Phil's barn and the shore bulwark is crowded with people. Even Jack Hagerty and Richard Bates are there. Their police car is pulled alongside the diesel pumps and the lights twirl, though the siren is off. Already sawhorses block either entrance to the semicircular driveway and more neighbors have gathered behind.

'What happened? What happened?' Yve finds herself asking as she pushes through the crowd. They part and let her pass into the yard. Dora Schultz stands with Bea Hopewell, who holds Martin in her arms. The boy reaches out, and Yve goes to take him, but Dora says, 'Go on, honey, he's fine.' Yve goes on. She is having trouble understanding. Her senses provide data, but in discrete pieces only, and she can't process the information. The grass is damp and the few leaves left on the ground are wet and black. The *Pearl* pulls gently at her lines. At the edge of the breakwater, Edna

Larkin holds Yve's mother by the elbows as Alma strains forward on the balls of her toes, her body launching itself toward the boat. Her mouth is open, her hands are fists. She screams *No!* and the word trails into a string of sobs that sound as if she is dissolving into laughter, before she catches her breath and screams again. Yve's father stands on deck with Fitz and Officer Hagerty. They are looking down into the hold. Yve drifts past her mother, and then she is on the boat, and John is beside her saying something. She watches his lips move, but she can't follow what he says. He tries to take her arm. She brushes him off. He takes her arm again; he would keep her from the hold, but she is determined to look.

Her father shakes his head and reaches his hand to cover her eyes, and Officer Hagerty steps between her and the hole, but they move so slowly she is able to dodge them and make it around to the other side. Looking down on her brother, she feels as if she is floating. His skin is pearly as the salt-ice he lies upon. He wears long johns, and socks on both his hands and on one foot. His hair is messy, as if he's recently been wearing a hat, or else has just risen from bed. He's fallen in an awkward position – limbs splayed and bent. No one thought to close his eyes. Yve leans over the rail and vomits.

A rush, a roar. She is swallowed up and all goes blank. Then someone is pressing something wet and rough to her face. 'There you are; there you go.' Edna Larkin helps her sit. Yve leans against the soft bulk of her aunt. Edna holds a cold washcloth to the back of Yve's neck. 'Okay, hon? Okay?' She rubs Yve between the shoulder blades. She chafes her arms, peers into her eyes. 'You okay, now? You okay?'

Yve looks around. The scene has changed. 'Where is everyone? Where's my mom?'

'She's inside lying down. The doctor gave her something.'

Yve coughs and spits. 'Where's John? Where's Kate?'

'Kate's inside. She's inside. You want to go inside?'

'Where's John?'

'He's talking to Jack Hagerty.'

Yve looks and sees that John does indeed sit inside the police car, and she takes the shadow on the driver's side to be Officer Hagerty. Officer Richard Bates waits a few yards off, looking geekish. His uniform is misshapen by his paraphernalia: his gun, his notepad, his flashlight. Time has passed. The sun is down and shadows are spreading across the lawn. A few people still stand in the road, watching while Chris is loaded onto an ambulance. Yve brings her hand to her forehead and is surprised by her own touch.

'I don't feel so well,' she tells her aunt.

'Let's go inside,' Edna says. She presses Yve against her and walks her to the kitchen door.

26

The screen door rattles under John's knuckles. It is not yet late, but it feels late. Jack Hagerty questioned him in the car a long time, as the yard cleared, and the family went in, and now the house is quiet. He feels wiped out. Sometimes Jack asked him the same thing two and three times. John would like to take two aspirins, drink a beer, and put his head in Yve's hands. He'd like her to stroke his hair while they sit quietly together. Heavy steps rumble inside, and the inner door opens. Edna speaks through the screen.

'What is it, John?'

'Can I see Yve?'

The familiar odor of the Albins' kitchen – of coffee and mildew and strong cleansers – floats out.

'She's asleep,' Edna says.

'Are you sure?'

303

'It's late, John. It's been a rough day for us all.'

'Could I please just see her?'

Edna pushes the screen door slightly. Bea Hopewell sits at the kitchen table, her large breasts propped against the edge. Two mugs before her, a pot of tea. They have already begun taking over. By tomorrow there will be a phone tree, and collection cans, and casseroles baking.

The blinds are down. Someone took the time to pull them – probably Edna. She deals well with trouble; she knows all the proper forms to follow. John imagines all the beds in this house have been made up with fresh sheets – Chris's old bed for Kate and Martin, the sofa bed for Edna, and a cot for Walley in the basement – and that there are probably fresh hand towels and new soaps in the bathrooms.

'She's upstairs,' Edna says.

John climbs quietly. He expects to find Yve undressed and in bed, but she sits at her desk, looking at the shaded window. Kate sits upon Yve's bed, Martin on her lap. The boy has snuggled up against her shoulder and fallen asleep. A string of drool, fine as a cobweb, hangs between his lower lip and Kate's sweater.

He nods, says, 'Kate—'

Kate turns dry eyes toward him. Her skin looks translucent beside the reddened wings of her nostrils. She stands. Martin grapples in his sleep, clinging desperately to her sweater. She puts a hand on his back to steady him. He shudders, stills.

John steps into the room. 'Are you okay?' He is aware of the question's absurdity, but can think of nothing else to say. 'Can I do anything—?'

Kate drops her gaze to her son. She makes some small noise, a small clucking, a coo. She slips past John and out. Her footsteps creak the hall, take a turn into Chris's old bedroom. The door shuts. On the other side, shoes drop, clothes collapse to the floor in soft

304

piles. Martin whimpers slightly. Chris's old bed settles under the child's light weight. John listens for Kate, but hears nothing more. He wonders where she stands in the room, what she looks at. It is as Chris left it. Alma never touched anything, except to clean.

'Are you going to jail?' Yve asks without turning.

'No. What for?'

'For killing my brother.'

He steps just inside the door to close it. 'I didn't kill him.'

'Who did?'

'No one. He choked.'

'Is that what you told Jack Hagerty?'

He is as aware now of the thin walls of Yve's room as he used to be when he was a teenager. Phil Albin, after realizing he couldn't keep them apart, established a rule that John could escort Yve home and even come inside, up to her bedroom, as long as her door remained opened to the hall. They're too old for this room now, John thinks. They should be having this discussion at their own kitchen table.

'It's true,' he tells Yve.

'Why'd he choke?' She fingers the blind. It makes a plastic sound on the sill.

'He was sick.' When she doesn't answer, John adds, 'He was fucked up, Yve, you know that.'

'You told Jack that, did you?'

He told Jack Hagerty practically everything. He said that Chris went crazy, went into withdrawal. He told how Chris was throwing shit around and how Fitz had to physically stop him. Of course he left out that they tied Chris – but he only really lied about where they were, and why they were there. He moved them south of Canadian waters and claimed they'd been fishing. When Jack asked about the fact that there were no fish in the hold, he said because they couldn't very well sell fish that a dead body had slept on.

'I told Jack he was sick and he vomited in his sleep and we tried to save him but we couldn't.'

'How'd you try to save him?'

'Jesus, Yve—'

She turns in her seat. He sits on the edge of her bed so she doesn't have to look up.

'I did everything I could.'

'Did you call for help? I don't think you did. Because if you did, we would've heard. Someone would've heard and radioed it on and it would've gotten back to us—'

'What would that have done, Yve?' He leans forward, but she puts her head down. 'What would that've done?'

'I don't know! They could have sent a helicopter! They could've rescued him!'

He talks at the white comma of her parted hair. 'He was dead in minutes. No one could have rescued him.'

She puts her hands near her ears as if she would cover them, but she doesn't. 'Why didn't you call?'

'The radio was broken.'

'Before or after?' He doesn't reply and she asks again, 'Before or after?'

'Before.'

'Don't lie to me, John. Hagerty might believe you, but I don't.'

Yve knows he is lying, because she knows him. Something happened that he isn't saying. If they were married, this might be the moment when she'd consider leaving. This would be the moment when she would pull the blankets from the bed and go to the living room. Oddly, the idea of it makes her feel tender toward him, and she slides forward in her seat. She wants to lie next to him on the bed, with his arm around her.

'Let's go for a walk,' John says.

She slides back. 'It's late.'

'We can't talk here.'

306

'What do you want to say?'

'I don't know.' He looks blindly about the room, then he touches the air near her knee. She waits for his hand to extend a bit more, but it retracts, instead. His jaw is swollen and purplish.

'Who hit you?'

He touches his face. 'This? It's nothing. I fell.'

'Did you fight? You and Chris?'

'No. Not really.' He stares into the middle distance, and she knows he is remembering a fight. It flickers across his face.

He catches her eye. 'Oh, Yve, I fucked it all up. I fucked it up so bad.'

'Shh.' She puts her fingers to his lips and he quiets. She's suddenly no longer sure she wants to hear any more. If he tells her more, then she will be responsible for their shared knowledge. She might even feel the need to do something she has no desire to do, like keep a terrible secret for the rest of her life, or tell someone something terrible about John. She doesn't want to be responsible for such things anymore. He has this habit: he hands her something terrible, and then he forgets about it. Or maybe not forgets, but he halves the weight for himself, and she goes from carrying no burden to carrying half of his. It keeps her yoked to him.

'I don't want to know,' she says. 'I told you before you left the same thing.'

He looks stricken.

'It's not my responsibility anymore, John. I won't carry your garbage. You're like Martin. You finish your candy and hand me the wrapper.'

'Come on, Yve.'

'Come on what?'

'You're just saying that because it sounds good. That's how you win—'

'Win what?'

'Whatever – you say something like that and I just shut up.'

307

'You're still talking.'

'What am I saying, though? What are we even talking about?'

'I don't know.'

He looks at her seriously. 'This is stupid.'

'I know. My brother's dead.' As she says it, it
becomes finally true. Everything else seems small.
Someone, her aunt most likely, is moving about downstairs. Another woman's voice, then her aunt's. The
kitchen door opens and shuts. 'I want you to go now,
John.'

He waits for her to change her mind, but she doesn't.
He stands and she stands with him.

'Go on,' she says.

'Okay.'

She listens to his feet down the stairs. He lets himself out the front door. He doesn't have his truck, so
he'll be walking. Her window faces the back, the
water. She doesn't bother pulling the blind aside. She
knows how the curve of the drive and the boat ramp
will look white under the moon. She can imagine the
Pearl made off to the railroad ties that brace the shore.
The water is black, sprinkled with red and green
lights. The town is yellow lights, and at the end of
either spit, white lighthouse beams sweep away the
night at intervals of four and seven seconds.

27

Warren Fitz, walking down Center Street, finds the
bottle in his hand – a pint of J&B he picked up from
Garenelli's after leaving the Albins' – is empty. He
takes it by the neck and he tosses it in the air so it arcs
around a streetlamp and comes down a few yards
ahead, shattering on the cobbles. The broken glass
glitters wetly. From the outside, the Wind looks like a
dark cave, empty but for a few diehards huddled

around their pints like little flames. Fitz watches them through the wrinkled panes of the foyer door. Sal Liro and Israel Titus are at their regular booth. Jimmy Daly hangs on a faraway stool by a thread. At a table on the dining side sit the crew of sailors off the schooner restoration. The young Stewart girl is with them, and so is Dora Schultz. Otherwise the place is empty. Fitz pushes through and feels immediate relief from the familiar, sour stink, the dim bulbs further softened by the low blue smoke, his friends' hoarse voices. They've been in the booth all day, and evidence of their labors crowds the table. The sound is down on the TV and the juke is quiet – someone has pulled the plug so its garish lights are off.

'Fitz,' Izzy says.

Sal kicks a chair free of the table. 'Fitz Fitz Fitz Fitz Fitz.'

Warren sits. He gets a slap on the shoulder from Sal.

'We heard,' Izzy says, 'over the radio.'

'Bad news,' Sal says.

Fitz takes a few bills from his pocket.

'Put that away. Dora!' Sal calls her from the sailors' table. She swings herself off a lap and saunters behind the bar.

'What?'

Sal circles his hand over the table. Dora comes with the bottle and pours into their old glasses, sets a fresh shot and pint for Fitz. She sits down with them.

'How's the family? How's Alma?'

Fitz puts his whiskey down. 'Alma—' Again he sees Alma screaming on the lawn, Edna holding her. 'Bad. Right there in her backyard. With the police.' He twirls his fingers like the police lights and the ambulance lights.

'Poor lady, Jesus.'

'What happened?' Izzy asks.

'We don't have to talk about it,' Dora says.

'He go over?'

309

'No.'

'You bring him home?'

'Yeah.'

'That's always better.' Sal takes a respectful moment. 'Caught in the net?'

Fitz shakes his head. The movement feels tarry, as if the air has grown thick. He is terrifically drunk, has been drinking since Hagerty released him from questioning. He makes a vague motion around his throat. 'Sick, you know, with the withdrawal.'

Both Sal and Izzy sit back. 'Stupid bastard,' Sal finally says.

'I shouldn't've let him go out,' Fitz says. 'I should've seen how it was and turned right around.'

'You couldn't've known.'

'It was my job to know, goddammit!' Fitz downs his shot. 'I let things get out of control. I lost control. My boat, my responsibility, right?'

'I don't know, Warren.' Sal drains his pint, looks in the empty bottom. He is already quite drunk himself.

'John—' Fitz stops himself, wonders what he was about to say, wonders whether he will say something damaging before the night is out. Perhaps he actually wants to say something damaging, get caught in something, pay the piper – he suddenly feels the urge to defend himself. 'Those boys, they just want to do things their own way.'

'Everybody's got to do things their own way, you ever notice?' Sal pours himself another beer, then he hovers the pitcher over Fitz's untouched pint. He puts the pitcher down and looks at Fitz mournfully. 'Come on, you're never gonna catch up.'

'How's Kate?' Dora asks.

Fitz waves her question away.

'I'm gonna give her a few days off,' Dora says. 'I'll call her tomorrow. You think I should call her tomorrow? I should call Edna first. I'll tell her we can have the wake here.' She pours herself a shot.

310

From the sailors' table comes a burst of laughter, then one of them starts singing. '*The old man shouts and the pumps stand by – leave her, Johnny, leave her! Oh we can never suck her dry—*'

'Hey hey!' Sal shouts.

'Keep it down, guys,' Dora says. She gets up and walks around the divider, drink in hand. 'You know no singing.'

'Sorry.' Ed ducks his nose into the neck of his shirt, stifling a giggle. 'We're just having a little celebration.'

Jefferson flails a limp-armed cheer. 'We're almost done! Woo-hoo!'

'Some respect, Jeff, okay?' She stares him quiet. 'That old man lost a crewmember, you know?'

'You find out what happened?' Wen asks.

She sits beside Hank, leans in. The men lean around her. 'You know Chris Albin?'

Jenny Stewart, nestled under Rob Ames's arm, gasps. Ed and Jefferson look blankly at her.

'Yve's brother,' Wen tells them. 'That's why she wasn't at dinner.'

'Jeez, I didn't know she had a brother.'

'I didn't even know her last name.'

'Her older brother,' Jenny Stewart says importantly. 'I went to school with him.'

'Poor kid,' Charlie says.

'Yeah,' Dora says. She gives Hank a little squeeze on the knee.

'How?' Wen asks.

'Dope, something, I don't know.'

'I almost dated him. He was always a mess,' Jenny Stewart says. 'That whole family is a mess.' She snuggles deeper into Rob's armpit.

'That's fucked up,' Ed says. He shakes his head, sits back. He drums a brief tattoo on the table's edge. 'That's fucked up, yo.'

'Yve's brother took drugs?' Charlie looks to Wen. Wen shrugs. He doesn't know any more than the rest of them. He wonders what else he doesn't know about Yve. He is vaguely relieved that he never slept with Kate. Wife of a junkie explains a lot, he thinks, then he wonders what he means by that.

28

The house is too full. It is as if the walls are breathing, dripping with the fogged exhalations of her extended family. Yve lies awake, counting the sweep of light-house beams. Four, seven, eight, twelve, fourteen, sixteen, twenty, twenty-one. She is too aware of the shape of her room, its rectangularity. The way its dark, unseeable corners pinch whatever light bleeds around the blind. She lies on a pallet in a box, which is stacked upon another box and lined beside other boxes, all organized in the box that is her parents' house . . .

Unable to sleep, she leaves early for work. It is so cold, the breath hardens in her nostrils and chills all smells but a whiff of vagrant woodsmoke. The yard dogs huddle near the back door of the CARP office, perhaps for a bit of escaping heat. The yard weeds are freeze-dried and rattling. They catch at her skirt as she passes. She climbs the clanging fire escape, swiping frost from the railing with her mittened hands. A thin red line spreads over the bay. She is glad to have work. At least she knows how the day will go. The sun will rise and the black bay will turn purple; by the time the men have eaten, the sea will fade to a grayish-green, the frost will melt, evaporate, and the railing will turn a flat black. She'll throw the breakfast scraps to the dogs. They'll move out into the sun to sniff and fight and forget the cold.

Coat off, apron on. Water to boil. Beer bottles off the table, rinse them, sort them in their cardboard cases for the return. Mix juice, set out plates. Take eggs and

312

sausage from the refrigerator. Set the milk on low. Pour steaming water over the grounds.

In the living room, Charlie lights his pipe and starts coughing. He is generally the first up and in for coffee. The bathroom door opens and closes and there's the long wait before his piss hits the water. Charlie has prostate. The things one learns. He flushes. She snips sausage links between the knife and her thumb into the sizzling pan, expecting at any moment now Charlie's hand on her shoulder, but his footsteps go back to his room. She leans back so she can see out the door to the empty hall.

The meat is nearly done and no one is yet up. She wants to hold on the eggs till at least Hank has come in. When he comes in, the others soon follow, because he's so loud. Eggs take only two minutes to fry and five to get cold and rubbery; she likes to do them last minute. And the toast. It's no good cold. She takes the butter out to soften and stops a moment, standing in the dark kitchen, butter dish in hand, caught by a forming thought. She looks at the clock. Six-thirty. She takes the sausage pan off the burner and lowers the milk so it won't froth over. She goes down the hall, past the naked ladies – now some sport mustaches, bras drawn over their naked breasts, bikini bottoms. She knocks on the living-room door, pushes it open. Hank is still in bed, reading a magazine. Charlie is fumbling with his shirt.

'So am I making breakfast for no one?' She tries to smile and sound chipper.

'We're getting something of a late start.' Charlie follows her to the kitchen, buttoning his shirt. He sits at the table. 'You okay, love?'

'Yes, fine.' She keeps her back to him, flipping eggs. The yolks quiver and threaten to break. The eggs sputter in the sausage grease and the milk rises in its pannikin. She pours some in a mug with coffee and takes it to Charlie.

313

He puts his hand on her wrist. 'We were at the Wind last night. Dora told us. We're sorry about your loss.'

'Thank you.'

'We really didn't expect to see you today.' He looks sheepish. 'You know, after your news.'

'Oh.' She feels as though she's come upon a brick wall in a previously clear road. 'Oh. Well, I'm here, so you may as well eat.'

She goes back to the stove. Hank shuffles in and helps himself to coffee. He sits, reading his magazine and waiting for his eggs. A weather radio starts up behind the door to Wen's room. The toast pops, startling Yve. She gets it, sets it down, her heart beating quickly.

'Should we wake the others?'

'Maybe we should let them sleep,' Charlie says.

Hank cups his hands to his mouth and yells at the ceiling, 'Get up, you lazy bastards!' He throws his magazine at Wen's door. 'We got a boat to paint!'

Someone, Ed, hollers from above, 'Shut the fuck up!' But the door in the ceiling is opened and Yve can hear Jefferson complaining in his soft drawl about his jesuschristing head being broke. There is more rustling in the attic. They are all up now. Neil comes in through the hall, dressed neatly as always, and pours himself tea. He says good morning to Yve, takes a slice of toast, and goes back to his room.

'He's disgusted with us,' Ed says. He and Jefferson pull up their chairs.

Yve fries more eggs, a whole dozen. They crackle and sizzle and stink. When she brings their eggs and meat over, Jefferson's cheek is on the table and Ed is taunting him, feeding him bits of toast as if the man is a bird fallen from a nest.

'You don't look so good,' Ed says to her.

'You don't look so good yourself.' She pours coffee for the two men. It smells burnt. She holds the skin

314

on the warmed milk back with a spoon as she pours.

'We were at the Wind,' Ed says. 'Three sheets to it.'

'Where's Rob?' she asks.

'Peg Boy won't be joining us.'

'He's a bit under the weather.' Jefferson lifts his head just enough to move his jaw for speech.

'He's a bit under Jenny Stewart,' Ed says.

Jefferson laughs, then moans.

Wen's door opens. He totters out, rubbing his eyes. He is naked to the waist and further, a plaid shirt wraps low around his hips like a skirt. The dangling sleeves graze his ankles. The line of hair below his navel looks pomaded, and she can't stop herself from following that line to the denser patch over the sarong-like knot of his shirt. A blue vein shows through the skin inside his hipbone. She realizes where she is staring and she lifts her eyes to his face. He doesn't look at her. He moves slowly about the kitchen, fetching a glass from the dishrack, then standing in front of the refrigerator a long time, long enough for the cold to reach across the room to Yve. He says nothing to anyone, as if he imagines himself to be alone. He doesn't look at her. She feels she is standing at the edge of something – she looks about the stove for a clue as to what she is supposed to be doing. Then she forgets, and she turns again to watch him. His spine bumps down his back and disappears in the low-slung wrap. She would like to lay her hand on his back and have him stand and look at her. Then he would say that he, too, is sorry for her loss.

He finally pulls the orange juice from the refrigerator. He pours himself a glass, then another, the second swallowed with two aspirins and a B12 from the bottle he keeps on the spice rack. He stares out the kitchen window awhile. During the last few months his hair has grown dreaded in back.

'We have to finish today,' he says. 'They're talking snow.'

The men around the table look at her as if it is up to her to answer.

'Yes,' she finally says. 'Come eat.'

He stays at the window. She says, 'I might need tomorrow off.'

'You can take today off, too — leave after breakfast.' He gets himself a cup of coffee and starts back for his room.

'Oh, I don't need today off.' She goes to the stove to check on the milk, crossing his path and making him stop for a moment. The coffee slops from his cup.

'Sorry.'

'It's okay.' She kneels at his feet to wipe it up. He stands still while she cleans.

'We're just about done,' he says to the top of her head.

'I'll cook extra today and leave heating-up instructions for tomorrow. You did fine the other night I left early, right?'

'You don't need to stay.'

She goes to the sink and rinses her sponge. 'I'm happy to work. I'd rather work.'

'You don't have to,' he says. 'I mean, there are leftovers and I'd just as soon have you leave with the rest.'

'Leave?' She rinses the sponge again.

'I'm letting all the extra help go. We'll finish before lunch.'

She turns. He's standing by the pantry, fiddling with a useless hinge.

'Are you letting me go?' she asks.

'Yes.'

'Uh-oh,' Ed says.

Wen shoots him a look. Then he turns back to Yve. 'You knew we couldn't keep you. We're rehiring in the spring if there's a sailing season.' His shoulder hitches and he goes into his room. She follows him. He closes the door behind her.

316

'I don't understand.' She stands in the middle of the room, waiting. 'You didn't say anything about this yesterday.'

'You ran out of here pretty quick.' He looks at her uncomfortably. 'I'm sorry—'

She waves her hand. 'It's okay,' she says, though she has no idea what she means by this. She is not yet used to sympathy. Though she cleans frequently, there is little free space on the floor, between the nests of clothes, and *Wooden Boat* magazines, and stacks of Patrick O'Brian paperbacks. He unties the shirt and lets it drop into the dirty pile. His skin looks gray in the early-morning light. He pulls a pair of long johns from another pile. He smells them, then puts them on.

'Is that why you're letting me go? Now? Today?'

He looks at her. 'This has nothing to do with anything, Yve, but money.'

'I don't care about the money.'

'Joe Ames is tired of paying the extra crew, and we can't keep you. That's all.'

'I could cook part-time for part pay. I could just come in for dinners.'

'Come here,' he says.

She goes over to him, and he hugs her. He smells sour from drinking, and warm from not washing. She can smell herself on him. She lifts her hands to hug him back.

He steps away from her. 'Hey, I heard a joke. A baby polar bear says to his father, "Dad?"' Wen deepens his voice. '"What is it, son?"' He raises his voice an octave for the baby. '"Are you sure I'm a polar bear?"' Then deepens it again. '"Why of course you're a polar bear, why do you ask?" "Well, because, because—"' He hunches his shoulders and chatters his teeth. '"I'm just so c-c-cold!"'

She doesn't laugh.

'You don't like it?' He does the baby again. '"I'm just so c-c-cold!"'

'I guess I don't get it.'

'I thought it was cute.'

'It's cute, but it isn't funny really.'

'I thought it was hilarious.' He puts on a T-shirt, the plaid shirt he was wearing as a sarong, and a sweater. He sits to pull on socks.

She sits beside him. 'So I guess I should just clean up breakfast and that's it.'

'That's it.'

She wonders what her face must look like, because he adds, 'Aw, come on. It's not like I'm moving away. We're gonna be here all winter.'

'Will you be here in the spring?'

'Probably.' He stops pulling on his socks. 'Yve. It's just a job. We're laying everyone off. Really.' He pulls her onto the mattress, then rolls so he is on top of her. He bounces her shoulders a little on the mattress, as if to shake that expression off her face.

She wiggles a little. 'Really?'

'Really.'

She wiggles a little more. 'Okay.'

They do it quickly, without fully undressing, and when he's finished she can still hear men moving around in the kitchen.

'What they must think,' she says.

'They must think we just fucked.'

'Oh Jesus,' she says.

'Well, we did, didn't we?' He touches her waist. Her skin feels as if it belongs to someone else. She wants to ask if they will fuck again, but she feels it inappropriate, or indelicate, considering. Then suddenly she's thinking about Chris and something white and spongy fills her lungs. She would like to run her hand down the center of herself, as if scooping the gizzards from a chicken, and scoop herself clean.

'I have to go, or they won't work.' He kisses the top of her head.

She waits until the men have left. Then she dresses

and straightens Wen's bed. She goes out into the kitchen and cleans it. She makes a list of things in the refrigerator that they have ready to eat, and a list of things they should buy the next time they go shopping, and she magnets these lists to the refrigerator. She cleans the bathroom one last time, and makes one more sweep through Charlie's, Hank's, and Neil's rooms. She doesn't want to leave. It is strange, leaving before lunch. It feels a little sad. It's odd, how she feels sad about her job, yet cannot access an emotion for Chris. It is as if she keeps forgetting he's dead. They hadn't spoken for so long. She was so used to him not being around, she saw him so rarely since he left home, and now it feels as if he is just fishing, and she will see him soon enough, at Thanksgiving. He will be there with Kate and Martin, cleaned up and well-behaved for the few hours it takes to get through the afternoon.

She takes her coat from the hall hook. When she steps onto the fire escape, the dogs look up. She spreads her arms to show she has nothing for them. As she passes, they nose her legs and she holds her hand so they can run their heads under her palm. She winds the chain through the gate. Instead of heading straight home, she decides to go down to the yard to see them put on the last coat of paint.

'There's Yve,' Phil Albin says to Helio Carreiro. She doesn't see him, he is at the window in the shiploft, looking down on the shipyard and the schooner below. This morning, his house crowded with women, Phil couldn't find a comfortable spot, so he wandered out. As with birth, it seems death belongs to women. They have a thousand little jobs surrounding it: cutting vegetables, folding napkins, making telephone calls, and running errands here and there. Everything needs to be turned upside down and cleaned, and suddenly people don't stay in their own houses,

319

and there's company in every room. The sofa's been taken over by shoe boxes filled with photos, and someone's begun a project with posterboard, pasting up snapshots of Chris and mementos from his life: blue ribbons and writing samples and pictures he drew as a child.

'She's not at work,' Phil says.

'Captain probably let her go. He's letting everyone go today, except his crew.'

'Oh.'

Helio stays at the draft table, sorting through ship plans. He unrolls them, throws torn ones to one side and good ones in a box. He points a paper tube at Phil. 'You know how much Ames says this is worth?'

Phil shrugs.

'Five dollars. He says he gives me five dollars for every single one I got. And thirty if I got a model to go with. I got a box of them! Maybe you should go through your barn. Maybe he gives you money for those ice tools. You not gonna use those.' He moves to the shelves along the wall, where more ship plans lie amid the warped battens. Webs of faint lines show through the scuffed floor paint – the measurements of hulls drawn, painted over, redrawn, painted over. Helio comes up and looks out the window.

'Lucky boys, no snow. Still, in the morning there's a frost, and that's bad. The paint, you know, gets weak.'

'How many hours they give between coats?' Phil asks.

'Coat a day. Finish in the morning, dry in the afternoon.'

'That's no good. It isn't sunny enough.'

'They don't wanna keep her on the ways.' Helio rubs his fingers and thumb together to signify money. 'What can I do?'

In the yard below, the men are tamping the lids down on their paint cans and putting away their tools. They bought everything from Service Marine, Phil can see the logo from here. 'That captain's green,' Phil says. 'He doesn't know anything about anything.'

'It's not the captain. He's not such a bad man. Ames wants her for the Thanksgiving parade. Captain says to me, I can't make her stay if Ames don't wanna pay more.'

'Joe's a penny-pinching bastard.'

'These days, who isn't?'

'You got anything over the winter?'

Helio clicks his tongue. 'I'm thinking I shut down a few months maybe.'

Phil nods.

'I hear you got Fitz over down your way. What he's paying you, if you don't mind me asking? Maybe I put in a pier, over there.' He waves at the derelict piers where the fleet once docked. 'Buy those, fix them up. There gonna be some boats needing dockage soon.'

'The fish are gone, Helio.'

'Ah, there's always something to catch.' He laughs. 'Yesterday's trash, tomorrow's delicacy.'

'If I were you, Helio, I wouldn't bother. I don't think there'll be many boats come spring.'

'Yachts maybe.' Helio laughs again. 'You sell for the yachts, I dock the yachts, fix them up in my yard.'

'I don't know. Charlesport has that sewed up pretty tight, I think.'

'They squeezing us. You, me, and everybody. This town – no old business gonna survive.' Helio shakes his head. 'How much you say you charging Fitz?'

'Nothing.'

There's a respectful silence. Already, Phil thinks.

'I'm sorry about your son,' Helio says.

'It's okay.'

'How's Alma?'

'Not good. She'd like to see more done.'

'Is there gonna be more done?'

'I don't know. Karl down at the funeral home says he clearly died of choking, like John said. Jack Hagerty came by this morning, said something about an investigation, if I want.' He mentioned to Phil that there were some bothersome details, like the spent fire extinguisher and the broken radio, and John's bruises, but John had explained about a fight. Jack offered to call for an autopsy, to impound the boat, but Phil said no, it wasn't necessary. Still, Jack said, there're other things to look for. I'm sure there are, Phil said, but I don't want Chris making any more trouble for anyone else.

'He's been trouble for us all a long time,' Phil tells Helio now, meaning Chris. 'I told Jack, There's no point in going around, poking around. John's got it hard enough; Kate, Martin. Everyone. We all still got to live here.'

'Fitz is taking it hard,' Helio says, as if to comfort.

'Yeah? I haven't seen him.'

Helio makes a sign of drinking. 'Like a crazy man, Dora says.'

Phil puts his hands in his pockets. Then he pulls one out and shades his eyes. His daughter stands near the henhouse, rocking from foot to foot as if she is cold. He could go down and take her out to lunch. Take her over to the Wind for a burger. She looks at the schooner as if watching paint dry is something to see. 'That paint'll peel off in sheets, soon as they put her in the water,' Phil says.

'Not my problem,' Helio says.

29

First thing in the morning, John drives to Charlesport to pawn what is left of his mother's jewelry. He gets only a couple hundred dollars, mostly from her engagement ring and a string of pearls she'd inherited from her mother, his grandmother. John knows the pieces would get much, much more if he were to sell

322

them outright, but Fitz wouldn't forgive him. He puts the bills in a white envelope. Then he drives back to the Albins'. Edna Larkin comes to the door with Martin on her hip. She says Yve's at work and Phil is out. He explains he wants to see Kate. She says Kate has gone home for clothes, so he drives over to Kate's.

He buzzes the cracked doorbell; it sounds like a game show. Someone shifts in the house. No one comes to the door, though. He tries to look in the window, but the curtains are drawn. He stands so near the screen he can smell it. It smells like exhaust. Behind him, the yard has turned brown. The roses are cut back and leaves have been raked over their roots. Kate's porch still houses a Halloween jack-o'-lantern, though now the pumpkin is withered and sunk around the lid and eyes. A truck of Martin's has been driven up to the mat and parked. John toes it aside. He wears his deck boots, but his jeans are clean. He's brushed his hair and shaved, and changed the shirt under his sweater.

'Hello?' He opens the screen door and bangs the knocker, a brass whale with *Welcome* on its belly. 'Hello? Kate?'

He puts his mouth to the window and says, 'Kate, it's John.' His lips taste like screen now, like ashes. The tumbler in the lock clicks open, but the door remains shut.

John pushes the door open. He peeks around into the living room. 'Kate?' He steps in.

'Hey John.' She is on the couch, watching TV.

'I brought you something,' he says, and he's immediately embarrassed by the envelope he holds out. She takes it from him and holds it against her stomach. The backs of her hands look white and wet; she wears a pair of Chris's old soccer sweats and crocheted slippers with rabbit ears and a face near the toes. Alma made a batch of them last Christmas. The men got dogs, the women rabbits. Yve used hers as puppets for Martin.

'I appreciate that you brought him home,' she says. She doesn't move her eyes from the screen.

John doesn't know how to reply, but then she goes on and he doesn't have to. 'I realize you could've just tossed him over and made less trouble for yourselves. Say he fell over.'

'Come on, Kate.'

'Jack Hagerty was over Albin's this morning. Asking all kinds of questions.'

'Yeah?'

'He told Phil he wants to search the boat.'

'Okay.'

'Would he find anything?' Her voice is hard.

'I don't know.'

He wants her to say something less hostile before he comes farther into the room, which is dark but for the blue light of the TV. Scattered all around, on the couch, the floor, the table, are photos. It is too dark to see the images, but he can imagine all the times that cameras came out. Kate was always one for taking pictures. She liked arranging them in albums, noting the when, where, and who. Sometimes adding those funny bubbles, as if the people were cartoon characters saying funny things.

'What's all this?'

Kate waves at the albums. 'Edna has this idea, for the wake. Posters around the room, give people something to look at.'

'I'm sorry—'

She holds up her hand. Then she tucks her hair behind her ears; it needs a wash. She doesn't take her eyes from the TV, bending forward and finding her cigarettes and lighter amid the litter on the coffee table as if she were blind and working from memory.

'Come on in,' she says.

He steps all the way in, across the room to the fireplace. Kate would just have to lift her eyes a little to see him there. He watches her watching. The TV

324

music lounges and dribbles from the dull speakers. His fingers stroll the mantel, picking up things and putting them down. Except for the photo albums, the room has a bare look, and he only finds small things to touch, paper clips and a book of matches.

'Sit,' she says. Besides the sofa, there is no other chair. He crosses the floor, treacherous with Martin's toys underfoot. As he sits, dust floats up, blue in the blue TV light.

'I remember this,' John says of the video. 'It's your wedding.'

'Yeah. I'm corny like that.' She lights another Salem. On the screen, blue people dance past the round tables of the Charlesport Charthouse. Chris and Kate slow-dance under a circle of light. The song is 'Always a Woman.' In another verse, John will get Yve out on the floor, too late for them to really enjoy it.

'Somebody called,' Kate says.

'What?'

'They didn't say anything.'

'What do you mean?' He half-turns from the TV, but the picture sucks at him, and he can't get his eyes to move to her face.

'I said, He's dead, and they hung up. That's why I didn't answer the door.'

Now he looks fully at her. 'Who do you think it was?'

She stays watching. 'Whoever you were working for. I don't know. But you better give them what they want.'

'Who were we working for?'

'You're kidding me, right?'

'No.'

'You don't know?' She almost laughs. 'Well, I don't know! Chris didn't tell me anything. I've just figured something was up from—' She waves her cigarette, as if there are clues scattered about the room.

'I don't even know what we were doing out there, Kate. We met this one guy—'

'Well, he didn't say anything.' She doesn't add that Chris might have, had she given him half a chance. She doesn't tell John that. 'We didn't talk before he left,' she says.

John feels something seep out of him. 'Mind if I open a window?' He reaches behind and pushes back the curtains so the sun fills the room with dusty light.

'Close that. It kills the picture.'

He closes the curtain. On the TV, Kate is about to throw the bouquet. They watch the women gather in a pastel flock. It strikes John that all weddings are so similar, so redundant, he wonders why people get so worked up over this or that, as if these flowers or that dress will make any kind of memorable difference.

'Do you think we're in trouble?'

'I don't know. Why don't you call the guy?' Kate says, blandly.

'What guy?'

'The guy you met.'

'I don't have his number.'

'You have his name. There's information.' She opens her hand slightly; the roam phone is on the coffee table. John takes it up, and it too smells ashy.

The electronic woman asks, What city, please?

'Miquelon.'

Immediately a live woman comes on. 'What city?'

'Miquelon. It's a French island near Canada. How do I get information for there?'

There's a few seconds of dead air. John watches a blue shadow of a girl he knew from high school – Irene Daly, her name comes to him from nowhere – jumping up and down with Kate's bouquet as the other women, open-mouthed, clap. The operator comes back on and gives him another information number. As he dials, the men at the wedding line up and TV Kate removes her garter and hands it to Chris. A French woman comes on.

John says, 'LaFortune.' Chris flicks the garter and the men lean away, but it hits Walley in the shoulder.

The French operator says in English, 'I'm sorry, there is no such listing.'

'For LaFortune?'

'I'm sorry, there is no listing for LaFortune.' She clicks off.

In the video, poor Walley sweats the garter up Irene's stockinged leg while the band plays a titty-bar vamp.

'Well?' Kate says.

'No listing.'

'I'm not surprised. All I can say is, you better find out what's up, before they come looking for you.' She leans forward. 'Look at me, I was huge.'

John looks. On the TV, the vampy song is ending and Chris has spun Kate into a precarious dip. She is hugely pregnant.

'Do you think they'll come here?'

She shrugs.

'Maybe you should go back to Albin's.'

'Edna was getting to me. I'll go back soon.' The tape ends suddenly, and Kate hits rewind. They all dance backwards, fast and frantic, through strips of blue static. The video machine whirs. Kate watches this as carefully as she watched the actual video.

John waits a bit, then says, 'I don't know who called you, Kate. Chris set it all up. I don't know what they could possibly want. What they gave us was empty.'

She puts her hand on his knee. 'I can't help you there, bucko.'

He feels ill. He needs to sleep. He says, 'I'm going, then. I'll see you tomorrow.' He stands; her hand falls off his leg and lies on the couch, palm up. She doesn't look up. Her eyes are fixed on the backward action.

'Watch with me,' she says.

John sits back down.

The rewind finishes and Kate hits play. She leans

her head on his shoulder. They watch her march down the aisle with Phil Albin standing in for her father.

'Look at me,' she says. 'What a cow.'

After he leaves Kate's house, John drives back to the Albins'. The boat is undisturbed since he left it last night. He goes over every surface. He palpates the mattresses, pillows, and life vests; he opens every food container, every carton, even the cans. He dumps their contents overboard, and the water beside the boat turns soupy. He goes through all the spare parts in the engine cubby, the boxes of belts and oil filters. He unrolls charts and opens books. He empties the emergency stores in the lazarette and lifts every sole board and peers around with a flashlight. He unscrews pipes. He can't find where it is hidden, if it is in fact even there, and though he feels frightened searching, he can't stop. He wants to find something and he doesn't want to find something. It is a creepy and uncomfortable feeling, as if he is a child rooting through his parents' drawers. As a last-ditch effort, he begins shoveling the ice from the hold. He is hoisting a bucket when he sees Jack Hagerty peering down.

'Cleaning up?'

'Yeah,' John says. He isn't sure if that is the wrong thing to say.

'Can we talk? I just have a few more questions.' His face is dark with the sun directly overhead, and John can't read his expression. His voice is flat and friendly as always.

'Sure.' John climbs out. They walk to the road and away from the house. Jack has parked the police vehicle out front instead of in the drive. He stops for a moment to say something to Dick Bates, who sits inside the idling car.

'The funeral's Wednesday,' Jack starts once they get a few yards away.

328

'Yes.'

'Viewing tomorrow.'

'Yes.' John paces his steps with the sheriff's. Here the road, a mix of shell and gravel, is loud under their feet.

'I stopped by to see Karl.'

'Yes,' John says. Karl Ostrood is the undertaker.

'How's your jaw?' Jack asks suddenly. John touches his jaw and Jack goes on, 'There was something that concerned Karl. And me, when he showed me.'

'Yes?'

'Is there anything you forgot to tell me?' Jack stops again. They've come to the place where the road turns under the pines and heads out to the lighthouse at the tip of the spit.

'About?'

'About Chris. When he choked. You said he was in bed.'

'He was. He was in my bunk because he was sick, and we didn't want him climbing up to his. We were worried he'd fall out.'

'How worried?'

'What do you mean?'

'How worried were you about him falling?'

'I'm afraid I don't understand,' John says.

'He has some marks.' Jack circles his fingers around his wrist. 'We found them strange.'

'I don't know about that,' John says.

'About what?'

'I don't know.'

They stroll awhile without talking. John has known Jack Hagerty his whole life. The man is not much older than he, just enough that they never were in school together – when John was in the grade school, Jack was in the junior high. Still, Jack's was a name he always heard. Peggy, Jack's younger sister, was in John's class. As they walk the smell of pine and of the ocean comes on heavily. Beyond the trees, waves burble into granite pockets. John thinks back through the questions, all the way to Jack's first one. 'Are you going to postpone the funeral?' he asks.

'We don't have to. We've got photos.'

'Oh,' John says. He can't keep himself from asking. 'Am I in some kind of trouble?'

'Are you?'

'I don't know,' John says honestly.

'Let's walk back,' Jack says. 'There's going to be a lot going on, with the funeral and all.'

'Yes,' John says.

'You're not going anywhere,' Jack says. It is more a statement than a question.

'Okay.' John wonders what Jack thinks he knows and what he might be waiting for John to do. He wonders how much observation he is under. 'I'm not going anywhere.'

If there is anything on the boat, John can't find it, but he doesn't trust that Jack won't look and have better luck. Because he has no other ideas, he drives over to the house on Pine. Both of the ladies are home, and they recognize him from the times he's come to get Chris, and they let him in without words. It is colder inside than out. A few windows are missing, and the walls in the living room are broken through in places, as if by a sledgehammer. There is even less real furniture here than at Kate's, but the space still seems full and ornate, because of the litter scattered everywhere. A lot of cardboard boxes, caseless pillows, and cheap blankets. Candles line the sills. A few are lit, softening the edges of the room and making the different patterns on the blankets jump.

The darker woman goes into the kitchen. Her hair is balding in patches in the back. John remembers she is Rea. He's rarely spoken to her; he usually deals with the lighter one, Dina. Today Dina wears a winter coat, a snorkel jacket, and she has it zipped so her face is framed by the raggedy fur. Dina says, 'Let's go in with Rea. It's warmer.'

The kitchen is warmer. The stink is worse, though, from the dishes piled in the sink. All the burners on the electric stove are on, and they glow in cheery spirals. The windows are covered with black plastic bags, and the room is dim but for the burners and a few candles.

'The landlord shut the water and heat,' Dina explains. 'But not the electric.' She lights a wand of incense off the stove and waves it around. John wants to ask her why they don't then turn on the lights, if they have electric, but it seems this house has some sort of powdery logic that he would never understand anyhow, and to ask would only point up his own naiveté.

'You John,' Rea says. She too wears a coat, of down-filled rolls. She sits on the table with her feet on a chair. Her eyes are fabulously made up. 'That Chris-boy's friend.'

John nods.

'What do you want?'

'Chris is dead,' he says, and Rea makes a fan of her fingers in front of her eyes.

'Don't be bringing that shit in here,' she says.

'I thought you'd want to know.'

She looks from the corner of her eye.

'What's gonna happen now?' John asks. He wonders, strangely, if he should offer her money.

'Dina, light a candle.' Rea waits until Dina lights a small white votive and places it on the counter beside the others. Then she asks, 'How'd he pass?'

John explains about the way Chris died, and about how they couldn't complete the job. He isn't sure what the ladies know or don't, so he tells them everything except the parts about throwing Chris's stash over-board and tying Chris up, because he thinks he might have betrayed some junkie etiquette and they might

331

judge him harshly, and refuse to help. He gives them LaFortune's name, and he tries to remember everything Chris told him about the plans, but that comes to little. He mentions the phone call Kate received. Rea nods her head knowingly, and holds her fingers folded before her face like a priest hearing confession. She makes occasional noises: small, kind *hnnnhs* to keep him going when he slows. He feels a sense of relief, spilling the whole story in one ear.

When he finishes, Rea says, 'So what do you want with us?'

'Chris told me we'd be getting paid through you. I thought you might be able to help . . .'

'I don't know nothing about all this.'

He wonders if she's lying. Her face doesn't change in any way.

'So, if you don't know anything about this, are you saying we went up there for nothing?' He stops short of saying Chris died for nothing. 'You're saying there's nothing on the boat?'

'Well, you got to figure there is, right?' Rea looks at Dina and Dina nods. The snorkel makes her movement slightly comical.

'Why?' John asks.

''Cause that's how it works. You the mule.'

'But what they gave us was empty.'

'Yeah, of course.' She puts the back of her hands to her hips.

'So you're saying it's there, but hidden.'

Rea looks at him as if he's stupid, saying something so obvious.

'So what am I supposed to do?'

'What you were supposed to do.'

'But I don't know who we were supposed to meet. Chris knew. And it's too late anyhow, they wouldn't be there anymore. We were supposed to meet some lobsterman—'

'What you first got to do is calm down,' Rea says.

'Like fifty percent of these things don't go right,' Dina says. 'You're dealing with some very flaky people.'

'You just got to make it right,' Rea says.

'With who?'

'Oh, I don't know that,' Rea says. 'You don't know that?'

He presses his fingers to his eyelids. 'I only knew that guy up in Miquelon. LaFortune.'

'The French Connection,' Dina says and Rea laughs. John wonders if she's heard a word he's told her.

'What do you know?' he asks her.

'Not much.' Rea brushes at a hovering fly. 'You might want to start with Vince LeHarve. It's probably him this end.'

'At least at some point in the scheme of things,' Dina says.

'What if it isn't?'

Rea says, 'Then you fucked, honey. You better hope whoever it is don't know your name.'

Dina peels the garbage bag back from the window and cold air streams in on a hairy column of light. There must be a cat somewhere. The window faces a cement backyard.

'Where's Vince LeHarve?' John asks.

'Bardot,' Rea says. 'He got a bar there, LeHarve's. Can't miss it.'

'The town is like this big.' Dina pinches the air.

'I've driven past it,' John says.

Rea looks at him accusingly. 'You been to LeHarve's?'

'No.' He meant the exit to the town.

'Don't go today,' Dina says. 'He's gone Mondays.'

Rea shakes her head. 'Not Mondays, Tuesdays. What's today?'

'Monday.'

'Then he's there.'

'No he's not.'

'Should I call?' John asks.

'Don't call. He's paranoid with the phone. Besides, he'll be gone already.' Dina's incense has burned down, and she holds the bare stick over Chris's votive. The splinters catch, curl into red embers, and burn out when they near her fingers.

'So I should go tomorrow?' John asks.

Rea says no and Dina says yes. Then Rea says, 'Get an early start.'

On his way out, John invites them to the funeral. Dina hunches her hands into her pockets. 'Yeah, we'll be there. Sure.'

'It's Wednesday at St. Peter's at two. There's viewing tomorrow at Ostrood's.'

'Yeah.' Dina peers at him from the depths of her snorkel jacket. 'Tell the widow sorry from us. She's a nice lady. What's her name again?'

'Kate,' John says. 'The kid is Martin.'

'Oh yeah.' Dina smiles. 'He's a cutie-pie.'

John looks at the house, but Rea has disappeared. Or else she's listening behind the door. He whispers, 'No one gave you anything?'

'People give us shit all the time.'

'No, I mean for me, or Chris. No one called?'

'We ain't got a phone.'

John tries to see down her snorkel. 'No. I suppose you wouldn't.'

Her voice softens. 'You go see Vince. He'll take care of you.'

He nods. He goes out to his truck. Before driving off, he notices she's still on the porch, so he rolls down his window. He leans over to catch her words.

'Fucking cold, right?' She makes a shivery motion as if she is some kind of normal person, talking about the weather.

30

Karl Ostrood did an excellent job; that's what everyone keeps telling Kate. She has quieted down – when she first saw Chris something ripped out of her, and her body moved as if she didn't own it. Her mouth stretched and she sobbed. She doubled over, clutching her stomach, until Yve pulled her upright. Now Kate sits on her folding chair as if glued. The effort to take the hands extended down toward her exhausts her. It's the pills. Dr. Briggs gave her an umber bottle, covered with little stickers. She keeps it in her purse. The bottle rattles when she moves. She's not high exactly, but the world does feel padded in cotton.

Martin couldn't sit still, so Edna had to take him back to the Albins'. Somewhere beside Kate, a million miles away – no, beside her – sits her mother-in-law. Yve is on the other side, dry-eyed. A little rhyme that. Side, dry-eyed. Kate turns to whisper it to Martin, and remembers once again that Edna has taken him home. It is strange how her head can't hold a thought. Her head can't hold a thought, her eye can't hold a tear. Something is wrong with her eyes. They feel burnt, as if someone has held a cigarette to her pupils. She makes a conscious effort to look about. There, yes – her eyeballs still move, still see. Good. Dark panels, quiet carpets. Very respectful. The flowers are beautiful. It's slow now. Everyone's already stopped by, perhaps; now they have to get home for dinner. Saw the body, time to heat up yesterday's leftovers. No. It's not like that. People have been kind. Dora says she'll bring the flowers to the wake, not to worry. Kate'll have to remind Chris to show up – no of course not. Of course not. She knew that was wrong even as she was thinking it, but she let herself think it anyhow just to feel as if he were alive for a moment. How unfair of him. Leaving before anything was figured out. Unfair, unfair. She could up and die too, if she wanted. She

335

could be that irresponsible. He's a quitter. He's always been a quitter. She could quit too, she could. She could get off this chair, or she could kill herself. This morning she lay in bed thinking she could take a leak or she could kill herself. She could get out of bed, drink a cup of coffee, find clean clothes for Martin, or she could kill herself. She could eat a slice of toast, take a shower, or she could take a handful of Valium. She doesn't feel like making even that much effort, she doesn't particularly feel like being dead, she just doesn't wish to get up and do all the little things you have to do when you're alive. If only there was a way to take a vacation from your life. Hire someone to come in and live it while you go south and sit on a beach. You can come back ten years later and find they did a wonderful job, keeping things going. You could decide to extend the vacation. Maybe never come back. That would be something, wouldn't it? Taking a vacation from your life.

Someone, Phil, is taking Kate's arm. It is time to go. They pass by Chris again, look in, there he is. Why is the makeup always so bad? It is a cliché, the unmatched foundation, the line at the jaw, the improper lipstick and blush. Men don't make up in life; why should they in death?

'Come on, dear. There you are.' Phil tucks Kate in back. Yve also slides in the back, leans to lock Kate's door. Phil then gently guides his wife into the passenger seat. He walks busily around to the driver's side, jingling his keys; heel-toe, heel-toe, his walk a self-important rush, as if to communicate his satisfaction of getting this little bit of business, seating the women, over in a timely and efficient fashion.

The town rolls past the window. Kate plays with her focus, looking at the street, then at the dirt on the glass, then back to the street.

'I wonder where John was. I didn't expect Warren, but I'm surprised at John,' Alma says. Phil keeps his

336

eyes on the road; Yve looks to one window, Kate to the other.

'I hope Edna's gotten Martin to sleep,' Alma says. She opens her purse and fingers the few items. It isn't her regular purse, it is her dress purse, the black leather, and so it is relatively empty. Lipstick; tissues, used and unused. She left her wallet home. She always leaves her wallet home when she goes out with Phil. He handles the money.

They pass the Finast, and the cardboard cutout tree with its colorful paper turkeys.

'Oh, Thanksgiving!' Alma bleats. She'd forgotten it entirely. Suddenly the holiday bobs before her, bloated, white, to be dealt with. It cannot be ignored. Ignored, it won't go away. It will still be there, floating about, stinking. 'What should we do? Phil?'

'Whatever you want, dear.'

'Oh,' Alma frets. 'Girls? Any idea? Yve?'

'I don't know, Mom.'

'Martin wants to see the boat go in,' Kate says, in the soporific monotone of the drugged. 'I promised.'

What an awful situation, Alma thinks. She's invited people. They'll all be at the funeral. Should they be asked to come back again, a day later, to eat turkey? And talk about what? There are no rules for this. Do you honor holidays after your son has died? Why bother? It seems more than a person should have to do.

31

On Rea's advice, John leaves early, before sunup, and drives north along the coast. It's a long way, nearly four hours north. He hears but can't see the ocean until the sky lightens and the milky streaks on the wind-shield go from pink to gold to white. Hard patches of old snow crop up along the side of the road. He is near Canada now. The scenery here is all black and white.

337

The sky is white, two white cables of guard rail hum by, and farther off the marbled sea is white on black.

As he approaches Bardot, a little bit of hope bubbles up inside him. It feels like a nervous tic. Perhaps he can make things right with this LeHarve and be done with it. He has felt sick since this all began, he realizes now, and he is ready to be done. If he can make things right, whatever is on his boat will be off. He'll happily accept any amount of money they offer, he doesn't care. In his mind, he explains this to whatever God might be listening. To ensure things go right, he makes other promises: that the money will go mostly to Kate and Martin, and he'll be more generous to Walley and Edna, and he and his father will take almost nothing, maybe just enough to get his mother's jewelry back and to get through the next month, maybe just enough for a down payment on a ring for Yve – this last promise causes a sinking feeling. He berates himself. A ring now feels like a trinket. She isn't speaking to him, and his picture of her opening a small box, and of her face brightening and her arms going around his neck, is false and borrowed. It's been cheapened. In the past, there have been so many times he could have and should have bought her a ring, and it would have meant something. She expected one the birthday she turned twenty-one, and again that Christmas, and again at twenty-five – when he remembers this his chest feels like a tunnel with air rushing through. For a moment, he fosters this discomfort, then it, too, becomes stale. He never planned on marrying her. He tries memories of Chris, in hopes of stirring up something more genuine, then he gives up altogether. Even hating himself feels secondhand. He turns on the radio.

Bardot is a black-and-white town. The houses are painted white with black shutters and roofs. Every third one has a sign posted in the shallow snow: *For Sale, Hunneman and Co., Innovative Realty.* He follows black-and-white signs to the waterfront district. They picture a three-masted schooner, but there are no schooners in the harbor and there are few draggers. He parks on what he supposes is Main Street, though there is no sign anymore, just a headless post. It's the only street with storefronts, though the sidewalks are empty, and most of the buildings have soap swirls obscuring their windows like cataracts. Grainy snow wraiths over the unplowed pavement. It is blindingly cold. John's eyes fill with tears as he steps from his truck. He's had no sleep. He left Rea and Dina to search the Pearl again, unsuccessfully. At home he drank beer and watched TV until his father wandered in. Then he lay in his bed waiting for the white numbers on his clock to click over. He crunches over the snow, and his steps sound like chewing, as if he must eat the road between himself and the door that says, in small print, *LeHarve's*. There's no other sign. This building, too, is blind. The windows are painted gray from the inside. It is still quite early, just after nine, but the door opens, and miracle of miracles, a bell bounces on the chain; tinkling like Christmas.

'You're open,' he says. No one answers. He blinks, waiting for his eyes to adjust. There are two men – one behind the bar, one sitting on a stool, watching him. They are like him: in their early thirties, white. By the size of their hands and shoulders, they look as if they do some kind of manual labor. Perhaps they fish, or used to. 'It's early,' he adds.

The one behind the bar wears dark trousers and a dark button-down shirt, both of which look too thin for the cold. The one sitting on the bar stool wears a wool suit jacket, the greenish black of a faded tattoo. He's working a slip of paper with a small eraserless pencil; at his elbow waits a glass of beer. He's intent on the TV in the corner. From this angle, John can't see the screen. He can see the screen of the TV in the other corner: football. The man on the bar stool says,

339

'Shit,' crumples his paper, and throws it on the floor. He digs another slip from a plastic holder on the bar.

'Come in or don't,' the bartender says. His tone is the same Dora takes at the end of her shift, as if he's been there hours, pouring drinks. John wonders if they, too, have been up all night.

'We don't bite,' the bartender adds. 'Much.' He laughs. The other man doesn't.

John steps farther in, peers at the screen the other man is so intent on. This other man is playing keno, but he has no money down. He circles numbers on his paper, holding his hands close around the slip as if it's a test and they may cheat off him.

'Ah, fucker!' the keno player says. He tears the slip to shreds. He pulls another slip without looking at the plastic holder.

'Didn't win, I guess,' John says to the other one, the one behind the bar.

'No, he did,' the bartender says. 'I tell him not to play without money, but he does it every time. Hurts to win without winning, you know?' He smiles as if this is a little joke the two of them can share.

'I guess.' John sits on a stool. He puts a few bills on the bar. The screen blinks: *Three Minutes to Next Game!!!* The bartender nods at John's money and John says, 'Harp.'

The bartender brings his beer, takes his money. 'He promised his old lady he won't gamble, ain't that right, Denny?' They both turn to Denny.

Denny says nothing. He is busy watching the screen, so they watch the screen, and after a while the numbers come up. Denny scratches the ones he gets right. Then he slams his pencil on the bar. 'I coulda had that one.' He talks at the screen. 'I had four in a row.' The screen erases and blinks its three-minute warning. Denny starts filling out another sheet, and the bartender faces the football game on the other screen.

The beer is flat, but John drinks the whole glass

anyhow. He twirls a bit on his stool, looking for some-where to settle his eyes so it doesn't seem he is watching these men as closely as he is. On the wall a pair of cardboard Pilgrim children cavort with a card-board turkey. Their cheeks are rosy and their hair is blond. Someone has bent their hinged limbs into impossible positions. Denny curses softly, and crumples another paper.

'A real winning streak,' John says.

The bartender comes back over. 'Can I get you any-thing else?' He sounds suddenly annoyed, as if John has pulled him away from the game.

'Yeah.' The coaster beneath John's glass is damp, and little bits come off in his fingers. 'Do you know a man named Vince LeHarve?'

The bartender brings another glass of beer, though John hasn't asked for it, and he pulls another bill from John's small pile. He rings and puts a quarter down.

'You're not him by any chance?' John feels cloddish asking.

'What if I was?'

'I have something for him.'

'What d'you have?'

'Something.'

'What?'

'Are you him?'

'No.'

'Is he?' John indicates Denny and hopes he isn't somehow named both Denny and Vince, because of the small jokes he's made at this man's expense. Given an appropriate amount of time, Denny does not identify himself as Vince, so John asks the bartender, 'Do you know where he is?'

'Not here.'

'Not here?'

'Do you see him?' The bartender spreads his big hands.

341

'No, I suppose not.'

Denny breaks his small pencil and immediately gets himself another. 'What?' he says to John.

'Nothing,' John says.

'You looking at him? You looking at him?' The bartender laughs at himself saying this.

'No.'

'You looking at him?'

John shakes his head. Something buzzes behind his eyes, as if a fly is trapped in his skull. He feels suddenly very tired. It's the beers so early, after so little sleep. He's tired. He has had it. He is done. He will drive home and make up some tale to tell Jack Hagerty; he will rip the boat apart from stem to stern and if he finds nothing, then there is nothing to find. He will hitchhike to Alaska and change his name. He will go to bed and never wake up. He will put an oar on his shoulder and walk inland till someone asks what it is. He will do anything but this. Anything but this. He takes the last bill and leaves the two quarters. He walks the two steps across the rotten floor and jingles the door open, before the bartender-not-Vince says, 'If you got anything for Vince you better show me.'

'I should show you.' John turns. 'Who are you?'

'Vince's cousin.'

'How do I know?'

'You don't. But I don't know who you are either.'

As if this evens things out, John comes back. He sits on the stool. He says, 'I'm a friend of Chris Albin.'

'Chris Albin. Denny, we know a Chris Albin?'

Denny doesn't answer.

'Why should we know a Chris Albin?'

'I guess you shouldn't.' John starts to get up again. 'I'll go somewhere else.'

'You got nowhere else to go.' The bartender laughs saying this and Denny laughs with him, repeating, *Nowhere else to go*, with the same inflection. The

342

bartender says, 'I know who you are.'

John keeps his face slack in hopes the man will say something more convincing.

'You're a dumb fuck fisherman, aren't you? Why do we work with these yokels?' He says this to Denny; he expects no answer from John.

John waits, overly warm in his sweater and flannel-lined trousers. He wishes the windows weren't painted over. He'd feel more comfortable if he could see his truck.

The bartender turns back to him. 'What do you have?' When John doesn't answer right away he says, 'You don't even know.' He says to Denny, 'He doesn't even know.' He watches the game a second, but the players are just walking around the field.

Skag, John thinks. H. Horse. 'Heroin,' he whispers, feeling a fool.

'How much weight?'

'I didn't ask.'

'He didn't ask,' the bartender tells Denny. Denny shrugs. The bartender turns back to John. 'How much were you getting?'

'Forty thousand.' The inflated number springs from his mouth automatically.

The man laughs again. 'Forty.' He laughs and Denny laughs and says, 'Forty.' Then they laugh some more. Finally the man wipes his eyes and says, 'I can't do that for you.'

'What can you do?'

'Half.'

'Half won't do.' John gets up. The plywood beneath his feet feels springy.

'Denny?' the bartender says.

Denny stands up. He grabs John and swings him, headfirst, into the bar. Things go red, then black. John feels pain where his cheek presses against the wood, and pressure from the man's hand on his skull. Eventually the dark water drains away and his vision clears. He looks at the world sideways and sees the lapel of Denny's jacket.

'I should do you right now, just take it. You're probably dumb enough to have it on you. You probably got it in your truck, dumb fuck.'

John recognizes the bartender's voice, and he wonders if these lines, too, have come from a movie.

'You got it on you, you dumb fisher fuck? I should do you right now. Stupid shit. What d'you have to say for yourself? Huh?'

'I don't—' The words come out funny, and they laugh. His lips are squashed together like the childhood chubby-bunny game. He doesn't want to say anything else and make them laugh again. His mouth fills with spit, and he has to keep swallowing. His tongue tastes like aluminum foil.

'Huh? Huh?' The man keeps saying this one thing, *huh*, as if there's some answer to it, as if there's something John could suggest to make him happy. John closes his eyes. It brings a small peace. A little less input, that's what is needed. Sometimes there's just too much coming in, and shutting down one sense – his head is lifted up by the hair, then slammed back to the bar. This happens a few more times till the ocean roars in his ear like a shell. He feels his head lifted again and he knows this is the last time. Once more and he'll pass out and then who knows?

He says, 'Wait.'

They pull him sitting. He opens his eyes, and the room goes swimmy. Little lights spark in the corners of his vision.

'You got it here?' The bartender waves around, pointing *you* and *here*.

'No.' John licks his lips. He finds it difficult to think. 'Do you have the money?'

The man laughs again, joylessly. 'You kill me, man. Denny, he wants the money. You got the stuff?'

'No,' John says. Denny slams him again and

344

pulls him back sitting. He wants to pass out. His head hurts. He would do anything to be home now. He wants not to vomit, or piss himself, or faint.

'Where is it?' the bartender asks.

'On the boat.'

'Where's that?'

'Rosaline.'

'You want us to go all the way to Rosaline?'

'Do you want me to deliver it?'

'No, man.' The bartender chuckles. 'We'll come get it.'

'Okay,' John says. 'Okay.' His head hurts terribly. 'Will we still get the money?'

'Yeah, yeah.' The bartender nods and Denny steadies John's head for him. 'You just give me your address and we'll stop by.'

Denny hands John a keno slip and a pencil. 'You can write it here.'

'Can I talk to Vince, maybe?' John says. 'I'm not sure how I feel about you coming to the house.' He is sure this will get him another head-slamming, but it only warrants a blank stare. 'It's not my house,' he explains.

'He's out of the country,' the bartender finally says. 'He's in Marseilles. Listen, I'm in contact with him all the time. I know who you are, don't worry. You're a friend of that guy, that – Chris. If you'd just said that – it just took me a while.'

'How do I know you won't just kill me?'

'Why would we kill you?'

'So you wouldn't have to pay me?' John looks around the bar. The Pilgrim children cavort and contort with the turkey. He is having problems figuring out his options.

'How about tomorrow?' the bartender suggests.

'I have a funeral tomorrow.'

'How about Thursday, then?' Denny says.

'Okay. Thursday morning.' There is something wrong with Thursday, but John can't remember what.

345

His head hurts. 'Make it early,' he says, to be on the safe side. He writes down: *The Pearl, Albin's Marina, Rosaline. Early*. He slides it over the bar. 'Just don't come into the house, okay?'

The bartender chuckles again, reading the keno slip. 'You slay me, you know that?'

'I guess so,' John says.

'He says don't come into the house,' the bartender tells Denny. 'He says early!' Denny is back at his numbers, circling. There is one minute to the next game. That is what the large print says, though the digital numbers in the corner already say 0:51.

'Early.' The bartender walks down to the service end and starts watching the game.

'Can I go now?' John says.

'Yeah, we'll see you.'

'Okay.' John stands a few moments by the door. He can't quite believe they'll ever allow him to leave. Yet when the bell jingles him out, no one grabs him.

He crunches back over the snow and sits in his truck a few moments, letting it warm up. He looks at his face in the mirror. It shows no new marks, just the purplishness at the jaw where he took out the fire extinguisher. He puts his hands on the wheel and sees them trembling, and he is overwhelmed with nauseated relief at being in his truck. He throws her into reverse and spins across the snow, then fishtails away from LeHarve's. He feels like a man already freed. He grins dopily. He rolls down the window and opens his mouth to the frigid air. When he reaches the highway he's almost tempted to hit the horn, but he slaps the dash with an open palm instead.

By the time John gets home, it is too late to go to the viewing. He drives by Ostrood's and the door is locked. He wonders if Jack Hagerty was there, wondering where John was. He wonders what the Albins think. Should he stop by, pay some kind of respects?

346

He isn't sure he'd be welcomed. With that thought come thoughts of the impending funeral. Seeing Yve and Alma, Kate. He considers going to the Wind, finding his father, but he can't face Sal and Izzy and that whole crowd. Instead, he drives to the package store and gets a case of beer and a bottle of Beam. He drinks till he passes out, sleeps like a dead man. At 4:24, he springs awake. He told the men where the boat was. He invited them to the Albins'. He invited them. Suddenly he is afraid. He is afraid they'll come before the appointed hour. He's afraid they've already come in the night. He doesn't want Phil or Alma to have to deal with these men. He dresses without lights, quietly, so as not to wake his father on the couch. The adrenaline of yesterday comes back with a ragged edge. He drives the gray streets too fast; cresting Cherry, the truck catches a hiccup of air. It's just five when he parks. The Albins' house is still dark. Heading straight for the *Pearl*, he already knows something is wrong.

It is in the wheelhouse. He sees the problem and his heart stops, and his breath and thoughts stop, and the gaps where breath and thought and heartbeat were fill with something heavy. Someone has turned the EPIRB right side up in its rack. It's always stored upside down – it shouldn't be righted except for extreme emergencies. The Emergency Position Indicating Radio Beacon. Righted, it automatically signals distress and its GPS location, and the Coast Guard comes looking. And if they come looking, what will they find? His heart jump-starts, and he hurries to snatch the capsule up, but as he takes it from the wall, it comes apart in his hands. He turns on the red overhead. The internal electronics have been carefully removed. The emptied cavity is the perfect shape and size. He knows immediately what has happened. The knowledge washes through him like an icy wave. He slides to the floor and sits for a while under the red light, with the gutted device in his lap. Then he fits it back together and restores it to its proper place. It makes sense they'd hid the package here: the EPIRB is the one thing on a boat you hope never to touch. It sits on the wall gathering dust. The only time you deploy it is when you're going down.

He climbs from the boat. He looks out at the water, then he walks to the road and looks around. It is still very early, and the neighbors' houses are dark. The bells have yet to ring for six a.m. Mass. Everything that should be white – the shell drive, the road, the Albins' house – glows bluely. He wonders what time Denny and the bartender came by. His breath comes in short blue puffs as he trots back to the boat. He looks carefully now at the ground along the shore as if he has the skill to decipher clues from the bent blades, the scuffed frost, but all he sees is his own trampling. When did they leave? How early did they come? Are they still here? A light comes on in the Albins' kitchen. He runs to it. The screen door sounds like a shot.

Yve looks up, startled. She sits at the table with Martin, bent over his *One Fish Two Fish* story book, a cup of coffee at her elbow. 'He can't sleep,' she says.

'Was anyone on the boat?' John asks her. 'Last night or this morning? Your dad? Jack Hagerty maybe?'

'No.'

'You sure?'

'I didn't see anyone.'

'Can you ask your dad?'

She gives him a strange look, but she goes upstairs. John sits at the table. Martin offers him the book, but John stares at the wall calendar, the free one from AAA Salmon and Sons that comes around every Christmas. They have the same one at home on the fridge. Disjointed thoughts flit through his mind. Was it the men from LeHarve's? If so, they owe him money. But if it wasn't, if it was taken by someone else, then

the bartender and Denny aren't people he wishes to
see ever again. They will think him a welcher. What if
it was taken by Jack Hagerty – but it couldn't be Jack
Hagerty, could it? He wouldn't just take it; he'd
impound the boat and be waiting there to arrest John.
Through the ceiling he can hear the soft voices of Yve
and her father.

Martin holds the book out again.

'No, Martin, not now.'

The boy throws the book down. Then he swipes his
hand back and forth on the table. The book goes over,
then Yve's coffee flies out and hits the wall. He grabs
the table with both hands and shakes. Coffee drips
down the wallpaper. He looks at John accusingly.

'Calm down,' John tells him.

Martin screams, and Yve comes running. She heads
straight for Martin, lifting him from his chair and
holding him against her chest. 'Did you burn your
handies? Let me see, did you burn yourself?' She
rocks him back and forth and kisses his palms. Her
back is to John, and Martin stares over her shoulder at
him.

'What's the matter?' Phil says as he comes in. He
means with the boat, and the two men go out together.
The shadowed dragger lifts and sighs. John directs
Phil to the wheelhouse.

'That.'

Phil takes the EPIRB from the wall and turns it over
in his hands. It feels oddly light. John gestures him to
open it. Phil does. He looks awhile at the emptied
capsule, then he screws it back together, remounts it.
He puts his hands in his pockets. 'We've never had a
break-in before,' he says.

'Did you see anyone? Two men maybe? Hear anything?'

'If I heard anything, I'd've come out. Do you want
me to call Jack?'

'No.' John fingers the EPIRB. 'No need.'

Phil looks at him curiously. 'Are you in some kind of trouble?'

'I don't know. Probably not. I don't know.'

Phil gazes out over the flat water. The sky is lightening in the east. 'What two men?'

'What two men?' John says back.

'You said two men. Did I see two men.'

'I don't know. I must've meant Jack and Richard.'

'Why would someone do this?' Phil asks it as if he's thinking aloud. 'It's a strange thing to take.'

'I don't know,' John says.

Phil eyes him. 'Let's get some coffee. Maybe we can figure it out.'

'There's nothing to figure out,' John says.

The screen door bangs and Yve comes out, bundled up in her coat and scarf. She carries Martin on her hip. She tells her father, 'I'm going to take him for a runaround, try to tire him a little.'

'Okay. Be back soon to help your mother.' Phil keeps going on in, but John stops. He puts his hand out to Yve.

'Can I talk to you?'

'Not right now.'

'It's important.' He drops his voice to a whisper. He's not sure what it is he wants to tell her. There is so much she doesn't know. Things have been moving so quickly. If he could sit with her awhile, things might slow down.

'They took it,' he tells her. 'It was in the EPIRB and they stole it.'

'I don't need to hear this right now, okay?' She rocks Martin. 'Let's just get through the funeral.'

She leaves him standing in the middle of the lawn, and she tells herself she won't look over her shoulder until she gets to the end of the drive. Then at the end of the drive she makes herself not look. She will see him later on. They'll be together for hours, through the funeral, the wake. She doesn't want to see him ever again, after this. Every time she sees him, she feels as though her arms and legs are missing. She shows Martin their long, morning shadows. They make monster hands and walk funnily. She won't let him run, because he wears his new suit under his winter coat; it was the only clean thing he had left.

Their walk is long, all the way to the old waterfront. At first Martin plays by himself, balance-walking on the curb, kicking leaves and garbage. When he becomes bored, Yve pretends they are on an adventure. They are hunting tigers, she tells him, and he excitedly peeks down alleys and around cars. Then he becomes tired, and insists on being carried.

At the crewhouse, Charlie answers the door. He is still in his sweatpants, as if he's just woken.

'He's not here,' Charlie tells her.

'Oh?'

'He's down at the yard, painting.'

She rocks Martin on her hip. He is heavy, like a sack of potatoes. Behind Charlie, in the hall, the coat hooks are mostly empty.

'I thought you were done. He laid everyone off.'

'Yeah, well, he called them back.'

'Really,' Yve says. She puts Martin down on the fire escape. He crouches to point his fingers through the iron slats to the dogs. 'What happened?'

'Joe Ames took us into Charlesport for a little celebration last night, and when we got back, red paint everywhere. All over the hull.'

'Really.'

Charlie rubs his face. His nails are yellow and horny, and the gesture looks staged. 'I was up all night. We were worried they'd come back and do worse.'

'They?' Yve asks. 'Who would do such a thing?'

He shrugs. He doesn't meet her eye, and she is sure he's spent the night speculating. His suspicions would, of course, include people she's known her whole life.

351

'Someone broke into the *Pearl*,' she says, defensively. He looks at her blankly. 'Warren Fitz's boat. The one my brother was on. It's docked at my father's.'

'Busy night.'

Martin pulls against her hand. 'Well, I'm sorry I woke you.'

'No problem.' He waits a moment. 'Well, then,' he says.

'Yes, thank you,' she says, as he shuts the door. She stands there, feeling foolish for thanking him. For what? Why thank him? She should just go home, help her mother. Kate is probably still in bed. All she does is sleep now. And it's going to be a hard enough day. And Martin needs a nap. But she doesn't feel like going home. She doesn't feel like sitting inside and eating cold cuts and drinking coffee until she's ready to burst, murmuring little responses every so often to her mother or aunt. It is beautiful out: there's a light wind, smelling of snow. The tips of her nose and ears are cold. Football weather, her brother used to call it, though he played soccer. She doesn't want to go home. Not yet.

On the way, she stops at Garenelli's for doughnuts and coffees. She comes into the shipyard cheerily announcing breakfast. The men have the scaffolds out again, the paint and their long-handled rollers. She passes around the cardboard box top and the waxed-paper sack. They take their doughnuts and coffees and thank her, but they don't chat or joke. They go back to their painting quickly. Something has been written all over the port side in red letters. Yve can pick out *We Fish* and *Go Hom*. From the few other letters still uncovered, it is clear there were some obscenities. Whoever did this knew what a mess red would make and how difficult it would be to cover before the parade. Wet white on wet red. Pink roller strokes radiate in every direction.

352

She circles around the schooner. Martin wants to play in the water lapping up the ways, so she has to carry him around the stern. The starboard side is still clean, which makes sense: only the port side of the hull will be facing the shore as the *Shardon* parades to the Museum Pier tomorrow. Yve wanders forward, then comes around again, unable to find Wen. Jefferson whistles and points. Above her head, in the bow net as if in a hammock, lies the captain. His legs cross at the ankle, he has one hand behind his head, and with the other he slaps paint on the prow.

'I brought breakfast!' She holds the bag and last coffee up to show him. He doesn't respond. She calls to him again, then is too embarrassed to call again louder, with the other men there. He's unreachable from even the nearest scaffolds. If she wants his attention, she'll have to climb the ladder to the catwalk, cross the gangway, and pass him his coffee from the deck.

'Come on, Martin, want to go on the boat?'

Martin looks at her uncertainly.

She puts the coffee in the bag, puts the bag in her teeth, then has Martin wrap his arms and legs around her neck and waist. 'We have to give the captain his breakfast,' she tells him. She climbs, one hand for herself, one for Martin, and the boy starts whimpering after the third rung. He twists in her arm, looking fretfully at the ground. 'Hold tight,' she tells him, though she doesn't have to. By the time she reaches the deck he's pale and sweaty.

'I brought coffee,' she announces.

Wen doesn't come from the bow net onto the deck. She leans over the rail and looks down on him. Her face shades his, and he removes his headphones from his ears.

'I brought you coffee.'

'I don't have anywhere to put it.' He gestures at the bow net and his full hands.

353

'I guess not, huh?' She feels silly. She wishes he would just stop painting and come onto the deck. When it is evident he won't, she puts the coffee bag on the squared butt of the bowsprit. She tells Martin, 'Don't touch,' but of course he leans over and pretends to touch, so she puts it higher, on the samson post where he can't reach. Then she leans her elbows over the rail again. Someone talks from the earphones of Wen's Walkman.

'What're you listening to?'

'Portuguese station.'

'I didn't know you spoke.'

'I don't.' He concentrates on the spot he's painting. His eyes look crossed from the close focus. 'But it's a sexy language, isn't it? It reminds me of Russian. I could listen to a Russian woman reading an agricultural report, and it would turn me on.'

'Oh,' Yve says. She has no idea what he is talking about. Martin is wandering aft, so she takes hold of the tail of his jacket. He pulls against her hand and sits down hard and begins to fuss. She pulls him to her lap.

'Your coffee's getting cold,' she says over the rail.

He doesn't look up at her. 'Oh well. Gotta paint.'

'Will it dry in time?'

'I don't know.'

'It's pretty cold,' she says, meaning the weather.

He doesn't answer. White splatters the black net, his hair.

'The funeral's today,' she tells him. 'At two, at St. Peter's.'

Martin still fusses, so she puts her back to the rail and bends her legs at the knee so he can lean against her thighs, facing her. She takes his two hands in hers and makes clappy actions, all the while talking loud enough for Wen to still hear, if he is listening.

'We had the viewing already,' she says. 'Everyone came. I bet the whole town came—' She stops, starts

354

again. 'It was strange. We just sat there while people walked by and peeked in, like he was on display or something. Which I guess he was – I mean, it was a viewing. I kept thinking we should've had a basket and charged them fifty cents a pop.' She jounces Martin. Trot trot to Boston, trot trot to Lynn. 'Kate's really out of it. The doctor's got her all doped up.' If the pony goes too fast we *all fall iiinnn!* She spreads her legs so Martin almost falls through, then she catches him just in time. She leans back over the rail.

'You could've come. John wasn't around.'

Wen sits cross-legged in the net now, spreading the bristles of his pinked brush with a dieseled rag. A small can bowlined to the bowsprit dangles beside him, and the paint inside is also pinkish.

'Will you be there this afternoon?'

'I don't know.'

'Why not?'

He inspects the brush as if he can make the bristles go white again if only he is thorough enough. Suddenly he throws the brush over his shoulder. It flips a couple times and splats on the ways.

'Heyhey!' Ed calls from below.

Wen ignores him and swings himself over the rail and onto the deck. Yve stands and pulls Martin to standing also. She goes nearer Wen, and he recoils slightly.

'What do you want from me?' he asks her.

She's surprised. It takes her a moment to find an answer. 'I just wanted to know if you'd be there. I'd like you to be there. Is that so strange?'

'I have to paint this fucking boat.'

'You could just come to the wake. It's at the Wind, after.'

He looks off, over her shoulder, as if he's grown impatient with her. He sighs. 'I'm sorry about your brother, but I didn't know him, and he won't miss me.'

'I'll miss you!' The outburst is so childish she's

ashamed. She quiets herself. 'Are you worried about John?'

He holds up a silencing hand.

'Because if you are—'

His hand pushes the air. He speaks calmly. 'I just don't think I'd be very welcome.'

'I don't care what John or any—'

He closes his eyes, and she knows she's mentioned John too many times for Wen to believe her.

'Please come. I want you to come.'

'Don't make this into something.'

'What am I making it? What am I making it? It's my brother's funeral, for God's sake!' She can't find strong enough words. 'I just want you to come to his stupid funeral!'

'Shh. Shh.' He strokes the air near her arms. The drop cloth pulls at its tape as he walks aft. She picks Martin up and starts to follow, but he goes below. She peers down the midships hatch.

To Wen, her face looks white and unattractive, sagging as it does from the upside-down position. She can be pretty sometimes – she could have been beautiful, maybe, or at least faked it well if she'd lived differently. If she lived in a different place, a city maybe, somewhere where she would've been inspired to make an attempt. Instead, she appears middle-aged, already. He thinks it's a shame, really; her chance at youth, liveliness, beauty, has been thwarted. He doesn't blame her, it isn't her fault. She hasn't had enough exposure to anything that would have helped her realize her potential. She's been somehow stunted – as if she's been constantly pruned back, like an espaliered tree, bent and tied, this way and that. He does like her, did like her, in an abstract way, but he knows she is bound here and he is not, and she will never get out from under her family, this town. She won't leave. He will. And it is not his job to rescue her, though she peers down at him

356

with her pinched, white, expectant face.

'Come on, Yve, give me a break. Okay?' He looks up at her from the base of the companionway with a frustrated expression. She pulls her head back and blinks at the bright deck. They'll have to pull the tarps up, probably, before the schooner makes her trip to her new pier. He must have a lot to do. He must be angry about the red paint. She wonders what the graffiti said, and who did it.

'Okay,' she says to no one in particular. 'Okay.' She guides Martin off the gangway and along the catwalk. She descends carefully with him clutched fretfully to her waist and neck. Her landing on the ways makes a hollow pop. She sets the boy down. A wave sweeps in and she lifts Martin by his two hands out of the ocean's way, and he picks up his feet and says, Wheeee. Then he wants it again. She picks him up and swings him off onto the rocky scree. She looks back at the boat, but it is shaded against the white sky, and she can't tell if Wen is on deck or not. She feels as though something unswallowed sticks in her throat. Nearly thirty, she thinks, and she understands nothing.

When Yve gets back with Martin, her father and John are in the living room. They sit opposite each other – her father in his chair, John in her mother's chair – dressed in their dark suits and saying nothing. Warren Fitz is on the sofa. His suit hangs off him and a rusty nick shows on his throat where he cut himself shaving. Yve says hello, and Fitz nods back. He smells like Listerine. All morning he's been drinking water, one glass after another. Edna finally gave him a pitcher so he wouldn't keep bothering her.

John follows Yve into the kitchen. He has the nervous energy of a man who has been waiting. At first he was almost relieved to find the package gone, and not in the hands of Jack Hagerty, then his relief gave way to annoyance, then anger at being duped so easily.

He tells himself he'll go back tomorrow and get the money. He doesn't know if he should see Dina and Rea or the men at LeHarve's for it, and he doesn't know how he will get them to pay, but he has to make himself this promise, or feel like a fool. He's been waiting for Yve to come so he can tell her. In his mind, they go upstairs to her room, and while he's telling her the whole story, she wears a concerned and worried look, and she leans forward and asks him to please let it go, and he says, I can't. The heroics of this last statement embarrass him – so he goes back to the beginning part that pleases him most, the part where Yve is listening. He leans in the kitchen door, watching her wander the room, picking at leftovers. The house has been filled with donated food, and platters cover the counters.

Edna Larkin, at the sink, says to him, 'Make yourself useful, John. Clear the table.' Yve gives him a small glance. She looks terrible, as if she's been crying.

'You done?' John asks Alma.

Alma nods. She sags over her plate. Her face is pale and drawn. She's had a headache since they brought Chris home. Sometimes it's so bad she sees little lights behind her eyes and things go black and she has to lie down with a cloth over her face.

Walley, at the table with Alma, rolls his good eye from John to Edna. 'I'm done,' he says hopefully.

Edna doesn't rescue him. Someone has to sit with Alma, and she's a little tired of her sister's hysterics herself. Grief is one thing: she grieved when Abel was lost, and there isn't one day she doesn't think about him, but you have to go on. You can't fall apart so. There are living people to care for. Edna always knew it would end like this. Her sister has always had an unnatural relationship with her son – there's never been room for anyone else – she was saying just as much the other day to Bea Hopewell: if Alma hadn't spoiled Chris so much—

'Where's Kate?' Yve asks.

'Upstairs, getting dressed.' Edna jerks her head. 'Go bring her down.'

Yve plunks Martin beside her mother and goes up to Chris's room. When her brother moved out, her mother left his personal items exactly as he had. She cleans weekly, moving nothing except to dust. The room has an aseptic quality, as if it has been recently unwrapped from plastic. Kate stands by the window facing the backyard and the harbor. She's dressed in a black suit and a lacy scarf she found at the SnugHarbor Free Store, and she looks like a paper silhouette cut from the wintry light.

'Knock, knock,' Yve says. She feels awkward. 'You look pretty.'

'Do I look like a widow?'

'No. I don't know.' The question flusters Yve. 'What's a widow supposed to look like?'

'Edna. Dora.' Kate picks her purse from the bed and puts it down again. 'I don't feel old enough to be a widow. Do I look old enough?'

'Of course not.'

'I'd rather be a divorcée. It sounds better.'

'Edna says come down.'

'I guess if Edna says—' Kate almost smiles.

It's strange, Yve thinks. She only ever sees Kate without Chris anyhow.

'Look what I found the other night,' Kate says as they are going downstairs. 'We can watch it while we're waiting for the cars.' They are supposed to be picked up by a pair of limousines at ten minutes to two.

In the living room, Kate starts the video. 'Come on, everybody, come and watch.' The wedding march begins tinnily. 'Come on, Walley! You're in this.'

'You can go,' Edna tells Walley. He gets up from the kitchen table, visibly relieved.

'There's a funny part with you and that girl,' Kate tells him.

359

'Irene Daly,' Yve says. Their voices carry easily through the small house.

'Whatever happened to her?' Edna calls from the kitchen.

'She went to Portland to study secretarial skills,' Yve calls back. 'Her father's still around.'

Edna elbows John drying dishes beside her. 'Go on in with the young people.'

In the living room, Yve now has Alma's chair, where John was before. It makes her back look stiff. There are no other seats, so John sits at her feet and leans against her shins. He reaches over his shoulder for her hand, but she doesn't give it to him. He tilts his head against her knees and looks up in her face.

'Am I hurting you?' he asks.

'My knees. You're heavy.'

'Sorry.' He gets up and looks around, unsure of where to sit. Behind the half-lidded blinds, the windows look dull. The room is dark. Fitz and Kate have the sofa and Phil Albin the armchair. Walley's on a chair he's brought in from the kitchen. Martin sprawls on the floor, his ark animals all around. John lies on the rug beside him. He shows Martin how to launch the sheep with a teeter-totter made from a coffee spoon and a prone lion as the fulcrum. The boy is delighted. He makes little explosions under his breath, and Fitz looks over every time Martin whooshes his lips, as if each time this repetitive noise is made anew.

'John,' Kate says, 'you're not a window.'

'Sorry.'

She pats the cushion beside her.

He joins Kate on the couch. Martin crawls into his lap. The little boy is hot and smells sour. Something sour about the dye in his black suit. John pushes Martin off and sees his own suit trousers are wrinkled.

The video music pulls Alma from the kitchen. She stands in the door, her shoulder against the jamb. Phil

360

rises from his seat, but she shakes her head and he sits back down. She stays in the doorway, lightly swaying. From where she is, she can't see the screen; still she says, 'That's the wedding video.'

'Yeah.' Everyone answers for Kate.

'He looked so handsome. Remember, oh—' Alma puts her hands to her cheeks, and her eyes widen as if she'll laugh, but she exhales and drops her hands. She begins crying again.

'Alma, enough,' Edna says from the kitchen. Alma turns to stare at her sister a few moments, then she crosses between the couch and TV and goes outside. Edna takes a few steps after her. The door slams. Edna tells them, 'She's making herself sick.'

Walley twists in his seat and tilts the blind. 'She's sitting in the limo,' he reports.

'The limos are here then,' John says. He feels foolish, stating the obvious. He brushes at the wrinkles in his trousers. 'I suppose we should go.'

Edna grunts and starts gathering Martin's animals into her purse. As she bends, her dress tightens across her backside. People reach for bags and suit jackets.

'Who's in which car?' Phil asks. He offers Kate a hand. She stands, Walley stands. Yve stays in her seat.

John offers his hand to Yve. She takes it. Something in his chest surges, then falls back as she drops his hand and lets the screen door shut between them.

After the service, they go in the two limos to the cemetery. Alma falls twice climbing the hill: it's slippery on the grass with new soles and her heels sink in. A white tent stretches over the site at the top. It wasn't cheap, this plot, but Kate wants Chris to have a view of the harbor. Alma wishes they could all be together, but she and Phil have plots in the old section, near her parents. She never thought to buy for her children. Now she regrets it. From now on, she will advise people to consider these things. She made Phil buy two plots beside Chris for Kate and Martin, so when the time comes they can all be together. She made sure he checked the box for Care in Perpetuity. Are you sure there are no more in the old section? she'd asked Karl Ostrood. That's where everyone is. And what if Martin marries? There's a spot for him beside his parents, but what of his wife and children – That's enough, Phil said. It was confusing: where should a child lie? Beside his parents or his wife? Now Alma worries if they did the right thing.

Under the tent, rows of folding chairs face the grave. Green plastic turf lines the hole and covers the mound of bare soil beside. For a few minutes there's some scrambling – early arrivals have taken all the chairs. When it becomes apparent there aren't nearly enough seats, chairs must be given up for older folks and family. Alma's proud of the turnout. They filled St. Peter's. Now they're filling the tent and spilling onto the lawn. Alma and Phil, Edna, and Kate with Martin on her lap, all sit in the first row. After some coaxing, Yve sits with them; she wanted to stand. At least they got a nice stone, Alma thinks: bright white marble.

Everyone turns. John, Warren Fitz, Walley, Sal Liro, Israel Titus, and Sandy Hopewell are climbing the hill with the box. Fitz looks particularly worn from it. The casket is heavy; Alma had it lined with lead – she doesn't want anything getting at her son. She clutches her purse on her lap and thinks she doesn't care if Fitz has a heart attack: she blames him. After the service, on the steps, he had the audacity to take her hand. His other hand trembled on top. He said, It was an accident, Allie. I loved him – you got to know that – like a son. She said, Then I'm sorry for John. She walked away from him and has since stayed away.

The casket arrives and is placed on the straps and Father Dominic clears his throat. He says a few words no one can hear. He's old and his voice is weak; he leans against the stone. Once he begins with *I am the resurrection and the life*, Alma stops trying to hear. She fiddles with her purse strap. There is nothing the priest can say to make it better.

The wind lifts the scalloped edge of the tent. Yve looks under and out. Another section of cemetery is being built on the other side of the hill where Moseley's farm used to be. A chain-link fence sets off the area, and a couple pieces of heavy equipment – earth movers and shovels and such – sit idle. As teenagers they used to go into Moseley's field to drink and look at the stars. Once Chris told Yve he was going to get her high. He made her smoke pot until she fell back into the grass laughing.

They stand and sing 'There's a Wideness in God's Mercy Like the Wideness of the Sea,' then Karl Ostrood toes a lever and the aluminum rollers let down the straps, lowering the coffin. Then comes the walk-by with handfuls of dirt, and some people throw flowers. Kate gives dirt to Martin – he enjoys the throwing of it so much he wants to go back for more. When Kate swings him on her hip, he begins crying and stretching his hand for the mound. Without thinking, Yve takes John's arm and lets him walk her back down the hill. She holds his hand by habit, and they ride together in the limo with Walley, Kate, and Martin.

They take the long way through town, going first down to the waterfront for a little extra memorial. It is a long procession of cars and trucks, but there is little other traffic on the road. Alma gets out of her limo, supported by Edna and Phil, to throw a wreath on the water. Everyone else stays in their cars. Facing the water, behind the museum, a grandstand of aluminum bleachers has been erected for the parade, and a wooden platform stage takes up the parking lot. The fleet, festooned with protest banners, is still docked on the pier in direct defiance of the notice Joe Ames mailed the beginning of the month. By midnight, the

Coast Guard can legally tow any boat still there. 'Are they going to move their boats?' Yve asks no one in particular.

'Just off the pier,' Walley says. 'They want to block the channel.'

'They'll get penalties,' John says.

Yve almost tells them about the graffiti on the *Shardon Rose*, but then feels private about it. They don't talk the rest of the way to the Wind.

Outside, Dora has posted a sign: *Closed Due to Death in the Family*. It's like fighting a floral tide just to get through the door; the entry hall has no room for coats because a grand and gaudy wreath from CARP takes up half the space. None of that crowd – the mayor, the Ameses – have shown, but they bought a savings bond for Martin and sent it to Kate with condolences. Now the ladies go in with Phil Albin and Warren Fitz, while John, coats weighting his arm, pushes aside lilies for hooks. Their perfumed coats smell as heavy as they feel.

Inside, more flowers: on either end of the bar, on all the tables, standing on easels in the corners. All the lights wear black bowties, and the glass dividers sport black drapes over the boat etchings. So much money gone to crepe and flowers. What a waste. It makes John angry. His anger starts at the decorations and spreads outward, like an oil spill darkening the edges of his vision. He feels the fury rolling off him in waves, and he half expects to see people moving away as he walks past, but they still reach out and touch him, patting his arm or back. Everyone's dressed in black, or at least their darkest blues or brown. There is a general quiet, and the unlikely presence of children and babies and old widowed women who rarely set foot in the bar. And the regulars are on their best behaviors, at least for now: less smoking and no cursing or playing of the juke. John finds himself angered by the fact that everyone's dressed well, and that the women are made up.

He hates their politeness. It would be more appropriate, he thinks, if they wore their worst clothes and went around cursing and breaking things.

'How're you?' Dora, in black satin, pours him a whiskey.

'Fine,' John says.

'No you're not.'

'Don't worry about me.' John gets the bottle and a fistful of tumblers off her.

Yve and the rest are down the bar near the food. Dora worked all morning with Susan Furlong and the Jameison women, cooking turkeys and hams and a roast beef. In addition to the cold-cut platters from Garenelli's, and the two six-foot heroes with toothpicks holding the cut pieces together, there are cheeses, olives, pickles, fruit plates, cut vegetables, and dips on all the tables. Crackers and rolls surround chafing pans brimming with sausage, meatballs, and chicken breasts smothered with cream and canned mushrooms.

John hands glasses around, and even Alma takes one in her pale, shaking paw. He raises his glass and they all drink to Chris. This is all he can say – 'To Chris' – and he hopes it's enough. He pours again.

Sal Liro stands and says, 'He was a good fisher. I'da worked with him any day.'

'Hear, hear.' The two booths of fishermen stand and drink even though none of them would have had Chris on their boats. But the toasts are going now, and truth doesn't matter. Everyone in the bar has to tell some story of him- or herself with Chris to prove their right to eat the free food and drink the free drinks. For the first few rounds, people tell serious anecdotes, but as the stories continue they go for laughs or embarrassing moments. It comes back around to John. He says his bit, but he can't remember his words, even as they stream from his mouth. Worse yet, he suspects his empty toast is bleeding him. The unfelt speech pulls memories from his brain like ribbon from a ticker-tape machine. The tape is torn off and passed around by nodding others, then balled and tossed, and he spits more. He can't drink fast enough to replace what he's losing. He drinks and drinks and can't get drunk.

Yve makes the mistake of trying to keep up. She drinks too much too early. She throws up in the head and comes back for more, her mascara smeared and lipstick wiped on the back of her hand. She puts her sour finger under his nose, in the dent she calls the Angel Kiss. It's a game they haven't played in ages.

'Angel Boy. My mom—' she hiccups – 'called Chris that, remember? He had all that soft, white hair.'

He swats her finger. She replaces it. 'Angel Kiss—'

He takes her hand from his face and holds it down. 'You're really drunk, Yve.'

'I am.' She twists her fingers inside his. 'Do you still love me?'

He closes his eyes. He opens them. 'Time for you to go home.'

'No,' she says. She pushes against him. 'No. You can't just say go—' Her sentence dribbles off unintelligibly.

He takes her glass and puts it on the bar. 'Time for bed.' He puts his hand between her shoulder blades and she resists. He pushes her through the ship-wrecked room. It has grown late. Outside, beyond the backward writing, the sky is black and the constellations look like photographs. Abandoned jackets and ties flop on the backs of chairs. No one eats anymore. The crackers have cracked and crumbled and sogged into alcohol puddles, the Sterno has burned away and the sauces congealed around the meats. Everything has gotten uglier. At some point Phil Albin dragged his wife – cursing Fitz and crying for an investigation – out by the elbows. Edna followed with Kate and Martin. The other widows and children left soon after and some of the old guys got down to a good cleansing

366

cry. It is all a blur to John and he doesn't care to remember clearly. He steers Yve toward his father, who sits at his usual booth with his usuals: Sal, Izzy, Walley, Pete Hopewell, Helio Carreiro, and a couple of local drunks.

'Sit, sit.' Fitz waves at them. They don't sit. The table is littered with the flotsam of the night: a bottle of single-malt and a batch of tumblers, two pitchers with beery foam drying up the side and around the mouth, some half-pint glasses with the same stains. The ashtrays overflow with Newports and Pall Malls and Winstons. A stogie rests on a saucer. Someone's ordered tea and forgotten it. The milk has separated out in a pasty swirl.

'Come on, Dad. Time to go.'

'Go, what go?' Fitz fumbles through the litter, squeezing Cellophaned cigarette packs. 'The night is young. Have a drink with us, for chrissake.' He finds a carton of Owls and pulls one free. Then the fumbling search begins for a light.

'It's late.'

Fitz ignores him. He is searching for a clean glass now.

'Dad.'

Fitz slaps his hands on the table. 'For chrissake, can't you ever leave a man drink in peace!' He starts coughing. He wipes his wet face, then lays his cheek on his arm.

'I'll get him home,' Sal says.

'Okay then.' John looks around for Yve. She has tottered to the door and now is talking to a bunch of men there. John recognizes the captain off the *Shardon Rose*, and some of the others as the crew members. One has his arm around Jenny Stewart. Jenny sees John and turns red, and when John comes up, she murmurs condolences.

John says to the men, 'There's a sign.'

'Sorry.' The captain holds up his palms as if surrendering. 'We just came by for a drink.'

367

'It's okay,' Yve says. 'I invited them. Stay, Wen.'

'No, no. It's okay, we'll go.'

John looks around the place. It is mostly empty, except for the fishers. But still, there are all the flowers and black drapings. 'We got a wake here,' he says.

'It's okay,' Yve says. 'I invited them.'

'We'll just go.' The captain makes motions to round up his men.

'Is there a problem?' Dora comes over from the bar, lays a hand on John's jacket. She nods at the sailors. 'Hey guys. Jen.'

'I wanted a drink,' one drawls.

'Shut up, Jefferson,' the captain says.

'Come on. Go on now.' John indicates the door with his head. Behind him, the table grates. John turns and Sal is standing.

'What's going on?'

'Nothing,' John tells him.

'We're leaving,' Wen tells Sal.

Sal takes a few steps forward. Ed and Jefferson step to meet him. Yve gets between. 'Come on.' She pats Sal and Ed on their chests. 'No trouble.'

'Who's making trouble?' Sal says. He looks at the captain. 'Why're you still here?'

'Come on, Sal,' Yve says. 'It's okay.'

'Didn't you get our message?' Sal says. 'Or can't you read?'

'You fat fuck!' Ed jumps and Sal falls under him. The table screeches, bottles and tumblers break on the floor. Ed and Sal roll across the glass, hands caught in each other's shirt.

'Stop it!' Yve flings herself at Wen. 'Make them stop!'

John can tell by the way she fits her body against the captain's it's not for the first time. And by the way the captain turns slightly from her, John knows he's tired of her. He's seen that look before. The captain's fucked her, and now he's done with her. She just doesn't know it yet.

'Get off her!' John pulls the captain by his collar. He knows it's ridiculous, she's the one throwing herself on the captain, but he yells this at the man anyhow, and then he finds himself shaking the man. The insult is unclear – is it worse that his girlfriend is a slut, or that this bastard thinks she isn't good enough anymore? It doesn't matter. Such questions are too complex right now. His earlier anger churns up, spills over. His father and the others hurry to join the brawl, but John can't be bothered with them, he's too busy squaring off with the captain.

'Calm down, man. Calm down.' Wen holds up his hands as if he'd calm John. He leaves himself wide open.

John swings. He watches the man's head snap back. His hand feels wet, as if it's been licked. He checks and finds he's cut his knuckles on the captain's teeth. He waits for the man to stumble, regain his balance. He wants the captain to get the idea of things, to ball his fists.

'Come on, now,' John prompts him. The man is much smaller than he, and John is more than a little embarrassed, hitting someone so small, until the captain obliges him with a neat blow to his gut. John bends to catch his breath. He smiles a little. 'That's right, you bastard.' The captain hits him in the temple. 'That's right,' John says. They fall into a natural rhythm, trading blows. As he hits and is hit, John talks to the man. He tells him just how long he and Yve have been together, and he asks him who does he think he is? He says his best friend is dead, and that this is his wake. But the captain doesn't listen as well as he fights and John's knuckles grow sore from the beating, and his right eye swells shut and there's a great roaring in his ears like the roaring he heard at LeHarve's. His lip splits and bleeds, and soon his jaw stops working, and he can only get one word out with each breath, but he chooses these few carefully. He tells the captain that

369

this is his home, his bar, his town. He and his kind are not welcome. Then the captain loosens John's teeth so he's reduced to spitting his words in blood to be read later. The captain flails on the floor and John puts his knee on the man's stomach and tries to get him to understand just how much he's lost and how unwilling he is to lose one thing more. Yve pulls at his elbow, making the job harder. She screams in his face. She is hysterical.

Dora brings a baseball bat down on the bar. The men freeze. Dora glares at them, stern as a nun. 'I'm calling the cops!'

'You wouldn't,' Sal says.

'Don't make me.'

John lets the captain go. Wen falls back on the tiles, panting. The other men separate. Some crawl to a clean spot on the floor, some lie where they are to catch their breath. John slides over to the bar, and he leans his back against it. He watches Yve wipe the captain's nose. It makes John feel sorry for her. She is so out of her league, and so miserably drunk, and she wants so desperately to salvage something that she never even had, that he pities her for the futility of her actions. He pulls himself to standing, then he goes over and pulls her up too.

'Come on,' he tells her. He finds her coat and her bag, and puts them on her. He takes her by the arm. He walks her into the street.

She sways a bit, looks around. She seems surprised at being outside. 'I'm sorry,' she mutters.

'It's okay.'

The walk to the Albins' is quiet; the cold wakes John up a bit, but Yve is drowsy and limp. She lets him hold her up, and she leans heavily against him. When he gets to her house, he opens the door carefully, and puts a finger to his lips to shush her. They go up to her room, he undresses her, then himself down to his boxers. He gives her a nightgown. He folds their clothes neatly on the chair, though they smell of cigarettes and grease and will need to be washed. On the other side of her wall, Alma and Phil breathe evenly. In Chris's room sleep Martin and Kate. Somewhere in the house – in the basement, most likely – are Edna and Walley. They are all here, together in one place for perhaps the last time. Yve is a small lump under the covers, curled on her side, clutching the air by her cheek. He sits awhile at her desk. The breeze seeping through the cracks of the window smells like steel: it will snow in a few hours. Outside, the *Pearl* pulls against her lines. Inside, the panes have iced. He holds his fingertips to this inside ice until it warms and slips. He puts his fingers on his jaw; the wet cold feels good.

He thinks she will be asleep when he climbs in beside her, but she is awake, with open eyes.

'Do you hate me?' Her breath is bad.

'No.'

'Do you love me?'

'Yeah.'

'Say it.'

'I love you,' he says. In her pupils are small reflections of his face, so he brings himself nearer to blot them out. She puts her hand on the back of his head and pulls him to her. Her chest rises and falls against his. After a while, she loosens her hold and rolls over, and tucks herself into him like a spoon. John puts his arm around her waist. He lies there thinking of how much he loves her, and how terrible it feels – as if his lungs are filled, and he can't exhale.

Dora, in her barroom wisdom, tells the men they must exit separately – the fishermen first, then the sailors can go once the road has cleared. Things are changing, and she can't afford to anger future customers. She watches as the fishers wander down the street aimlessly, neither looking over their shoulders nor looking farther ahead than their next steps. Then she turns to serve the sailors.

The Bethel clock chimes quarter past midnight, halting the fishermen. Their draggers must be moved. 'Or turn into pumpkins,' Izzy says and they laugh. Sal suggests they all go down together, and so they do, walking to the waterfront with the extra care of drunken men. At the pier, they climb into their separate draggers and Fitz volunteers to throw docklines. He watches them motor off and into the bay. The water is dark and pocked like charred foil. Sal is the first to let his anchor run. From where Fitz stands, the sound of the links pouring out is like the plastic piddle of toy money. He waits a while longer, but none of the men come back in. He grows cold and bored with waiting. He figures his friends have gone to sleep on their separate boats, and he considers how he might go out and join them – Sal or Izzy or Pete or someone – so the night needn't end, but all the plans he comes up with involve the work of going to the Albins' and getting his skiff or his dragger going and the idea of it makes him tired. And he'd have to walk to get anywhere, because they arrived at the funeral in limos that have long since gone. He wishes he could be back in the bar. He thinks the problem with this town is that there is just one fishers' bar, and when it's closed it's closed. He sits on the playground bench and considers this. The toy lighthouse, the dory, the capstan, hulk in the shadows and take on different shapes. He plays with his eyes – when he looks at them directly, they disappear; when he looks away, they re-form in the margins of his vision as people kneeling, or standing, or squatting. He thinks he will lie down on the bench awhile to clear his head. He wakes briefly to snowflakes big as pillow feathers tumbling from the low sky – blanketing snow, muffling snow – swirling past and hissing into the black water.

32

Yve wakes needing water and aspirin, but she doesn't want to get up from the warm blankets. The light shining around the edges of the window blind is white. The foghorns are blowing, though there is no fog, only snow, tapping softly on the glass. Snow in general all up and down the seaboard. John has his leg over hers, and his chest to her back. Still sleepily amnesic, she knows there is something to remember about last night, about the past few days, the past few weeks, but it hovers dimly on the horizon, and she is unwilling to look for it just yet. She'd rather think of how nice it is to wake before another person, so you can be aware of going back to sleep next to them. She closes her eyes and lets her thoughts come in half-dreamt fragments. John puts out heat like a radiator – there was a story, something about her grandmother, when she was a girl up in Hebron, and how her whole family used to huddle together in one big bed, like dogs, for such heat. Now it's only the adults who get to sleep with other people. Funny how children, the ones most afraid of the dark, are made to sleep alone – when she has children she'll let them in the bed until they're too big, and then she'll get them dogs to huddle with—

The mattress sinks, then rises as John gets up.

'Where're you going?' she asks.

He is putting on his clothes from last night, and the odors have mutated to something goatish. 'Your father wants to see me downstairs.'

She opens one eye. Her father stands in the doorway. He seems unsurprised that John has stayed the night. Her tongue tastes like paste. 'Get me water?'

'Sure,' John says, but she has already rolled over to his side of the bed.

In the hallway Phil whispers, 'I'm calling Jack Hagerty.'

All the doors to the other rooms are shut, and no light seeps under them. John wonders if the rest of the family are still sleeping. 'I wish you wouldn't.'

'Jesus, John. Who is he? What the hell have you gotten us into? This is still my house—' Phil looks old and small in his bathrobe, and John sees that he is frightened. But he can't say anything more – they have reached the landing, and in the living room stands the bartender from LeHarve's.

'John Fitz,' the bartender says. Over his thin suit pants and button-down shirt he wears a cotton sweater, and on his feet are worn loafers. They look cheap and too thin for the weather. 'Come with me,' he says.

John doesn't step from the landing, and neither does Phil. Seeing the bartender now, in the yellow light of the Albins' living room, John is surprised to find him a rather small man who, given a different haircut, could be some innocuous foreign cousin. He does have a foreign look, after all, a certain way of holding his lips politely around his teeth. He looks almost benign standing there, beside the mantel, fingering the ridiculous Thanksgiving centerpiece of chrysanthemums and autumn-colored leaves, with its incongruous calico scarecrow doll. Alma put it up before they brought Chris back, and it has remained this whole time. This is what was wrong with Thursday, John realizes, too late. It is today. It is Thanksgiving. He wonders if Denny is around, in another room, outside, maybe.

'Promise me you won't call the sheriff,' John tells Phil, though he knows it is not within his rights to ask.

'Jesus,' Phil says.

They exit through the kitchen. Alma sits at the table, and she, too, looks frightened. John wonders if she came down to make the coffee and found this man in the house. He wonders what the man might have said to her. He thinks it is unfortunate that the one time he

374

would have been happy to see Edna Larkin bustling about, butting in, she is somehow missing. Then he realizes she is probably already out of the house, already down at the Museum Pier, organizing her SnugHarbor Ladies' Auxiliary for the parade protest. Today is the Holly-Day Festival, after all. He had forgotten that, also.

Phil starts to exit with them and John tells him, 'Stay inside.'

'You'll holler if you need me?'

'I won't need you.'

The shrubs and diesel pumps are rounded with snow. Snow covers the whole yard in blue-white drifts and continues to fall. It is thick, heavy snow, and by the time they reach the *Pearl*, they're dusted about the shoulders and hair. Half-filled footsteps lead from the bulwark to a Volvo in the drive.

'I told you not to come into the house,' John says.

'I had to get you. You said early.'

'To be honest, I didn't expect you to come back.'

'I find that slightly insulting,' the bartender says.

John doesn't answer. He leads the man into the *Pearl*'s wheelhouse so they can speak in something more like privacy. Though he is sure Phil is at the window, waiting and watching. He wonders if Phil has called Jack yet.

'We don't have a lot of time,' John says. 'Did you bring the money?'

'Do you have the package?'

'What do you mean?'

'The product. The weight. Show me the shit, I show you the money.'

'What are you talking about?'

'Are you going to be an asshole?'

'I'm not being an asshole. I just want to see the money.'

'We're not communicating, John Fitz.' The bartender holds his hands cupped between them. 'I need to see

375

the package before you get the money. Do you understand what I am saying to you?' He has a way of speaking slowly, as if John is too dimwitted to follow. Nevertheless, what he's saying makes no sense.

'You're saying you don't already have it?'

'Exactly.'

John glances about the wheelhouse, as if it might provide some clue. It looks as it has for days now – the broken radio, the emptied EPIRB screwed back in place. A coffee mug from their trip back still sits, unwashed, on the chart shelf. Outside, snow swirls from a blank white sky. There is nothing here. Whatever was here is gone. If the bartender doesn't have it, then Denny must have come alone. He must have come alone and not told the bartender.

'Where's Denny?' John asks.

'Don't worry about Denny. Denny's at the bar.'

'You might want to ask him where your package is. Ask him where he was night before last.'

The man squints. 'He was with me. All night.'

'Where?'

'What the fuck do you care?'

'You're saying you weren't here the night before last? You're saying you didn't take something off this boat? Denny didn't either?'

The man lays his finger on his nose. 'Are you saying someone took it off the boat?'

'It was hidden,' John starts to explain.

'Do I look like I give a shit?' The bartender offers a blank expression, to illustrate that he does not, in fact, give a shit. But of course he does. His face may be slack, but his muscles are tense under his sweater. The man may be small, but he is clearly crazy. Only a crazy man would run a bar in an empty town; only a crazy man would be out in this weather in those clothes asking for something already gone. It is gone. He must have it. Or Denny must. *Think*, John thinks, but he's unable to. His head aches and his face feels like one big scab. There are so many conflicting bits of information. He wishes he could go back over a few things, straighten it out. But the bartender is impatient.

'Did you know where it was hidden?' John asks.

'What are you asking me?' The bartender frowns. 'I find this conversation very disturbing, John Fitz. I'm beginning to wonder what kind of setup this might be.'

John realizes he has made a terrific mistake. It is suddenly clear. He should never have gone to LeHarve's. That was a mistake. He should never have gone to see Denny and the bartender. Denny and the bartender were the wrong people. The right people were whoever emptied the EPIRB. Whoever came in the night knew where it was hidden. They knew where to look. It was emptied by whomever they were supposed to meet – perhaps it was the lobsterman, perhaps it was some stateside contingent of LaFortune's – it doesn't matter who it was, but it wasn't the bartender or Denny. Whoever called Kate, when they heard Chris was dead, knew they'd have to come get the package themselves – and of course they knew it was on the *Pearl*. It couldn't've been hard to find out where she was docked – in the backyard of Chris's parents. In his greediness and cowardice to be free of the troublesome package, he has brought a worse trouble upon himself; he has brought a worse trouble into the Albins' backyard.

The bartender ticks his tongue.

'What if I told you it's not here anymore?' John asks.

The bartender looks grave. 'I would say you are in very bad shape.'

'I think I might have made a mistake.'

The bartender touches his hip. 'Maybe we need to go into the house and ask your friends about this. Do you think maybe they can help us out? Maybe they've been taking things that don't belong to them? Do you think?'

'No.' John can't think of what else to say. He'd hoped

they'd be even – the bartender doesn't get the package, so John doesn't get the money. But the bartender, John understands now, never had any plans of giving him money. He clearly has no money on him. He just wants the heroin, and he wants John to tell him where it is. And if John won't tell him, he'll begin questioning the Albins. He is already looking back at the house. He is already turning away, stepping off the boat. John doesn't want this man in the house again. He wants to get this man as far from Phil, Alma, and Yve as possible.

'They don't have it,' John says.

The bartender stops halfway between the dragger and the bulwark. He steps back onto the boat. He looks at his sodden loafers in disgust. He looks at John. 'Then where is it?'

'With someone else.'

'We'll go see this someone else together.'

'Tomorrow is better.'

'No. Now.' He says this with a finality that does not invite contradiction.

'Okay.' At least, John thinks, he can get this man off of Phil's property before things go south. He blinks snowflakes from his lashes. He is not so much afraid as in a state of hovering disbelief. He can't believe his actions have brought him here. He has no idea where to take this man. He feels blind – yet when he looks about, he can see the snow sweeping over the silvery water. Everything else is obscured. Somewhere behind the snowy curtain is the bay, filled with his friends' anchored draggers, and beyond them the town. He wishes he could see the lights. For some reason, that would be a comfort. He wishes he were there with Yve and Kate and Martin, watching for Santa on the *Shardon Rose*. He wishes he were there with Pete Hopewell and the other fishers, waving some goofy placard. He imagines the state troopers have arrived to take their stands along the barricades, and the waterfront is filling with spectators.

378

'Okay,' John says.

'We'll take my car,' the bartender says.

'No.'

'Why not?'

'It's on my friend's boat. Anchored out.'

'Where?'

John points in the general direction of town. From here, nothing can be seen but thick swirling snowflakes and water. The presence of another boat must be taken on faith. Still, the bartender nods.

'Then we'll take your boat.' The bartender climbs back aboard.

John gets him to take the wheel while he throws the lines, then he jumps aboard and takes over. The man seems pleased with this turn of events. He seems to enjoy being on the water. He stands beside John looking out the window as they head across. The snow spirals past the wheelhouse, enveloping them in white. White snow, white sky behind. He doesn't seem to feel the cold air. John wonders if he should try to converse with the man. According to the clock glued to the panel above the GPS screen, it is already 9:42. He has been with this man only fifteen minutes, less than that, since they left Alma's kitchen. It will be another eight or so minutes across the bay, maybe ten, because they are slowed by poor visibility. The parade is supposed to start at ten. It strikes John that it is fortunate that the bartender did not, in fact, arrive early as asked. Perhaps his concept of early is different from John's. Still, they were all sleeping late. All except Alma and Phil. The reds and greens of the channel markers come dully into view. Shadowed draggers begin to materialize. As they get closer, the man becomes agitated.

'What the fuck is all this?'

Ahead, as if a veil has lifted, the bannered fleet shows through the snow. On the decks roam dark blots of fishermen. The fireboat from Charlesport is in the channel, firing off all its hoses. Beyond, the museum and the crowded waterfront appear. Faint music comes from speakers onshore.

'Where are we going?'

'To see my friend.'

'This is bullshit.'

'It's a parade. It's Thanksgiving,' John says. The bartender's cheeks are a high red, from cold or anger, John doesn't know or care. He feels oddly gleeful. He worries he may laugh. He knows this hilarity is only adrenaline. In fact, he should be afraid. But the worst has already happened – he broke his promise to take care of Chris and he tied him up, and now Chris is dead, so what could be worse? Whatever happens now is just mopping up the mess.

'Turn around. Now!'

'We're almost there.' John punches the throttle and the *Pearl* speeds up.

'What the fuck is wrong with you? Are you stupid? Do you hear?' The man looks confused and angry. Down at Carreiro's yard, the dim silhouette of the *Shardon Rose* rides the marine railway into the bay. They are going to launch her. John can't quite see, but he imagines the figures on the catwalk, and one of the CARP women – maybe Rita Barrett – harnessed to the rails of the walk, ready to swing a bottle of champagne from a silk ribbon. A small cheer rises from the shadowy grandstand in front of the museum. As they near, the music grows clearer. It's a traditional chantey covered by a current band. John knows some of the words. *Lucky's boat is painted green* – but this group pronounces Lucky as Loo-key, frenchifying the first syllable – *the prettiest boat that you ever seen! Aha, me boys, a riddle-aye-day!*

'Turn around,' the bartender says.

Something cold screws under John's sweater and presses his spine. He realizes it must be a handgun of some kind, and a calm part of him marvels that he can

380

know this, having never had a gun pressed to his spine before.

'Do you want to die?' the bartender asks.

'Not really,' John says, driving into the channel.

A Coast Guard cutter emerges from the snow. It is white and official, the real thing this time, with its blue and orange stripes and emblematic seal. John heads directly toward it. An officer tells them through a megaphone that they must remove themselves from the channel. 'You have entered an Established Safety Zone,' the officer announces in a thick, metallic voice.

'I am going to kill you,' the bartender says.

'I know,' John says.

But the man hesitates. Perhaps he is worried about the sound his gun will make and that the Coasties will most certainly hear. Or perhaps he is afraid of witnesses on the other draggers; now that they are in the channel, John can see his friends clearly. There's also a crowd onshore: Edna Larkin and her SnugHarbor Coalition – fishermen's wives and daughters and grandchildren chanting and shaking their fists; the CARP businessmen and -women, on their aluminum grandstand with their plastic cups of champagne; Mayor Barrett on the miked podium and the soundman behind; Reverend Dowd and Father Dominic on hand for prayers in their blessing-of-the-fleet robes, the priest shaking his holy-water rattle and the Reverend with only his waving hand. Even Santa Claus is there, on the *Shardon Rose*, attended by a full complement of sailors. As the restored schooner travels slowly past the shore, cheers and boos rise over the booming chantey. *Oh Lucky's rolling out his grub, ah me boys.* People hold up signs. Some throw streamers, others snowballs. A cable van with a tall transmitter is parked by the museum and a cameraman trolls about, picking up local color.

'This is your second warning,' the Coastie says. 'You

are committing a federal violation. Remove your vessel from the channel.'

'I'm serious,' the bartender says.

'I'm sure you are,' John says. He doesn't mean it sarcastically; he is sure the bartender is serious. As he waits for the shot, he wonders what it will feel like. Probably cold – he has heard of things being so hot they feel cold, and he figures that it must be this way with bullets. He only hopes he is close enough to the shore for people to hear. He wants to be sure the bartender is caught – he wants to make sure the man can't go back to the Albins', can't bother them again. He keeps the Pearl steady, heading for the Museum Pier. Time slows, turns liquid: it repeatedly breaks, wavelike, on the same moment. All around the snow-swirled air grows heavier and closer, and he feels as if he is floating and swirling himself. The *Pearl* motors forward and the *Shardon Rose* motors forward and the point at which their two courses will intersect shines before him like a beacon. Surely the Coasties see it too, surely they will stop him, board him, rescue him, before that moment. On the decks of the other fishing boats, his friends have begun cheering. Pete Hopewell on the *Lady Bea*, Izzy Titus on the *Lizzie*, the lobstermen – RayRay O'Buck, Tomas Dugan, Jim Salvatore – blast their horns in support. A bell rings on the T*hree Marias* and the engine rumbles and a ball of violet smoke bounces off the waves as Sal Liro charges the channel.

Ashore, the chanting splinters into confused shouts. Some are for John, some against. According to the speakers on either side of the stage, Loo-key is still rolling out his grub. *One split pea in a ten-pound tub!*

'This is your third warning,' the megaphone squawks. 'Prepare for boarding.'

'Get the fuck out!' the bartender shouts.

The crew on the Coast Guard cutter put fenders over the side—

aha me boys

—but Sal leads the fleet in an attack, storming the Coasties and cutting them off from the *Pearl*.

'Out! Now!' The bartender looks wild. Something about this last command sounds final, and John thinks: How bad can it be? All the fear is in the anticipation – it is like waiting to jump into cold water. His only disappointment is that he feels unprepared. He wishes he had a few seconds to compose his thoughts, and perhaps to remember some of the things that are important to him, people maybe, and places. The *Shardon Rose* looks beautiful: they have cleaned up the deck and put some of the rigging on the mainsail and jib, so it seems she could sail if they wished. She is close enough now for him to see the crew clearly – the two old ones; the two younger ones; Joe Ames's nephew, who Jenny Stewart likes; the pompous first mate, who didn't throw a single punch last night; and, of course, the captain, looking the salt in a worn peacoat, his lower lip swollen and the bridge of his nose well bruised. It strikes John that he can remember none of their names, these men who have lived in his town for months. He can see the surprise on their faces. He can see that Santa Claus is just Joe Ames in a bad costume.

He knows everyone onshore: there is Edna Larkin and Bea Hopewell; there is Mabel Dowd with Walley Larkin beside her; there, on the aluminum bandstand, sit the whole Stewart family. There is Peter Gusek, and farther down sits Lou Cerosky, the man who wants to put a yacht club by the old fish plant. There, of course, stand Jack Hagerty and Richard Bates, holding back the crowd. And there is Yve, running for the pier. Behind her come her mother and father, Kate and Martin – their coats thrown over their pajamas. They must have driven down as soon as John left. How did they know he would end up here? It doesn't matter; he's glad they came. He looks at everyone. It seems he

383

can see the whole town at once. People's mouths look like black holes – they holler and wave. It seems they have all come for him. The pressure of the pistol changes against his back and he knows this is it. He punches the throttle, and as the *Pearl* plows into the *Shardon Rose*, and the sailors fall forward, there comes a tremendous crack.

AFTER

'Can I have it?' Martin asks Yve of the battleship in the window.

'We'll see.'

The boy hangs back.

'Come on, Martin, I have to get to work.'

It's an awesome model, full detail down to the rivets.

'Fine then,' Yve says.

He's too old for her to grab his hand. He's six now, and in the first grade since September. He lets her walk a bit without him – past the soaped windows of the Woolworth's, and of Kiernan's Hardware. (Martin's grandfather bought everything in the store for a song because Mr. Kiernan drove his car to the end of the southern spit, doused himself in gas, and lit a match. Jimmy Kiernan stopped coming to school after that.) Martin catches up with his aunt at Stewart's Pharmacy.

'I need a few things,' she says. 'You can come in or wait here.'

'Wait here.'

There's an electric train in the window: under blinking blue lights, over white felt hills, it travels a loop of track shaped like a bean. Colognes, pen-and-pencil sets, other things squat in the peaks and valleys, but they don't interest Martin as much as the small frozen men and the mirror sea. Everything is sprinkled with

387

Cellophane glitter. The train travels around and around, a sign in the boxcar suggests Stewart's for All Your Holiday Needs.

His aunt comes jingling out. 'Chop chop!' She carries a brown paper sack.

'What'd you get?'

'Nothing for you.'

He skips alongside, trying to peek into the top of the bag. She holds it higher. If he jumps, his face is nearly to her chin. When he stands still he is tall as her boobies. That's a word she doesn't like him saying. Boobies. Titties. He feels himself blushing. She's shorter than his mom. They all live together in a rented apartment on Cherry Street, and every time they come home after dark his mother says, Be careful – the neighborhood's going to the dogs. His aunt complains about the rent. She works in a bakery, the Black Cod, with a sign like a black fish over the door. Last year, he got ten dollars for posing in a sweatshirt with the black fish on it for their calendar, and his aunt said, I always knew you'd be famous. Now she pats his bobbing head and reaches in her bag.

'What's this?' She opens her mouth and eyes wide with false surprise. He jumps to see. She pulls out a string of jawbreakers. 'You can have one now.'

He takes the long Cellophane chain and selects the best one from the middle, and returns the rest to his aunt's waiting hand. The candy makes a hard sweet ball between his cheek and gum and he pretends it is a plug of tobacco, like those deforming the jaws of the men who, during the summer, wait out front of the yacht club for day work, spitting. He is not allowed to play down there, his aunt says, but he sometimes goes anyhow, to look at the boats.

Now past Orsten's Stationery, now past Garenelli's deli. Now past the lot with the sign *Clean It or Lien It*. What does Lien It mean? he asked his aunt after he learned to read, and she said, Sometimes people hold on to land waiting for the price to go up, and then other people see the empty spot and think it's a good place for garbage, and so the land becomes a dump, and it's unhealthy, so the government wants the owners to come in and do something with the land instead of leaving it empty. But what is Lien It? He pictures a bunch of two-by-fours propped against the brick walls on either side of the garbagy lot, like his grandfather has propped against his barn because it's leaning as if it is going to fall.

'How's your jawbreaker?' his aunt asks him now.

'Good. They all taste the same after the top part's sucked off. But they make your tongue different colors, see?' He shows her his tongue.

After school his aunt always picks him up and walks him to his mother's job, then goes to work herself. His mother's boss, Dora, is a nice lady, but Dora's husband is a shit, his mother says, though she hates when he says shit. His mother told his aunt once that Dora said Hank's a real disappointment. I'm not surprised, his aunt said back.

Now on the cobbled roads, where the buildings get shorter and closer together. They come to the Whiskey Wind. It is pretty from the outside, with the big gold letters on the window and the Christmas lights showing through. The door jingles when they come in, then shushes shut behind. He pushes the inner door, holds it open for his aunt.

Dora, behind the bar with his mother, says, 'Look at you, little man, when'd you get so big? What are you feeding him?' His aunt and mother laugh. The shit is sitting in the booth with Mr. Fitz and Mr. Daly and otherwise the place is empty, because it is still only four and the dinner crowd hasn't come in yet. Sometimes Mr. Fitz scares Martin – he's really old and his breath is terrible and he has a hole in the tip of his nose from part of it freezing and turning black and falling off. His mother always tells him

389

to be nice to Mr. Fitz, he's had a hard time.

'What do you have there?' His mother opens his mouth. Her finger is soapy on his chin. He shows his blue tongue. 'No more before dinner,' she says. 'Go tell Pee Wee what you want.' Martin goes to the service window. Standing on his toes he can get his elbows on the aluminum shelf. What he always wants is a hamburger and fries. What his mother makes him eat is the lettuce and tomato that come with it. He shows his tongue to Pee Wee and Pee Wee pretends shock. He invites Martin into the kitchen to dress his bun.

'You're gonna give him cavities,' Kate says to Yve.

'He'll get them anyhow.' Yve sits at the bar and takes the coffee Kate pours. 'The place looks nice, Dora.' Big colored bulbs light the mirror and red bows line the brass poles along the glass divider.

'Yeah. I'm gonna get a big wreath for over the cash register. They got them for fourteen bucks apiece at Handleman's, but I think I'll wait for Edna's.' Every year, Edna Larkin sells wreaths to raise money for the SnugHarbor Scholarship Fund. Every year, they send a fisher's son or daughter to vocational school. Cosmetology and auto mechanics are most popular.

'I like the lights,' Yve says.

'Yeah, Hank did them.'

'Nice lights.' Yve nods to Hank. He's gotten fat over the years. He is the only one of the sailors who stayed after the *Shardon Rose* sank. Though the museum raised her and repaired her, she doesn't go sailing. She stays docked at the museum, and you can walk around the deck for an extra buck fifty.

'Yve, come over here.' Warren Fitz waves at her. 'C'mere. How's your mum?'

She stays at the bar. 'Fine. Everyone's fine.'

'Give'r my respects.'

'Will do.'

'C'mere.'

'Nah, I can't, Warren. I've got work.'

390

'Come on. Lemme buy you a drink.'

Yve rescues Kate's cigarette from burning itself out in the ashtray. She takes a few drags, blows smoke rings at the old man. 'Tomorrow maybe.'

'Tomorrow.' He winks slowly. 'I'll be here.'

'No worries there,' Kate says. She takes the butt back. 'Last night he passed out in the head, and Dora couldn't get the door open 'cause he was blocking it. Hank had to take it off the hinges.'

Yve smiles, though she doesn't find it funny. She feels sorry for the old man. He's lost everything: his son, his house, his boat – now he lives in a single-room-occupancy on Pine, and he doesn't have much to do all day.

'I've got to go,' Yve tells Kate, though she doesn't have to be at work for another hour. 'Bye, Martin.' Her nephew's too busy wolfing down his dinner to wave. She nods at the others.

Kate makes a face and points at the boy. Don't forget, she mouths. Yve gives her the okay. She's supposed to bring the battleship home. They're going to stay up and watch *It's a Wonderful Life* and get drunk and wrap presents.

On her way to the bakery, she stops for the ship model. At Orsten's she gets a box of cards, at Garenelli's the bottle of wine, and a few blocks down the video. The video store is crowded and the shelves have lots of blank spaces. Lots of harried mothers are renting movies. *It's a Wonderful Life* is out, as is *Miracle on 34th Street*, and Yve finds this frustration enough to get her oddly teary. She shakes her head at her silly sentimental self. She's become a bit of a softie these past few years. And the Christmas season is always difficult. Holidays in general, what her mother calls 'family days,' are difficult. They remind you of everyone missing. Most of the old crowd is gone, of course. They've sold out and moved on – the Jameisons, the Furlongs, the Hopewells, Sal and Maria

391

Liro, the Tituses. You couldn't expect them to stay after property values got so high.

The Black Cod is down by the Historic Waterfront, in the new Economic Opportunity Zone – which as far as Yve's concerned is just a fancy name for taking over condemned buildings, slapping a coat of paint on them, and charging an arm and a leg rent. The whole area has been rebuilt into a pedestrian mall. Mayor Barrett got the man who did South Street Seaport and that place in Baltimore to draw up the design. All the nicer shops have sprung up down here. White fairy lights fill the trees along Water Street, and boughs of evergreen and holly are tied with stiff gold ribbons to each streetlamp. A horse and buggy waits to tour the square. The driver wears red carnations in his hatband and lapel.

Yve turns the corner onto the Titus Fish Pier, which she hasn't visited since they began reconstruction. It is now lined with small shops. The low sun reflects off the creamy white boutiques with a wonderful brightness. The effect is dazzling. Poinsettias and paperwhites fill the window boxes, and the displays behind are bountiful and opulent. She glances at her watch; she still has a half hour before work. Perhaps she can find something for her mother, or Kate, here.

The first store is filled with pretty, frivolous things. Yve walks carefully around the laden tables. Glass ornaments tinkle against each other – frog princes, mermaids, fruits and vegetables thin as onionskin and twenty dollars each. Christmas-tree china, gold-leaf wrapping papers, chenille scarves, silk eye-pillows, herbed bath oils. She touches things, smells things, she stops before a large oval mirror and a tree of cut-velvet hats. She's never seen anything like them, and she tries on a purple cloche.

'They're fifteen percent off.' A saleslady comes over. She tugs the fabric around Yve's face, then strokes her hair forward along her cheeks. 'That's very flattering. You have lovely bones.'

Yve looks at herself in the mirror. She turns her head three-quarters and pulls in her breath. She could wear it to visit John. She is planning a visit downstate the day after Christmas. They won't allow visitors Christmas Day, perhaps because most of the guards want Christmas off. They are arbitrary like that. Sometimes she'll ride the whole way down – four hours on the bus – and find the whole place is in lock-down because of some fight in the cafeteria, and she has to turn around and go home without seeing him at all. The men are rough sometimes – John won't tell her what goes on inside. He says it's too unpleasant to repeat. She doesn't need him to tell her. She hears enough of the stories anyhow. She's become friends with many of the other prisoners' wives. If someone told her four years ago that someday she'd be hanging out with convicts' wives, smoking cigarettes in a prison waiting room, she would've laughed in her face. Life is strange. It is funny what you get used to. A couple of the women even took her out after John and she got married. They split a pu-pu platter at the Moonlight Lounge and got high on Alabama Slammers. It was very odd, the wedding ceremony – holding hands through the Plexiglas cutout in the visiting area, while the other men talked with their wives and girlfriends as if nothing was happening. She had to buy the rings herself, from a pawnshop. And no engagement ring. She didn't mind; they didn't have the money after the legal fees and all. Oh, they threw the book at him – fines for crossing into the Coast Guard's Safety Zone, civil suits brought for personal injury and property damage, reparation to the museum and the city equal to the cost of raising and repairing the *Shardon Rose* (Fitz scuttled the *Pearl* to pay for it all, and he still had to declare bankruptcy). But it was the eight counts of assault that landed John in prison – one for each crewmember, one for the captain, and one for Joe Ames. They called his boat a deadly weapon. His sentence was lightened by a sympathetic judge, who persuaded the prosecution not to make John any more of a martyr than he already was. His defense claimed momentary insanity, brought on by undue stress, but the jury thought the act premeditated. Everyone believed he had rammed the *Shardon* in protest of the fishing regulations and the loss of dockage. The bartender – John told the court he was a friend of a friend – jumped bail and, as he was never found, was subsequently forgotten about. A few witnesses had reported hearing a pistol shot, but no gun, nor evidence of one, ever turned up, and the noise was attributed to collision and confusion. John was a hero for a while; he even made the *New York Times*, and *All Things Considered* did a twenty-minute story on him.

He's up for parole in two years. In two years she's thirty-four. Enough time still to start a family. Sometimes he says if Denny and the bartender are still looking for him, he feels safer in jail, and she tells him, Don't be silly. He says, We might have to run away to Alaska, break my parole. She says, I'll move anywhere you say; now hurry up and get out. She smiles and kisses his fingers through the Plexiglas cutout. She's waited for him before, she can wait still.

'What do you think?' the saleswoman says.

The hat is attractive – Yve faces herself full on.

'It's reversible.'

'I don't know.' Yve removes the hat. The price is exorbitant. 'I have to think about it.'

The outside air feels good after the overheated store. She walks just to feel the refreshing cold, and finds herself at the end of the pier. In the last shop window, crystal icicles catch and refract white spotlights, spinning beckoning beams out into the darkening street. She stops. From silver branches hang brassieres, panties, teddies, and sleep sets. She considers a pair of embroidered slippers for her mother, or a robe. The robe definitely. It's thick as a quilt and her mother's is old. Then she sees the price. Such things always cost an arm and a leg, Yve thinks. How ridiculous to spend so much on underwear no one ever sees. She continues to search the display, though, as if there is something she could possibly want. Then she sees it. In the corner, in a brown-and-white-striped box, packages of colored hose burst from a bed of tissue. That, Yve thinks, is the perfect gift for Kate. The notion feels like a triumph. She will go into this store and buy Kate ten pairs of French silk stockings.

The door jingles and the salesgirl looks up from the counter. 'May I help you?'

'Yes.' Yve goes to the window display. 'I'd like those.' She points.

The woman takes the stockings from the window.

'Oh, don't spoil your display—'

'It's no problem.' The salesgirl holds the box up. 'Gift-wrap?'

'Please.'

The girl disappears into the back and Yve waits by the window. There seems to be a small hole where the box was removed, but perhaps that's just because Yve knows what used to be there. Maybe if you'd never been here before, and you just now came upon this scene for the first time, you wouldn't notice the difference. You wouldn't miss what is gone. Because really, other than that, everything looks lovely. And it is just as lovely from inside looking out as from out looking in. Lovelier even, with the street turning blue in the twilight, and the shoppers scurrying hopefully by, in search of some elusive last-minute gift.

THE END

THE PROPERTY OF RAIN
Angela Lambert

'HER MOST AMBITIOUS [NOVEL] TO DATE . . .
GRIPPING, PASSIONATE AND INTELLIGENT'
The Times

The date is 1921 and the Great War is over, but
its aftermath casts a long shadow. That year, six
thousand miles apart, two children are born. Sam
Savage, the youngest child of a farm worker, grows up
in a tranquil Suffolk village where apparent serenity
hides poverty, hunger and brutality. Lakshmi is the
unwanted fourth daughter of a sweeper, living near
Kanpur in north-west India in a settlement of
Untouchables. At the age of fifteen, these two come
together in extreme circumstances, in the midst of a
monsoon – an encounter that will have tragic and
lifelong consequences.

'ANGELA LAMBERT WRITES WITH PASSION AND
PRECISION, BRINGING GENUINE EMOTIONAL
POWER TO HER EVOCATION OF TWO DEGRADED
ENVIRONMENTS AND ONE TRAGIC INCIDENT'
Sunday Telegraph

'SHADES OF E. M. FORSTER COLOUR A DEEPLY
SATISFYING ACCOUNT OF A COLLISION OF
CULTURES AND THE PERNICIOUS EFFECTS
OF HATRED'
Daily Mail

0 552 99738 2

BLACK SWAN

ALL BONES AND LIES
Anne Fine

'A DEEP, THOUGHTFUL NOVEL'
The Times

Colin is in many ways an ideal citizen. He works for
the council. He visits his aged mother, Norah, cooks
for her, and listens to her grumbles. He also keeps in
touch with his sister Dilys, long estranged from her
mother, in a vain attempt to maintain family ties. But
neither Dilys, Norah nor Colin's colleagues know
about his other, secret life – which involves a garden
shed, a circus acrobat, a much adored three-year-old
charmer, and a certain Mr Haksar's penchant for
squabbling with his neighbours.

What Colin does not know is that, thanks to an
incorrectly filled in house insurance policy, his two
lives are set to collide, and there is nothing he can do
to stop them.

'SPLENDID . . . CLEVER, CRUEL AND FUNNY . . .
THIS IS A HEARTWARMING BOOK'
Evening Standard

0 552 99898 2

BLACK SWAN

A HEART OF STONE
Renate Dorrestein

'A LITERARY NOVEL WITH A DARK SECRET IN ITS
HEART THAT MAKES READING COMPULSIVE'
Kate Atkinson

Precocious Ellen is the only one of the four close Van
Bemmel children who dreads the arrival of the new baby.
She has told her parents to call the baby Ida, the ugliest
name she could think of, and is secretly afraid that the
curse she has put upon the unborn child will come true.
Her parents, eccentric and devoted to each other, seem to
the outside world to be loving and caring, but after one of
the children has a shocking accident a horror descends
upon this happy household which leads to a disaster even
Ellen is powerless to prevent.

Twenty-five years later a pregnant Ellen returns to the
family home, where she is haunted by the voices of her
dead family. She imagines the questions her own child will
one day ask: 'Mummy, why don't I have a granny? Why no
grandad? No uncles or aunts? Why not?'

A Heart of Stone is an elegant, passionate but chilling
novel from Holland's bestselling writer.

'A WONDERFUL FRESH VOICE WITH A STARTLING
AND ULTIMATELY REDEMPTIVE TALE TO TELL. HER
WRITING IS SUPREMELY CONFIDENT AND INTIMATE.
A HEART OF STONE IS A LITERARY NOVEL WITH A
DARK SECRET IN ITS HEART THAT MAKES READING
COMPULSIVE'
Kate Atkinson

'NOT ONLY HIGHLY EMOTIVE AND COMPELLING, BUT
HUMOROUS TOO. I COULD NOT PUT THIS NOVEL DOWN'
Marika Cobbold

0 552 99836 2

BLACK SWAN

IDIOGLOSSIA
Eleanor Bailey

'HIGHLY ORIGINAL AND BEAUTIFULLY WRITTEN...A BRILLIANT
IMAGINATION AND GENUINE PSYCHOLOGICAL INSIGHTS'
Sunday Telegraph

For four generations of women from the same family, madness is
a potent legacy. It tempts, it persuades and it destroys. But it can
also bring a strange kind of freedom. . .

Aggressive, demanding, eccentric, Great Edie curses the
psychological weakness that runs through the family like a fault.
No one would suspect that her psychic powers were anything
more than a business, security for her old age.

Her daughter, Grace, has languished in a mental institution for long
spells of her adult life, after a tragedy years ago. Grace's only child,
Maggie, grew up, working with her father on a fading cruise liner.
But the golden age of ocean travel is over, and a relationship with
the mysterious comedian, Rudi, leaves her pregnant and alone.

Now Maggie's daughter, Sarah, is truly dispossessed and, through
gratuitous sex, seeks revenge on her loveless childhood. She
rejects the world of overused clichés and overpriced coffee but
can see no alternative – except to let go. . .

'RELENTLESSLY BUILDING BENEATH AN ENTERTAINING AND
WELL-WRITTEN STORY, THE READER IS MADE AWARE OF
THE RELATIONSHIPS WHICH BIND US, NOT ONLY TO OUR
FAMILY BUT ONE BEING TO ANOTHER'
Daily Mail

'[BAILEY'S] UNSENTIMENTAL BUT SYMPATHETIC
LANGUAGE PENETRATES THE PRIVATE WORLD OF
THE EMOTIONS IN AN IMPRESSIVE WAY'
The Times

'A BRILLIANT ACCOMPLISHED DEBUT . . . SLICK AND
CLEVER, HEARTFELT AND DEEP . . . BAILEY'S OBSERVATIONS
ARE STARTLING AND FRESH . . . THE SORT OF READ WHICH
HAUNTS YOU FOR WEEKS AFTERWARDS'
Sunday Express

'BAILEY IS AN INTELLIGENT WRITER, ELOQUENT ABOUT
MEMORY AND WOMEN'S STORIES. HER GRIP ON POETIC
LANGUAGE IS AN ASSURED ONE . . . AN AMBITIOUS FIRST
NOVEL'
Independent on Sunday

0 552 99860 5

BLACK SWAN

A SELECTED LIST OF FINE WRITING
AVAILABLE FROM BLACK SWAN

99588 6	THE HOUSE OF THE SPIRITS	Isabel Allende	£7.99
99820 6	FLANDERS	Patricia Anthony	£6.99
99734 X	EMOTIONALLY WEIRD	Kate Atkinson	£6.99
99860 5	IDIOGLOSSIA	Eleanor Bailey	£6.99
99922 9	A GOOD HOUSE	Bonnie Burnard	£6.99
99684 X	THE WATER IS WIDE	Pat Conroy	£6.99
99767 6	SISTER OF MY HEART	Chitra Banerjee Divakaruni	£6.99
99836 2	A HEART OF STONE	Renate Dorrestein	£6.99
99587 8	LIKE WATER FOR CHOCOLATE	Laura Esquivel	£6.99
99898 2	ALL BONES AND LIES	Anne Fine	£6.99
99851 6	REMEMBERING BLUE	Connie May Fowler	£6.99
99759 5	DOG DAYS, GLENN MILLER NIGHTS	Laurie Graham	£6.99
99801 X	THE SHORT HISTORY OF A PRINCE	Jane Hamilton	£6.99
99800 1	BLACKBERRY WINE	Joanne Harris	£6.99
99867 2	LIKE WATER IN WILD PLACES	Pamela Jooste	£6.99
99738 2	THE PROPERTY OF RAIN	Angela Lambert	£6.99
99959 8	BACK ROADS	Tawni O'Dell	£6.99
99909 1	LA CUCINA	Lily Prior	£6.99
99777 3	THE SPARROW	Mary Doria Russell	£7.99
99918 0	MUSIC FOR THE THIRD EAR	Susan Schwartz Senstad	£6.99
99865 6	THE FIG EATER	Jody Shields	£6.99
99819 2	WHISTLING FOR THE ELEPHANTS	Sandi Toksvig	£6.99
99872 9	MARRYING THE MISTRESS	Joanna Trollope	£6.99
99864 8	A DESERT IN BOHEMIA	Jill Paton Walsh	£6.99
99673 4	DINA'S BOOK	Herbjørg Wassmo	£7.99
99723 4	PART OF THE FURNITURE	Mary Wesley	£6.99
99797 8	ARRIVING IN SNOWY WEATHER	Joyce Windsor	£6.99